James Craig has worked as a journalist and consultant for more than thirty years. He lives in Central London with his family. His previous Inspector Carlyle novels, *London Calling*; *Never Apologise, Never Explain*; *Buckingham Palace Blues*; *The Circus*; *Then We Die*; *A Man of Sorrows* and *Shoot to Kill* are also available from Constable & Robinson.

For more information visit www.james-craig.co.uk, or follow him on Twitter: @byjamescraig

Praise for *London Calling*

'A cracking read.' BBC Radio 4

'Fast paced and very easy to get quickly lost in.' Lovereading.com

Praise for *Never Apologise, Never Explain*

'Pacy and entertaining.' *The Times*

'Engaging, fast paced . . . a satisfying modern British crime novel.' *Shots*

'*Never Apologise, Never Explain* is as close as you can get to the heartbeat of London. It may even cause palpitations when reading.' *It's Crime! Reviews*

SINS OF THE FATHERS

James Craig

Constable • London

CONSTABLE

First published in Great Britain in 2015 by Constable

Copyright © James Craig, 2015

The moral right of the author has been asserted.

*All characters and events in this publication, other than
those clearly in the public domain, are fictitious
and any resemblance to real persons,
living or dead, is purely coincidental.*

A CIP catalogue record for this book
is available from the British Library

ISBN 978-1-47211-519-5 (paperback)
ISBN 978-1-47211-520-1 (ebook)

Typeset in Times New Roman by TW Typesetting, Plymouth, Devon
Printed and bound by CPI Group (UK) Ltd, Croydon, CR0 4YY

Constable
is an imprint of
Constable & Robinson Ltd
100 Victoria Embankment
London EC4Y 0DY

An Hachette UK Company
www.hachette.co.uk

www.constablerobinson.com

For Catherine and Cate

Tomorrow do thy worst, for I have lived today.

'Happy the Man', John Dryden

ONE

A famous American writer had died a few days ago. The guy was so famous that even Julian Schaeffer had heard of him. Julian even thought that he **might have** read one of his books. At least, he was fairly sure that he had seen the film of one of his books – the one with Danny DeVito in it, along with the Scientologist actor who seemed more interested in flying planes than appearing in movies. The pilot/actor was really famous, but at that particular moment, Julian couldn't recall his name. The more he tried, the more he could feel it slipping away from his grasp.

Stress does that to you, he supposed.

Taking a sip of his coffee, Julian finished reading the newspaper obituary and calculated how old the author had been when he had keeled over. It irritated him immensely that they didn't just spell it out in the text of the story. When they turned to an obit, the first thing that people asked was: How old was he – or she – when the Grim Reaper came calling?

Did they, as the English liked to put it, have a good innings?

That's what the reader wanted to know. Why make them have to work it out for themselves?

So how old had the guy been when he snuffed it? Julian did the maths, hovering between eighty-six and eighty-seven for a few moments before deciding on the latter.

'Hmm,' he muttered to himself. 'Not bad.' Making it to eighty-seven made you a winner in Julian's book. In his view, life was a competition. How long you survived was one of the most important measures of winning or losing. If life expectancy for a man was seventy-eight or -nine, anything over the average eighty surely meant that you had won.

Getting almost an extra decade over the Average Joe? He would take that. Of course, twenty years would be better but, in Julian's book, beating the norm was the main thing. As a bare minimum, he wanted his fair whack. He didn't want the last thought fizzing through his brain before he keeled over to be *I've lost*.

Finishing his drink, his gaze slipped to a box below the obit in which was listed the author's top ten tips for writing.

1. Never open a book with the weather

Only an American could say that. You simply couldn't get away with a rule like that in England. Here, the weather was a national obsession.

Dropping the newspaper on to the bench beside him, Julian looked around the large playground in search of his daughter. After a few moments he caught sight of her, laughing with some other children as they played in the sandpit. Julian felt a wave of irritation at the thought of Rebecca getting her clothes dirty in the damp sand. Then he remembered that his mother would take care of it later and the emotion subsided as quickly as it had risen.

Looking up at the sky, he shivered. It was the kind of day where the conditions seemed to change constantly. Every time you looked up it was totally different, clear blue or slate black. One minute it was early January, the next, May. The heavens were never at peace, not unlike the city sprawled out uneasily below it.

Right now, it was more like January. Sighing, Julian gently lobbed his empty paper cup towards the wastebin, his shot missing by a good six inches.

'Damn.'

Wearily pushing himself up from the bench, he took three half-steps to his left and bent down to pick up the cup, feeling a slight spasm in his back as he did so. It was an old squash injury that flared up occasionally, each time taking slightly longer to pass than the time before. Straightening up slowly, he dropped the cup into the bin before gingerly massaging the base of his spine as he returned to the bench.

Glancing at his insanely expensive watch, Julian saw that it was already after 11 a.m., in other words, the heart of the working day. Right about now, he should have been in a meeting with Josh Samuels of Harring Wootton Mackenzie. It was a meeting he needed to take. Yet here he was, babysitting Rebecca.

He tried to recall whether the Samuels meeting had been formerly rescheduled. Again, his mind was blank, the details of his calendar replaced by the mixture of pleasure and guilt that he felt at not being at his desk.

The laughter of a group of children playing on a climbing frame twenty yards away drifted past him on the brisk wind. Buttoning up his macintosh, he re-opened his copy of *The Times* and turned to the business section. Ignoring the usual filler about interest rates (low) and bankers' bonuses (high), he struggled through a story about the UK's bribery laws before he became conscious of someone approaching the bench. Looking up, Julian smiled at the only other man he had seen in the park since sitting down. It was good that at least one other dad was on duty today. Somehow, it made him feel slightly less of a failure.

Dressed head to toe in black – Converse All Stars, jeans, leather jacket – the man looked tanned and relaxed. Aged thirty, give or take, he was around six feet tall, with wispy blond hair and a day's stubble on his chin.

You look very full of yourself, Julian mused, feeling somewhat dowdy by comparison.

Glancing to his left and right, the man took a step closer. Bouncing on the balls of his feet, he kept his hands in his pockets.

'Schaeffer?'

A sense of discomfort cloaked Julian's shoulders. 'Yes.'

The man nodded.

'Forgive me,' Julian asked, 'but have we met?'

By way of reply, the man pulled out a small pistol, pointing it straight at Julian's face.

'Who are you?' Julian tried to stand but his legs refused to work. 'What is this?'

'This,' said the man, relaxing into his task, 'is you dying.'

'But—' Over the man's shoulder, Julian saw a woman chasing a toddler by a cluster of recently planted trees. Off to the right, Rebecca was still happily playing in the sand with her new-found friends. Thanks be to God, she had no interest in her father whatsoever. Before he could move, there was a smacking sound as the newspaper jerked in his hand, and then another, pushing him back into the bench. Looking down, he could already feel the blood seeping through his shirt and onto the newsprint.

Another burst of laughter swept past him on the breeze, followed by a popping noise. This time, Julian felt conscious of the sharp pain spreading through his chest. The disintegrating paper fell from his grasp, its pages instantly carried away on the wind.

Satisfied that the job was done, the gunman turned and walked slowly away. Tasting the blood in his mouth, Julian gazed imploringly towards his daughter, who played on, blissfully unaware of what had just happened. He tried to cry for help but all that came out was a low hiss that he himself could barely hear over the sound of the wind.

TWO

Inspector John Carlyle sniffed the air apprehensively as he looked up at the darkening sky. It had been blue when he'd left his flat, scarcely half an hour ago. At least part of it had. *It's going to piss down*, he thought morosely, *and you've come out without an overcoat*. Almost fifty and he still couldn't manage to dress himself properly, always wearing what he should have worn for the conditions pertaining to the day before. It was the one thing – the only thing, really – about the city that really hacked him off. The famous weather: always too cold, too wet, too hot, too dry – never just right.

Carlyle looked up at the fine figure of Thomas Coram.

'So who did it then, Captain?'

Coram stared down at the inspector, looking decidedly unimpressed. If the pioneer in the cause of child welfare had seen the shooter, he was keeping his own counsel.

'Suit yourself,' Carlyle mumbled. Leaning against the base of the statue commemorating the founder of London's first Foundling Hospital, he scanned Coram's Fields. Barely five minutes' walk from the hustle and bustle of the newly revamped King's Cross, the park was a grass and concrete square covering a city block of seven acres at the top of Lamb's Conduit Street. On one side, a long, single-storey building contained a café, a nursery, sand pits, a playground and a drop-in centre; on the other, a collection of pens kept a selection of moth-eaten farm animals and domestic pets. At the back, behind a row of massive oak trees, was a collection of climbing frames, a big slide, some swings, a zipwire and, behind a wire fence, a number of five-a-side football pitches. Coram's was a welcome oasis in the middle of London where unaccompanied adults were not allowed and kids could play with relative freedom in relative safety.

Not today, of course, but most of the time.

The inspector always thought of Coram's Fields as a summer venue. He had brought his daughter, Alice, here hundreds of times over the years; sitting on a bench, watching the world go by while she played with the friends that always seemed to be knocking about. Of course, Alice was way too old now for the place. That time in their lives had gone. He missed it, but there was nothing that could be done to bring it back. Feeling more than a twinge of sadness, he pulled a tissue from the pocket of his jacket and wasted several seconds cleaning the lenses of his glasses. Over the last few years, they had gone from being an occasional reading aide to an omnipresent necessity. Another sign of his advancing years. Placing the specs carefully back on his nose, he watched his sergeant, an annoyingly handsome Mancunian smartarse named Umar Sligo, walking slowly towards him.

Almost twenty years younger than the inspector, Umar could still, just about, claim to be in his prime. With an Irish father and a Pakistani mother, he was living, breathing proof of the benefits of the multicultural society. He had arrived at Charing Cross via Kassim Darwish Grammar School for Boys ('*the true measure of a good education is to explore the limitations of your knowledge*') and a first-class degree from the University of Manchester in Politics and Criminology. A successful spell in the Greater Manchester Police saw him become a sergeant when he had just turned twenty-three.

Umar had arrived in London a little over a year ago. At the time, Carlyle was on a dismal run, having just lost his second sergeant in quick succession. To lose a third would have been deemed more than careless, so he had made an effort to keep hold of Master Sligo, even when the young man repeatedly had seemed more interested in chasing WPCs than chasing criminals.

Just why Umar had decided to up sticks and move to the capital had never become clear. The inspector, who, perversely, lacked the basic curiosity of your average person, had made no effort to find out. Having grown accustomed to working with him, Carlyle was comfortable enough with the younger man. He considered their relationship as 'okay', no more than that.

'Boss.' Umar waved his notebook by way of greeting.

'Sergeant.'

'Not a great start to the day.'

'No,' Carlyle agreed, ''specially not when it's supposed to be my day off.'

'Oh, sorry.'

'Not your fault.' Carlyle nodded towards the rather pathetic looking white tent, about thirty yards off to his left, which denoted the crime scene. 'Who's the victim?'

'A guy called . . .' Umar glanced at his notebook 'Julian Schaeffer. He was here with his daughter, Rebecca. Apparently they came here quite often. A couple of the mums knew the kid from parties and things.'

Carlyle's heart sank.

'She's fine,' Umar said hastily. 'Well, I mean she wasn't injured or anything. She didn't see the actual shooting, as far as we can tell. Which is a mercy.'

A very small mercy, Carlyle thought.

'We haven't tried to interview her yet. A doctor is checking her out and one of the PCSOs is looking after her.'

Carlyle sucked in a breath. He had a low opinion of Community Support Officers – 'plastic policemen' as they were known – but looking after a child for an hour or so should be just about do-able. 'Where is she?'

'Over there.' Umar pointed at a series of illuminated windows off to his right. 'In the nursery.'

'Okay.' Carlyle knew he would have to speak to the child and he was already dreading it. In a situation like this, dealing with adults was bad enough. 'They're also sending a child psychologist.'

7

'Good.' He would wait until the shrink arrived before launching into an interview. 'What else have we got?'

'The whole thing has caused quite a commotion.' The sergeant gestured over his shoulder towards a group of twenty or so women and children. They were huddled on the far side of the park, around the tiny café, as far from the tent as possible. A trio of female uniforms went between them, taking statements.

'Obviously.' Carlyle sighed heavily. 'A hit man walks into a playground and shoots a bloke reading his paper while his daughter plays nearby. I can see how that might cause a bit of upset among the yummy mummies and their little ones.'

'Not many yummy mummies round here,' Umar observed sadly. Carlyle glared at him. 'We've conducted the initial canvass,' he added, clearing his throat.

'And?' Carlyle never ceased to be amazed how quickly the sergeant could completely exhaust his reserves of patience before the day had even started in earnest.

'They all want to go home.'

'Apart from that?'

'It would appear that no one saw anything.'

Carlyle let out a frustrated yelp. 'But the guy was shot three times.'

'A couple of people heard what, presumably, were the shots, but they just thought it was a car backfiring. How many people would know the difference? Anyway, it's probably just as well. If anyone had noticed what was going on and tried to intervene, they might have been killed as well.'

'Fair point,' Carlyle conceded. 'What about CCTV?'

Umar shook his head. 'The space doesn't really lend itself to it.'

Must be the only space in London that doesn't, Carlyle observed. He pointed at a tall building towering over the park, a block to the west. 'What about them?'

Umar looked round. 'I don't see why they'd be filming a playground, but we can ask.'

'You know the drill. We need to check any cameras from the

8

surrounding blocks that might show the guy entering or exiting.'
A thought struck him. 'By the way, how did he get in?'

Umar scratched his ear. 'Through the gate, I suppose.'

'I thought only adults with kids were allowed in? Presumably he
didn't bring a child along to facilitate the hit.'

'It's not exactly tight security. The place relies on volunteers.
There doesn't seem to have been someone on the gate this morning. Anyone could just walk in.'

Carlyle nodded. Now that he thought about it, he could not
recall ever being challenged when he'd come into the park, even
if he was alone and Alice was already playing inside. 'So, in the
absence of witnesses, CCTV or anything else, what *do* we have?'

'The victim was found by a boy called . . .' Umar glanced at
his notes then closed the book and stuffed it in the back pocket of
his jeans, 'Harry Scott. Aged six. Young Harry saw that the guy
had dropped his paper and went to retrieve it for him. When he
approached the bench, he got a bit of a shock.'

'I bet he did.' Carlyle idly wondered if someone might be on the
end of a compensation claim as a result of young Harry's trauma.
Deciding that, even if the youngster's parents did turn litigious,
he personally would be in the clear, he let the question slip from
his mind.

'Even then, it took them a few minutes to find out what he was
screaming about. They thought he'd had a fall or something.'

'Kids do a lot of screaming,' Carlyle said sagely, 'as you are
about to find out.'

Looking glum, Umar nodded. His girlfriend, Christina, was due
to give birth to their first child in a few weeks' time. 'Actually . . .'

'Yes?' Carlyle watched a couple of young boys arrive at the front
gate. The taller had a football under his arm. One of the uniforms
stopped them. There was a brief protest from the boy with the
ball before they headed off towards the public gardens next door.
It wasn't as good as Coram's but it would do for their kickabout.

'We wanted to ask you a favour.' Umar stared off somewhere
beyond Carlyle's left shoulder.

Let me guess, Carlyle thought sourly, *you're going to leave me in the lurch by taking a monster holiday.* The government had just brought in new legislation allowing fathers to take up to twenty-six weeks' extra paternity leave. Half the coppers in the Met were probably desperately trying to get their old lady up the duff as a result. He tried not to scowl. 'Sure.'

'Thanks.'

'Depending on what it is, obviously,' Carlyle added hastily.

'Yes.'

'I mean, if I can.'

'Would you be my best man?' Umar blurted out.

This time the inspector did scowl. 'What?'

'Christina and I are getting married next week.' Umar gestured past a couple of goats in the direction of St Pancras station. 'Just up at Camden Town Hall. Nothing fancy but we need a couple of witnesses. I wondered if you and Mrs Carlyle would be prepared to do the honours?'

Mrs Carlyle? For a second, the inspector was stumped. Technically, there was no 'Mrs Carlyle'. After their nuptials, Helen had kept her own name, mainly as a matter of principle but also as a partial hedge against him turning out to be a totally hopeless husband.

'We need two witnesses,' Umar repeated, 'to sign the register.'

Carlyle looked his sergeant up and down suspiciously. Him and Helen? The only guests at the wedding? What about family and friends? Casual acquaintances? Passers-by, even?

'You know this is supposed to be a celebration, don't you?'

'We just want to get married with a minimum of fuss.'

'Well,' the inspector observed, 'you're certainly going the right way about it.'

THREE

Carlyle had first come across Christina O'Brien during a police raid on Everton's, a strip club located on a grubby side street near Holborn tube station, in search of illegal immigrants. Taking offence at having her work schedule interrupted, the American pole dancer had become an instant legend by battering an innocent constable senseless with a monster dildo, while wearing not a single stitch of clothing. The assault, captured for posterity by a police cameraman, was well on the way to becoming an Internet sensation, having been viewed more than 900,000 times before some killjoy Met lawyers managed to execute a series of takedown notices, depriving future generations of the chance to see Christina in action.

As far as Carlyle could recall, no illegal immigrants were arrested in the operation. For the feisty Ms O'Brien, however, assaulting a police officer brought not only the threat of arrest, but also of deportation back home to the United States. Not wishing to return to the land of the free and the home of the brave, Christina had offered Carlyle 'a freebie' in one of the Charing Cross interrogation rooms in exchange for help to get the charges against her dropped. Always one to resist temptation, the inspector had declined, keeping the matter to himself. He had never told Helen; it wasn't the kind of thing you recounted as an amusing anecdote when you got home.

In the event, the charges were dropped without the need for any bartering of services. A combination of a smart lawyer and the embarrassment of the Metropolitan Police at one of its officers being beaten up by a naked Amazon meant that Christina was quickly released and allowed to stay in the country. Soon thereafter she hooked up with an understandably smitten Umar, gave up the stripping for a job in PR and got up the duff. Not necessarily in that order.

Not knowing how to respond to this most unexpected of invitations, Carlyle looked around the empty playground. 'Coram's Fields will be handy when you've got the kid,' he mused. 'It's a good place. Apart from the odd shooting, of course,' he added.

'It's too far away. We're living up in Archway.'

Unlucky, Carlyle thought. With the best will in the world, Archway was a soul-destroying dump. 'You can always get the bus,' he ventured.

'Maybe.' Umar's expression suggested he was contemplating the loss of his Sunday mornings for the next ten years or more.

'Worth keeping in mind.'

'True. Anyway, we've got to get married first.'

'Indeed.'

'It's just going to be a very small thing. A quick ceremony, sign the register, a couple of photographs and then maybe we could have some lunch. I thought we could go to the Champagne Bar at St Pancras.'

'Well . . .' Carlyle had no idea what to say. The poor bugger must be desperate to be asking him to be his best man. Not to mention the fact that the reception was going to be held in a train station. 'When is it?'

Umar gave him the date. 'We need to be at the Town Hall at eleven.'

'Okay.' Carlyle scratched his head.

'You'll do it?' A look of relief and gratitude spread across Umar's face.

'Um . . .' Then: *Don't be such a git*, the inspector told himself sharply. *The kid is getting married; it's a big deal. Be a supportive colleague for once in your life.* 'I'm sure it will be fine. I'll talk to Helen.'

'Great.' Umar smiled nervously.

'And congratulations to both of you.' He tried to think what Helen would say in a situation like this. 'Good luck.'

'Thanks.'

'Just one thing.'

'What?'

'When it comes to Helen, don't call her Mrs Carlyle. It's Helen Kennedy. She didn't change her name when we got married and getting it wrong wouldn't go down well.'

'Good tip,' Umar grinned.

'She didn't say anything about obeying me either,' Carlyle grumbled. 'Something to do with "the vicious hegemony of the patriarchy" and the "terrible shortcomings of the antediluvian wedding vows".' Still listening to similar complaints thirty years later, he could recount Helen's charge sheet verbatim.

Umar's grin grew wider. 'I don't blame her.'

Carlyle shot him a look.

'Sorry,' the youger man apologized. 'I just didn't think anyone said "obey" these days.'

'No. Back then refusing to say it was a bit more of a statement.'

'Christina is going to change her name, though.'

Bad move, Carlyle thought. *If you get a divorce, she'll just have to change it back again. Why bother with all the hassle?* Trying to shake all the negative thoughts from his head, he thrust out a hand. 'Well done.'

Umar shook it warmly. 'Thanks.'

'I hope it all goes well.'

'I'm sure it will.'

You never know, Carlyle thought, *maybe it just will.* Giving Umar a reassuring pat on the shoulder, he began walking towards the small group of parents and children congregated by the café. 'C'mon,' he said cheerily. 'Let me buy you a cup of tea to celebrate.'

Before he could reach the café, however, a familiar figure appeared from inside the tent and beckoned him over. Desperately needing an injection of caffeine, Carlyle tried to ignore the signals until Umar, bringing up the rear, gave him a tap on the shoulder.

'Boss, I think they need you over there.'

Muttering to himself, Carlyle reluctantly changed course. As he approached the tent, a smiling Susan Phillips held up a small clear plastic evidence bag containing a wallet and a watch. Under a transparent plastic body suit, he could see that she was wearing a pair of worn jeans and a Cure T-shirt. By the pathologist's usual standards, it was a very casual ensemble.

Perhaps I wasn't the only one on a day off, Carlyle mused.

'I know you don't like the sight of blood,' she smiled mischievously, 'so I thought I'd bring these out for you.'

'Thank you very much.' Carlyle grinned, looking sheepish. 'That's very considerate of you.' His squeamishness was a well-known joke around the police stations of Central London. He took the bag. 'What have we got?'

'It clearly wasn't a robbery,' Phillips said, scratching the end of her nose with a latex-gloved hand. 'There's several hundred pounds in the wallet and the watch looks expensive.'

Carlyle nodded. 'Umar told me his name was—' Too late, he realized that he had forgotten that particular detail.

'Julian Schaeffer.' A bead of sweat ran down the side of Phillips's face. 'There's a business card in the wallet which gives his profession as "financial consultant". He was reading *The Times* when he was shot.'

'I'm more a *Mirror* man, myself. The question is: what was he doing here in the middle of a working day?'

Phillips wiped away the sweat with her forearm. 'Maybe he couldn't get childcare. It is half-term, after all.'

Carlyle was less than convinced. 'Guy who works in finance, expensive watch, well dressed?'

Phillips added, 'Expensive suit.'

'Not the kind of bloke you would expect to sign up to do the child minding.'

'Well, it looks like he did today.' Phillips started back to the tent. 'I'll let you know what else I find out, but you can reasonably assume it was the shots to the chest that killed him.'

'Thanks,' said Carlyle cheerily. As she disappeared back inside, he felt a big fat raindrop land on the top of his head. Keen to avoid a soaking, he began jogging across the grass in search of cover.

The Kipferl Austrian café at Coram's Fields was basically a few sheltered tables in front of a counter at the end of a colonnade. Sitting at one of the tables, Umar was finishing a Coke. Damp and out of breath, the inspector could feel his blood sugar plummeting and his temper fraying. Consulting the menu, written up on a large blackboard, he turned to a hassled-looking girl in a red bandana behind the counter.

'What's a Grosser Brauner?'

'It's like a double macchiato,' the girl replied.

'Perfect. I'll have one of those, please.' Carlyle stuck a hand in his pocket, in search of some change. Fortunately, he appeared to be in funds.

'Anything to eat?' The girl shuffled behind the counter while Carlyle peered at the selection under the glass. Cee Lo Green's 'Forget You' was playing on a small DAB radio stationed on top of a fridge. The alternative, rather more explicit version of the song was a current favourite of Alice's; she liked to play it loudly, on a regular basis, in an attempt to irritate her parents.

Carlyle watched the girl handle the shiny Gaggia coffee machine behind the counter quickly and expertly. When she handed him the coffee, he pointed at the sign by one of the plates in the display.

'Why is it called *Jewish* applecake?'

The girl shrugged without replying.

The rumbling of his stomach suggested that the origin of the name was an irrelevance, compared to the succulent-looking apples encased in enticing pastry. The inspector pulled a selection of coins from his pocket. 'I'll have a slice of that too.'

The cake was delicious. More importantly, the coffee was excellent – hot, sharp and envigorating – just the way it should be. It

15

took Carlyle less than two minutes to polish off both. The inspector liked to consider himself an aficionado in such matters and he was happy to pronounce himself more than satisfied. He licked the crumbs from his fingers and wondered if another Grosser Brauner was in order.

Umar watched his superior's questionable table manners with obvious distaste. 'What shall we do now?'

'I'd better go and talk to the kid.' Carlyle gestured towards a woman in a business suit marching determinedly towards them carrying a briefcase. 'Presumably this is the shrink.' He waited until she had almost reached their table before getting to his feet.

In her buttoned-up jacket and a skirt that came down below her knees, the woman looked like a character out of a 1950s B-movie. Tall and slim, she had short black hair and brown eyes behind tortoiseshell glasses that rested neatly on her cheekbones. It was an austere look but not unattractive.

Stopping in front of Carlyle, she offered a hand and they shook.

'Sergeant Sligo?'

Umar tittered. 'That's me.'

'I'm Carlyle.'

She looked at him blankly.

'Inspector John Carlyle. I'm in charge here.'

'Good to know that someone is. I'm Moira Aust, Central Family Support. Sorry it's taken me so long to get here, but I was giving a lecture at UCL when I got the call.'

'What was the lecture about?' Umar enquired, preparing to ramp up the charm.

'Well . . .'

'Let's not worry about that now,' Carlyle interrupted. 'Let's go and see the girl.'

'Of course,' Aust nodded. 'What's her name?'

'Er . . .' Carlyle looked at Umar.

'Rebecca.'

'Good,' said Aust primly. 'Let's go and see Rebecca.'

FOUR

Standing in the empty classroom, Carlyle glared at the scruffy woman in a dirty uniform sitting on a desk, jabbering away into her phone.

'You know what? I'm not sure I fancy a Mexican tonight – maybe some Thai.' The PSCO looked up at Carlyle as if to say *I'm on the phone here, do you mind?* 'No, definitely not Indian, not after last time.'

Somehow Carlyle resisted the temptation to give her a smack round the ear. 'Where's Rebecca?' he demanded.

'Hold on a sec.' The woman broke off her conversation to point over towards the door. 'She went to the loo.' She immediately returned to her call. 'Sorry about that. Yeah, Thai probably.'

Shaking his head, Carlyle left the classroom and headed back down the corridor to the reception. Off to the right were male and female toilets.

'Let me go and check.' Aust hurried past him and ducked into the ladies. Seconds later, she came back. 'Not here.'

Umar dived into the gents, returning almost immediately, alone.

This cannot be happening. Carlyle felt the applecake begin to weigh in his stomach. 'How many people have we got on site?' he asked Umar.

'Including us? Four. Plus one on the gate, the PSCO back there, the forensics team and Dr Aust.'

Oh sweet Jesus, now he really was beginning to feel sick. 'Okay.

I'll search the nursery. You take the doctor and organize a sweep of the rest of the site. If we've lost this kid we're in real trouble.'

'So, where is Rebecca?' Hands on hips, Umar stared across the deserted park. After more than an hour searching, they had come up with nothing. Aust had wisely departed the scene, citing another appointment.

Carlyle ran a hand across his neck. His head could roll for this. What a way to end a long if not particularly distinguished career – losing a small girl in a park in the wake of her father's murder.

In his hyper-anxious state, the inspector suddenly became conscious of his mobile starting to vibrate in his pocket. Praying for some good news, he lifted it to his ear.

'I need you to come to my office.' The voice on the other end of the line was cool and insistent.

The inspector felt his anxiety spike. 'Now?'

'I promise that it won't take very long.'

How long does it take to get sacked? Carlyle wondered if his next call should be to a Police Federation Rep. 'We are in the middle of—'

'I know what you're doing,' Commander Carole Simpson snapped. 'I'll expect you in the next hour.'

The line went dead. Carlyle said to Umar, 'Looks like I need to go over to Paddington Green.'

An expression of severe dismay crossed the sergeant's face. 'What – now?'

The inspector gave him an *I'm only obeying orders* kind of shrug.

'So what do you want me to do?'

'What do you think? See if you can get a lead on what happened to the kid.'

The background hum of children playing was immensely soothing. Sitting on a bench by the café outside the Diana Memorial Playground in Kensington Gardens, Daniel Sands watched the endless flow of people entering the park through the wrought-iron gates off to his right. The sun had come out. A couple of boys, aged six or seven, rushed past, shrieking as they headed for the wooden pirate ship that dominated the play area. A pretty blonde woman followed behind, carrying their jackets. Daniel Sands smiled at the woman as she passed. The woman eyed him warily, conscious that he was an old man sitting on his own outside a space that was commonly the domain of small children and young parents. Understanding her thought process, Sands refused to take any offence.

Taking a sip of his tea, he scanned the front page of that morning's *Telegraph*. The main story concerned a 'super-injunction' that had been taken out by a so-called 'leading businessman', in order to prevent the media reporting details of an alleged affair with a reality TV star turned model. What hope was there for the media, he wondered, when even the *Telegraph* – previously the most staid and conservative of titles – was obsessed by this kind of rubbish? The reason he bought the paper in the first place was because he expected it to insulate him from the kind of base behaviour that the rest of the world seemed to wallow in.

'Mr Sands?'

'Yes.' Folding up his paper, Daniel looked up at a tall, well-built man standing in front of him, his face partially concealed behind a pair of aviator sunglasses. He was younger than Daniel had expected, probably not yet out of his twenties. His shaven head and no-nonsense demeanour made him look like a soldier.

Getting to his feet, Daniel extended a hand and they shook. 'I'm Daniel Sands.'

'Dominic Sandbrook.'

Daniel caught the glint in the man's eye. 'DS,' he chuckled. 'The same initials as mine, and I like the "Sand" bit. That's not your real name, is it?'

'No, of course not.' The man calling himself Sandbrook took a seat on the bench. 'But it will do.' A broad grin spread across his face. 'Unless you would like to call me something else?'

'No, no, that's fine.' Daniel gestured towards the café. 'Would you like a drink?'

The man shook his head.

'Well . . .' Suddenly unsure of what to say, Daniel sat back down.

Behind them came the sudden sound of a child's scream, followed by a series of sobs which were slowly absorbed back into the general hubbub. The newcomer stared into the middle distance, waiting for the relative calm to return. 'We are ready to proceed,' he said, not looking at Daniel. 'Have you come to a decision?'

Daniel suddenly felt like a fool. An old man unable to put the past behind him. It was all so long ago. What was he doing?

The man waited patiently.

Letting the emotion pass, Daniel watched a squirrel jump on to the next table, sniff the remains of a discarded muffin and scoot away. 'Yes,' he said finally, 'I want him brought back.'

'That is the harder option.' The man looked at Daniel with compassion. 'Not to mention more expensive. A bullet in the head is far cheaper and a lot more . . .' he groped for a word, '*definitive*.'

A calm descended on Daniel; he had made up his mind. 'But this is not about revenge,' he said. 'It is about justice.'

The man calling himself Sandbrook bit his lower lip. 'If it was me, it would be about revenge.'

Daniel smiled sadly. 'Just be grateful that it isn't you in this position.'

The man nodded. 'You have the bank account details?'

'Yes. I will make the transfer today.'

'Good. In the absence of any unforeseen developments, we will make the delivery within fifteen days of receipt of funds. We will call you twice: once when we have the package in our possession and then to confirm its safe arrival in the UK, ready for collection.'

The package. Daniel grinned. It was like being in a bad spy movie. That would make him who – Alec Guinness? 'How will you get the package into the country?'

The man got to his feet. 'Does it matter?'

'No, I suppose not.'

'As I said, this is the harder option. Better that you don't know the details. It is not as easy as it would be on the continent, obviously. The border controls here are stricter. It can be done, but failure to repatriate is one of the risk factors. Success is not guaranteed.'

'I understand.' Daniel wished that he hadn't asked the question.

'And if we do successfully repatriate, the courts may not hold him.'

'There is an outstanding arrest warrant.'

'Which has never been vigorously pursued,' Sandbrook gently pointed out.

A look of disgust passed across Daniel's face. 'The Italians – they do not care. They have a killer living in their midst and no one bats an eyelid. The Germans and the French declined to help. The Swiss wouldn't even open an investigation.'

Sandbrook nodded. 'Everyone has their own priorities.'

'Priorities?' Daniel let out a harsh laugh. 'You don't have children, do you?'

'I have a couple of nieces.'

'It's not the same. When you have your own child, you will understand. When you are a parent, the only priority can be your child. He has to be brought back here. The English have jurisdiction: the English will try him.'

'Yes, but the alleged crime was a long time ago. And then there are the circumstances in which he is being brought back. A good lawyer will have plenty of room for manoeuvre. It will be a media storm and, even if he loses, there is every chance he will be let out on appeal.'

'I will have a good lawyer, too,' Daniel ground out. 'English justice is the best in the world. There can be no going back.'

'It is good that you believe that,' the man said quietly.

Daniel turned in his seat to better look him in the face. 'And you? What do you believe in? Only the money?'

'Not at all,' the man said evenly. 'My colleagues and I, we have to pay the bills but we are fortunate in that we can choose our clients. We would not have taken you on if we did not believe in your case.'

Daniel thought about the large sum he would be transferring later this afternoon. It would pay for a lot of expenses. 'Would you have taken me on if I had no money?'

The man smiled. 'That is a hypothetical question. How can I answer that?' He gave Daniel a gentle pat on the arm. 'We approached you, remember?'

'That's right.' Daniel remembered when a man very much like the one now sitting next to him had arrived at the door of his Notting Hill townhouse. It was late one night and the air was fresh following a recent thunderstorm. The man was a 'friend of a friend' – he gave Daniel the name of a mutual acquaintance – and he claimed that he represented a group of men who had been moved by Daniel's plight. They could help resolve the problem that had been eating away at him for years. They wanted to help.

The two men had talked late into the night yet, at the end of it all, nothing about the man or his group had been explained. It seemed that they were a band of brothers – mercenaries? vigilantes? – who existed only in the shadows. No proof was offered that they could do what Daniel required.

As he was leaving, Daniel's mysterious guest handed him a scrap of paper containing the number for a mobile phone. Daniel had initially been sceptical. The whole thing sounded like a scam. Still, he had spoken to his acquaintance and taken up references he had been given and made a few enquiries of his own. If the results were not enough to give him a complete picture of his would-be saviours, it was enough to reassure him that they had the necessary skills and training to do the job. The seeds of hope had been sown. Anyway, what did he have to lose? Only money. He didn't know what he was going to do with his wealth. Without a child to pass it on to, it seemed an almost intolerable burden.

After hesitating for several days he had called the number. Now here he was, a man who had never had so much as a parking ticket discussing a kidnapping.

'We are not in this to make money,' the man insisted. 'Equally, there are costs involved in the project. If things go wrong, there can be no refund.'

'I understand,' Daniel repeated. 'What do you think of our chances?'

The man stared at the horizon for several moments before venturing his opinion. 'I am more of a pessimist than some of my colleagues, so I would say small.'

Inwardly, Daniel groaned. 'How small?'

'Small but not zero.' The man gave him a reassuring smile. 'Don't worry, we will not let you down. I know that you have waited a long time for this.'

'Yes,' Daniel mumbled. 'Yes, I have.'

'Keep your phone switched on. We will be in touch.'

Watching the man walking away, heading towards Kensington High Street, Daniel pulled a tattered photograph from the pocket of his jacket. Blinking away a tear, he stared at the image of his daughter; his daughter, as he liked to remember her, an inquisitive, happy thirteen-year-old girl in jeans and a T-shirt, sitting on the steps of the National Gallery, drinking from a Coke can. It had been the first time that Lillian's mother had let her come back to London to stay with her father, and he could recall every minute of their outing. When the picture had been taken, they had just been to see Georges Seurat's *Bathers at Asnières*, for part of a school project that Lillian had been doing. From there they went off to have a pizza on Regent Street, followed by a trip to the theatre.

It had been, by some margin, the best day of his life.

It was the last time he saw her alive.

Daniel Sands felt the tears roll down his cheeks as he gazed at the picture. It was the only thing of value in his life. He would take it with him to his grave.

FIVE

The inspector popped the last of the banana into his mouth and chewed it unhappily, wondering what to do with the skin. Sighing audibly, Commander Simpson pointed to a waste-bin by the side of her desk. A true status symbol in the twenty-first century hierarchy, since everyone below the rank of Chief Superintendent had had their bins taken away. It was supposedly an initiative to encourage recycling but mainly to do with cutting costs and avoiding the embarrassment of having cleaners who turned out to be illegal immigrants.

Getting out of his seat, the inspector dropped the skin into the bin. 'Thanks.'

Waiting for him to sit back down, Simpson clasped her hands together, as if in prayer. 'Dino's asked me to marry him,' she said abruptly.

Jeez, Carlyle thought, *why does everybody suddenly feel the need to tell me about their nuptials?* He raised an eyebrow. 'You're not going to ask me to be a bridesmaid, are you?'

'What?' Simpson's face clouded and she looked like she was already regretting raising the subject. Sitting behind the desk in her office at Paddington Green station, she glanced around the bare walls. Apart from the cheap, threadbare furniture, the place was empty. Over the years he had been coming here, Carlyle noticed that the personal touches were becoming fewer and fewer. It was almost as if Simpson didn't want her colleagues to know that she existed outside of the uniform.

'Nothing,' he replied hastily. 'Well, that's great, I suppose. Congratulations.'

'I haven't said "yes" yet,' Simpson muttered testily.

'Mm.'

She grimaced. 'What does that mean?'

'Nothing.' For some time now, Carlyle had wondered whether Dino Mottram, an old-style entrepreneur, ten years or more Simpson's senior, was in line to become the second Mr Carole Simpson. The couple had been stepping out together for a while now and, initially, it had seemed to the inspector like a good idea. Husband number one – Joshua Hunt – had crashed and burned quite spectacularly: a conviction for fraud and jail, followed by terminal cancer, bringing the Commander's career progression in the Metropolitan Police to a grinding halt as a result.

On the bright side, professional catastrophe had made things easier between Commander and Inspector. Once Simpson had accepted that her climb up the greasy pole was over, she relaxed considerably. Since her troubles with Joshua, Carlyle had found her much more agreeable, both professionally and personally. He liked the idea that their relationship had improved as her career had nose-dived. Being more than a little perverse, it made him feel slightly less alone working inside the Metropolitan Police Force.

Carlyle knew that he should keep his mouth firmly shut but his resolve lasted less than ten seconds. 'I suppose you've discussed a pre-nup?' he grinned. Dino, well known as a serial monogamist, was a regular presence in the various 'Rich Lists' so beloved of Sunday newspapers.

'It's a common enough practice these days,' Simpson observed. 'Anyway, it's not like I need his money.'

'Not very romantic, though,' Carlyle chided her, 'is it?' If anyone deserved a bit of domestic bliss it was Carole Simpson. However, over the last year or so, the inspector had first-hand expereience of dealing with Dino and his company, Entomophagus Industries, on a professional basis. Now that he had seen the man in action, he wasn't so sure that the Commander wouldn't be better off staying single.

Simpson gave him the gimlet eye. 'You don't like Dino, do you?'

Carlyle mumbled, 'I don't really have a view . . .'

'John, I know you. You are incapable of bullshitting your way through things like this.' A smile crept across her face and she immediately looked ten years younger. 'When they were handing out diplomacy genes, you simply didn't get any.'

Carlyle laughed. 'Seriously, I *don't* have a view on Dino. I don't have to have a view on Dino. It's not me that he wants to marry.'

Simpson drummed her fingers on the table. 'That's hardly a ringing endorsement.'

Sitting up in his chair, Carlyle spread his arms in frustration. This wasn't what he had come here to discuss. 'What do you want me to say? You're a grown up, you have to make your own decision.'

Simpson looked down at her desk.

'If things are going so well with Dino,' he burbled, trying to fill the silence, 'why do you need to get married? It's hardly a big deal.'

'You're married.'

'True.' Carlyle shifted uncomfortably in his seat. How did the conversation get round to *him*? 'But Helen and I lived together for years before that. In the end, we formally got married just before Alice was born.'

Simpson smiled. 'A shotgun wedding?'

'Not at all.' Carlyle sat forward in his chair, feeling quite defensive now. His family was his family. He didn't need to explain it to anyone. 'It was just a bit of fun. The sun shone and we had a picnic in Hyde Park. It was a beautiful day. I'm happy to be married but it doesn't really mean anything. It certainly didn't change anything at home.' He broke into a grin. 'Helen has remained firmly in charge.'

Simpson gestured at his hand. 'Is that why you don't wear a ring?'

'Not really.' Carlyle rubbed his ring finger with his right hand.

Looking across the table, he realized that the Commander was still wearing a simple gold wedding band. 'I don't like jewellery, that's all.'

Simpson thought about it for a moment. Her gaze belatedly fell on the Clash *London Calling* T-shirt that he was wearing.

'I was on a day off,' Carlyle explained, scratching his stomach.

Simpson couldn't have cared less. 'Tell me about Julian Schaeffer.'

'Shot in the chest at close range. No messing about. From what we can tell so far, it looks like a professional killing.'

Simpson frowned. 'In a kiddies' playground? This is London, for God's sake, not . . .' she tried to think of somewhere suitably dangerous, 'Mexico.'

'It's a strange one,' Carlyle agreed. 'The priority at the moment is to find Mr Schaeffer's daughter.'

He glanced at the screen of his BlackBerry. While he had been on the tube, it looked like Umar had finally come up with some additional information.

Simpson nodded, waiting for him to go on.

Squinting, he read from the screen. 'Rebecca Schaeffer is six. She was an occasional visitor to the drop-in centre at the park. According to one of the volunteers who works there, the parents are separated, maybe divorced, we don't know yet. It appears the father was looking after her for half-term.'

'The sins of the father,' Simpson muttered, 'laid upon the children.'

'Boss?'

The Commander said briefly, '*The Merchant of Venice*.'

'Hm.'

'You should really know your Shakespeare, John.'

Carlyle realized that now was not the time to mention that he had given up English Lit before O level. Worse, rude mechanical that he was, he considered the Bard ridiculously overrated. 'We just have to discover what the particular sins of the father were, in this case.'

27

'Find the girl first. What happened to her? Do you think she was abducted by the shooter?'

Simpson clearly didn't realize that the girl had gone missing *after* the police had arrived at the scene. Carlyle wondered if he might yet survive this latest cock-up.

'Er . . .' Unable to come up with a watertight lie, he simply said, 'We've got a full search underway.'

'Do we have a photo of her?'

'Not yet.'

Simpson looked suitably unimpressed. 'Next steps?'

Carlyle stood up and allowed himself a stretch. 'I need to go and speak to the wife and then visit Mr Schaeffer's office.'

'What did he do?'

'Something in financial services.'

Simpson smiled sadly. Her former husband had been 'something in financial services' and the phrase did not inspire any sort of confidence. 'That narrows it down.'

'I'll find out more.'

'Keep me informed.'

Carlyle nodded. They both knew that his track record of keeping his boss in the loop was extremely patchy. 'Of course.'

As he turned towards the door it opened and Simpson's executive assistant walked in. Dressed in a pair of sandals, skinny white jeans and a printed blouse, Ellie Harris was twenty-five, five foot nine and blonde; in short, drop dead gorgeous. With a father in the House of Lords, a First Class law degree from King's College, London, and a part-time modelling career, she had been the talk of the station within five minutes of arriving at Paddington Green. With immense force of will Carlyle tried not to gawp as she stepped up to Simpson's desk and handed the Commander a single sheet of A4 paper.

'Inspector, I thought you might want to see this.'

'Thanks.' Simpson quickly read the contents and offered it to Carlyle.

Ellie smiled at Carlyle as she left the room.

'*John*.' Simpson waved the piece of paper impatiently at him.

Carlyle grinned. 'Is she any good?'

Simpson ignored the question. 'A girl has been involved in a traffic accident on Rosebery Avenue.'

Rosebery Avenue was less than ten minutes' walk from Coram's Fields. It could be Rebecca.

Carlyle skipped towards the door. 'Is she hurt?'

Simpson shook her head. 'That's all I have. There are no other details yet.'

'Okay. I'll get over there now.'

'Take a car from downstairs.'

'Thanks.' Ducking out of the door, he nodded at the lovely Ellie in the office outside as he rushed towards the lifts. Flicking through a copy of *Vogue*, with a mobile wedged between her shoulder and her left ear, she didn't look up.

SIX

The rain had cleared and the sky had returned to a cautious blue, with temperatures reaching the low twenties, high for London for the time of year. Discharging his driver on Clerkenwell Road, Carlyle made his way on foot through the backed-up traffic towards the police tape. Almost immediately, he felt sweat soaking into his shirt as his body temperature rose. The inspector was not good in the heat and he quickly began to feel oppressed and lethargic. As he progressed, the cacophony of horns grew louder and the air grew thicker with exhaust fumes. A dull headache gripped the back of his neck and he felt an acute need for some water. Halfway up the road, he passed a number 38 bus. It was stuck between stops and the passengers were arguing with the driver, who was refusing to open the doors so that they could get out. Carlyle watched a man in a suit and tie kick one of the doors in fury while a baby in a buggy started screaming its head off; just another fun journey for happy travellers in the big city. He ducked inside a newsagent shop and bought a chilled half-litre bottle of Evian, chugging down half of it before continuing on his way.

A couple of minutes later, he reached the ambulance parked outside the Sadler's Wells theatre. Carlyle stepped off the pavement and looked up and down the avenue. The traffic had been stopped in both directions; the bleating of the horns dying away as drivers realized that no one was paying any attention to their predicament. A handful of passers-by stood behind the tape, chatting amongst themselves, watching what was going on as if they were a bunch of tourists watching one of the performance artists in the Piazza in Covent Garden. Feeling suitably disgusted, Carlyle pushed his way past and ducked under the tape.

In the middle of the road, a red Royal Mail van stood inside the cordon. In front of the van, two paramedics – a man and a woman – were working on a girl sprawled on the tarmac. As he approached, Carlyle could see that they were working slowly and methodically. There was no urgency in their actions and they were grimly silent. It was clear that they had not been able to save the child.

Carlyle took a deep breath. He felt a hand on his shoulder.

'Inspector.'

Turning, he faced a short blonde woman. He was fairly sure that she was a sergeant at the Holborn station but her name escaped him.

She offered her hand. 'Jill Hughes. I did a stint at Charing Cross last year. I work out of Tolpuddle Street.' She pointed up the road in the general direction of Islington.

'Of course.' Shaking her hand, Carlyle realized that he must have been thinking of someone else.

The paramedics carefully lifted the girl onto a gurney, covered her with a blanket and wheeled her towards the ambulance. Hands on hips, Hughes said sadly, 'Fifteen years old – bloody hell.'

Not my girl, Carlyle thought. *Thank God. Way too old*. He took another swig from his water bottle in a futile attempt to keep his headache at bay. This was shaping up to be one of those days you spent chasing your tail across the city to no effect whatsoever.

'The driver had just come out of Mount Pleasant,' Hughes continued.

'Yeah.' Largely disinterested now, Carlyle could make out the sorting office at the top of the road. An identical red van came out of the front gate and edged into the traffic that was now backed up along Farringdon Road, heading for King's Cross.

She gestured towards the ambulance. 'He says the girl just walked straight out between a couple of parked cars.'

Carlyle caught sight of the driver, a young white guy, unshaven with straggly brown hair down to his shoulders; his sky-blue Royal Mail shirt was heavily creased and open at the neck. A packet of Drum rolling tobacco was sticking out of the breast pocket of the shirt. Leaning against the side of his van, the driver was playing a game on his mobile phone, oblivious to the body being loaded onto the ambulance a few yards away.

'It's always easy to blame the victim,' the inspector mused, 'especially when they're dead.'

'Excuse me, sir.' A uniform ushered Carlyle out of the way as he moved the police tape to allow the ambulance to head off down the now-empty southbound lane.

'Going to Barts?' St Bartholomew's Hospital was a five-minute drive away.

'I expect so.' The constable put the tape back in place, to the annoyance of the waiting drivers.

Carlyle finished the last of his Evian and crunched the plastic bottle in his fist. His head was pounding and he felt sick. It would take him about half an hour to walk back to the station at Charing Cross. Public transport would take twice as long. At least. All he wanted to do was take three Ibuprofen tablets and lie down in a dark room with an ice pack on his forehead. Crossing to the far side of the street in search of some shade, he walked wearily away.

The earlier rain had cleaned the streets, washing away the lingering odour of piss from the doorway of the boarded-up betting shop on Agar Street, at least for the time being. Hands thrust deep into his pockets, Carlyle waited for a taxi to barrel past, heading up the road at a ridiculous speed, before crossing the street.

His mind blank, he looked up at his place of work as if seeing it for the first time. Below a small and grubby royal crest, the sign said CHARING CROSS POLICE STATION. One of a hundred and forty Metropolitan Police stations located across London, the nick covered some of the most expensive real estate in the world, a block north of the eponymous train station. It was a squat, featureless building, rising six economical storeys high, bristling with CCTV cameras on every corner, peppered with windows too small for its bulk; windows for seeing out of rather than for looking in through. The half a dozen old-fashioned blue police lamps that appeared to have been placed in random locations around the building looked just as fake as they actually were. The same blue lamp used to be found outside all police stations, reminding the public that the police were always ready to serve. Now they were just design accessories.

The station building was painted in an off-white colour that always looked dingy. The finishing touch was a small portico, as if copied from the nearby church in the Piazza, framing the front entrance and making it look more like a provincial town hall than a major cop shop. This had been his home from home for the past fifteen or so years. Ignoring the phone vibrating in his pocket, he climbed the front steps, walked past the blue lamp stationed at the front entrance and entered the outer foyer of the building. This was where the public would wait on wooden benches, playing with their mobile phones, reading the Crimestoppers posters on the wall, feeling uncomfortable and wondering what everyone else was there for. Eventually, they would be buzzed through a set of glass doors which led further into the building and the main lobby.

Behind the glass doors stood the front desk, the desk sergeant and the beginning of what was usually either a short and unhappy or a long and very unhappy brush with the best of British official-dom. Someone once said that all police stations smell of shit and fear. In the case of Charing Cross, the normal combination was a mix of body odour and boredom. It was like a hospital without the nurses, or a school without the kids: soulless, bureaucratic and depressing.

At any given time, the benches were usually the domain of tour-ists who had been robbed, rickshaw drivers complaining about unpaid fares, run-over cyclists and other slow-motion road-rage cases. There was also a steady stream of assault cases, the unlucky victims of random, invariably drink-fuelled violence. All in all, the flotsam and jetsam from the shallow end of the gene pool, Carlyle reflected. These were the people he'd signed up to work for, thirty years ago. The inspector was long since resigned to the fact that nothing ever changed. As one wag once put it, the clowns may change but it's still a bloody circus. What did that make him? A trapeze artist? A lion-tamer? Charing Cross Station was his Big Top. Even so, he liked to spend as little time inside the building as possible.

At least this evening the place was largely empty. One of their regulars, a dosser from the Parker Street halfway house on the other side of Covent Garden, was asleep in a corner; two benches along, a fat woman sat with her hand in a bag of peppermint creams. Next to her a young boy, maybe nine or ten, was engrossed in a game on his PSP. Both of them seemed perfectly content. A couple of yards away, a silver-haired Japanese guy in a suit and tie sat, elbows on knees, staring into space. *You're a bit overdressed for here, sunshine*, Carlyle thought as he tapped on the glass and waited to be buzzed through. Presumably a businessman who'd had his wallet nicked.

It took him a few moments to get the attention of Angie Middleton, the desk sergeant, who was busy arguing with an animated bloke standing at the desk – another unhappy punter. Finally, he caught her eye. Middleton hit the release button and Carlyle pulled the door as it clicked open. As he did so, he caught sight of Umar heading towards him, on his way out. A look of frustration crossed the sergeant's face as he saw his boss and realized that his departure was going to be delayed.

'We need to have a catch-up,' said Carlyle by way of greeting, pointing back into the bowels of the station.

'I've left a note on your desk.' Umar tapped his watch. 'We've got an antenatal class tonight. Christina will kill me if I'm late again.'

Carlyle grimaced. The last thing he needed was Umar buggering off early. On the other hand, he knew from his own experience of family life that some things during pregnancy were fairly non-negotiable. Helen had insisted that they go to some National Childbirth Trust classes in Kentish Town before Alice was born. The whole thing had been horrendous, stuck in a room with a dozen or so middle-class couples who had their C-section in the diary and were already worrying about schools and music lessons. Worse, the teacher who was a cross between Andrea Dworkin and Enid Blyton. Carlyle had found the whole thing embarrassing and tedious in equal measure. But, rightly, it had been Helen's call. It hadn't killed him to go.

Even now, the memory of pelvic-floor exercises and pain relief (he wasn't offered any) made him shudder. He took a deep breath and squeezed out a grin. 'Is it all sitting on bean bags talking about the end of life as you know it?'

'My God.' Umar made a face. 'It's far worse than that.'

'Been there, done that.' Carlyle gave him a consoling pat on the back. 'Sometimes you just have to take one for the team.'

'Yeah. It's all bollocks.'

'Of course it is,' Carlyle agreed, 'but if it keeps Christina happy that's what counts.'

'Mm,' Umar said dully.

'My view,' Carlyle was usually reluctant to go about dispensing advice but, for once, he easily slipped into the experienced older bloke role, 'is that you just have to wait for it to come out and then get on with it. Nothing can prepare you for it; I wouldn't bother with any books or any advice.'

Umar's face broke into a grin. 'Other than yours, of course.'

'Of course,' Carlyle smiled. 'Trust me, for I am The Oracle.'

'Ha ha.'

Carlyle spread his arms wide. 'Take it to the bank, my friend. The only thing you have to do is keep the missus as happy as possible and roll your sleeves up on the big day.'

'Okay.'

Feeling increasingly comfortable riding his high horse, Carlyle went on with his lecture. 'Above all, as soon as the crap starts flying, literally in this case, you'll have to get busy changing those nappies.'

35

'Of course.' Umar looked offended. 'I'll be doing my share.'

'No, no, no, no, no.' Carlyle glanced over at the desk. Middleton and her unhappy punter appeared to have reached a stalemate. 'You have to do much more than that. I remember my dad watching me change one of Alice's nappies. Standing back at a safe distance, the old bugger happily boasted how he'd never had to change a single nappy in his life. Those days are long gone.'

'I know,' Umar said, already bored by the inspector's reminiscences.

'Good. And I'll speak to Helen about the wedding tonight.'

'Thanks.'

'No problem. Give me a call when you've finished comparing birthing pools and baby buggies and we can work out a plan of action.'

'There is a hell of a lot to go through here, though.' Hopelessly caught between the proverbial rock and a hard place, Umar nervously fingered his mobile phone. 'Maybe I should give Christina a call and tell her I need to work late.'

'Nah. It's okay. You'd better get going.'

Umar looked nonplussed. 'Er, thanks.'

The inspector gave him a sad smile. 'Good luck.' As he watched his sergeant head out of the station, it crossed Carlyle's mind that twenty-six weeks of paternity leave added up to six months. How long did he have when Alice was born? A week? Certainly no more than that. The world was going mad. He'd need to find yet another bloody sergeant; Simpson could hardly blame him for Christina getting knocked up but she would still be pissed off. He was getting through sergeants at a ridiculous rate. At least he would know in advance to look for a new one. The trick was to find a suitable candidate before some no-hoper was foisted upon him.

Carlyle quickly flipped through a list of possible replacements in his head, but no one immediately came to mind. He realized that he would have to give the matter some very serious attention.

SEVEN

'But this is simply not good enough.' The man at the desk waved an exasperated arm in the direction of Angie Middleton. He was about the same height as Carlyle, with jet-black hair that ended neatly just above the collar of his shirt. The accent was the kind of mid-Atlantic nothingness of someone who had lived in the United States for an extended period of time.

Careful, mate, Carlyle thought, *or you'll get yourself nicked.*

'Sir.' A massive black woman, Middleton lurched back on her heels to avoid getting a smack in the mouth. It crossed the inspector's mind that if she gave the guy a smack back he might not wake up for a week.

Another wave of the arm. 'We have been waiting for almost two hours.'

Carlyle's brain told him to keep walking but, hesitating, he made the fatal mistake of making eye-contact with Middleton. A relieved grin spread across her face as she gestured towards him.

'The inspector here will be able to help you.'

The man turned, nodded at Carlyle and extended a hand. 'Hiroshi Takahara.'

Reluctantly, Carlyle shook the man's hand.

'Mr Taka . . .' Middleton looked down at a business card lying on the blotter on her desk, 'Takahara here works at the Japanese Embassy.' She pointed at the old guy who was still sitting on the bench, staring into space. 'He's here about Mr Nino . . . miya.'

Takahara nodded again, or maybe it was a small bow. 'His daughter.'

Carlyle gave him a blank look.

'Mr Ninomiya's daughter appears to be missing,' Middleton explained. She was busying herself in paperwork, not looking up in case Carlyle tried to return the hospital pass. 'He would like to find out how the investigation into her disappearance is going.'

What investigation? A jolt of panic kicked the inspector's brain into gear. The Japanese Embassy was in Piccadilly, close to Hyde Park Corner. 'Isn't this one for West End Central?' he asked, more in hope than expectation. West End Central, on Jermyn Street, was a lot closer to the Embassy than Charing Cross.

Middleton wrote something on her sheet of paper, shaking her head as she did so. 'The girl was living on John Adam Street when she went missing, so it was kicked over to us.'

'So who's dealing with it?' the inspector asked wearily.

Middleton finally looked up and gave him an apologetic shrug. 'Inspector Watkins.'

'Great.'

Sophie Watkins had gone on maternity leave a fortnight ago. As far as he could remember, this would be her third or maybe even her fourth kid. A perfectly pleasant but totally uninspiring woman, she must have spent less than two years out of the last six actually working. Popping out that many sprogs in quick succession while staying, untouchable, on the company payroll was, to Carlyle's view, taking the piss bigtime.

Especially when, all around, police spending was being slashed and jobs were being cut.

But then again, he was just your average, insensitive middle-aged bloke.

'There's a report on the system. Oh, and your wife called. You need to phone her.' Middleton turned and disappeared behind a door at the end of the desk before he could start whining.

Hiroshi Takahara looked at him expectantly, a fresh business card in his hand.

Carlyle reluctantly took the card and looked the diplomat up and down. Fresh faced, if a bit crumpled after a couple of hours waiting on the benches outside, Takahara looked to be in his early thirties. London was doubtless a plum diplomatic posting, so he must be a 'high flyer' of some sort.

High flyers usually meant trouble.

The inspector felt an overwhelming urge to run. His mobile started vibrating once more but he didn't have the energy to answer it. Pushing up his glasses, he rubbed his eyes.

'We have been waiting a very long time.'

Turning the business card in his hand, Carlyle let his glasses fall back into place and held up a hand. 'I'm very sorry about that sir,' he said gently, gesturing at the man on the bench. 'If you could go and get Mr . . .'

'Ninomiya,' Takahara reminded him. 'Naohiro Ninomiya.'

'Ninomiya.'

Takahara nodded.

'Apologies for my pronunciation.'

Takahara nodded again.

'If you could go and get Mr Ninomiya, I'll take you upstairs and we will see what we can find out.'

Having installed the two Japanese in a first-floor meeting room, Carlyle printed off a copy of Sophie Watkins's original report and nipped down to the canteen in the basement. Armed with a paper cup of green tea, he sat down at an empty table and quickly scanned through the notes on the disappearance of Ayumi Ninomiya.

Ayumi Ninomiya, twenty-two, shared a flat in an Art Deco block called the Little Adelphi just south of the Strand, next to the Embankment Gardens, close to the Thames. She had come to London from Nagasaki two years ago to study fashion at Central Saint Martin's College of Art and Design and to work on her English. Carlyle thought about that for a moment. Even before college fees, the girl's expenses must have amounted to more than two grand a month. Ayumi had worked part-time in a bar just off Regent's Street, but that would scarcely pay her pocket money.

The family must be loaded, Carlyle assumed, to be able to pay for the trip.

Whatever.

Friday night six weeks ago, Ayumi had gone to a Covent Garden nightspot called the Lawnmower Club. It was Seventies' Night. Her friends last saw her about two o'clock in the morning. Off their faces, they didn't realize that Ayumi wasn't around until leaving time, 5.30 a.m. Even then, they assumed that she had just gone home.

The walk back to the Little Adelphi should have taken less than ten minutes.

She never turned up.

Ayumi Ninomiya's flatmate – another Japanese girl called Miki Kasaba – walked into Charing Cross and reported her missing at three minutes past four on Sunday afternoon. The police had swung – slowly – into action. Carlyle scanned down the list of people that Inspector Watkins and her sergeant had interviewed over the next week – the flatmate, the friends, people at the club, people at the college, neighbours. Nothing.

It crossed his mind that, with Sophie Watkins away, her sergeant, a quiet guy from Wimbledon called Ed Savage, might be free to step into Umar's shoes, if required. The inspector filed the idea away for future reference. At the very least, Savage could get back on this case. Presumably he wasn't on duty this evening or Middleton would have dropped it straight into his lap.

Carlyle thought about giving the sergeant a call before he spoke to the father but decided against it; he knew that Savage would not be able to add anything to the report. It would be touch and go whether he remembered Ayumi Ninomiya at all. That was not a criticism; it was just the way it was – there was more than enough to keep you busy when you moved on. Six weeks was like a lifetime ago. No copper could keep their brain filled with information that was essentially of historical interest only.

Skipping through the remaining pages of the report, he wondered what he would tell the girl's father. The Initial Investigating Officers – Watkins and Savage – had done everything that you would expect: Ayumi had been logged as 'missing' on the Police National Computer, and the National Policing Improvement Agency's Missing Persons Bureau had been contacted. They had also compiled details of friends and relatives and listed the places that she frequented. Having searched the Little Adelphi flat, they had taken a toothbrush so that there was a DNA sample on record.

A nice little tick in every box.

But no Ayumi.

There were two photos in the file. The first, a standard black-and-white passport photograph, showed an elegant girl who looked as if she could be anything from eighteen to thirty-five. She had a strong jawline, a friendly gaze and an expensive-looking bob haircut. The second was a snap of Ayumi and another girl standing in front of one of the lions in Trafalgar Square, both of them giving the thumbs-up to the camera. A scribbled note on the back identified the other girl as the flatmate, Miki Kasaba. They were dressed for winter and it looked cold; Ayumi's hair was longer than in the passport snap but it wasn't clear which was the more recent picture.

Carlyle was distracted by his phone buzzing in his pocket again. Reluctantly, he checked the text. It was from Helen: *Give me a call.*

He laboriously typed a reply – *Tied up at the moment. Home in an hour* – hit send, and dropped the phone back in his pocket.

Ayumi had no known medical problems. As far as they could tell, she hadn't had an accident. At least, she hadn't turned up at any hospital in the city, or at any morgue. The initial hope in these situations was that the 'missing' person was just off partying somewhere. After six weeks, however, most people had managed to make it home. Equally worrying was the fact that there had been no withdrawals from her bank account in the month following her disappearance.

The family had consented to publicity. Carlyle scratched his head, trying to recall if there had been anything about the disappearance in the media. Not that he could recall, but then he didn't pay much attention. Anyway, it looked like after an initial burst of activity, nothing had happened. Ayumi Ninomiya had been added to the list along with the other quarter of a million people who go missing in the UK every year; she would either turn up or she wouldn't. There was not much that anyone could do about it either way.

Except now her father had travelled six thousand miles to find out what was going on.

Carlyle felt a sudden flash of empathy with the old man. For a moment, he tasted Naohiro Ninomiya's boundless fear. If Alice had gone to Japan and disappeared, he wouldn't wait six weeks and then sit politely on a police bench being ignored for hours on end. He would stomp around and raise merry hell; he would try to do *something*.

That's what he would do.

Closing the file, he finished his tea. Getting to his feet, he dropped his empty cup into a rubbish bin by the till and headed upstairs.

EIGHT

Placing the file on the desk, Carlyle took a deep breath and sat down in front of Hiroshi Takahara and Naohiro Ninomiya. Both men looked extremely tired. The diplomat looked annoyed. The father looked determined. Up close, he was older than Carlyle had first supposed, probably in his mid-to-late sixties.

In the lift, the inspector had run through what he was going to say. It had sounded quite good in his head. But now, his mind was blank. Playing for time, he cleared his throat.

The two men looked at him expectantly.

'Gentlemen.' Carlyle forced himself to sit up straight. 'First, again, I must apologize for the delay downstairs.'

Mr Ninomiya gave a gracious nod.

'If we had known you were coming . . .'

'The Embassy contacted the station three times,' Takahara cut in, his voice strained, 'but we did not get any reply.' Leaning forward in his chair, he gestured towards the door. 'And then the woman downstairs . . .'

Ninomiya put a calming hand on the younger man's shoulder as he fixed Carlyle with a firm stare. 'You do not need to apologize, Inspector, these things happen.' His voice was low and clear, the English precise, with only a slight accent. 'But now that we are here, what can you tell me about your search for Ayumi?'

'Well,' Carlyle tapped the file with his index finger, 'I have to tell you that, up to this point, I have not been part of this particular investigation.' A look of disappointment clouded Ninomiya's grey eyes. 'However, I promise you that I will liaise with the investigating officers going forward.'

What the hell are you saying? a voice in his head started screaming. *You've got more than enough on your plate at the moment as it is.*

'But it has been six weeks now,' Takahara protested. 'This lady is a Japanese citizen. The government of Japan expects you to take all necessary steps to find her.'

Gritting his teeth, Carlyle focused solely on the father. 'The investigation to date has been conducted in a thorough and professional manner.' He tapped again on the file. 'We have searched Ayumi's flat, spoken to her known friends and associates, and we have visited where she studied and worked.'

In short, we've got nothing.

Under Mr Ninomiya's unwavering gaze, Carlyle forced himself to maintain eye-contact. 'Your daughter has been listed as missing on the Police National Computer, and she has been placed on the National Policing Improvement Agency's Missing Persons Bureau.'

'So,' Ninomiya asked, his voice staying low, 'do you think you can find her?'

Carlyle let out a breath. The statistics suggested that there was only one answer to that question. But now was not the time for statistics. 'The one thing I will not do, sir, is make promises that I cannot keep.'

Takahara opened his mouth to complain then thought better of it.

'I cannot promise that we will find your daughter,' Carlyle continued. 'What I can promise is that we will do our best. Having become aware of the case, I will personally do what I can.'

Ninomiya nodded again. He seemed to be visibly aging before the inspector's eyes.

'I know that you have already given us what help you can,' Carlyle said gently, 'and we are very grateful for that. But if there is anything else that you think might be relevant, nothing is too small to be worth considering.'

In response to this, Takahara compressed his lips angrily. So much for the inscrutable Japanese, Carlyle thought.

Ninomiya did a better job of keeping his emotions in check. 'Have you spoken to Miki?'

Miki? It took Carlyle a moment to drag the name of the flatmate – Miki Kasaba – from the pile of partially digested information in his head. 'Of course,' he replied, 'and we have spoken to all the people she suggested might be in contact with Ayumi.'

A spark of defiance flickered in Ninomiya's eye. 'And when was the last time that you spoke to her?'

'I would have to check.' Opening the file, Carlyle flicked through Sergeant Savage's notes. 'It would be approximately two weeks after she reported Ayumi missing.'

Ninomiya drummed his fingers on the table. 'I spoke to Miki almost every day, up until last week. Since then I have not heard from her.'

'Are you saying she has gone missing too?' Carlyle asked.

'Aren't *you* supposed to tell *us*?' Takahara asked.

'I am not aware that she has been reported missing.' Carlyle wasn't aware of much. 'But I will look into that.'

'Good.' Ninomiya abruptly got to his feet and extended a hand. 'Thank you for your time, Inspector.'

Relieved that he had got through the meeting, Carlyle jumped up and shook Ninomiya's hand.

'I shall be staying in London for at least a week, so we shall meet again.'

Carlyle's heart sank.

'Next time, I hope that you will have more information for me.'

'I will do my best,' Carlyle repeated. Resisting the temptation to bow, he handed out a couple of business cards of his own.

Slowly getting out of his chair, Takahara glowered at the inspector. Ninomiya gave Takahara an admonishing look before turning back to face Carlyle.

'The Embassy has been extremely gracious in the assistance it has provided. However, I am sure that we can now deal directly, man to man.'

Carlyle resisted the temptation to smirk at the diplomat. 'Of course.'

'I am staying at the Garden Hotel, do you know it?'

'Yes.' Carlyle knew the Garden well. The hotel was located just around the corner from the station, on St Martin's Lane, and the concierge was a good contact.

'I will return tomorrow for an update,' Ninomiya stated firmly.

Don't push me too far, Carlyle thought. 'Let's say this,' he suggested as he ushered the two men out of the room and towards the lifts. 'I will make various enquiries and then I will call on you at the hotel tomorrow evening, some time around seven.'

The two men exchanged a few words in Japanese.

'That is acceptable,' Ninomiya declared. 'I will see you then.' Ignoring the lifts, he headed for the stairs with Takahara in tow.

Enya Etchingham, it turned out, was an earnest young woman with no kids of her own. She went through the various NCT modules in a careful but rather bloodless manner. No anecdotes, no reminiscences, nothing to suggest that her knowledge of the process of childbirth came from anywhere other than a book.

She was a good-looking woman, though, Umar decided.

Enya caught him staring and smiled. 'How are you doing with your breathing exercises, Mr Sligo?'

Busted. Gripping Christina's hand tighter, Umar watched as his girlfriend did a passable impression of an asthmatic goldfish. According to the clock above the door, the hour had been up at least five minutes ago.

Following his gaze, Enya clapped her hands together. 'All right, everybody,' she said cheerily, 'let's finish there for tonight. Remember to keep practising the drills at home and I'll see you next week.'

Jesus. How did anyone ever manage to have a kid before

antenatal classes were invented? Struggling out of his orange bean bag, Umar got to his feet and helped Christina up. A pained expression crossed her face.

'I need to go to the loo.'

'Okay,' Umar shrugged. Pulling out his mobile, he called Carlyle's number as he watched her head for the door. As he let it ring, Christina fell into conversation with the only woman in the class – apart from the teacher – who didn't seem to be pregnant. Together they disappeared down the corridor as the inspector's voicemail kicked in. Umar left a perfunctory message and hung up.

'What do you think of the class?'

Umar turned to see a heavily pregnant blonde standing by his shoulder. Her green eyes twinkled mischievously.

'It's . . . interesting,' he said.

The room had emptied quickly. Apart from a Japanese couple talking to Enya, they were the only ones left. The blonde gestured towards the door. 'What does your wife make of it?'

'She's not my wife,' Umar blurted out.

The blonde grinned. 'Karen thinks she's very nice.'

'Karen?'

'My partner.' The woman held out a hand. 'I'm Joanna.'

'Umar.'

They shook and she made a point of holding on to his hand longer than necessary. 'The one thing they don't tell you,' Joanna giggled, checking to see that Enya wasn't listening, 'is how horny you get.'

'Um.' Umar was suddenly conscious of a dull ache in his groin. Christina certainly wasn't horny and hadn't been for some time.

'I just want to have sex,' Joanna whispered, 'all the time.'

'I see,' he gulped.

'I could do it right now.' Reaching into her bag on the floor, Joanna pulled out a business card and thrust it into Umar's hand. 'But maybe it would be better if you called me.'

'Er, right.' Unable to take any more of this particular

conversation, Umar stuck the card into his trouser pocket and bolted for the door.

The meeting with the Japanese had been as smooth as could have been expected. Still, Carlyle felt drained as he headed up to the third floor and sank into the chair in front of his desk. For the umpteenth time, his phone started vibrating in his pocket. Knowing that it would be Helen complaining about his tardiness, he let it go to voicemail.

In front of him was the impressively thick report Umar had compiled on the Schaeffer shooting. Flicking it open, Carlyle was surprised to see Susan Phillips's preliminary report on the top. Leaning forward, he squinted at the contents, worrying that an eye-test was overdue. Trying not to think about how much a trip to the optician's might end up costing, he flicked through the report which confirmed that Julian Schaeffer had died from gunshot wounds to the chest.

'That usually does the trick,' Carlyle mused.

The shots had come from a small-calibre weapon; the bullets had been recovered from the corpse.

'Handy if we find a bloke walking down the street with a gun in his hand . . .' Not wishing to wallow in the gory details of Phillips's prose, he moved swiftly on. Umar had filed a preliminary report of his own, including details of the interviews collected at Coram's Fields and background information on the victim and his family. A search of Schaeffer's flat and office had turned up nothing of note. They would have to go back to both locations for a more thorough look tomorrow.

The mother of the still-missing Rebecca had been identified as one Iris Belekhsan. Ms Belekhsan was a dentist. Apparently she was out of the country on holiday and had yet to be contacted. One of her colleagues had confirmed that she had left London a week ago.

Handy for an alibi, was Carlyle's first thought.

Picking up a pencil lying next to his landline, the inspector scribbled a note to check with Border Control. He noted with a wry smile that the co-worker had refused to speculate on Ms Belekhsan's domestic arrangements. However, going on holiday without your husband, or your child for that matter, suggested its own story.

At the back of the report was a list of other names and telephone numbers, people that the police hadn't been able to get round to speaking to on Day 1 of the investigation. Carlyle stopped counting when he got to twenty names. There was more than enough to be going on with – even before he thought about Mr Ninomiya. The work was piling up. That's just the way it happened. Cases were like buses. Nothing would come along for a while and then they'd get three or four all at the same time. He felt both energized and swamped. At least Umar was stepping up to the plate. 'Good effort, matey,' Carlyle smiled. Maybe impending fatherhood was encouraging the boy to up his game. In any event, he hoped it continued.

Tidying up the various bits of paper, the inspector shoved them back in the folder and slipped it into a drawer. Then he composed an email to Ed Savage, Sophie Watkin's sidekick, saying that he would call him in the morning. Sending that off into cyberspace, he got to his feet and at long last headed for home.

NINE

Paul Fassbender sat in the darkness in his study, steadily sipping from a large measure of Lagavulin Distillers Edition, a copy of *The Leopard* by Giuseppe Tomasi di Lampedusa lying unopened on his lap. In the distance, he could hear the wind whipping across Lake Garda and the Sirmio peninsula. Not yet 10 p.m. and Sirmione was closed for the night. Not for the first time, Fassbender asked himself why he had retired to Italy. It had been his wife's idea – the folly of letting a woman tell you what to do. These days, she spent more time in Marbella with her sister than she did with him. All alone in Lombardy, he sometimes wondered if he was not dead already.

His morbid musings were interrupted by what he imagined was the sound of footsteps in the hallway. Getting old was a bastard; his hearing, like all of his senses, played tricks on him on a regular basis.

The footsteps came closer. Taking a large mouthful of whisky, Fassbender slowly turned his head towards the door just as it creaked open.

He squinted at the shadow in the doorway. 'Who are you?'

The man stepped into the room. He didn't look like much, but he had youth on his side.

Half-rising from his seat, Fassbender hurled his glass towards the intruder, covering himself in Lagavulin in the process.

The man easily ducked away from the missile. 'You are the doctor?' he reached forward and placed a firm hand on Fassbender's shoulder, pushing him back down into his chair.

'I *was* a doctor,' Fassbender snapped, his English barely accented. 'I have been retired for several years now.' Nodding, the man took a step back, reaching into the breast pocket of his jacket as he did so.

'What do you want?' With his eyes accustomed to the darkness, Fassbender had no difficulty in making out the small syringe in the man's hand. A sick grin crept across his face. 'That stupid old fool,' he hissed. '*He* sent you, didn't he?' Once again, he tried to force himself out of the chair, only for the younger man to hold him down with his free hand.

'No more questions,' he said calmly. 'You need to relax.'

Fassbender hardly felt the needle as it sank into his thigh. Damn Italy, he thought bitterly, it really was like being dead already.

When the phone began ringing, Daniel Sands fumbled with the handset, almost dropping it. Recovering his composure, he was able to reply, 'Yes?'

'We have taken delivery of the package.'

Did he recognize the voice? He wasn't sure.

'Do you understand?' the caller asked.

'Yes, good. Thank you. This is quicker than I expected.'

'You will receive another call in two days,' came the terse instruction.

Daniel felt his hand shake violently. 'I will be ready.'

Out on the street, the inspector made his way towards the Piazza, weaving through the thinning crowds in front of St Paul's Church. Known as 'the Actors' Church', it was currently flanked on one side by a sunglasses store, and on the other by a bank. Inigo Jones, the architect, would doubtless be proud, Carlyle thought, to see his celebrated creation now keeping such august company. God would probably be quite chuffed, too.

Cutting across the Covent Garden Piazza, he passed an imposing mansion standing in the north-west corner, at number 43 King Street. Back in the nineteenth century, it had been one of London's first boxing venues. Then, as now, the fight game was so bent that many of the bouts descended into farce. One of the most famous King Street matches ended in chaos with *both* boxers taking a dive even before a single punch had been thrown. Not surprisingly, the disgruntled punters sought to take their frustrations out on the two pugilists, one of whom had the presence of mind to feign blindness in order to escape a beating from the mob. Legend had it that the 'blind' boxer was declared the winner and awarded the purse as well.

Carlyle spotted a poster of Iggy Pop advertising car insurance and tutted to himself. Whatever happened to live fast, die young? he wondered to himself as he thrust his hands in his pockets and upped his pace.

It took him less than five minutes to make the journey from police station to home, a two-bedroom apartment on the thirteenth floor of Winter Garden House, near Holborn tube station, at the north end of Drury Lane. Pulling the key from the lock, he stepped into the hallway, quietly closing the door behind him. From the far end of the hall, behind Alice's bedroom door, he could make out the strains of the Clash's version of 'Police on My Back'. A couple of years ago, Alice had borrowed all of his old Clash CDs. Now she knew their back catalogue far better than he did. Carlyle wondered what her friends at school made of it. Smiling proudly, he slipped off his shoes.

'Where the hell have you been?'

Carlyle smiled wanly at his wife who had appeared in the living-room doorway. Arms folded, she had a face like thunder.

'Tough day,' he told her.

Helen couldn't have looked any less sympathetic as she ground out, 'I've been trying to get hold of you for hours.'

For God's sake, he thought, *give me a break*. Gritting his teeth, he said, 'I know, sorry. But I—'

Not interested in his explanation, she turned and stalked off.

Down the hall, Joe Strummer had moved on to 'Midnight Log'.

Rubbing his eyes, Carlyle counted to ten and followed his wife into the living room.

'John.' Alexander Carlyle placed his half-empty bottle of Peroni beer on the coffee table.

'Dad.' Carlyle looked his old man up and down. Short and wiry, he was clean-shaven, with his white hair longer than Carlyle remembered it. Wearing jeans and a grey Fred Perry polo shirt that Helen had bought for his last birthday, he looked considerably younger than his seventy-odd years. The inspector thought back to the last time he had seen him – not since a Fulham game at Craven Cottage before Christmas. A listless Fulham had been thumped by another bunch of no-hopers. His dad had insisted on leaving twenty minutes before the end. They had gone for a drink in the Lemon Tree on the New King's Road but the conversation had been sparse and they had spent most of their time watching the football reports on the pub's TV. There had been a mass brawl in the Man United–Arsenal game and the referee had sent off three players.

It's funny what sticks in your memory.

Had he spoken to the old fella since then? Once, twice tops. Not about anything of note.

'John,' Alexander repeated, struggling out of the sofa.

'What brings you here?' It had to be more than a year since his father's last visit to Covent Garden, despite the fact that he lived only twenty-five minutes away, in West London.

The old man stepped forward and placed a hand on his son's shoulder. 'It's about your mother.'

Carlyle glanced at Helen, who was still scowling in the corner. She was his usual source of information about Lorna Gordon, his mother. As far as he was aware, his parents, who had divorced a few years earlier, hadn't even spoken to each other for more than six months.

Alexander cleared his throat. 'She's dead, son.'

Carlyle looked at him blankly. There had been nothing wrong with his mother. She kept herself in reasonable shape and she had the best part of a decade to go, statistically speaking, before her time was supposed to be up.

53

'What happened?'

Biting down on her annoyance, Helen came over and gave him a hug. 'She had a heart attack.'

His father hovered close by. 'She didn't suffer.'

Feeling incredibly self-conscious, Carlyle stared at the floor. What was he supposed to do? Burst into tears? He just couldn't play that game.

Alexander picked up his bottle and drained the last of the beer. 'I'm about to get all the arrangements in hand.'

Stepping free from his wife, Carlyle smiled at his father. 'Of course.' In that moment, he felt a huge affection for the old man; the practical Scotsman getting on and dealing with the situation. He took the empty bottle from his father. 'I think I'll have a beer myself. Want another one?'

Alexander thought about it for a moment. 'Just the one more,' he said finally. 'Thank you.'

Helen followed Carlyle into the kitchen. 'Are you okay, John?' she asked, watching him pull a couple of beers from the fridge.

'Yes.' Carlyle found a bottle-opener in the cutlery drawer and prised open the two bottles. 'I'm sorry it took me so long to get back.'

She reached over and kissed him on the cheek, all anger now gone. 'I understand.'

'And I'm sorry to leave you stuck with all of this.'

'It's fine. Your father has been great.'

Leaning against the fridge, Carlyle sucked down a mouthful of beer. 'So what happened?'

'I got a call at about five o'clock this afternoon.' Helen lowered her voice, 'From Ken Walton.'

Carlyle was surprised. 'Ken Walton?' The latter had been his mother's – well, boyfriend, when she had split from his father. As he recalled, Walton had ditched her after about six months. 'I didn't know that they were still seeing each other.'

'I think they met up now and again,' Helen said evasively.

Carlyle grunted. Under the circumstances, it didn't really matter.

'Ken called your dad.'

Maybe it did matter. 'Christ.'

'He's okay about it.'

Carlyle took another swig from his beer bottle. 'I bet.'

Helen patted him on the arm. 'Anyway, we need to get on.'

'Yes.' Carlyle gazed out of the kitchen window, across the Thames, towards the lights of the South Bank. He had a sudden, overwhelming urge to step out into the night, get pissed and explore the city's bounty. Waiting for it to pass, he turned back to his wife. 'How is Alice taking it?'

'She was a bit upset, but she'll be fine. She'll miss her grandma, of course, but they didn't see each other that much any more. I think she found Lorna too overbearing as she got older.'

I know the feeling. Carlyle just managed to avoid turning the thoughts into words. 'I'll go and have a chat with her.'

'Leave her.' Helen pointed to the clock on the wall by the door. 'It's a school night. Let her get to sleep. You should speak to your dad.'

Carlyle made a face.

'I thought he could stay here tonight,' Helen continued.

'Good idea.'

'I'll make a bed up for him on the sofa.'

'Okay.' Carlyle finished his beer and grabbed another from the fridge. Then, with a fresh bottle in each hand, he went off to talk to his dad.

TEN

'Come on, man, this has gone beyond a joke.' Calvin Jacobs hawked up a large gob of phlegm and spat it out onto the concrete floor. He had been kneeling on that floor for more than an hour now and his knees ached terribly. But the pain in his legs wasn't what was causing Calvin such immediate concern.

Nor was it the fact that his hands had been tied behind his back with plastic cuffs so tightly that he could no longer feel his fingers.

What was really stressing Calvin out was the blade hovering in front of his face, so close that he could clearly make out the logo: *Fiskars Splitting Axe X25*. Looking up at the hulking figure in front of him, Calvin tried not to burst into tears again. 'It wasn't me, man. I wasn't even there.'

The blade appeared three inches in front of his nose. It didn't appear very sharp. The man smiled maliciously, as if he was reading Calvin's mind. 'Don't worry,' he whispered. 'Fiskars have been making tools like these since 1649; it will get the job done.'

'I wasn't there,' Calvin wailed.

The man took a half-step forward, wiggling the axe handle as if he was lining up a particularly tricky golf shot. 'Don't lie to me, Calvin. You lie to me, I get mad. I get mad, I lose my concentration.'

Calvin felt the tears come again, hot and sticky, running down his cheeks and dripping off his chin. 'Please.'

The man stuck his tongue between his teeth, his eyes nothing more than two dark holes that had receded into the back of his skull. 'I get this right, your head comes all the way off, first time.

Minimizes any pain. You probably won't even know what happened.' The tongue disappeared back inside his mouth. 'But if I don't get a clean shot, need to hack at it a few times – well, I'm afraid that all bets are off.'

Calvin tried to scream but all that came out was a shrivelled groan. Anyway, he knew it was pointless. He'd spent the last hour shouting his head off and no one had paid any notice. That was the thing about this damn city, someone could be committing a murder twenty feet away and everyone ignores it; nobody cares. Bastards.

'Okay. Let's see how this goes.'

The blade disappeared from his line of vision. Closing his eyes as tightly as he could, Calvin Jacobs cried for his mother.

Careful not to steal the whole duvet, Carlyle rolled over and squinted at the clock on the table by his side of the bed.

2.12 a.m.

He couldn't remember the last time he had felt this wide awake. The adrenaline was coursing round his body and he knew that sleep would not come before dawn. Beside him, Helen started softly snoring. He gave her a gentle dig in the ribs and the snoring stopped.

2.13.

In a situation like this, he would normally slip into the living room and watch Sky Sports News for a while until he felt his eyelids begin to droop. Tonight, however, with his father on the sofa, that was not an option. Scratching his head, he stared at the ceiling.

2.14.

He thought he could make out a scuffling noise. It sounded like the mice were back. A ubiquitous problem for Londoners, rodents were something that Carlyle had always happily ignored until one evening a fearless little creature had darted up onto the sofa to enjoy an episode of *The Killing*. Carlyle had jumped a foot into the air and immediately got on the phone to the council. A few days later a man came round with some traps and some poison and there had been no more sightings for a while. But, deep down, Carlyle knew that where there was one, there would always be more. And they would never be gone for good.

2.15.

Ignoring the scuffling, he tried to focus on the hum of traffic outside. If you concentrated, you could just about make out the steady stream of traffic that headed up and down Kingsway, despite the late hour. Should he get up? Or should he just lie here, still, hoping that sleep might eventually come?

A memory of his mother drifted into his mind. He must have been fifteen or sixteen; they were standing in the kitchen of the family's council flat in Fulham. Carlyle was wondering how he was going to scrape together the cash for a cassette of the new Clash album before it went off special offer at the Our Price record store on the Fulham Road. His mother, meanwhile, was wondering why he couldn't grow up.

Arms folded, scowling, Lorna Gordon adopted a familiar pose. She was wearing a truly horrible blue and white knitted sweater that his father had bought as a Christmas present. She hated the sweater but wore it anyway. Looking her son up and down, the annoyance on her face was obvious. 'You'll be leaving school before you know it.' The last vestiges of the Glasgow accent mixed with the anger in her voice.

Carlyle gripped a rolled-up copy of the *New Musical Express* tightly in his left hand, the ink seeping into his fingers. He had bought the NME earlier in the day. It looked good – Paul Weller, Richard Hell, Iggy Pop and Bruce Springsteen – and he wanted to head off to his bedroom to read it in peace. 'I know.' He knew that his parents wanted him to settle on a career as early as possible, but life wasn't like that any more. There were no more jobs for life, wasn't that what everyone was saying? Joe Strummer screaming 'Career Opportunities' blasted into his head and he laughed.

Lorna looked at him in horror. 'What's so funny, boy?'

Boy.

Jesus.

The truth was, Carlyle *had* been thinking about what he might do when he left school. He was spending time in the Careers Office there – something not totally unconnected to the fact that it was run by the sultry Mrs Jennings – and he even had a list of possible vocations. He'd ruled out university on the grounds that even if his grades were good enough, his motivation to spend another three years in a classroom was lacking. He'd had an uncle in the Army but that seemed either too boring (like school, but with guns) or too dangerous. He wasn't going to let himself get blown up by some crazy Irish terrorist complaining about what happened to his ancestors three hundred years ago.

Joe Strummer sang on, listing all the other things he didn't want to do.

One thing young John was thinking about was the police force. Thinking about it seriously, too. But he didn't want to get into that with his mother right now.

Lorna leaned against the sink and lifted her mug of Tetley's tea to her lips. 'It's always going to be a struggle for you, son, isn't it?' She blew on the tea and took a sip.

Staring at the floor, Carlyle banged his copy of the *NME* against his leg.

'You have to get on, life won't wait for you.'

'No, Ma. I know it won't.'

'You're living in a dream world.'

2.18.

More scuttling noises came from the darkness. Realizing that he had been holding his breath, Carlyle exhaled deeply. Even after all this time, he still felt embarrassed by the conversation with his mother. Somehow, he felt ashamed.

With a small cry of complaint, Helen turned back towards him and stuck a warm arm across his bare chest. 'Upset about your mum?' she asked, her voice thick with sleep.

'Nah.' He kissed her. 'Just restless. Go back to sleep.'

She nuzzled closer, her hand slipping between his legs as she made a half-hearted attempt to take his mind off things, not protesting when he moved it away. 'I'm sorry, sweetheart.'

Carlyle kissed her again. 'I'm fine. Go back to sleep.' Not needing a second invitation, Helen grunted as she pulled the duvet over her head. Soon the gentle snoring resumed.

2.21.

He wondered if his father could sleep tonight. What must the old man be thinking?

There was no denying that Lorna Gordon had been a difficult woman. A few years ago, she discovered that Alexander had been guilty of a brief, decades-old infidelity and kicked him out of the family home. Carlyle had always thought that she used the affair as a convenient excuse, and that the truth was she had just grown fed up with her husband. His father had gone meekly into a bedsit; maybe he had just grown fed up of the marriage too.

2.22.

Whatever.

It wasn't that he had any regrets. Now that his mother was gone, Carlyle was able to admit – if only to himself – that his life would not really be affected one way or another. Next to the radio alarm he found his spectacles. Putting them on, he slipped out of bed, retrieved his clothes from the floor and headed into the bathroom. In the darkness, illuminated by the orange glow of the streetlighting below, he took a piss, aiming at the side of the bowl so as not to make any more noise than was absolutely necessary. Finishing up, he didn't flush.

After pulling on his clothes, Carlyle washed his face and gave his teeth a half-hearted brush. Stepping out into the hallway, he stopped outside Alice's door. Nothing. Moving along, he picked up a pair of trainers and let himself out, quietly closing the front door behind him.

Sitting on the top step of the landing, he pulled on the trainers and tied the laces in a tight double knot. Getting to his feet, he yawned. Now, of course, he felt incredibly sleepy. Not bothering with the lift, he made his way down the stairs.

* * *

Slowly regaining consciousness, Paul Fassbender felt his head smack against something cold and sharp. His curses caught in the gag in his throat and he fought the urge to throw up. His head was groggy and he felt like hell. Getting his breathing under control, he took a moment to take in his circumstances. Bound hand and foot, with a hessian sack over his head, he shivered in the freezing darkness.

The sound of traffic buzzed around his ears. Up front, inside the car, some mindless pop music blared from the radio. The driver bounced through another pothole and he hit his head again, this time without swearing. Shoved in the boot like a rag doll, every bone in his body ached and he badly needed to use the toilet. Despite all that, he was smiling.

He knew where he was going.

Well, well, he thought to himself, the old bastard had finally done it. Daniel Sands had finally snapped. Even after all this time, he couldn't leave it alone. Even worse, he didn't have the balls to do it properly. If he had been a real man, Fassbender would be in a shallow grave by now, a bullet in his brain, his flesh already beginning to rot.

The song on the radio ended and a DJ, speaking in French, gave a traffic update, warning of delays on the A7 heading towards Lyon. *I must have been asleep for a while*, thought Fassbender The plan, presumably, would be to drive him to the coast and then try to get him across the Channel on a ferry or maybe by train.

Closing his eyes, Fassbender brought up an image of Sands prattling on about 'justice'. Did he never learn? Even if they managed to get him to England, he was confident that he would be back home within a week. Meanwhile, his abductor and his accomplices would be facing lengthy jail sentences for assault, kidnapping and false imprisonment.

Fassbender chuckled to himself. Now *that's* what you called justice.

The pressure on his bladder increased. He stopped trying to

hold it in and felt the warm amber liquid spreading down his legs. It would go cold soon enough but he didn't care – one more problem for his captor to sort out. Snickering to himself, he tried to engineer a bowel movement. After a while, he conceded that nothing was going to come out. That was no surprise; he had been constipated for weeks and a satisfying bowel movement was no more than a distant memory. Ah well, maybe later. A car horn sounded somewhere behind them. Making himself as comfortable as he could manage, Fassbender settled in for the rest of his trip.

ELEVEN

Joe Rowan, a refugee from the Ealing police station, was the desk sergeant on night duty. Buzzing the doors open, he looked relieved to see the inspector, saying, 'Bloody hell, that was quick.'

You should have stayed in bed, Carlyle admonished himself, *you berk.*

'Huh?'

'I only called you about two minutes ago.'

'Huh?' As Rowan spoke, Carlyle felt his mobile vibrating in his pocket. He pulled it out, glanced at the screen and groaned. Six missed calls. How in the name of all things technological was that possible? The inspector knew of no one on the entire planet Earth who was less in tune with the digital revolution.

'You called me?'

'Yeah.'

'I was on my way in.' Wearily, he scanned the unanswered numbers. Two were from Umar and one was from Rowan on the desk. The rest were his voicemail trying to call him.

'Well, anyway,' Rowan said hastily, 'thanks for covering this.'

Covering what? Dazed, Carlyle accepted the slip of paper that Rowan thrust into his hand.

'They're waiting for you.' A phone on the desk started ringing. 'By all accounts, it's really quite something.' Rowan turned away and picked up the phone. 'Hello?'

Carlyle looked at the address written on the sheet of paper. SE1? Then he recalled that Stamford Street was just a quick walk over Waterloo Bridge. He could be there in less than fifteen minutes.

'Uh-huh, yeah.' Rowan looked up, surprised to see Carlyle still standing in front of him. 'That's right.' The sergeant's tone suggested that this was a private conversation, one he didn't want the inspector listening in on. He put his hand over the receiver and gestured at the paper in Carlyle's hand. 'Sounds like a good one.'

'I've got enough of those already.'

Rowan gave him a *What do you want me to do?* shrug and returned to his phone call.

Knowing when he was beaten, Carlyle turned away and headed back out into the night.

Waterloo Bridge was one of his favourite spots in the whole of London. Crossing the river, Carlyle looked past St Paul's towards the bright shining lights of the skyscrapers of Docklands. On the other side, looking west, was the London Eye and the Houses of Parliament, shimmering in the orange glow of the streetlighting. Dropping down off the bridge, he huried along the pedestrianized walkway beside the dirty brown river, heading east, past the National Theatre. Further along, lights were blazing on the ground floor of the South Bank Television Centre. A woman sitting at her desk, talking on the phone – one of the producers or researchers of a breakfast show that went on air at six every weekday morning – watched the inspector as he went past. Journalists at work near the scene of a crime; he wondered if any of them might have seen something. Probably not. Apart from anything else, they weren't that type of journalist; their show was all about celebrities, diets and holidays, rather than crime or other 'hard' news. Carlyle had never watched the programme but knew from various newspaper stories that it had undergone a disastrous, hugely expensive revamp a few months earlier. The obvious lack of chemistry between the two main presenters and a slump in viewing figures meant that speculation was rife that studio bosses might pull the plug after less than a year.

Reaching Gabriel's Wharf, he took a right, away from the water, passing through a small knot of pizza restaurants and trinket shops, before coming out on to Stamford Street, which ran parallel to the river between Waterloo and Blackfriars Bridges. Immediately he saw the police vans and cars about a hundred yards further down the road. A spotlight illuminated one of the houses, and various people who had come out to see what had happened were clustered around a couple of uniforms on guard in front of the police tape that ran across the south side of the street.

Number 172 stood in the middle of a row of half a dozen Georgian houses that had survived the war and remained in splendid isolation, facing towards the river. The rest of the street had been bombed out in the Blitz. Urban renewal and gentrification had taken more than fifty years to reach this tiny neighbourhood, and still had only done so in patchy fashion. The far end of the street was home to a block of expensive 1990s flats, all PVC windows and tiny balconies. In the middle of the row there was still a gap where maybe fifteen or twenty houses had been flattened by the Germans. The undeveloped ground was still being used as a temporary car park, as it had been for at least the last forty years. In one corner was a burnt-out estate car. As he walked past, Carlyle saw a dosser sitting in the driving seat, watching proceedings. His possessions were piled up in a shopping trolley that stood next to the car. Some kind of mongrel was asleep under the cart. The touching scene reminded the inspector of 'Dog', a well-known drunk who used to hang around Covent Garden, giving tourists a sob story about his lost pet as he hustled for change. The dog, of course, was fictitious. The drunk was, for a while, a regular on the benches at Charing Cross station. Carlyle grinned at the memory.

What was the guy's name?

Walter Poonoosamy.

To his pleasant surprise, it came to him almost immediately. Then again, Walter Poonoosamy *was* a fairly memorable name.

As he approached the police tape, Carlyle was mildly surprised to see the familiar figure of Sergeant Ed Savage appear from behind a van.

Savage held up the tape to let him through. 'The desk said you were coming,' he complained, 'half an hour ago.' An inch or so taller than the inspector, he was in his early thirties, still in reasonable shape. With short blond hair and a firm jaw, he had a boyish air that had not been totally washed away by having three kids under six. Carlyle and Helen had met the Savage family at a police social a few months earlier. He remembered how Mrs Savage, who worked as a nurse, had looked completely shattered. By comparison, her husband looked like he was coping just fine.

Carlyle ignored the complaint. He had worked with Savage a couple of times in recent years and knew that he was basically okay. Moreover, if he might want him to replace Umar, there was no point in having a spat now. 'What have we got?'

Turning away, Savage gestured for the inspector to follow. 'You're going to love this.'

Always the big build-up, Carlyle thought wearily. He chased after Savage, almost walking right into the back of the sergeant as he stopped next to a blanket draped over the railings in front of the house.

'*Voilà!*' Savage removed the blanket with a flourish.

'Holy shit!' Carlyle took a step backwards, almost falling off the pavement and into the gutter.

'I told you you'd like it,' Savage smirked.

Carlyle squinted through his glasses. 'Is that real?'

Savage pointed at the blood on the paving stones by their feet. 'It sure is.'

Ignoring his squeamishness, Carlyle moved back towards the head. It looked waxy, like something out of Madame Tussauds' waxworks. The gore hanging from the neck looked real enough, though. So did the greasy black hair that no longer had any shoulders to fall on. The gormless expression on the victim's face also had more than an air of realism about it.

Savage gestured back along the street. 'The bloke sitting in the car found him about one thirty. He went and told one of the security guards at the TV station, who called it in.'

A forensics team arrived, led by a pathologist Carlyle hadn't met before. After the necessary introductions had been made, Savage handed over the blanket, and the policemen retreated to allow the technicians to get on with their job.

'Why would someone chop a bloke's head off and stick it on public display like that?' Carlyle thought he might as well ask the question.

Savage gave him an amused look. 'Isn't that what *you're* here to tell us?'

'All in good time, Sergeant,' said Carlyle cheerily. He had only been at the crime scene for a couple of minutes, but already he was confident of a quick result. Clearly, passion and violence were at play here, not premeditation and cunning. It wouldn't take long to catch whoever did this. 'All in good time.' He winced as he watched one of the technicians carefully open the guy's mouth. 'Do we have an ID?'

'It's a head,' Savage protested.

'So where's the rest of him?'

'We haven't found that yet.' Savage pulled a packet of Benson & Hedges from his jacket pocket and offered one to Carlyle.

The inspector shook his head. 'No, thanks.'

Savage put a cigarette in his mouth and began fumbling for his lighter. 'He was killed inside, for sure.' He gestured towards the house. All the lights were on and Carlyle could see more technicians at the first-floor window. 'Whoever did it decapitated him on the first floor and dragged the body down the stairs and out of the front door.' Finding his lighter, Savage lit up and took a long drag.

'So where is it now?' Carlyle asked again, stepping away from the smoke.

Savage exhaled thoughtfully.

The inspector gestured at the head. 'He certainly wasn't trying to hide him.' He looked up and down the street. Outside every property was a collection of black bin liners awaiting the arrival of the bin men.

Savage followed his gaze and cursed.

The inspector tried to look sympathetic. 'You'd better start with those. The house-to-house can come afterwards.'

'Yes, sir.' Savage stalked off to find some uniforms to search through the rubbish.

'Oh – and Sergeant?'

Gritting his teeth, Savage turned back to face Carlyle. 'Yes?'

'Is there anywhere I can get a decent cup of coffee around here?'

TWELVE

Carlyle brought a cup of filter coffee from a 7-Eleven on the corner of Duchy Street and returned across the rough ground of the car park, taking care not to step into any of the potholes in his path. As he approached the burnt-out car, he could see that it had once been a VW Golf, or something similar. The tramp was still in the driver's seat, watching as half a dozen uniformed officers went slowly along the street.

'They'll be looking for body parts, I expect,' he said matter-of-factly, as the inspector approached. 'So far, all they've got is the head.'

Thirty yards down the road a WPC stuck her hand in the air and signalled for one of the technicians to come over.

'Looks like they've found something.' The tramp's gaze fell on the cup in Carlyle's hand.

'I thought you might like some coffee.' Stepping forward, Carlyle stuck his hand through the space where the windscreen used to be and carefully placed the cup on the dashboard. He dug out a couple of sachets of sugar and a mini-carton of milk and placed them next to the cup. 'It's hot.'

The tramp looked at the coffee with some distaste. 'I'd rather have some Strongbow.' He gestured back in the direction from which Carlyle had come, towards the all-night 7-Eleven. 'They've got a good offer on at the moment – six cans for ten quid.'

'Bargain,' said Carlyle, nonplussed. Sticking out a hand, he introduced himself.

'Oliver.' The tramp ignored the inspector's hand. 'Oliver Mackenzie.' Sitting in the wreck of the motor it was hard to get a good view, but on first glance, the guy looked fresh-faced and clear-eyed for someone living on the streets. 'My friends call me Olly.'

Carlyle nodded. 'Well, Mr Mackenzie, what happened here?'

The tramp leaned forward against the steering wheel and let rip with an enormous fart.

Carlyle took an involuntary step backwards.

'I needed that.' Oliver settled back on the springs that were all that remained of the driver's seat. 'Too many beans at the soup kitchen. I counted three different kinds tonight.'

Why do I bother? the inspector wondered. 'Uh-huh.'

'Beans, beans, beans; nothing but bloody beans. I told them, "More meat, fewer beans, or you won't be seeing me again".'

Technicians were now inspecting a trio of black bin bags which had been lined up under a streetlight.

Carlyle folded his arms. 'Tell me what you saw.'

Oliver tried to give him an ingratiating smile. 'Did I mention the Strongbow?'

'What did you *see*?' Carlyle snapped.

From under the shopping cart, the dog growled.

'Now you've woken Peanut.' Oliver looked hurt.

Peanut? 'Mr Mackenzie . . .'

Realizing that it was all he was going to get from the policeman, the tramp reached up and grabbed the coffee. Sticking the cup between his legs, he lifted off the lid, before adding the sugar and the milk. After stirring it with his finger, he took a sip. 'Ahh.'

Carlyle waited patiently.

After a couple more mouthfuls, Oliver put the lid back on the cup. He looked up at Carlyle. 'I saw the head.'

'Yes?'

'And that was it.'

When Carlyle returned to the crime scene, the head had been

removed – along with several of the bin liners – for further investigation. Having gone through the rubbish, the uniforms were starting their door-to-door enquiries. More box ticking. The likelihood of coming up with anything useful was slim; witnesses were as rare as they were unreliable.

He found Savage sitting in the passenger seat of a Police Range Rover having another cigarette. He watched warily as Carlyle approached, and asked: 'Get anything from the wino?'

The inspector placed a hand on the car roof and leaned towards the open window. 'Nope.'

'Never mind.' Savage grinned maliciously. 'At least you didn't fall in a pothole.'

Carlyle looked around. 'This won't be difficult, will it? A nutter putting a head on a spike.'

Savage took a long drag on his cigarette and flicked it out of the window, past Carlyle's right arm.

'Naohiro Ninomiya came to the station last night,' the inspector told him.

Savage pretended that he couldn't place the name.

'The Japanese guy,' Carlyle pretended to remind him. 'His daughter went missing. You and Watkins chased it up.'

'What did he want?'

'He was with a guy from the Japanese Embassy. They were after an update on the investigation.'

'Why didn't he bloody call me then?' Savage said, the petulance clear in his voice.

'They said no one had returned their calls.'

'Well, Watkins is off now.'

That doesn't stop you picking up the bloody phone, though, does it? Carlyle tried to keep the annoyance from showing in his face.

'Anyway, we chased everything up, by the book. It's a dead end.'

'Are you going to tell the father that?'

Savage grinned. 'That's above my pay grade.'

The inspector glanced up at the burnt-out car. Oliver Mackenzie had gone, along with his trolley and his dog. It would be getting light soon. Maybe he was a vampire. Maybe the dog was a vampire dog. Carlyle chuckled to himself. He looked back at Savage and his smile vanished. 'I thought you might say that.'

Belatedly, Savage realized he was pushing his luck. 'Sorry, Inspector.' He held up a hand. 'It's Watkins's job really.'

'Doesn't bloody help me much,' Carlyle groused. 'Does it?'

Sticking another cigarette between his lips, Savage said nothing.

Carlyle pulled his mobile phone out of his pocket to check the time. It was too late to go back to bed. The working day had begun. 'Finish up here and meet me back at the station – we can see what we've got.'

As he walked away from the car, he heard Savage mumble something that sounded like, 'Whatever.'

Sod you too, thought Carlyle. Head down, he marched along the road, walking in the direction of Waterloo. Almost immediately, he was conscious of someone falling in step beside him. Looking round, he saw a young man wearing a Take That T-shirt under a parka. Tall and thin, he was carrying a Tesco plastic bag containing what looked like a selection of microwave meals. His eyes were two dark pinpricks, marking him out as a stoner.

'I know who did it,' he said.

'What?' Carlyle stopped.

'The bloke who had his head stuck on the railings, I know who did it.' The youth did a little dance on the tarmac. Unshaven and gaunt, he had a mop of curly hair that looked like it had been casually plonked on the top of his head. An unused cigarette was stuck behind his left ear.

Please God, Carlyle offered up a silent prayer, *not another nutter*. 'Yeah?'

The man nodded eagerly. 'Yeah.'

Carlyle let out a long breath. 'I tell you what,' he pointed at Savage, who was still sitting in the car, 'go and talk to Sergeant Savage – the guy in the Range Rover. He is in charge here.'

The man looked at Carlyle doubtfully.

'He will want to take a full statement,' Carlyle insisted. 'Go on.' He watched as the man headed reluctantly towards Savage, before continuing on his way at a brisk pace.

Under the railway arches by the Royal Festival Hall was the 93 Coffee Bar. It was not yet 5.15 – sunrise was still the best part of forty-five minutes away – and the Closed sign was still in place. But the lights were on and as he approached, Carlyle could see activity inside. Reaching the door, he knocked firmly on the glass and waited. After a few moments, a tired-looking blonde woman stuck her head out of a doorway at the back.

'We're closed,' she shouted, without looking up.

Carlyle grinned and knocked again.

'I said . . .' Finally glancing in his direction, she stopped in mid-sentence and smiled. Wiping her hands on a tea towel, she hastened to the door, turned the lock and pulled it open. 'What brings you here?' Standing on her toes, she reached over and gave him a peck on the cheek.

Carlyle gestured back towards the river. 'Long night.' Stepping inside, he explained about the head on the railings as she re-locked the door.

She put her hand to her mouth to stifle a giggle.

'It's not funny, Laura,' Carlyle said with mock seriousness. But he was laughing too. It was good to see a friendly face. He would have liked to go home and jump into bed, but that was not an option so at least he could meet the working day with a full stomach.

Laura Stevenson read his mind. 'Full English?'

Carlyle thought about it for a moment. 'Eggs, chips and beans. White toast, no butter. But with some green tea, if you have it.'

Laura raised an eyebrow. 'Green tea?'

'Green tea,' Carlyle grinned. 'My one concession to healthy living these days. Sometimes.'

'Fine. Just give me a minute.'

'Thanks.' As she nipped behind the counter, Carlyle looked at the small montage of photos on the wall behind the till. He soon found the one he had been looking for, in the top right-hand corner where it had been for the last thirty years or so. A teenage Laura was standing on a crowded Brighton beach with her arm round her father. The sun was shining and the sky was blue, and both of them were smiling. Carlyle had taken the picture.

John Carlyle had only been two years on the Force when he had helped Eamonn Stevenson track down his daughter. Laura had been 'kidnapped' by her mother, who had whisked her off from the family home in Bermondsey to a squat in Kilburn. Social Services wouldn't intervene, so Carlyle had gone with Eamonn to get her back. When the mother's new boyfriend had put up a fight, Carlyle had busted his kneecap with a length of lead pipe. From then on, he became an honorary member of the family. He still remembered that day out at the seaside. Outside of moments with Helen and Alice, it was one of his happiest memories.

'How's your dad?' Carlyle asked.

'So-so.' Laura reached into a box of green tea bags. 'When was the last time you saw him?'

Carlyle couldn't remember. He smiled ruefully. 'Not for a while.'

'He's almost seventy-four now.' Laura dropped four slices of bread into an outsized toaster. 'He's doing okay, considering, just getting a bit slow.' She caught his eye. 'He'd love to see you.'

Carlyle sighed inwardly. It was impossible to keep up with everyone. Eamonn and Laura had sorted themselves out and moved on. So had he. Carlyle had had his own life to lead. Between pounding the beat and his assiduous courting of the reluctant Helen, there had been precious little time left for much else. Occasionally he would drop into the café, which Eamonn had taken over from his uncle, only to leave embarrassed by the fact that he would never be allowed to pay for anything. Carlyle knew that Eamonn's gratitude was genuine, but it made him uncomfortable. It was hard enough making a living from the café without handing out free meals, and he didn't want to feel like a freeloader.

'How's Sean?' he asked, moving the conversation on. Sean Taylor, Laura's husband, was a copper, a sergeant working out of the Streatham station. Husband and wife worked like dogs to send their daughter to a private boarding school for girls in Kent.

'He's fine, a bit worried about the cuts.'

'Aren't we all.'

Nodding, Laura handed him a mug and pulled the toast out of the machine in one fluid movement. 'Lightly toasted, just the way you like it.'

Carlyle nodded happily.

'We can't afford any problems at the moment. Julie's going to university soon. The fees are ridiculous.'

'I know.' Carlyle sipped his tea. It burned the back of his throat and he purred contentedly. 'Ridiculous.'

Laura dropped the toast on a plate and turned her attention to the eggs and chips. 'Wait till it's Alice's turn.'

I'm absolutely dreading it, Carlyle thought. Helen had already started saving for the possibility. At the current rate of progress, Carlyle had calculated, they would be able to cover the first year's fees in about thirty-five years. Moving away from the counter, he picked up a copy of yesterday's *Metro* from a rack on the wall and took a seat at a table by the window. Flicking through the news pages, he read a story about a gang smuggling illegal immigrants into the country in specially built compartments in lorries.

'If people are that desperate,' he said to himself, 'let them bloody come.'

Laura appeared with his food and put the plate carefully onto the table. 'What are you muttering about?'

'Nothing, nothing.' Moving the paper to one side, he licked his lips.

'Careful,' she warned him, 'it's hot.'

'Okay, thanks.' Carlyle grabbed a bottle of ketchup and applied it liberally to his chips. Right on cue, his stomach started rumbling and he began unceremoniously shovelling food into his mouth. Flipping the Open sign at the door, Laura slipped behind the counter to get ready for the morning rush.

As the clock crept around towards six, a steady stream of

customers appeared – a mix of roadsweepers, bin men and some construction workers, along with a few early office workers and the odd jogger in search of a caffeine boost to help them on their run. Laura had cleared his plate away and Carlyle, his belly now more than full, was lingering over a second mug of green tea as he finished reading yesterday's paper. London's new mayor was promoting a new cycle scheme while reducing Congestion Charging, making it easier for people to clog up London's streets with their Chelsea Tractors and other vehicles. Typical bloody politician, Carlyle thought. Over the years, he'd had several run-ins with the previous mayor; it was good to see that the new guy was keeping up the time-honoured tradition of being totally useless.

Closing the paper, he folded it neatly and put it back on the rack. He took his empty cup over to the counter where Laura was taking the order of a couple of traffic wardens. Placing the cup on the counter, he reached into his jacket pocket and took out his wallet. Ignoring Laura's shake of the head, he removed a tenner and dropped it into the tips jar by the till.

Their order taken, the traffic wardens retreated to their table. Laura gave him a pained look. 'John.'

Carlyle fished a couple of pound coins out of his trouser pocket and added them to the jar. 'Those university fees are a killer.'

She smiled. 'Thanks.'

'No. Thank *you*. That was just what I needed.' Reaching over the counter, he kissed her on the forehead. 'Say hi to Eamonn for me. I'll try and get to see him soon.'

'Will do.' The smile wavered slightly. They both knew that it wouldn't happen.

'I'll see you later.'

She turned back to the Gaggia coffee machine. 'Good luck with the head.'

'Luck?' Carlyle laughed as he reached the door. 'Luck doesn't come into it.'

THIRTEEN

Out on the pavement, Carlyle turned left, heading towards the river. Climbing the steps by the side of the Royal Festival Hall he crossed the footbridge that ran alongside the railway bridge leading into Charing Cross train station. It took him less than five minutes to get over the river and walk down John Adam Street to the Little Adelphi apartment building. Ayumi Ninomiya and her flatmate shared Flat 5A. Looking in vain for the porter, Carlyle buzzed the flat.

No reply.

He stood on the pavement for a few seconds and tried again, longer this time, counting slowly up to thirty before stopping.

Still nothing.

Ah well, it was worth a try. What should he do next? The day stretched tediously ahead of him; Carlyle knew that he had a long To Do list, but he felt unable to prioritize. He was tired and finding it hard to focus. Usually, he liked to do the easiest and quickest things first, getting them out of the way so that he could chalk up a few wins while giving the harder problems time to solve themselves or, at least, go away. If the tricky things were still on his desk when he got around to looking at them, then at least they would get his undivided attention. This morning, however, there were no 'quick wins' on offer. The reality was that he didn't want to do anything.

His lassitude was interrupted by the phone ringing in his pocket.

'Carlyle.'

'It's Umar.'

'What's up?'

'I tried to call you last night.'

'I know, I know. I got waylaid.' Crossing the road, the inspector started towards Adam Street, which would take him on to the Strand. From there it was a short walk to the police station. 'How did the antenatal class go?'

'Fine, fine,' said Umar hastily, disinclined to explain to his boss how he'd been hit on by a lesbian mum-to-be in the crudest manner imaginable. 'I'm at the station. Did you read my report?'

'Yes.' It took Carlyle a couple of moments to recall the basic facts of the Schaeffer case. 'We've got a lot to do.'

Umar grunted. His boss was becoming a master at stating the obvious. 'Where do you want to start?'

Carlyle's reply was drowned out as a red Porsche 911 Turbo roared down the street and came to a screeching halt outside the Little Adelphi.

'Inspector?'

Carlyle turned and began walking back in the direction he'd come from. 'I'll have to call you back,' he said.

'Okay.'

'No, wait.' Carlyle stepped into the middle of the road and squinted at the Porsche's numberplate. Lowering his voice, he read out the registration. 'Find out who owns that car.'

'Sure.' Umar read it back.

'That's it.'

'Okay. I'll check.

Umar clicked off the call.

Keeping the phone stuck to his ear, Carlyle walked slowly past the Porsche as a rotund, red-faced guy in his sixties struggled out of the driver's seat. Leaving the door open, the man jogged round to the passenger side and offered a hand to his young companion as she climbed sleekly out of the car with a spectacular array of shopping bags. The man looked exhausted but he smiled brightly as he lined the bags up in front of the entrance of the apartment building. Once the shopping was all present and correct, the girl dutifully leaned forward to let the man kiss her on the lips. The man grinned and said something that Carlyle couldn't hear before jumping back into the car and disappearing round the corner. Carlyle waited until the girl had picked up all of her bags and was keying in the code to open the front door of the building before he strolled over to her.

'Miki Kasaba?'

Pretty but tired, her face encrusted with far too much make-up, the girl looked at him blankly. If she was surprised at being accosted by an unknown man in the street, it didn't show. The lock clicked open and she pushed the door ajar.

Carlyle flashed his ID. 'I'm from the police. I wanted to ask you about Ayumi.'

A flicker of concern crossed the girl's face. 'Have you found her?'

Carlyle shook his head. 'No.'

'Help me with the bags.' Pushing the door fully open, Miki slipped into the lobby, leaving the inspector to follow.

By the time he reached the lift, laden down with the shopping, she was holding the doors open for him, muttering something under her breath in Japanese. Stepping inside, Carlyle put the bags down on the floor and waited for the doors to close behind him. 'Her father has come to London,' he explained, once they were on their way. 'He was trying to get hold of you.'

Miki nodded but said nothing. On the second floor, the doors pinged open and she strode out, once again leaving the inspector to pick up the bags. Carlyle followed the girl down a long, dimly lit corridor. Stopping outside 5A, she fished a key out of her jacket pocket, saying, 'It's been a long night.'

Carlyle nodded. *Tell me about it.*

She looked at him, as if for the first time. 'What is your name?'

'Carlyle. Inspector John Carlyle.'

Miki stuck the key in the lock. 'Last time it was a woman.'

'Yes. She has gone on maternity leave.'

'Of course,' Miki giggled, pushing the door open. 'I remember now. She was *big*. Maybe she should have been more careful. Stopped work earlier.'

Carlyle said nothing. Trained in his new position, he picked up the bags and followed Miki inside into the hallway. Kicking off her shoes, she hung her coat on a peg on the wall and moved off down the corridor. 'I need a shower.' She pointed to a room off to the left. 'Put the shopping in there and make yourself a cup of tea if you want. I won't be long.' Before he had a chance to respond, she disappeared into the bathroom, closing the door behind her.

Dumping the bags in the middle of the room, Carlyle dropped onto a black leather sofa and kicked off his shoes. Yawning, he did a quick audit of Miki's shopping. Most of the brands were names which he didn't recognize but there were three large carrier bags with the legend *Louboutin* emblazoned on the side. Carlyle knew what they were, even before he clocked the two shoeboxes inside each bag. He let out a low whistle. Clearly Miki, or more likely Miki's gentleman friend, had spent several thousand pounds on some pretty heavy retail therapy. Leaning back into the sofa, he stretched his toes on the wooden floor. With his stomach still full of breakfast, he felt heavy and lethargic. Maybe he should make himself some tea?

Someone was talking. But they weren't talking to him, and they weren't talking in English. Shaking himself awake, Carlyle slowly focused on Miki Kasaba standing in the doorway in a pair of jeans and a grey T-shirt, talking on her mobile. Giving him a cheeky grin, she said something in Japanese and ended the call.

'Looks like I'm not the only one who had a hard night.' Freshly scrubbed, without the make-up, she radiated youth and health.

Getting to his feet, Carlyle grunted.

'Did you get some tea?'

Stretching, he shook his head.

'Let me make some.' Crossing the room, she stepped into the open-plan kitchen.

'Thanks.'

Leaving her mobile on a worktop, she filled and switched on the kettle. 'What kind of tea would you like?'

Carlyle sat back down. 'Green tea – if you've got it.'

'I have.' Miki opened a cupboard and took out a couple of mugs.

Carlyle gestured at the carrier bags. 'That's a lot of shopping.'

Miki took two tea bags from a box and popped one in each mug. 'Dan took me to Paris.'

'The guy in the Porsche?'

Miki looked at him coyly. 'Yes.' The kettle came to the boil and she poured water into each mug. Then she picked up both mugs – with the tea bags left in – handed him his and sat down with hers at the opposite end of the sofa.

'Thanks.' Carlyle took a careful sip.

Grasping her mug with both hands, Miki stared into her tea. 'He'd been pressing me to go for months.'

Feeling an admission coming on, the inspector stayed schtum.

'Ayumi always told me that I would have to sleep with him if I went.' She gestured at the bags with her chin. 'It was only a question of the price. We used to joke about it. Ayumi always said that six pairs of Louboutins was the absolute minimum.'

For her, Carlyle wondered, or for you? Feeling himself blush, he tried to think back to any reference to a sugar daddy in the casefile. He was fairly sure that there wasn't any. 'Who's Dan?'

Miki rubbed her nose on her wrist. 'I thought you were here about Ayumi?'

'You need to help me here,' Carlyle said gently. 'Did Ayumi date Dan before you?'

'I told everything to the other officer.' Miki picked at a nail. 'Ayumi met a lot of different guys online.'

'Which website did she use?'

'There are a few. The best one is called Leafhopper. Ayumi said the guys on there at least had plenty of money.' Miki stifled a sob. 'She isn't coming back now, is she?'

It doesn't look like it. Not for all the Louboutins in the world.

Carlyle made a non-committal gesture. 'If she went off with someone from this website, where could she be?'

'You tell me.' Miki placed her mug on the floor. 'I need to get some sleep.' She looked the inspector straight in the eye. 'It's a big bed; big enough to share.'

Carlyle jumped to his feet. 'I have to get to work.'

Putting a hand on her hip, Miki gave him a fake little pout. 'Your call.'

Carlyle gestured at the shoes. 'Anyway, you're way out of my league.'

The pout gave way to a cheeky smile. 'Everyone likes to slum it once in a while.'

Taking a deep breath, Carlyle returned his mug to the kitchen counter and set off for the doorway. 'I'll tell Mr Ninomiya that he can give you a call to arrange a meeting.'

She gave a tiny sigh. 'I suppose so.'

'Good.' Carlyle stared at the floor. 'Thank you for the tea.' Fishing a business card from his pocket, he placed it on the television stand by the door. 'Do get in touch if you can think of anything else.' Without waiting for a reply, he ducked into the hall and fled towards the relative sanctuary of Charing Cross police station.

Waiting for the traffic lights to change so that he could cross the Strand, Carlyle scrolled through his latest list of missed calls:

Umar

Helen

Simpson

Susan Phillips

Two unknown numbers

The inspector scratched his head. That was about right for a few hours' AWOL. No one had left a message. He looked up in the direction of Trafalgar Square. As usual, the traffic was crawling along at no more than a couple of miles an hour. The air was still and he could taste the exhaust fumes in the back of his throat.

Three feet in front of him, a stationary taxi driver laughed into his Bluetooth headset as the meter ticked over to £42.20. In the back of the cab, a frustrated-looking businessman tapped angrily on his BlackBerry as his money burned away.

Belatedly the inspector tried to organize the rest of his day. Who should he call first? As the lights changed, the taxi edged on to the pedestrian crossing, blocking his way. Cursing, Carlyle resisted the temptation to give it a kick as he slalomed between the cab and a hotel shuttle bus. Safely reaching the north side of the road, he hit Phillips's number as he strode towards the police station.

She answered on the first ring. 'I was wondering where you had got to.' Bright and cheery.

'Busy,' said Carlyle gruffly.

Susan Phillips got the message and immediately toned down the cheer. 'Did you see my report?'

'Yeah. Thanks for getting it over so quickly.'

'It will take me time to work up the final verdict but I don't think there'll be much new in it.'

'Okay.' Carlyle stood by the red phone box outside the station entrance and listened politely while the pathologist reprised some of the highlights of Julian Schaeffer's murder. He liked Phillips well enough to make a few encouraging and grateful-sounding noises but, in truth, he wasn't much interested. The bloke had been shot in the chest at close range; that was all he really needed to know.

At least the snooze on Miki Kasaba's sofa had refreshed him enough to boost his civility levels. When Phillips had finished her monologue, he was polite enough to ask a question.

'Anything interesting about the bullets?' It wasn't really her area, but seeing as she had dug them out of the stiff, he thought he might as well ask. He knew that Phillips was a team player who showed more interest than most of her colleagues in the cases she worked on. She didn't just cut up corpses, write up her notes and go home. It was one of the things he liked about her.

'Not really. The ballistics check was done this morning.' She reeled off a list of technical details that went in one ear and out the other.

'Standard ammunition,' Phillips concluded. 'Could have been used in a wide variety of handguns. Find the weapon and they can run a comparison.'

They both knew that wasn't going to happen. This was a professional killing; the gun used to kill Schaeffer would have been stripped and its component parts individually destroyed. Carlyle nodded at a WPC he knew coming out of the building and passing him on the pavement. 'I'd better get on with it, then.'

'Good luck.'

'Thanks.'

'Oh,' Phillips said hastily, before he could hang up on her, 'and there's the other thing.'

Head bowed, Carlyle kicked the toe of his shoe against the phone box. 'What other thing?'

'Pippa Collingwood.'

Carlyle scoured his brain but nothing came out. 'Who?'

Phillips sounded surprised. 'Weren't you up on Rosebery Avenue yesterday? The girl who was run over by the postal van.'

'Oh that, yeah. Nothing to do with me, though.' He tried to remember the name of the sergeant from Islington who had been in charge but – again – his mind was blank.

'Ah, okay.'

'Why?' Peering inside the phone box, the inspector counted eight prostitutes' calling cards stuck on the back wall above the phone with Blu-Tack. He shook his head. Having sex with a prostitute wasn't illegal but solicitation was. The guys who went round sticking up the cards could be arrested and fined. The council had a team that was supposed to remove the cards as soon as they were put up. It was a 'quality of life' issue. But they couldn't even enforce the law right next to the police station.

'Well,' Phillips cleared her throat, 'it wasn't just that she'd been run over. When we looked at her there was evidence that she had been the victim of violence over a period of time.'

Carlyle grimaced. 'Sexual abuse?'

Phillips coughed. 'Yes. It looks like she'd been raped. More than once.'

Carlyle felt sick to his stomach. He rubbed his face. 'Like I said, nothing to do with me. Listen, I'm going to have a catch-up on Mr Schaeffer now. I'll call you later if I have any questions.'

'Good luck.'

'Thanks.' Ending the call, he headed inside.

FOURTEEN

After a trip to the canteen for a restorative cup of green tea, Carlyle went upstairs to his desk on the third floor. There was no sign of Umar, so he called his wife. Like Phillips, Helen answered on the first ring. Clearly, this was his day for getting hold of people.

'Where have you been?' Her voice was concerned rather than angry.

Carlyle felt himself relax. He explained what he had been up to, leaving out the part about the nap on Miki's sofa. 'What are you doing?'

'I took the day off, so that I could hang out with your dad.'

'Okay.' He was grateful for this kindness and also because she didn't raise the fact that the idea of taking some 'personal time' would never even have crossed his mind.

'I think he's happy for me to make the arrangements for the funeral.'

I bet he is. 'It's good of you,' he mumbled.

'He is your dad, John. It is your mum we're talking about.'

Once again this morning he felt embarrassed. Although there was no one else around, he lowered his voice. 'Yes, of course.' He scribbled some notes on a pad on his desk as Helen talked through some of the details. The funeral was expected to be set for tomorrow week. 'The thirteenth?'

'The fourteeth,' she corrected him.

'Okay.'

'Does that make a difference?'

86

'No, no,' Carlyle said hastily. 'You have to take pretty much what you're given, I suppose.'

'Pretty much.'

'The law of supply and demand,' he mused.

'What?'

'Nothing.' Out of the corner of his eye, he saw Umar heading towards him. The sergeant was making a winding-up motion, telling him to get off the call. Carlyle held up an index finger to signal that he would be but a moment.

'It's going to cost about six grand.'

'What?' Carlyle did a quick mental audit of their various bank accounts. Helen was in charge of the family finances and she liked to point out that they didn't have a savings account. Rather, they had a buffer zone for when times got tough. It looked like the buffer zone was going to get wiped out.

'That's what it costs,' she said defensively.

'Of course, of course.' He backed off, not wanting her to think he was being cheap or petty at a time like this. 'Let's just hope that no one else keels over any time soon.'

'That's not funny, John.'

Jesus, me and my big mouth. Umar was hovering and Carlyle waved him irritably away. 'Sorry. Anyway, we can take care of the cost, no problem. It will all be fine.' Watching his sergeant retreat a few feet, arms folded, he lowered his voice further. 'You are doing a great job on this. I really am very grateful. It's a big help.'

'Mm.'

'Look, I've got to go. Crap day. There are a lot of people chasing me. I'll give you a call as soon as I know how the rest of the day is panning out.' He dropped his head so low it was almost under the desk. 'I love you,' he whispered but she had already ended the call. Tossing the mobile on his desk, he realized that he hadn't even asked Helen how his father was getting on. 'Your Son of the Year Award is in the post,' he mumbled to himself.

'Sorry?'

Rubbing his temples, the inspector looked up at his sergeant, who had surreptitiously crept back towards the desk. Umar looked as excited as a child in a sweetie shop. Normally he only got like that when he was chasing some skirt.

'Nothing.' Carlyle smiled wearily. 'What have we got?'

'We've found the girl.'

Carlyle stood up. 'Ayumi?'

'Huh?'

'Sorry, wrong investigation. Which girl are we talking about?'

A look of profound annoyance flashed across Umar's face. 'Rebecca Shaeffer. The girl that disappeared from the playground. Who else?'

'Oh, yes. Of course.'

Umar looked at him like he was mad. 'Despite it being half-term, we managed to track down the headmistress of Rebecca's school. They had contact details for a grandmother in Primrose Hill, so I sent a couple of uniforms round there and bingo, there she was, drinking cocoa and watching *Tom and Jerry*.'

Tom and Jerry. Quality. Carlyle hoped it was some of the old ones – they were so much better. 'So the girl's there,' he said slowly, 'but the grandparents didn't know about the father getting shot?'

'They do now,' Umar admitted. 'One of the uniforms spilled the beans.'

The inspector was disappointed but not surprised. 'In that case,' he groaned, 'we'd better get up there, sharpish.'

Rebecca Schaeffer sat on the sofa eating a toasted teacake covered in butter and strawberry jam. She chewed slowly and deliberately as she turned the pages of a paperback – *Tasha the Tap Dance Fairy*. Carlyle recognized the cover. It was one of a series called *Rainbow Magic*, featuring the adventures of two girls, Rachel and Kirsty, and their fairy friends.

It was amazing what stuck in your brain.

When Alice had been Rebecca's age, or maybe a bit younger, she had devoured the various series which, in total ran to something like sixty or seventy books. At £3.99 a pop, there was something like £250-worth of fairy books stuffed in various boxes in Carlyle's cramped flat. The inspector had often daydreamed of bumping into the author – the wonderfully named Daisy Meadows – and giving her a piece of his mind. He was extremely relieved when Alice discovered Holborn Library and moved on to the delights of older, 'tweenage', fiction, such as the *Vampire Diaries* and *Zombie Blondes*.

'Do you like the book?'

Keeping her eyes glued on the pages of the book, Rebecca's nod was almost imperceptible. Picking the teacake from the plate next to her on the sofa, she took a small bite and chewed thoughtfully.

'My daughter used to like the *Rainbow Magic* stories,' Carlyle persevered.

Frowning, Rebecca turned the page, hoping that he would take the hint and go away.

'When Rebecca gets into her book, she doesn't like to be disturbed.'

'So I see.' The inspector looked up at the old man who had appeared from the kitchen with a steaming mug in each hand. 'They're nice books.'

'There's certainly a lot of them.' Ronald Connolly didn't quite manage a chuckle. 'Here you are.' Handing Carlyle a mug, he wrapped both hands round the one he had kept for himself.

'Thanks.'

Connolly looked tired and drawn. At least he was in better shape than his wife. Anna Connolly had retreated to her bedroom immediately after the first police officers had arrived. Several hours on, she showed no signs of coming out.

Connolly looked at the girl and smiled sadly. 'Are you all right, sweetheart?'

'Yes, Grandpa.' Still Rebecca didn't look up but Carlyle could see the look of determination in her face that she was not going to cry.

Connolly took a hand from the mug and gestured towards the doorway. 'Maybe we should go and talk in the back.'

'Good idea.' Taking a sip of his tea, Carlyle let his host lead the way to a large kitchen with French windows, which opened out on to a small patio garden. Sitting at the kitchen table, Umar was munching on a teacake of his own, while scribbling down some notes onto a sheet of paper.

Placing his mug on the table, Connolly pulled out a chair and gestured for Carlyle to follow. 'Take a seat, please.'

Carlyle sat down and Umar shovelled the last of the teacake into his mouth, saying, 'That was lovely, thank you.'

Somewhat miffed that he had not been offered a teacake, Carlyle shot his sergeant a dirty look.

'You're most welcome,' Connolly smiled. Somewhere in his late sixties, he looked fit and comfortable, notwithstanding his difficult day. The man was, Carlyle observed, a pretty good poster boy for the retired Baby Boomer generation, people who had spent their entire lives living beyond everybody else's means. Wearing brown corduroy trousers, a white shirt with blue check and a grey cardigan, he had the healthy glow of a happy retiree. 'Would you like another one?'

Umar contemplated his empty plate and was about to say 'yes' when he finally caught the disapproving glare of his boss. 'No,' he said somewhat reluctantly, 'I'm fine. One was plenty. Thank you.'

'My pleasure.' Connolly turned his attention to Carlyle. 'I'm sorry about my wife not being down here, Inspector. But I can assure you she's in quite a state. Please don't hold it against her.'

'That's fine, sir,' Carlyle said stiffly. 'Obviously we will want to talk to Mrs Connolly at some point but we understand that she needs some privacy right now. Everybody reacts differently to this type of situation. I know she will do whatever she can to help us in our investigation.'

Connolly nodded. 'Of course. But obviously this is a lot harder for her than it is for me.'

Carlyle glanced at Umar. The boy had a ring of crumbs around his mouth. The inspector gestured for him to wipe them away.

'Anna and I married nine years ago,' Connolly explained. 'I am her third husband. Julian came from her first marriage.'

Ah yes, thought Carlyle, *the joys of the ever-evolving family unit*.

'Julian's father died decades ago, before I'd even met Anna. He was their only child but she had twins, a boy and a girl, with husband number two.'

'I have all the details,' Umar interjected, more for the old man's benefit than for the inspector's. 'The other family members are in the process of being informed and we will talk to them as we make our enquiries.'

'Good,' Carlyle was relieved that his sergeant could at least occasionally *sound* efficient. He turned back to Connolly. 'Why don't you just explain to me what you know about what happened in the last twenty-four hours.'

'Of course.' Connolly took a mouthful of tea and placed the mug on the table, as he composed himself. 'Well, I was out. I'd gone for a swim at the local pool and I got home about six o'clock. When I got in, Rebecca was sitting here at the table, eating her tea. Anna had made her some spaghetti – it's her favourite.' He paused to take another mouthful of his tea.

'Weren't you surprised when she turned up?'

'Oh, no,' Connolly said brightly, 'we were expecting her.'

Carlyle raised an eyebrow. 'You were?'

'Yes. She had been due to come and spend the night. Julian said he had some work event that he had to attend.'

'And you believed him?' the inspector asked.

'I didn't really think about it,' Connolly admitted. 'We're always happy to have Rebecca to stay.'

Carlyle scratched his head before turning to the question that had been troubling him. 'How did she get here?'

Fingering the handle of his mug, Connolly looked at him blankly.

'You're in Primrose Hill. Rebecca had to come all the way up here from Coram's Fields. How did she manage it?'

'The bus, of course.'

Carlyle was shocked. Alice didn't use public transport on her own until she was ten. Rebecca Schaeffer wasn't yet seven.

'She got a 168 from Southampton Row. It takes about half an hour. There's a bus stop at the end of our road.'

'You let her travel on her own?' Carlyle asked, incredulous. He was all for allowing children greater responsibility as they got older, but this seemed to be taking things too far. Way too far.

'It's not the first time she's done it,' Connolly explained. 'Rebecca knows to come here, if . . .' he paused for a moment, thinking about how far to go, 'if there is a problem with her parents.'

'The divorce,' Umar interjected.

'Yes, well,' Connolly gazed into his mug, 'the separation. I don't think the divorce has actually been finalized yet.'

'Amicable?' Carlyle asked.

Connolly shook his head. 'Oh goodness me, no. That is not an accurate description of the process at all, I'm afraid.' Pushing back his chair, he got to his feet. 'More tea?'

'No,' said Carlyle quickly, not giving Umar the chance to respond. 'We're fine, thank you.'

Connolly tipped the remains of his drink into the sink, rinsed the mug and upended it on the draining board before returning to his seat. 'I've tried to stay out of it as much as possible, but Anna got very upset about it all. I told her that she had to let them sort it out between themselves, but Julian is her son, so she found it very hard to leave alone. And, obviously, she – like me – was very concerned about the impact on the child. It's all a terrible shame.'

'Yes,' said Carlyle, injecting as much synthetic sympathy into his voice as he could manage. 'When Rebecca arrived here yesterday, what did she say?'

Connolly let out a long breath. 'Nothing in particular. That's why we were so surprised when we got the news this morning. Anna was hysterical.'

The inspector was beginning to feel a bit hysterical himself.

'Didn't you try to ring the parents last night?' he asked.

'Anna tried to speak to Julian but she wasn't surprised when she couldn't get hold of him. He's often very busy at work.'

'And the wife?'

'Anna refuses to talk to her. Anyway, we knew that Iris was on holiday abroad with her new boyfriend.'

Bloody hell, what a mess.

Carlyle was trying to order the plethora of questions zooming through his brain when the doorbell sounded.

Umar jumped to his feet. 'That'll be Social Services.'

A look of alarm spread across Ronald Connolly's face, prompting the inspector to place a comforting hand on his arm. 'Don't worry, it is only a matter of routine. I'll make sure that they leave Rebecca with you.' He nodded to Umar to get the door.

'Thank you.' Connolly smiled weakly. 'I think the poor child has been put through enough already.'

'That is absolutely correct, sir,' said Carlyle with feeling. 'Absolutely correct.'

FIFTEEN

It didn't take the inspector long to realize that he liked Ronald Connolly just fine. Here he was, standing in a pile of crap not of his own making, and yet the step-grandfather was just about the only person focused on the sole thing that really mattered here – looking after Rebecca. It was a good effort by the old man.

Which reminded him, he needed to talk to his own father.

Carlyle's musings were interrupted by the sound of a small altercation coming from the hall. He was halfway to his feet to investigate when the kitchen door flew open and an imperious woman strode in with Umar trailing in her wake.

'What the hell?' Carlyle fell back into his chair.

The worried look returned to Connolly's face.

'Nice to see you too, Inspector.' The woman smiled at the old man like a fox contemplating a chicken. 'Mr Connolly, my name is Abigail Slater. I am Iris Belekhsan's legal representative. I am here to talk to you about your situation.'

'My situation?' Connolly looked enquiringly at the inspector.

Slater made to speak but Carlyle held up a hand. 'I do apologize, sir,' he said quickly, his gaze locked on the lawyer's mischievous grey eyes. 'This is a highly inappropriate visit by Ms Slater. Perhaps you could go and sit with Rebecca for a few minutes while I deal with her.'

'Of course.' As Connolly got to his feet and shuffled through the door, Carlyle gestured for Umar to go with him.

Once they were alone, Carlyle sat back in his chair and folded his arms, making a show of giving the lawyer a good once-over. He had to admit she looked tanned and fit, with her hair pulled back into a girlish ponytail and only the slightest amount of make-up. Under a fashionably cut black jacket, she wore a pink blouse, with two buttons undone at the neck, not quite enough to offer up any distracting décolletage. The overall effect was relaxed but professional, not too corporate, a softer, more thoughtful look in which to arrive at a house in mourning.

Slater sat back and let him take it all in. The look on her face said that she could read the thoughts going through his tiny male brain as easily as a six-year-old's storybook.

'Long time no see,' said Carlyle finally.

She arched an eyebrow and said saucily, 'Have you missed me?'

Despite everything, Carlyle chuckled. He had first come across Abigail Slater when she had tried to stop him from bringing one of her clients – a paedophile priest – to justice. Thankfully, the wretched man had saved them both a lot of trouble by jumping from a church roof. In the years since then, Slater had become somewhat famous for being the mistress of the Mayor of London, Christian Holyrod. The relationship had ended with a fatal heart attack for the mayor while indulging in some al fresco frolics with Ms Slater – in the middle of the centre circle of one of London's biggest football grounds. There hadn't been a game on at the time but Carlyle's amusement could hardly have been greater as Slater had been found wearing nothing but a replica football shirt and a strap-on dildo. The newspapers had a field day. Assuming that she would be too embarrassed to show her face in polite society for a couple of decades at least, he thought that he had seen the last of Ms Abigail Slater.

Not for the first time in his career, he was proved wrong.

'I thought that you might have left the country,' he smirked.

Reddening ever so slightly, she shrugged. 'Poor Christian had a heart attack. What can you do?'

'It's tough luck,' Carlyle agreed, trying not to laugh.

'Precisely. Anyway, I had to get on with things.' She shot him a sharp look. 'After all, I was never a kept woman.'

'So what are you doing here?'

Slater mentioned the name of a legal firm that he'd never heard of. 'One of my colleagues is handling the divorce for the mother. They asked me to deal with anything relating to the criminal investigation.'

'Why should she have to worry?' Carlyle countered. 'She was out of the country. She has an alibi.'

Slater tapped an index finger on the table. Her pink nail polish matched the colour of her blouse. 'Of course she has an alibi, Inspector. But in a situation like this, who wouldn't be worried? She wants to make sure there are no issues over custody of her daughter.'

You've got to be kidding, Carlyle thought angrily. *You go off on holiday with a new squeeze and expect to come back and pick up your kid like a dog from the kennels?* He looked at Slater with renewed disgust. 'What do you want?'

Slater looked at her watch. 'The mother will be arriving at Heathrow in just over two hours. She has asked that I take Rebecca to meet her at the airport.'

Oh, has she now? Gritting his teeth, Carlyle got slowly to his feet. He could feel the anger rising up inside of him and he welcomed it. 'The child is being looked after by the grandparents,' he said, his expression grim.

'I have my instructions,' Slater said flatly.

'This is the best place for her right now.' Carlyle pointed to the door.

'Oh, so you're a child psychologist now?'

'No. And neither are you.' He seriously doubted if Slater could manage to look after the child, even for an hour.

'Are you going to prevent me from going about my business?' Slater shook her head. 'You always were such a total arse.'

Carlyle ignored the personal insult. 'You have no authority,' he said firmly.

'And you do?'

'You need to leave.'

Slater started to say something more, then thought better of it.

Carlyle watched her retreat from the room. 'Bring your client to Charing Cross tomorrow morning at nine. We can discuss it further then. Until that time, the child stays here.'

'Tomorrow.' Slater stomped down the hall and slammed the front door shut.

It took another couple of hours to get things squared off with Social Services and extract a formal statement from Julian Schaeffer's mother. Anna Connolly was monosyllabic, bordering on comatose. It was clear that she had been heavily self-medicating. Carlyle felt angry at the woman for being so wrapped up in her own grief and disappointment that she took herself to bed rather than look after her granddaughter. But he kept his feelings in check. After all, he told himself, Mrs Connolly was hardly unique. It often seemed that his whole working life was spent watching adults so caught up in their own dramas that they ignored the needs of the children around them.

On the other hand, the inspector's admiration for the reliable, stoical Ronald Connolly was increasing steadily. As he prepared to leave, he watched the old man sitting at the kitchen table with Rebecca. They were playing a numbers learning game called Ooky Spooky where the object was to get rid of all your cards. Carlyle remembered playing it with his daughter and recalled how Alice used to fly into a rage when she thought she was going to lose. He could tell the old man was trying to let the child win, without making it too obvious, just as he himself had done almost a decade ago.

From the doorway, Carlyle could see Rebecca's cards. She had a terrible hand and would struggle to win, even if her opponent was deliberately trying to lose. He could only hope that she was a better loser than Alice had been at that age. 'I will come back to see you tomorrow,' he said to no one in particular.

The old man nodded, not looking up from his cards. 'We'll be fine. Have a good evening, Inspector.'

In the hallway, he passed Anna Connolly sitting on the stairs, staring into space.

'I will let you know when we have any news,' he told her.

Lost in thought, she didn't seem to hear him.

He opened the front door to let himself out.

'What you've got to realize, Inspector,' she said softly, 'is that there is only one person who could have possibly wanted Julian dead.'

Carlyle turned back to face her. 'What?'

Anna Connolly's eyes shone brightly now, as though she had finally come out of her stupor. 'Only one person.'

Glancing down the hall, Carlyle stepped closer. He didn't want the kid hearing this. 'Who?'

'Iris.' The anger on Anna Connolly's face melted into pure hatred. 'His bitch of a wife.'

The day was almost done and Umar, close to home, cried off returning to Charing Cross, leaving the inspector to make the journey back to the station on his own. The Northern Line was its usual Third World self, leaving him plenty of time to ponder the merits of Iris Belekhsan. In murder cases, you always looked at the family first. Assuming that she wasn't the kind of dentist who moonlighted as a professional killer *and* could be in two places at the same time, Iris clearly hadn't pulled the trigger. On the other hand, she was the obvious person to have hired the hit man. From a purely practical point of view, Carlyle hoped that this was a domestic deluxe. Even with the crazy lawyer Abigail Slater trying to trip him up at every turn, he had no doubt that he would be able to make short work of tomorrow's interview. The whole thing could be wrapped up before lunchtime, leaving him free to get on with all the other crap currently on his plate.

Turning onto Agar Street, Carlyle saw a small knot of reporters and television crews standing on the steps of the police station.

'For God's sake,' he grumbled, 'what now?' Dropping his gaze to the pavement, he walked on.

'Inspector Carlyle!'

Looking up, Carlyle blinked. His foot had hardly touched the first step and some Amazonian reporter was shoving a microphone in his face. Who was she? And, much more importantly, how did she know who he was?

Her bosom bounced dangerously close to his face, forcing the inspector to jump back onto the pavement. 'What can you tell me about the arrest of Simon Collingwood?' she squawked, raising an eyebrow in a manner that suggested there was a lot that could and should be said. Three TV cameras zoomed in on the inspector's face as the rest of the media pack gathered round to hear his answer.

Who the hell was Simon Collingwood? Trying not to look like a frightened rabbit, Carlyle clamped his jaw shut and attempted to move past the woman.

Shuffling along the step, she refused to let him pass. 'I just need a comment from you about the current state of the investigation,' she insisted.

'Has Mr Collingwood confessed?' asked another woman.

Confessed to what? Carlyle wondered angrily.

'Where are the other bodies?'

Why do these muppets know more about what's going on than me? Carlyle braced himself. Smile and keep walking – that's what the Met's media trainers taught you.

Thinking that she was finally going to get her soundbite, the Amazon smiled back. Her teeth were white and even, and she looked like a shark preparing for lunch. Exhaling, Carlyle ducked under the microphone and onto the steps. Once again, she tried to block his path, but this time he extended his right arm to fend her off. Placing the flat of his hand just below her neck, he gave a gentle shove.

'Hey,' the reporter cried as she dropped her microphone and fell backwards into the TV cameraman behind her. All around them, camera motors whirred as snappers caught the moment for posterity.

'He hit me!' Sitting down heavily on the step, the reporter fumbled for her microphone.

Not nearly hard enough, Carlyle reflected. Keeping the rictus grin on his face, he pushed his way roughly through the remaining hacks until he was safely inside.

SIXTEEN

Approaching the front desk, the inspector's fake smile was quickly replaced by a real one as he came across the reassuring figure of Angie Middleton. Busy scolding an errant Community Support Officer, the desk sergeant was oblivious to his approach. Carlyle waited until the unfortunate volunteer had taken his lecture and had scuttled off before catching her eye.

'What's that all about outside?' he asked, gesturing back towards the front entrance.

Angie looked at him with a mixture of amusement and annoyance that suggested he was next in line for a good telling-off. 'Sergeant Savage is upstairs,' she replied curtly. 'He's been trying to get hold of you for ages.'

Carlyle moved to check his mobile but thought better of it. All it would tell him was that he'd somehow managed to miss another half a dozen calls. Just how did he get to be so totally useless in the mobile communications department? It was one of life's great mysteries.

'Your phone's no good if you don't bloody answer it,' Angie snapped. There was no malice in her voice. Both of them knew that he was a hopeless case.

'You need to get some uniforms out there,' he said grumpily, 'to sort that lot out.'

'You try getting those bloody PCSOs to get off their arses.'

No, thanks, thought Carlyle as he stalked off to find Savage.

* * *

Lying back in the dentist's chair, the man looked up at the LCD screen stuck to the ceiling directly above his head. On the BBC News Channel, a vacant-looking blonde presenter was talking about floods somewhere or other on the Indian sub-continent. God, wasn't going to the dentist enough of a pain already? Couldn't they choose something more fun to watch while you were stuck in the chair?

The door opened and he caught sight of a white coat out of the corner of his eye.

Iris Belekhsan stepped over to the chair, placed her hand on his crotch and gave him a gentle squeeze. That was one of the things he liked about Iris – she didn't mess about.

Immediately he began to stiffen as his pulse ticked up.

'We'll have to be quick, George,' she whispered, tugging at his zip. 'My next patient is due in ten minutes.'

That, he smiled to himself, *is not going to be a problem.* Undoing the button, he yanked at his trousers. 'Aren't you going to lock the door?'

'That would take the edge off it, don't you think?' She stepped into his line of vision and opened her coat. The white blouse underneath was buttoned almost to the neck. Similarly, her pencil skirt fitted the *professional woman at work* look. But when she hitched it up to display her new Brazilian, he gasped in appreciation.

Climbing on to the chair, she slipped him inside her. He was disappointed to discover that she wasn't wet, but her first thrust immediately ended any thoughts of pleasure other than his own.

After wiping herself, Iris Belekhsan dropped the tissues in a waste-bin and pulled a pair of fresh white panties out of the pocket of her coat. Stepping out of her pumps, she slipped on the knickers. In the corner, the intercom burbled into life.

'*Your next patient is here, Doctor.*'

Stepping back into her shoes, Belekhsan looked up at the clock on the wall and buzzed the receptionist. 'They're early,' she said. 'I'll come and get them in a minute.'

'*Very good.*'

She watched as he packed himself away. He had that dreamy, self-satisfied look that all men get when they've shot their load and have all their short-term needs catered for. Men were so simple – cretins really. It crossed her mind, as it often did, that it would make more sense to be gay, or maybe just be a nun. She crossed to the bench to check the notes of her next patient.

'The police will want to interview me about Julian,' she said casually.

'That's inevitable. Don't worry about it – they won't have anything. The cons are hopeless. They'll give up and the whole thing will be forgotten in a week or two.' Zipping himself up, the man gave her a sheepish grin. 'I'll see you later.'

'See you later, George.' She let him plant a kiss on her forehead.

'I'll give you a call,' he called over his shoulder, before disappearing through the door.

Alone in the surgery, Belekhsan buzzed the receptionist again. 'Okay,' she said. 'Show the next one in.'

Carlyle found his mood deteriorating sharply in the ten minutes or so it took him to find the sergeant. Far from being 'upstairs', as Middleton had suggested, a tour of the station finally located Savage in the basement, tucking into a plate of fish and chips in the canteen.

At least this gave the inspector the opportunity to get his hands on a king-sized Mars Bar. After handing over his cash to the guy at the till, Carlyle wandered over to Savage's table and took a seat.

Pushing away his empty plate, Savage let out a satisfied burp. 'Nice of you to turn up.'

Carlyle tore the wrapper off his bar and took a large bite, chewing quickly. 'What's all that bollocks upstairs?' he asked, careful not to spit any bits of chocolate onto the table.

Savage lifted a cup to his lips and loudly slurped his tea. His gaze went past Carlyle to a couple of other sergeants who were walking past, their trays groaning with food.

One of them grinned at Savage. 'Well done, Robbie.'

Savage's smirk grew into a full-blown smile. 'Thanks.'

Annoyed further by their love-in, Carlyle scowled. 'Robbie?'

'My nickname,' Savage explained, placing his cup back on its saucer, 'after the ex-footballer.'

Carlyle thought about it for a moment. 'The gobby sod with the ponytail? Went on that dancing show. Used to play for United when he was a kid.'

'Yeah.' Savage eyed him coldly. 'Although I don't think he's got the ponytail anymore.' Carlyle wondered if Savage might be a United fan. The possibility was enough to have him slipping down Carlyle's list of possible Umar replacements at a steady rate of knots. Supporting United was an extremely serious character flaw in the inspector's book.

'The journalists,' the inspector repeated. 'What are they chasing? There's loads of them.'

'Yeah.' Savage's face brightened again. 'They found out about our axe murderer.'

Before I bloody did, Carlyle thought angrily. 'How?'

Savage shrugged. 'You know how it is.'

Carlyle did indeed. Most police officers would sell bits of information to journalists in the blink of an eye.

'Lots of people would have known about it,' Savage said, somewhat defensively. 'We brought him in hours ago.'

'So this guy . . .'

'Simon Collingwood.'

'Who is he? Some kind of celebrity?'

'He's a rugby player.' Savage mentioned a team that played on the outskirts of London.

Carlyle made a face. As far as he was concerned, 'sport' meant football. Everything else was just pissing about, especially rugby, which was just a way for emotionally stunted middle-class boys to sublimate their homoerotic tendencies. 'Never heard of him.'

'And he was in the papers recently for going out with some bird from one of those talent shows on TV.'

'Okay,' Carlyle held up a hand. 'I get the picture.' He took another bite of his Mars Bar. 'How did you find him?'

'A bloke walked up to me at the scene just after you left and gave me the name.'

Damn. Carlyle thought back to the conversation he'd had just before leaving the crime scene. He'd told the bloke to speak to Savage. He'd given it to him on a plate. What a total berk. Robbie's collar meant Robbie's glory.

'Told me where I could find him, too.'

Obviously. Carlyle stifled an urge to scream. 'Has he said anything?'

Savage leaned back in his chair. 'Not yet – not that it matters. We found him with the axe. He's in Interview Room Six, all lawyered up and ready to go. I assumed you'd want to conduct the interview.'

'Okay,' said Carlyle, 'we'd better go and have a chat with him then.'

When he arrived in the interview room, the inspector was surprised to see a man on the floor doing press-ups.

'Mr Collingwood?'

The man grunted and went into the Plank position. Carlyle noted with some distaste that sweat was dripping from his brow on to the floor. Standing in the doorway, he shot a quizzical glance at the man's lawyer, a pretty redhead called Eva Walker. Their paths had crossed several times before and he had found her to be quite sensible – for a lawyer – not so much prone to the kind of theatrical behaviour enjoyed by so many of her peers. That gave her enough Brownie points for the inspector to indulge the idiosyncrasies of her clients. Up to a point.

Sipping demurely from the half-litre bottle of Evian, Walker nodded hello. Carlyle watched the man move into the Downward Dog as Savage appeared at his shoulder.

'He's not still doing his bloody exercises, is he?' the sergeant enquired loudly.

Carlyle self-consciously scratched his stomach. It was a while since he had made it to the gym and he knew he needed to get back in there as quickly as possible. He recalled how the boxer George Foreman had once been asked how he managed to still get into the ring in his forties. Foreman had replied that the trick was never to let yourself get out of shape. Never stop training. Do something every day. Carlyle was currently managing 'something' about every other week.

'C'mon,' said Savage, 'let's get started.' Pushing past his boss, he sat down at the table.

Grimacing, Collingwood dropped back into the plank before counting out a final ten push-ups. Jumping to his feet, he ducked his head to wipe his brow on the sleeve of his white T-shirt before taking the seat next to his lawyer.

Walker pulled a second bottle of water from her bag on the floor and handed it to her client.

'Thanks.' Collingwood flipped open the lid and took a long drink. The inspector noted that he was a short, stocky man, with a well-developed torso and over-developed biceps. Mid-thirties, give or take, with dark brown eyes and wispy, sandy hair that was thinning on top.

Collingwood caught him looking. He held the inspector's stare while he finished drinking his water. 'Ah.' Placing the bottle on the table, he cleared his throat.

'Ready?' Carlyle asked.

By way of reply, Collingwood sat back in his chair.

'Right.' Savage placed a Portable Digital Recorder on the table. 'Let's make a start.'

As he made to switch the machine on, Walker held up a hand. 'Before we do so, Sergeant, I would like to take the opportunity to say something on behalf of my client.'

The inspector liked the sound of that. It looked like more Brownie points would be coming Walker's way. The lawyer looked tired, flushed, as if she was going down with the flu. *She wants this to be over as much as we do*, he thought. 'Feel free,' he said, waiting to hear what she had to say.

'Off the record.' For the benefit of her client, the lawyer shot a look at each policeman in turn. All three of them knew that this was a charade – everything that went on in the room, both word and deed, was being recorded by the CCTV camera on the wall behind the inspector's head. However, a bit of theatre was often necessary to get the suspect comfortable with spilling his guts, and if this got them quickly done and dusted, the inspector was more than happy to play charades.

'Off the record,' he agreed.

Walker took another sip of Evian. 'Thank you.'

Leaving the machine where it was, Savage waved a hand in the air. 'Go ahead.'

'Okay.' Placing her hands on the table, Walker stated: 'My client admits responsibility for the killing of Kevin Wakefield, Calvin Jacobs, William Toms and George Fleming.'

There was a stunned silence in the room. Carlyle looked at Collingwood, whose face remained impassive, apparently oblivious to the conversation that was taking place around him.

'Four murders?' Out of the corner of his eye, the inspector could see Savage biting his lower lip in an attempt to stifle a whoop of delight. The look on the sergeant's face was that of a man who has just been told he has won the lottery.

'Yes.' Walker's voice was low and hoarse. 'That is correct.' The lawyer looked like she was about to throw up.

Shaking his head, Savage let out a low whistle. 'So far, we've only found parts equating to approximately two and a half bodies.'

Walker nodded as she took another swig from her water bottle.

'Presumably Mr Collingwood will tell us where the rest of them are?'

'Mr Collingwood will provide all the assistance he can,' Walker replied. Taking a couple of careful breaths, she ploughed on:

'However, it is important to him that his actions are put into their proper context.'

Here we go, Carlyle thought.

'These acts were committed under the most extreme duress. My client believes that these men were responsible for the gang rape and subsequent death of his daughter.'

His daughter? Carlyle belatedly made the connection with the girl who had been knocked down by the mail van.

'The girl who was run over on Rosebery Avenue?'

'Yes.' Walker's voice was now scarcely a whisper.

What was her name?

His mind was completely blank.

It's funny the things you forget.

Finally, Collingwood tuned back in to what was being said. 'Pippa.'

Meeting his gaze, Carlyle thought he could make out the mixture of hurt and defiance in the father's eyes. 'Pippa, yes.' Now he realized why there had been the media scrum outside the station. Even if this guy was the least celebrated celebrity you'd never heard of, the press would have a field day with the story for ages.

More than that, there would be a lot of popular support for the man who had – allegedly – chopped up the vile creatures that had violated and destroyed his daughter. What father, Carlyle mused, wouldn't want to do the same thing? Make the bastards pay for what they did. It was a natural human emotion.

The inspector felt a stab of empathy, maybe even admiration for the man sitting opposite him. Then again, Carlyle wasn't sitting in this room because he was a father; he was there because he was a cop. He turned his attention to the lawyer, who still looked like she wanted to puke on the table. 'With all due respect, Ms Walker,' he said gently, 'your client does not appear to be under too much stress now.'

'I have done what I needed to do,' Collingwood said, his tone even. 'It's over now.'

108

'If these men were guilty,' Savage asked, 'why not let justice take its course?'

Collingwood looked at him defiantly. 'This *was* justice.'

Savage snarled, as if he wanted to reach across the table and smack him: 'Who made *you* judge and jury?'

Shrugging, Collingwood dropped his gaze to the table. 'I'm not judge and jury,' he said quietly. 'Even if those bastards had been arrested, tried and found guilty, then what? The average term for rape offenders is eight years. Many get four years or less. The rules allow automatic release halfway through a sentence.' Looking up, he fixed his gaze on Carlyle. 'A couple of years – where's the justice in that?'

SEVENTEEN

The sky was changing constantly as the clouds scudded past on the gusting wind. Sitting morosely on the bed, Paul Fassbender watched a seagull hover outside the open window. Inside the room, the atmosphere was on the cold side of fresh. Realizing that he could smell the sea, Fassbender breathed in deeply; a simple pleasure, infinitely enjoyable despite the circumstances.

After an indefinite time, they had arrived at the coast. He guessed they were in one of the main Channel ports: Calais, Dieppe or maybe Zeebrugge. He knew that this would be the difficult part of the operation for his kidnappers, getting him back into England. There was a part of him that was genuinely curious to see how they would try to do it.

After a few moments, the seagull floated away. Using his free hand, Fassbender pulled the thin duvet around his shoulders. His other hand was handcuffed to the metal bedframe. Apart from the bed, the room in which he was being held captive was empty of furniture. There was no carpet on the floor and the garish patterned wallpaper looked as if it hadn't been changed in many decades. On the torn linoleum sat a tray containing the remains of his breakfast, croissants and coffee, which he had greedily demolished a little while earlier. Beyond that, as far away as he could manage to push it, sat the pot that served as his toilet.

Sitting on the bed, knees pulled up to his chest, he started to laugh. His body ached. He was tired and unshaven. He needed to brush his teeth and his body odour was most unpleasant. His soiled clothing had been taken away and he had been dressed in a cheap nylon tracksuit that made him look like the prisoner he was. Meanwhile, his wife, working on her tan in Marbella, probably didn't even realize that he was missing. It was an outrage. At the same time, he was fuelled by a sense of euphoria. For the first time in years, maybe decades, Paul Fassbender felt as if he were alive.

Initially, lying in the boot of the kidnapper's car as it sped north, his fury had known no bounds. Then he understood that he was being taken on a mission. This was the endgame. Perhaps he would arrive in England, perhaps not. Either way, he would face down his nemesis for a final time. Daniel Sands had played right into his hands. Once this little drama was concluded, it would be Sands who would end up in jail while he would be free to resume his gilded – if rather dull – retirement in the Italian lakes.

If the best revenge was a long and happy life, Fassbender was comforted by the near certainty that he would make it well into his nineties. His genes were good; his father and his uncles had made it to ninety-two, ninety-three and ninety-six respectively. And his grandfather had made it to a spectacular hundred and one. His mother's side of the family were rather less sturdy but still regularly made it into their late eighties. Fassbender had plenty of time left – twenty years minimum. There was no need to get worked up about what might happen over the next few days.

What was the worst-case scenario? A few more days of discomfort and a brief appearance in front of an English judge before being released in time to enjoy Sands himself being arrested on various assault and kidnapping charges.

He was distracted from this happy prospect by the sound of the key turning in the lock. The door opened and the same man who had invaded his home stepped into the room. Dressed in a navy fleece and camouflage trousers, he looked at Fassbender from behind a pair of large aviator sunglasses.

'Have you finished your meal?'

What does it look like? Fassbender watched the man retrieve the tray. 'Where are you taking me?'

111

'Where do you think?' The man stepped back towards the door.

'You know you will go to jail for this?'

'We'll see.'

The door closed. The key turned in the lock. Fassbender looked at the sky, perfectly content to wait.

Eva Walker finished the last of her water. 'The attack on Mr Collingwood's daughter took place two months ago,' she explained. 'The police have already mothballed the investigation. There appeared to be no prospect of any justice for Pippa's family.'

Carlyle shifted uncomfortably in his seat. 'Who was in charge of the investigation?'

The lawyer mentioned an inspector who worked out of the Islington station. The name did not register with Carlyle. He made a mental note to speak to Jill Hughes, the sergeant that he had met on Rosebery Avenue when Pippa Collingwood had been run down. 'The family home is near where she died,' Walker added, as if reading his thoughts.

The inspector looked at Walker and Collingwood in turn. 'Do you know for a fact that these men did it?'

Saying nothing, Collingwood just nodded.

'They were all known to the victim,' said Walker. 'They were team-mates of Mr Collingwood last season.'

'In that case,' said Carlyle, summoning up his most formal, bureaucratic tone, 'you should really have left the matter to us, rather than resorting to such a violent, vigilante-style attack.'

At this, the lawyer reared up, as if she wanted to reach across the table and give him a slap.

'The physical evidence was collected late and not processed properly,' she said grimly. 'Each of the men produced an alibi. My impression is that the effort involved in trying to pursue a prosecution was just seen as too much like hard work by the officers involved.'

'Okay.' Carlyle let out a long breath. He felt an overwhelming need to get out of this room, out of the building, and breathe some fresh air. 'Sergeant Savage will take your statement and write up a preliminary report to go to the CPS.' Even the Crown Prosecution Service couldn't mess this one up. However, rather than take a manslaughter plea, they might push for the unnecessary circus of a murder trial. 'It will be up to them to decide how they want to proceed.'

Neither Walker nor Collingwood responded. She knew how these things worked. He had no interest.

Getting to his feet, Carlyle patted Savage on the shoulder. 'Good luck,' he said to no one in particular, before scuttling out.

Assuming that the press would still be camped outside the front entrance, he ducked out of a side door and slipped onto the Strand, heading for home. When he reached the flat, he was surprised to see his father still sitting in the living room, slumped in front of an old episode of *The Sweeney* on an obscure satellite channel. Appearing from the bathroom, Helen gave her husband a hug and pulled him into the kitchen.

'We went to see the undertaker this afternoon. I think it knocked your dad a bit sideways.'

'Uh-huh.' Carlyle felt washed out. He just wanted to grab a bite to eat and flop into bed. Empathy was a struggle.

'Maybe you could take him out for a beer, have a chat.'

Nooo! Carlyle scrunched up his face.

'You need to talk to him, John.'

'But—' He was just about to start whining like a five year old when he realized that he'd completely forgotten about Naohiro Ninomiya.

Bed would have to wait.

Then an idea percolated through his brain; a way he could kill two birds with one stone.

Misreading his thoughtful expression, Helen thought that he was trying to weasel out of his obligations. 'John . . .'

'Okay, okay.' Kissing her on the forehead, he went to get his father.

* * *

The Garden Hotel was one of those super-cool, super-expensive places that always made Carlyle feel super-uncomfortable. Waiting for Naohiro Ninomiya to come down from his room, Carlyle pointed to a nearby sofa.

'Why don't you take a seat, Dad?'

'I'm fine.' Alexander stood staring at a couple of young women – a redhead and a brunette, sheathed in improbably short dresses – as they strolled through the lobby, heading for the Light Bar at the rear of the building. Their hard bodies and hard faces said 'Russian hookers'. Watching them go past, Carlyle idly wondered how long it had been since his dad had scored.

Not your problem, he told himself, quickly shaking the question from his head.

'I've got to speak to this guy about his missing daughter for a couple of minutes and then we'll go to the pub across the road.' The Robber Baron was a crappy tourist trap, always overcrowded, but at least the inspector could afford to buy a couple of drinks in there. Just about.

'Sure.'

One of the hookers caught Alexander staring at her and gave him a predatory smile. The inspector winced. She was definitely well beyond the Carlyle budget.

'Get your tongue off the floor,' he hissed, 'or I'll have to arrest you.' He was still glaring at his father when Naohiro Ninomiya appeared from nowhere to shake his hand.

'Inspector Carlyle,' he said pleasantly, 'I thought that you had perhaps forgotten about me.'

'My apologies, sir, for being so late,' said Carlyle, not wanting to sound too deferential in front of his father. 'It has been a long and difficult day.'

Ninomiya nodded sympathetically. 'Have you made any progress?'

'Some.'

'Good,' Ninomiya smiled. 'And who is this?'

114

'Alexander Carlyle.' Not waiting to be introduced by his son, the old man shook Ninomiya's hand and, the inspector was amused to notice, gave a small bow. 'I am John's father.'

'Naohiro Ninomiya.'

'We are going for a drink,' the inspector explained.

'In that case,' said Ninomiya, gesturing towards the bar, 'let's talk in there.'

Carlyle shook his head. 'I don't think . . .' But his father was already heading off in the direction of the Russian hookers.

Ninomiya signalled for the inspector to follow. 'Come.'

'Okay.' Carlyle reluctantly followed after his father, hoping that Ninomiya would put the tab on his room.

They squeezed around a table near the bar. Waiting to be served, Carlyle noted that the place was about two-thirds full; attentive serving staff flitted from table to table to ensure that the drinks kept coming. Over the chatter, he could just make out the strains of 'Sing' by My Chemical Romance coming from the speakers on the wall. The lights were kept low, to add to the atmosphere, but in the far corner, at the back, he caught sight of the Russian hookers canoodling with a couple of shady-looking blokes. Carlyle smiled to himself. They were never short of interesting folk at the Garden. Maybe he should ask the concierge about them afterwards.

After a few moments, a harassed-looking waitress came over and took their order. To Carlyle's relief, Ninomiya gave her his room number and indicated that he would indeed run a tab. Suddenly the delights of the Robber Baron were looking considerably less appealing.

Once the waitress had disappeared behind the bar, Ninomiya turned to the inspector. 'So, you haven't really found anything?'

'The investigation is ongoing,' Carlyle said blandly.

Ninomiya gave him a small smile. 'You will have to excuse me, Inspector. I am just an ordinary man. I have no particular understanding of these things. What does "the investigation is ongoing" *mean*?'

Carlyle glanced at his father for some moral support. All he got back from Alexander was a look containing equal measures of amusement and disappointment. It was the kind of look he'd seen a lot of, over the last forty-plus years. 'I spoke to your daughter's flatmate,' he offered. 'She is back in London and expecting your call.'

Looking decidedly unimpressed, Ninomiya was about to say something when the waitress appeared with three bottles of Tiger beer, three glasses and a small bowl of miniature rice crackers. Placing them on the table, she got Ninomiya to sign the bill and then moved on to the next table.

'Miki is looking forward to meeting you,' Carlyle lied.

'But she has no idea what happened to Ayumi.' The Japanese lifted a bottle and began carefully pouring its contents into a glass.

Carlyle watched in dismay as his father shovelled a handful of rice crackers into his mouth and then washed them down with beer straight from the bottle. Telling himself that he had to be as patient as possible, he took a deep breath. 'Miki has not come up with any more ideas about where Ayumi might be,' he said, choosing his words carefully, 'but she will do what she can to help.'

'Children.' Shaking his head, Naohiro Ninomiya smiled at Alexander Carlyle. 'They bring nothing but trouble and suffering.'

Still chugging down his beer, Alexander nodded sagely. 'That's very true.'

Maybe you were just bad parents, Carlyle thought sourly.

'This one,' Alexander gestured with his bottle, 'was always causing his mother no end of grief.'

Bollocks.

'She died yesterday, by the way.'

By the way? Carlyle was shocked by his father's casual admission.

'Your mother?' Ninomiya's eyes widened.

'Yes,' Carlyle mumbled.

'My condolences.'

'Thank you.'

'And you are still at work?'

116

The inspector shrugged. *What else am I supposed to do,* h wondered. His body ached with tiredness. Dumping half of his beer into a glass, he took a large mouthful. He knew he shouldn't be drinking but it tasted good.

'He was always very dedicated,' Alexander said. 'Never off sick, never using up his holidays.'

'Dad—'

Ninomiya caught the eye of a passing waiter and signalled for more beers. Lifting his glass to his lips, the Japanese man said softly, 'Ayumi's mother died three years ago. She had a stroke.'

'I'm sorry.' Alexander patted Ninomiya on the arm. 'And now your girl's disappeared. That's really terrible. Things have been really tough for you.'

Ninomiya nodded. It looked like he was about to burst into tears.

Sweet Jesus, Carlyle thought, *I can't take much more of this. I should leave them to it.* At the very least, he should call Helen and tell her what was going on. This had been her idea – kind of – but Carlyle knew that he would get the blame if he brought the old fella home too late or too intoxicated.

Pulling his phone from his jacket pocket, the inspector was just about to hit his wife's number when the mobile began vibrating in his hand. With no number displayed on the screen, he would normally have let it go to voicemail. This time, however, he hit the receive button with alacrity and barked into the handset, 'Carlyle.'

The voice on the other end of the line was almost inaudible.

'Hold on a minute.' He got to his feet and gestured at the phone. 'Excuse me, but I have to take this.'

Naohiro Ninomiya nodded.

Alexander Carlyle effortlessly finished his beer in anticipation of the next round.

EIGHTEEN

Moving through the hotel lobby, Carlyle headed towards the floor-to-ceiling glass windows that looked out on to the street.

'Sorry about that,' he said.

'Inspector, it's Brian Sutherland.'

Sutherland was Crime Editor at *The Times*. The inspector had known Sutherland for long enough to deem him okay, for a journalist, which wasn't saying much.

'Can you talk?'

'What can I do for you?' Carlyle asked brusquely, knowing what the answer would be.

'It's about Simon Collingwood.'

'Right.' Carlyle stepped away from the bouncers at the hotel's main entrance.

'Everyone's going crazy for this story. I hear it's your case.'

Normally, when approached by a journalist, Carlyle would have just said 'no' and ended the call. This time, however, he hesitated.

'Inspector?'

'Yeah,' he said, lowering his voice, 'I'm on that.'

'Good,' said Sutherland. 'I just wanted to check a few things.' On deadline, he was all business.

'Background,' Carlyle said.

'Of course.'

'No quotes.'

'Fine.'

'No attribution.'

'Yes, yes.'

'There can be no fingerprints on this,' Carlyle insisted.

'Absolutely,' Sutherland agreed. 'Nothing comes back to you.'

'Good.'

'But I will make a note of it in my favours book.'

'So will I,' Carlyle chuckled. 'So, what do you need?'

The inspector spent the next ten minutes talking through the Collingwood case and answering Sutherland's questions. When he had finished, Sutherland asked: 'What do you reckon?'

'About what?'

'Collingwood. Is he a psycho? Or a hero?'

Carlyle pawed the limestone floor with a shoe. 'Do you have any daughters?' Outside, on St Martin's Lane, a couple of taxi drivers were standing on the pavement, stretching their legs and sharing a joke as they waited for their next customers.

'Yes. Two,' the journalist replied. 'Seventeen and twelve.'

'Well, then,' Carlyle said gruffly, 'what do *you* think?'

Back in the bar, he found the two old men chatting happily, as if they had known each other for years. As he approached the table, his father started laughing. With some considerable embarrassment, Carlyle realized that he couldn't remember the last time he'd seen his old man in such a happy mood.

'What are you guys talking about?'

'Och,' Alexander waved an almost empty bottle in front of his face. His eyes shone and he was clearly well on the way to being pissed, 'just this and that.'

Carlyle turned to Naohiro Ninomiya. The Japanese also looked somewhat tired and emotional. 'Sorry about that,' he told him. 'I had to take the call.'

Ninomiya tried to clear his thoughts. 'Was it about my daughter?'

'No,' Carlyle said honestly. 'Another case.' He saw the disappointment in the man's face and looked away. The hookers were still at the table in the corner but the men had gone.

Alexander finished his beer and burped loudly. 'Pardon me.'

Trying to ignore his father's terrible manners, Carlyle focused his attention on Ninomiya. 'I will continue to make Ayumi's case a priority.'

Ninomiya nodded. His eyes were bright with the effects of the alcohol but he seemed to be holding his booze rather better than Alexander.

Carlyle spoke slowly but with a certain passion. 'I have more people I need to speak to. I don't believe that they have been interviewed by the police before. I cannot promise you that we will find anything new, but I *do* promise that things will be done properly.'

'Properly,' Ninomiya repeated.

'Yes,' said Carlyle firmly. 'As I would expect if it was my child.' It sounded trite but he meant it.

Ninomiya's eyes began to tear up. 'Thank you.'

'If I could just ask you one more thing,' said Carlyle quickly.

'Yes?' Ninomiya enquired.

'I know that you told my colleagues that Ayumi didn't have a boyfriend.' Carlyle took a mouthful of his beer and immediately regretted it; in his absence it had grown warm and flat. Ninomiya looked at him expectantly. 'But I wonder if she ever mentioned any male friends that you think I should talk to.'

Ninomiya shook his head rather too quickly. Clearly it was something that he didn't want to talk about.

'She must have known some men,' Carlyle persisted, 'even just as casual social acquaintances.' There had been remarkably few friends listed in the original report and they were all women.

The Japanese gazed at his beer bottle. 'She didn't mention any.'

She didn't mention much, Carlyle thought rather impatiently. 'Thank you for the drink, sir.' Getting to his feet, he tapped Alexander on the shoulder. 'Let's get going.'

His father, who had given the appearance of being half-asleep, jerked awake and scowled. 'It's not that late.'

'It is if you have to go to work in the morning,' Carlyle snapped.

With the air of a cheeky eight year old, Alexander grinned at Naohiro Ninomiya. 'I think I might stay for one more.'

Ninomiya nodded enthusiastically. 'Good idea.'

Hands on hips, Carlyle cursed under his breath.

'If it's a problem,' his father said sulkily, 'I can go back home tonight.'

'No, no, no,' Carlyle said wearily, knowing that, once again, he would get the blame for allowing the old fella to slink off to his bedsit when he was supposed to be enjoying the comfort and support of his immediate family.

Alexander grinned malevolently. His son had always been completely under the thumb at home and the old man knew that, drunk or not, he would be able to milk the goodwill of his daughter-in-law for a while yet. He patted his jacket pocket. 'I've got a key.'

'Fine,' Carlyle said, his voice terse. 'But don't be too late and don't make too much noise when you get in.'

'Don't you worry about me, son.'

'If you wake me up,' Carlyle hissed, 'I'll kill you.'

Ignoring their spat, Naohiro Ninomiya signalled to a passing waiter for more beer, leaving the inspector to head off into the night, in search of his bed.

Sprawled out on the sofa, Helen looked up from the TV news as he walked into the living room.

'Where's your dad?'

'I left him drinking nine-quid beers and leering at Russian hookers on St Martin's Lane.'

'What?'

'He stayed on for another drink.' Flopping on to the sofa beside his wife, Carlyle explained about their trip to the Light Bar.

Helen muted the sound on the TV. 'You left him with some Japanese guy?'

Carlyle shrugged. 'He seems nice enough.'

'But isn't that against the rules?'

'Huh?'

'Taking your dad to talk to a . . . I don't know . . . what would you call him?'

'Who, Ninomiya? I dunno, a client?' He chuckled disapprovingly as he contemplated the police force as a twenty-first century service industry. The world had changed in so many ways since he had joined the Met in the 1980s, not all of it for the better. Back then, the idea that they could ever become service providers, complete with KPIs, CRM systems and 'client focus metrics' was simply beyond the ken of most officers. Now the jargon was everywhere. Meaningless words – corrosive, too, reducing the police to the level of burger flippers. The bloody customers were never going to be satisfied. People always needed something to moan about, whether there was any justification for it or not: if you spent too much time worrying about that you would never do your job.

'Yeah, I suppose it's against protocol,' he said grudgingly, 'but so what? They seemed to get on okay; just two lonely old guys having a chat over a beer.'

'Mm.' But Helen sounded unsure.

Carlyle gently nudged her in the ribs with his elbow. 'You know what they say.'

'No. Tell me, Inspector,' Helen grinned, 'what *do* they say?'

'A disappointment shared is a disappointment halved.'

'Hardly.'

A soon-to-be-retired news anchor appeared on the screen. Struggling through the script on his autocue, he looked like he was stoned. *He sounds as pissed as my old man*, Carlyle thought. He grabbed the remote from his wife and switched over to Sky News, where a pretty blonde presenter was standing outside Charing Cross police station. At the bottom of the screen, a caption read: *Rugby star arrested*. Carlyle gestured at the screen with the remote. 'This is what I did at work today.' He gave Helen a quick run-through of events as the report showed a younger-looking Simon Collingwood scoring a try in a game played in an almost empty stadium.

'The poor man.' Helen shook her head sadly.

'He did kill four people with an axe,' Carlyle reminded her.

'What terrible pressure,' Helen clucked. 'He must feel like his head is exploding.'

'It's other people's heads that exploded,' Carlyle chortled.

'John,' she scolded, 'that's in very bad taste.'

'He seemed very calm and collected when I spoke to him earlier.' The news report ended and on came the weather. Apparently it was going to rain tomorrow. Carlyle made a mental note to wear his raincoat. He was always getting the weather wrong.

'He must be in a right state,' Helen murmured.

Carlyle pulled her close and slipped an arm around her shoulder. 'You sound like his lawyer.'

'He's admitted it?' she asked.

'They want us to agree to a manslaughter plea. I don't know if the CPS will go for it.' With the Crown Prosecution Service, you never knew. A single mum who hadn't paid her TV licence could get chased relentlessly through the courts at huge expense while an axe murderer could walk free for a whole variety of reasons.

'Under the circumstances . . .' Helen shrugged.

'Under the circumstances they might smell blood. I think it would be dangerous, though. He's bound to get a lot of sympathy from a jury.'

She looked at him. 'Do you reckon?'

'Sure, given what happened to his daughter.'

'And what about his wife?'

'Apparently she's been under heavy sedation since the daughter died. I'm not sure that she even knows what's been going on.'

Helen unwrapped his arm and pushed herself up on the sofa. 'Well,' she said grimly, 'if those guys raped that girl, they deserved everything they got.'

Carlyle laughed. 'Listen to you.'

'Well,' she protested, 'they did.'

'And here was I thinking that you were the liberal conscience of this family,' he teased.

She gave him a playful smack on the arm. 'Liberal doesn't mean weak.'

'You reckon?'

'Seriously, though, John, if that had happened to Alice, you'd want to do something about it, wouldn't you?'

Carlyle fell backwards on the sofa, staring at the ceiling. His head was buzzing and he ached with tiredness, so much so that he realized that sleep would almost certainly not come. And he still hadn't spoken to his daughter about the death of her grandma.

Getting to her feet, Helen prodded him with a toe. 'Well, wouldn't you?'

'First,' he pointed out, 'nothing like that is going to happen to Alice.'

'But—'

He held up a hand. 'Look at the maths. Statistically it's not going to happen. Even if it did, she has her Brown Belt and would happily kick the crap out of anyone trying to lay a finger on her.' For more than ten years now, they had insisted that their daughter attend weekly karate lessons in Jubilee Hall, on the south side of the Piazza. Packing a fearsome punch, Alice was now well on the way to becoming a Black Belt, to the immense delight of both her parents.

'There were four of them.'

'Second,' said Carlyle angrily, 'if something like that *did* happen, I would know exactly what to do. No one would find any of the bits and I wouldn't bloody confess, either.'

'I'm glad we sorted that out.' Helen helped him to his feet. 'Now let's go to bed.'

NINETEEN

It seemed like he had only been asleep for half an hour. Forcing his eyes open, Carlyle squinted at the radio alarm clock by the bed. Even in his myopic state, he could make out the funny green numbers glowing in the dark.

1.52 became 1.53.

He *had* only been asleep for half an hour.

Nooo.

The next problem: whose phone was going off? He desperately hoped it was Helen's but knew perfectly well that it wasn't.

So did his wife.

'Shut that thing up.' Giving him a firm kick, Helen pulled a pillow over her head.

Sitting up, Carlyle grabbed his specs and looked around. He finally located his phone, blinking violently under a copy of *L.A. Requiem* by Robert Crais that he had been slowly rereading.

'Sorry,' he mumbled, grabbing the phone and scuttling into the bathroom. Sitting on the edge of the bath, he looked at the screen.

Two missed calls.

Alex Miles.

Alex Miles's message.

Damn.

He hit the number.

The chief concierge at the Garden Hotel answered immediately.

'What's so urgent,' Carlyle hissed, 'that you're calling me at two o'clock in the morning?'

'I know what time it is,' said Miles testily. 'At least you were able to go to bed.'

'Okay, okay. What's the problem?'

'There's a Scottish bloke here claiming to be your father.' Miles gave him a quick description.

Carlyle stared into the darkness. 'He *is* my father.'

'In that case,' Miles said, 'you need to get over here right now.'

In little more than ten minutes, the inspector was back at the hotel. As he scurried through the lobby, Alex Miles appeared from behind the reception desk. Waving a pass key in his hand, Miles greeted him with a curt nod.

'First floor.'

They rode the elevator in silence. Outside Room 185 stood a tall, thin man, suited and booted, with sleepy eyes and a shaven head. He eyed the inspector warily.

'Tony McDowell,' Miles explained, 'our new head of security.'

Carlyle grunted a greeting of sorts. McDowell looked at him blankly. His eyes were sunken and he had excessively prominent cheekbones and looked like he needed a good feed.

Miles gestured for McDowell to move away from the door. 'I told you about the inspector. He works round the corner.'

McDowell grunted back.

Placing a hand on his arm, Miles shot Carlyle a look. 'We have an understanding.'

Carlyle cleared his throat. 'Yes, we do.' Miles and McDowell were both doing him a big favour. At some stage in the future he would have to pay the bill without any quibbles. He placed his hand on the door handle. 'Are they inside?'

'Yeah.' McDowell grinned nastily. 'The party's over, though.'

'There was a hell of a lot of shouting going on when we arrived,' Miles explained. 'They woke up half the people on this floor.'

Wishing he was still in bed, Carlyle took a deep breath. 'Okay. Let's sort it out.'

* * *

It had been quite a party, by the look of things. Leaning against the window with his arms crossed, Alexander Carlyle glanced up as his son walked into the room. 'Oh great,' he groaned. 'Look who's here. Dixon of Dock Green!'

The only person in the room to understand the antiquated reference, Carlyle looked his father up and down. The old fella looked haggard, green around the gills, while retaining the alertness of a man who realized he had dropped himself into some deep shit and was casting around desperately for a means of escape.

'What are you doing here?'

What the hell do you think? Carlyle thought angrily. Ignoring his father, he looked around the suite. Large by the Garden's standards, with six people now crowded inside, it was standing room only.

On the nearside of the bed sat the two hookers he had seen earlier. Each of them had a mobile stuck to her ear, squawking away in stereo in staccato Russian. They looked tired and very pissed-off.

'Ladies.'

The unhappy duo stared at Carlyle sullenly while continuing with their conversations. On the TV a porno film was playing with the sound muted. A couple of actresses were getting very familiar in the back of a taxi. Unable to spot the remote control, the inspector carefully stepped over the scattered remains of the minibar and switched it off at the power point.

In the far corner of the room, Naohiro Ninomiya slowly rose from his chair. 'I am sorry,' he said quietly.

Carlyle bit his tongue.

'It is my fault,' the man explained. 'My credit card didn't work.'

Still yakking away on the phone, one of the girls, the redhead, pulled a handheld chip and pin terminal from a bag at her feet and waved it at Carlyle. 'Is not working. The network go down or something.'

The brunette smacked her colleague on the shoulder with her mobile phone and muttered something indecipherable.

Carlyle looked at Miles.

The concierge grinned. 'The hazards of working in the service economy.'

'They owe us eight hundred fifty pounds. Five hundred for sex, three hundred fifty for blow job,' the redhead continued. 'No discounts for cash.'

Bloody hell, thought Carlyle, *that's an expensive blow job.* Glancing at his father, he wondered which service he had gone for and from which hooker, before pushing the prurient thought from his mind.

'We take euros,' said the brunette, somewhat optimistically.

'You'll take a trip to the police station if you don't behave,' said Carlyle irritably. Pulling a couple of business cards out of his pocket, he handed one to each girl.

The brunette stared at the card, shouted something down the phone and ended her call. 'I suppose you want freebie too?' she snapped.

Miles was grinning like a Cheshire cat and it occurred to Carlyle that he would have already tried what was on offer; Miles was known for making a point of personally checking out all of the girls who worked in his hotel. 'What I want,' he told them, 'is for you ladies to leave quietly. That way, you will avoid arrest.' The redhead opened her mouth in protest, but Carlyle held up a hand. 'You also have my card. If I can help you with anything in the future, call the mobile number on there.'

The girls looked at Miles, unconvinced.

The concierge tried to appear thoughtful before speaking. 'I think that is a reasonable deal.'

'Andrei will still want to be paid,' the brunette pouted.

Andrei would be their pimp, probably one of the men who had been in the Light Bar earlier.

'Let me deal with that,' said Miles hastily, not wanting to be discussing his business in front of the policeman. 'I will speak to Andrei. It will be okay.'

Realizing that there was no room to negotiate, the brunette stood up. The redhead, still talking on the phone, followed suit.

Unsmiling, Miles gestured towards the door. 'It's the best way.'

Pushing her friend in that direction, the redhead pointed an accusing finger at Carlyle's father, muttering something in Russian. She turned to Carlyle, a nasty glint in her eye. 'This old bastard – he can't even get it up.'

Catching a glimpse of his dad, head hung in shame, looking like he wanted the ground to open up and swallow him whole, Carlyle felt a wave of embarrassment wash over him. 'Listen to me,' he hissed at her. 'I can be your friend or I can be your enemy. You walk out of this room and everything is forgotten – then I am your friend and you can ask for my help when you need it. Otherwise, I am your sworn enemy. I will make it my number one priority to have you deported back to Siberia, along with your friend, plus your pimp and whichever bastard he's working for, too.'

For a moment the girl stared at him, nonplussed. Then she burst into laughter. 'I come from Bataysk.' She pointed at her pal. 'So does she. It is nowhere near Siberia.'

'And you want to go back there?' Carlyle asked.

'Okay, okay.' The redhead headed for the door. 'We have deal. Do not forget.'

Outside, father and son walked in silence back towards the Piazza. It was after two thirty and the streets were almost deserted. The city was theirs, not that either man wanted it right now. On Garrick Street, Carlyle stopped. His brain was hyperactive. There would be no point in going back to bed now. He gestured towards the Strand.

'I'm going back to the station.'

Standing in the middle of the road, Alexander contemplated his shoes.

At least he has the decency to look ashamed of himself, Carlyle thought. 'Don't wake Alice or Helen when you get in.'

His father looked at him sheepishly. 'You won't tell them, will you?'

Christ, Dad. Shaking his head, Carlyle stepped off the pavement and put a hand on the old fella's shoulder. 'Of course not.'

'I'm sorry.'

'I know, I know.'

The old man looked like he was about to cry.

'You had quite a night, but what happens in the Garden stays in the Garden.' A mail van appeared, heading north. The inspector pulled his father back on to the safety of the pavement. 'It won't go any further. And we will never discuss it again.'

'Thank you.'

'No problem.' Carlyle could feel himself welling up now. He couldn't think of another time when the old fella had thanked him for anything. 'So,' he cleared his throat, 'can you get back to the flat okay?'

Alexander nodded.

'Good. Get some sleep. I'll see you later.'

'All right.'

Standing on the kerb, he watched his father make his way along King Street, and then he turned and headed for the station. When he reached the front steps, however, he kept on walking. Making his way across the Strand, he strode down Villiers Street, next to Charing Cross train station, until he came to an all-night café run by a Dutch family and located under the railway arches. Jasper Braafheid had owned the Cross Café for almost thirty years. Carlyle was by no means a regular but he stopped by often enough. As he arrived, a man was taking early editions of the morning papers from a van, dropping his bundles outside the newsagents next door.

'Mate.' Pulling a fiver from his pocket, Carlyle bought a copy of *The Times*, the *Mirror* and the *Sun* before heading inside. The place was surprisingly full for the time of night; there were six or seven people all sitting on their own, going about their business. Behind the counter, a young man greeted him with a friendly nod.

Carlyle smiled back. 'Jasper not around?'

The kid shook his head. 'He doesn't do nights any more.'

'Don't blame him.' Carlyle ordered two large lattes and a couple of fried-egg sandwiches to go.

'Sure.' The boy disappeared into a little room at the back to cook the eggs.

While he waited for the food, Carlyle checked out the news-papers. All of them had large pictures of Simon Collingwood on the front page, along with lurid descriptions of his 'brutal revenge attacks' on the men who had violated his daughter. *The Times* had a sidebar about his rugby career (275 games for his club; 2 England 'B' caps), his job as a City broker and his private life. Carlyle raised his eyebrows as he read that Collingwood was a 'committed Christian' who tithed 10 per cent of his income to the Church of England. At the bottom, there was a teaser for a feature on page 34: *The vengeful father: hero or killer?*

'Or both?' Carlyle mumbled to himself. He flicked to page 2. Underneath a picture of a heartbreakingly pretty-looking Pippa Collingwood was a description of a bright, popular student at her school. Pippa played hockey, swam for the school team and was due to go on a working trip to Kenya to help build a primary school. All in all, she sounded like a great kid; a credit to her par-ents. He closed the paper before his eyes started welling up for the second time that night.

'Here you go.' The kid placed a paper bag on the counter. 'Seven pounds twenty, please.'

'Thanks.' Sticking the papers under his arm, Carlyle counted out the money and dropped a few extra coins in the tips box. Picking up his order, he walked out.

TWENTY

Sitting on the bed, with his knees pulled up against his chin and his back against the wall, Simon Collingwood said nothing as the inspector entered the cell. It was the middle of the night but there was no evidence that he had been sleeping. He looked tired but determined.

'Here.'

Collingwood hesitated for a moment then took the cup.

Squinting against the harsh lighting, Carlyle removed one of the rolls from the bag and placed it on the bed. 'Egg.'

'Thanks.' Collingwood took a sip of his coffee. Then, dropping his legs onto the floor, he gestured at the newspapers under the inspector's arm. 'Did I make the front pages?' he asked, his voice low, his embarrassment obvious.

'You sure did.' Carlyle handed them over. Folding his arms, he took up a position by the door. 'The coverage is not bad, considering.'

'Considering that I chopped up four men?' Collingwood smiled.

Carlyle stared at his shoes. 'There will be a lot of sympathy for your situation.'

'That's fine, but I don't need sympathy, do I?'

'We all need sympathy,' said Carlyle lamely.

Collingwood looked at each paper in turn. Placing them next to the roll, he said to Carlyle,'Can I keep these?'

'Yes.'

'Thank you.'

'They'll take them off you in the morning, though.'

'Okay.' Collingwood looked at him expectantly and Carlyle suddenly wondered why he had come.

Thinking about Pippa Collingwood being put in the ambulance on Rosebery Avenue, he shifted from foot to foot. 'Has your lawyer told you where you're going?'

Collingwood shook his head.

'Maybe she doesn't know yet,' Carlyle said. 'The likelihood is that there will be a court hearing later this morning, probably at Horseferry Road. After that, I would expect that you will be taken to Wormwood Scrubs.'

'For how long?' Collingwood unwrapped his roll and took a bite. 'I don't know.'

Collingwood chewed slowly and methodically before swallowing. 'So what do you need?'

'Huh?'

'Why are you here?'

'I just thought I'd bring you something to eat.'

Collingwood took another bite of the sandwich. Egg yolk dripped down his chin and he wiped it away with his hand.

Carlyle turned and banged on the door. 'I have to get going.'

Collingwood placed the remains of his food back on the bed. 'Do you have kids, Inspector?'

Footsteps came slowly down the corridor and the key turned in the door.

'A daughter.'

Collingwood nodded. 'So, faced with my situation, what would you do?'

'Good question.' Carlyle smiled sadly as the door swung open. 'I hope that I never have to find out.'

Upstairs, the inspector sat in front of his computer, gobbling his egg roll and washing it down with cold coffee. Going through his emails, he clicked on a survey from the Police Federation: 86 per cent of police officers in England and Wales believed that cuts to police budgets and a reduction in officer numbers would have a detrimental effect on crime levels and result in the public getting a poorer service.

'You don't say.' What the hell were the other 14 per cent thinking? Not so long ago, Carlyle had considered packing it all in himself. The redundancy or 'early retirement' offer on the table had been attractive but not quite attractive enough. Now, resigned to the fact that (a) he couldn't afford to take early retirement and (b) he couldn't do anything else, he saw himself staying at Charing Cross for as long as the Met would let him. On that basis, he didn't see much point in moaning about things.

He read down the press release, finding a quote from a Federation spokesman: *'The Federation is not opposed to change but this is a criminal's charter. Let's improve policing, not destroy it. We need a police service that is appropriate for the future and able to deliver what is expected of it.'*

Everyone's a politician these days, Carlyle thought sourly, hitting the delete button. The email was immediately replaced by another, from Umar, simply headlined *Porsche owner*.

The DVLA came through with the registration. The car is owned by a guy called Daniel Cedric Hutton.

There was a link to a Wikipedia page; Carlyle clicked on it and read through a version of Hutton's biography.

Daniel Cedric Murray Hutton, generally known as Danny Hutton (born 2 July 1948) is a businessman and philanthropist who founded DCMH Systems in 1973. In 1984, he married Maria Sunningdale, a society heiress and art collector.

Hutton has twice run for Parliament as a Liberal Candidate, both times losing his deposit.

Having sold his business to Zulu Anderson CMZE Global Inc. in 2007, these days Hutton is perhaps most famous for being the father of Electra Hutton-Sunningdale, the performance artist and social campaigner who founded the London branch of SlutWalkers.

Carlyle rubbed his temples. What the hell was SlutWalkers?

Forget it, he told himself, *that's not to the point*. He scanned down the rest of Hutton's biography. Unsurprisingly, there was no mention of a penchant for young Japanese girlfriends. Flipping back to the email, he scribbled down Hutton's London address on a sheet of paper lying on his desk. Under the address, he jotted down his To Dos for the day. It was a long list but he knew that he would find time to pay the sugar daddy a visit.

'You and Grandpa were out late last night.' Alice grinned cheekily as she shoved an almond croissant into her mouth and took a large bite. In her uniform – red skirt and white blouse – she looked about ten years younger than she did lounging about in a T-shirt and jeans at home perfecting her teenage sneer.

'Um, yes, well.' Not meeting his daughter's gaze, Carlyle stared out of the window of the Cowcross Milk Bar at the traffic that was backed up along Charterhouse Street on the north side of Smithfield. Citing unnamed 'logistical issues', Abigail Slater had bumped his interview with Iris Belekhsan back to 11 a.m. Displaying the immense chutzpah with which the inspector was only too familiar, the lawyer had also insisted that the meeting take place at her offices, rather than the police station. Normally Carlyle would have protested furiously. Today, however, he welcomed the extra time. Not only would it give him the chance to talk to his daughter about the death of her grandmother but, if he was quick, he would also be able to squeeze in his first session at the gym in more than a fortnight.

Across the road, nothing stirred. West Poultry Avenue was deserted. Opening for business from three in the morning, the market was already winding down by seven. Now, just before eight thirty, the working day was over and it was largely empty. London Central Markets, originally known as Smithfield, had been a livestock market for over 800 years, located at the city boundaries on the edge of St Bartholomew's Priory. It was also used as a venue for executing criminals – Wat Tyler, the leader of the Peasants' Revolt, died here, as did Scottish troublemaker William Wallace – as well as a location for fairs, jousting competitions and tournaments. The site was redeveloped in the 1860s, using the designs of

Sir Horace Jones, the architect famous for Tower Bridge. Now, in the midst of gentrification, the 10-acre site was ringed by a seemingly random mixture of fashionable bars and restaurants, along with a few cafés that belonged to a completely different era. It was in one of the latter – a greasy spoon that had somehow survived from the 1950s – that the two of them were having breakfast on the way to Alice's school.

'Were you drunk?' she asked matter-of-factly.

Carlyle hid behind his cup. 'Not really.' *Not me, anyway.*

'Grandpa made a right racket when he came in,' Alice giggled, wiping a piece of almond from the corner of her mouth. 'Banging and crashing around all over the place. Mum was really pissed off.'

Great. That was a conversation to look forward to when he got home. He finished his latte and got to his feet. 'C'mon. Let's get going.'

They reached Goswell Road in companionable silence, turning right and ducking into the Barbican complex on the corner of Beech Street. The eponymous arts centre and housing estate was located in an area bombed out during the Second World War. The City of London Corporation, the guys who ran the capital's financial district, opened the arts centre in 1982 as the City's gift to the nation. However, this was not a great period for architecture and what they came up with was a concrete ziggurat, a terraced pyramid with a multi-level layout so complex that it required different coloured lines painted on the ground to help theatre-goers and tourists avoid getting lost on its walkways. If ever a building had a personality bypass, this was it. To no one's surprise, it was later voted London's ugliest building.

For his part, Carlyle actually quite liked it. Back in the day – literally half a lifetime ago in Alice's case – he had always looked forward to being able to do the school run. The thirty minutes spent with his daughter as they meandered towards the Barbican arts complex, home to the City School for Girls, were among the happiest times of his life. On the way to school, they would pick up breakfast and he would listen to what was on Alice's mind. At the time, Carlyle could not think of anything he would rather do in the entire world than walk through the streets while listening to the random thoughts of his daughter.

The school fees had, for many years, soaked up a distressing proportion of their household income. In principle, Carlyle wasn't in favour of private schools. But Alice had loved it and his objections had waned long before she had managed to snag a scholarship, easing the pressure on his pocket. Standing on one of the elevated walkways, he leaned over the balcony and looked down at the school below. It was about a hundred yards away, on the far side of a large ornamental pond with a fountain at its centre.

Standing on her toes, Alice reached over and kissed him on the cheek. 'Thanks for breakfast, Dad. It was nice.'

'Yeah,' Carlyle smiled. The days since Alice had needed her parents to walk her to school had long passed, and Carlyle had been pleasantly surprised that she had let him tag along this morning. Clearly, however, this was as close as he was to be allowed to the school gates. His watch now said eight thirty-five. Alice wouldn't be late, but she wouldn't be particularly early either. 'You'd better get down there.'

In no apparent hurry, Alice shifted one of the straps on her backpack. 'Didn't you want to talk about Grandma?'

'Well . . .' That had been the plan. Now, however, Carlyle didn't really want his mother to muscle in on their time together. 'What do you think about it?'

Alice shrugged. 'Shit happens.'

Her father's daughter, Carlyle thought happily. 'Yes,' he laughed, 'it does.'

'After all,' she grinned, turning away from him, 'we're all going to die, right?'

'I suppose we are,' Carlyle agreed. But she had already gone, disappearing down a concealed stairwell, leaving him talking to himself.

The gym in Jubilee Hall, a converted warehouse on the south side of Covent Garden's Piazza, was largely empty. Looking up at the TV screens on the far wall, Carlyle stepped onto a Life Fitness cross-trainer and fiddled around with his iPod. Skipping through a succession of randomly selected tracks, he found something from the Prodigy that would get his blood pumping. Turning down the volume to something that he hoped wouldn't leave him deaf, he smiled as 'Invaders Must Die' began pumping through the head-phones and he stomped down on the machine in search of a rhythm and the endorphin rush that would surely follow.

Up on one of the screens, between CBBC and Sky Sports News, BBC 24-hour news was reporting on the Collingwood story from outside of Brixton Prison. Maybe he didn't go to the Scrubs after all, Carlyle thought. An earnest-looking reporter was struggling to keep her earpiece in place as the producer cut to pictures of the prison van leaving Charing Cross police station earlier in the morning.

'Good luck, sunshine,' Carlyle grunted as he upped the tempo.

Just under an hour later, suitably exercised, he was finishing off a berry smoothie in the gym's café when his phone started ringing.

'Where have you been?' Umar demanded.

Finishing his drink, Carlyle ignored the question. 'I'm just on my way to see Iris Belekhsan and Abigail Slater.'

'Want me to come along?'

Carlyle thought about it for a moment. Umar might act as a guarantee of good behaviour if Slater wound him up; on the other hand, it wasn't the best use of their meagre resources. 'Nah,' he said finally. 'You press on chasing down the husband's known acquaintances and we can compare notes later.'

'Fine.' Umar didn't sound too thrilled about it. Doubtless he had been looking forward to another Carlyle–Slater ding dong. 'By the way,' he added, 'Simpson's looking for you.'

'The Commander's always looking for me,' said Carlyle chirp-ily. 'I'll catch up with her later.' Ending the call, he skipped out into the Covent Garden crowds with the happy demeanour of a man already well satisfied with his day's work.

TWENTY-ONE

Stiff, Smithers & Mongolsson had state-of-the-art offices in a brand spanking new glass and steel tower block that had sprung up on Holborn Viaduct, near the Old Bailey. Abigail Slater's firm had taken the entire third and fourth floors of a development that had been 70 per cent built and zero per cent let as the financial crisis kicked in. The construction firm responsible for it had gone bust and it had taken almost six years before a new owner was found and the construction work was completed. The end result was that SS&M picked up 20,000 square feet free for six years, with a bargain rent for the next twelve. Despite the deals on offer, the place was still more than half-empty. Such were the vagaries of the London property market.

After being made to go through airport-style security on the ground floor, Carlyle was escorted to a lift and sent up to the SS&M reception where a dour-looking middle aged woman handed him a pre-printed ID badge. 'I've informed Ms Slater's office that you are here,' the receptionist said, already turning her attention to another visitor who was creeping towards her desk. 'Please take a seat.'

Stuffing the badge into his pocket, Carlyle did as instructed. Planting himself on a sofa, he turned his attention to the large plasma screen on the wall behind the receptionist's head. Sky News was playing. The sound was muted but he watched the now seemingly ubiquitous figure of Simon Collingwood being escorted into Horseferry Road Magistrate's Court for another hearing. Cameras flashed and TV crews pushed each other out of the way in search of the best shot. Patient, unhurried, handcuffed, Collingwood took it all in his stride, expressionlessly posing for pictures until one of the security guards finally bundled him through the front door.

Carlyle shook his head. 'What a bloody circus.' In the background, he caught a glimpse of Simpson and Savage. The Commander was hurrying up the steps of the courtroom. Letting her go on ahead, Sergeant Savage hesitated – hoping, no doubt, to be invited to say a few words to the cameras. Carlyle smiled to himself. Back in the day, Carole Simpson had been a major media tart. Then her career hit a brick wall and she had no use for journalists any more. Savage, it seemed, still wanted his fifteen minutes – or should that be fifteen seconds? – of fame.

This morning, however, Savage was to be disappointed. He was most definitely not the story. With Collingwood now inside, the attention of the Sky reporter turned to a group of young women who had gathered on the pavement. A few were carrying banners – *Go, Simon! Justice for Pippa! Rapists Must Die!!!* – to support the killer dad who was rapidly becoming a mini-celebrity in his own right.

The inspector picked up a copy of the *Daily Mirror* that had been left on a glass table along with the morning's other papers. When he was a kid, the *Mirror* had been a proper newspaper, interested in ideas, concerned about social issues and events in the wider world. Now it was just another dumbed-down tabloid, touting the usual crap. Sad, but there you go. The front-page story was about the rash of super injunctions that had been sought by a mix of footballers, actors and businessmen, in order to try to prevent their bad behaviour from being made public. 'Tossers,' Carlyle mumbled to himself as he quickly flicked to the sports coverage at the back.

'Inspector Carlyle?'

'Yes.' Carlyle discarded the newspaper and jumped to his feet. A young black guy, tall and good-looking, smiled at him. He was wearing a navy single-breasted suit with a grey shirt, open at the

140

neck. His head was shaven and a pair of heavy-framed Yves Saint Laurent-style glasses were pushed high up on the bridge of his nose. But the thing that really caught Carlyle's attention was the small diamond stud in his left ear. All in all, it was a very sharp look for a lawyer.

He stuck out a hand. 'I'm Kieron Sterling, Abigail Slater's associate.'

The inspector shook the young man's hand.

'Ms Slater is ready to see you now.'

About bloody time.

'We apologize for the delay,' Sterling cooed, with all the practised insincerity of his boss. 'It has been a very busy morning.'

'Let's get on with it then,' Carlyle sighed, gesturing for the youngster to lead the way.

Leaving the reception area, they walked in silence down a long, carpeted hallway with doors on either side. At the end of the hall, the associate took a left and opened a door to a large meeting room. Standing aside, he allowed the inspector to enter first. The room was dominated by a rectangular wooden table, with ten seats lined up on either side. In the event, there were only two people in the room, sitting on the far side of the table.

Carlyle pulled out a chair and sat down, giving Sterling time to scurry to the end of the table and plonk himself down with a notebook and pencil.

'Apologies for the delay, Inspector.' Scribbling furiously on a yellow A4 notepad, Abigail Slater did not look up. In an elegant navy jacket and a simple, pearl-coloured blouse, she was looking good. 'I presume that Kieron explained the circumstances to you?'

Carlyle grunted noncommittally.

Wiping a strand of hair out of her eyes, Slater waved a gleaming silver fountain pen in the air. 'Would you like something to drink?'

'I am fine, thank you,' said Carlyle stiffly. Reaching across the table, he offered his hand to the woman sitting next to Slater, who was equally well dressed in a simple black blazer and a grey silk knitted top. 'John Carlyle.'

The woman looked at him for several seconds before taking his hand with the greatest reluctance.

'Iris Belekhsan.'

Sitting back in his chair, the inspector took a moment or two to absorb Iris Belekhsan's distinctive features, for there were many: abundant jet-black hair which curled around her long, pale neck; the pale alabaster cheeks, the large dark eyes, the straight nose, the moist, well-formed lips bearing no trace of make-up. This was one good-looking woman – far too good-looking to be a dentist, surely?

'Inspector.' Slater dropped her pen on the pad and gave him a mocking grin. She was not used to being overshadowed by her clients and didn't much like it.

Ignoring her, Carlyle kept his gaze on Belekhsan. 'My condolences,' he said.

When she frowned, she was, if anything, even more beautiful. 'What for?'

'For the death of your husband,' Carlyle said gently.

'My soon to be ex-husband,' Belekhsan corrected him.

'I suppose,' Carlyle smiled thinly, 'at least you don't have to worry about the divorce any more.'

Belekhsan was about to say something further when Slater put a hand on her shoulder. 'Let's just get the ground rules of this meeting sorted out, shall we?'

Sitting back in his chair, Carlyle folded his arms. 'Go ahead.'

Slater nodded. 'Good. Ms Belekhsan has voluntarily agreed to meet with you. She is not a suspect.'

At this stage, Carlyle thought, *she is very much a suspect*. Avoiding Slater's gaze, he kept his mouth firmly shut.

'As you know, she was out of the country when this terrible event happened, on holiday in Cyprus. When informed of it, she immediately returned to the United Kingdom to be with her daughter and to help you in any way that she could.'

Yeah, right. 'Where is she now?'

'Who?'

'Rebecca.'

'She's with a friend,' Belekhsan explained.

Carlyle made a show of looking confused. 'Wouldn't it be better to let her grandparents look after her?'

Belekhsan looked like she'd just swallowed a wasp. Happy Families.

'Ms Belekhsan,' Slater ploughed on, 'was in the process of finalizing her divorce from Rebecca's father, Julian Schaeffer.' She fixed Carlyle with a cold stare. 'And just to be clear, SS and M had negotiated a very fair settlement on Ms Belekhsan's behalf, so there is no motive there.'

Getting into his stride, Carlyle decided to keep gently digging, like an archaeologist working away at the topsoil with a trowel. 'I will want to see that agreement.' Slater looked unhappy but consented. He turned back to face Belekhsan. 'Why were you getting a divorce?'

Her face darkened, tipping her beauty into something altogether more scary.

'The usual things,' she answered.

Placing his elbows on the table, Carlyle leaned forward, pushing the lawyer to the edge of his vision. 'Forgive me,' he said quietly, 'but I have never been divorced, so I don't know what "the usual things" are. Could you be a bit more specific?'

'We argued a lot.' Irritated, Belekhsan picked at a broken nail. 'Over money, sex, the child – as I said, the usual things.' Looking up, she smiled maliciously at him. 'Maybe you have a perfect marriage. Maybe these things are not usual for you and your wife.'

'Did he have a girlfriend?'

Belekhsan rolled her eyes. 'I would not know,' she said haughtily.

'But you have a boyfriend?'

Slater had her answer ready for that one. 'Ms Belekhsan and Mr Schaeffer had been separated for more than a year when the shooting took place,' she trilled. 'Ms Belekhsan has been in a new relationship for approximately three months.'

'Four,' Belekhsan corrected her.

'Four months,' Slater continued. 'The trip to Cyprus had been their first holiday together.'

'And what did Mr Schaeffer make of that?'

'I don't know,' Belekhsan shrugged. 'Anyway, it was none of his business.'

'You will need to let me have the boyfriend's details,' Carlyle responded. 'We will be wanting to speak to him as well.'

Belekhsan looked mulish at this, but she kept her mouth shut.

'It is just a matter of routine,' Carlyle explained.

'My client understands,' Slater nodded. 'She is a victim here too.'

Perhaps. Carlyle kept his gaze firmly on the wife. 'Who would have got custody of Rebecca when the divorce was finalized?'

'It would have been split.' Belekhsan sounded irritated. With the question? Or with the fact of having to share the kid? Maybe both.

'Isn't that unusual?' Carlyle enquired.

Pulling off a sliver of broken nail, Belekhsan flicked it on to the floor.

'Usually the mother wins hands down in these situations,' he went on.

Belekhsan looked at him blankly.

'It was an amicable agreement,' Slater interjected, 'that sought to put the interests of the child first.'

'I see,' Carlyle said. In situations like this, the interests of the child usually went straight out of the window, but he was in an exercise-induced good mood and prepared to let the lawyer deliver her spiel.

'It also took into account the fact that both parents were in full-time employment with demanding jobs,' Slater continued. 'All in all, everyone made a conscious effort to deal with this in a sensible and practical manner.'

Poor bloody kid, Carlyle thought. Throwing away the trowel, he reached for his spade. It was time to play the navvy, rather than the archaeologist. Belekhsan had turned her attention to another damaged nail. It struck him as surprising that such an elegant woman would be less than fastidious in the manicure department. 'So,' he said, his voice a model of idle curiosity, 'you have no idea why someone might want to shoot Mr Schaeffer three times in the chest in the middle of a playground full of children?'

Iris Belekhsan gave him a look which suggested that she was considering the question for the first time. Ten, fifteen seconds passed before she managed to shake her head.

Carlyle smiled sympathetically. 'Would you care to speculate?'

'I don't see how that helps,' Slater snapped.

'Maybe he annoyed someone at his work,' Belekhsan suggested airily.

Now it was Carlyle's turn to pretend to think things through. Umar had visited Schaeffer's workplace – it had basically been a desk in a serviced office – and as far as they could tell he had worked alone. 'But I thought he was a one-man band?'

Belekhsan looked nonplussed. 'Sorry?'

'He worked on his own,' Carlyle explained. 'Who could he have annoyed?'

The not-so grieving widow looked at him as if he was a naughty ten year old who was refusing to brush his teeth properly. 'His clients, of course.'

The inspector waited. When she didn't offer any more information, he prompted further. 'What exactly did he do?'

Iris Belekhsan idly scratched her left breast. Carlyle tried not to stare. 'He advised high-net-worth individuals on their investments, that sort of thing.'

'From what we have seen so far,' Carlyle reflected, 'his records do not seem to be anywhere near complete.'

Belekhsan made a face. 'I wouldn't know anything about that.'

At the far end of the table, Kieron Sterling gestured at his watch.

Slater gave her associate a nod. 'I'm afraid,' she said, turning to Carlyle, 'we are rather pushed for time this morning, Inspector. I think we are going to have to call it a day.'

'One final question,' Carlyle said evenly, refusing to let the lawyer end the meeting so quickly.

'Go on.'

'Did Mr Schaeffer have a will?'

Having the answer to hand, Slater smiled indulgently. 'Everything goes to the child. Once the estate has been dealt with, all the monies will be put in a trust that will provide for Rebecca's education. It will be turned fully over to her when she is twenty-one.'

Carlyle looked at Belekhsan. 'And are you happy about that?'

Belekhsan shrugged as if it was of no import. 'My will is exactly the same.'

'Fine.' Carlyle got to his feet. 'I will need to speak to you again in due course. I will also need to speak to Rebecca again.' Victim Support and Social Services had both spoken to the kid, to no effect whatsoever. Carlyle didn't think he could do any better but he knew that he would have to give it a go.

Slater gave him a look that suggested he should crawl back under the nearest rock, while Belekhsan's eyes twinkled with something that under different circumstances might have been described as mischief.

'Am I a suspect?'

It was a question that the inspector had been asked a thousand times before. The stock answer tripped from his tongue before his brain had time to engage. 'The investigation is ongoing.' He saw no reason to put her at ease.

Belekhsan glanced at Slater. 'If you need anything further, I am sure that Abigail will be able to help you,' she said.

'Of course,' Slater nodded. 'The inspector knows that I am always here to help.'

It sounded like a cue for laughter but he controlled his mirth. 'I'll be in touch.' Jumping from his chair, Sterling reached for the door but Carlyle shook his head. He could see himself out.

TWENTY-TWO

Taking a large bite out of a shiny green apple, Umar watched the inspector approach his desk. After several chews, he swallowed.

'How did it go?'

Sliding past, Carlyle settled into the chair at his own desk. 'Pretty much as expected.'

'Mm.'

'No one's saying anything, basically.'

'Do you think she did it?' Umar nibbled the apple.

Reaching forward, Carlyle switched on his computer. 'Well, she didn't pull the trigger, obviously, given that she was in Cyprus with her new boyfriend at the time. Whether she was behind the killing is another matter.'

'What do you think?'

'Look at the stats. When the husband is done in, you always have to look at the wife.' Carlyle grinned. 'By the way, how *is* Christina?'

'Urgh.' Umar took one last bite from his apple and tossed the core towards a small cardboard box that had been placed on the floor as an improvised bin. To his disgust, he missed by a ridiculous amount, at least six inches.

'Good shot,' Carlyle sniggered.

With some considerable reluctance, the young sergeant got to his feet, picked up the core by the stalk and dropped it among the collection of paper cups, crisp packets and sandwich wrappers already in the box. 'I can't remember the last time I had a proper night's sleep,' he complained. 'And the bloody kid hasn't even arrived yet.'

Carlyle tried not to smirk. The boy did look completely knackered, which only added to the strange sense of wellbeing he himself had been enjoying all day.

'Easy for you to look smug,' Umar griped. 'Those days are long behind you now.'

True, thought Carlyle happily, saying, 'Don't worry about it. You'll be fine.'

Umar looked around to check that no one was eavesdropping on their conversation before wheeling his chair towards Carlyle and lowering his voice. 'She's so bloody big. And tossing and turning the whole time. Moaning about how it's all my fault.'

'Well, it is, I presume?'

'I would kill for a full night's sleep right now,' Umar whispered. 'And one of the women at the ante-natal class started hitting on me.'

Carlyle raised his eyebrows.

'Right in my face she was, too.'

The inspector felt a familiar mix of jealousy and prurient interest. He'd never been hit on by a woman in his life, unless you counted Miki Kasaba, and he was beginning to think he must have dreamed that.

'Maybe I'll take her up on it, just to see if I can get a decent night's kip.'

'But isn't she up the duff as well?'

'Yeah,' Umar grinned. 'But quite foxy.' He left out the bisexual bit in case it all got a bit too much for the inspector's limited imagination.

Carlyle waved an admonishing finger at his sergeant. 'You need to get a grip.'

Umar gave him a sly look. 'You're just jealous of my pulling power.'

'Hardly,' Carlyle lied. 'Anyway, remember that Porsche licence-plate I got you to check out?'

Umar nodded. 'Yeah.'

'Well . . .' Carlyle began explaining the story of Ayumi Ninomiya, backwards, starting from Daniel Hutton's motor.

Umar laughed out loud when he got to the bit about Miki and her big bed. 'She's obviously got a thing for older men.'

Carlyle realized that he should have kept his stupid fat mouth shut.

'Maybe you should sign up to the website,' Umar grinned.

'Sod off.'

'Seriously,' the sergeant continued. 'You could go undercover to flush out the killer.'

'For a start, we don't know that the missing girl, Ayumi Ninomiya, is dead. Also, the point of signing up is to meet young girls, not other sugar daddies.'

Umar stroked his chin thoughtfully. 'Sounds good to me.'

Carlyle shook his head. 'That would go down well at home. Anyway, I don't think tired, broke, middle-aged coppers are quite what the young ladies in question are looking for.'

Umar looked his boss up and down. 'No,' he said finally, 'I suppose not.'

'Any more good ideas?' Carlyle asked, irritated now.

Reversing his chair, back towards his desk, Umar asked: 'What's the dating website called?'

'Leafhopper.com.'

Umar typed the name into his search engine. 'That's a tech company.'

'Eh?'

'Hold on, hold on.' Umar clicked on his mouse. 'Here we go. It's Leafhopper.org, actually.'

'Whatever.' The inspector felt rather uneasy that he hadn't done this simple check rather earlier in the proceedings.

Umar read from the screen. 'Discerning – elite – global.'

'Sounds like your kind of thing.' Getting up from his chair, Carlyle stepped behind his sergeant and scanned the site's home page. A blurb read: *The top location for sugar daddy dating*

– bringing together successful sugar daddies and beautiful sugar babies. However, the page itself was bland and functional, with the subscription options prominently displayed and a link for existing members to log in. Only a picture of a happy-looking blonde babe in an under-sized bikini hinted at the delights inside.

Carlyle sighed heavily. 'How did we get through life without the internet?'

Umar grunted. 'The guy with the Porsche, what was his name?'

'Hutton. Daniel Hutton.'

Umar scanned the page. 'Can't see any kind of search function. I guess you don't get anything until you've paid. Maybe we should just ask the site's owners to show us what they've got.'

'There's no way they'd play ball without a court order and we're never going to get one of those without something stronger than we've got at the moment.'

'Maybe I'll just sign up and see what I can find out.'

Carlyle pointed to the small print, which required a £275 signing-on fee on top of the £30 monthly subscription. 'Good luck getting that through expenses.'

'Maybe there's a free trial option,' said Umar optimistically as he bashed a few more keys.

'Forget it,' Carlyle said. 'We're wasting our time. Anyway, you're too young to be anyone's sugar daddy.'

'I suppose.'

'Besides, we've got more than enough on our plate.'

Umar flicked on to the BBC News website. The lead story was about yet another super injunction. 'So you're going to park this one?'

'No.' Carlyle shook his head. 'When I get time, I'll go and see Hutton and take it from there.'

'Okay.'

Carlyle stepped back to his desk. 'By the way, what's a slut walk?'

Umar sat back in his chair and placed his hands behind his head. It was a good pose with which to share a few pearls of wisdom with the tired old fogey who pretended to be his boss. 'It's a kind of post-feminist thing.'

Uh oh, thought Carlyle.

'To do with the right of women to wear what they want.'

'And can't they?' Carlyle gestured airily towards the outside world. 'It's not exactly Tehran out there.'

'No, no, no.' Umar clarified: 'This is about the right to wear *anything* you want. If you want to dress like a Soho streetwalker you should be able to do so without some pig of a man hitting on you because you're giving him the come-on.'

'But why would you want to dress like a hooker if—'

Umar held up his hand. 'Surely you know better than to even get involved in discussion about it?'

'Yeah, good point.' The inspector had learned the hard way over the years that anything to do with so-called 'gender equality' was best left alone. You just couldn't win.

'They go on demonstrations in their underwear,' Umar explained. 'It started in America, I think.'

'Figures,' Carlyle grumbled. 'I wonder what Germaine Greer would make of it all.'

Umar gave him a blank look. 'Who?'

Jesus.

'Christina's a feminist,' Umar mused, 'and she didn't bother with any underwear. Or outerwear for that matter.'

An image of the naked stripper smacking one of his PCs over the head with an outsized vibrator popped into his mind and Carlyle laughed out loud.

'Why did you ask, anyway?' Umar enquired, yawning.

'Hutton's daughter,' Carlyle told him. 'Apparently she's one of the leaders of the SlutWalk movement in London.'

'I see.' Umar thought about that for a moment. 'Shall I go and interview her?'

'Better leave her to me.'

Umar looked disappointed, but only for a second. 'By the way,' he asked, 'have you spoken to Helen yet?'

Carlyle looked at him blankly.

'About the wedding.'

Ah. He had completely forgotten about his sergeant's upcoming nuptials.

'Er, not yet.' This time, Umar looked genuinely disappointed. Maybe even a little hurt. He made to say something but Carlyle quickly held up a hand. 'I have an excuse,' he stammered, 'a very good excuse.'

Having explained about his mother, Carlyle launched into an extended monologue about his father and the hookers in the Garden Hotel by way of a little light relief. As he was reaching the conclusion, he saw that Umar had become distracted by something on the far side of the room. Looking round, he saw a furious-looking Simpson steaming towards them, with a sheepish-looking Savage in tow.

Oh great, the inspector thought. *What now?*

He didn't have to wait long to find out. Simpson's opening gambit was short and to the point. 'Collingwood's escaped.'

Carlyle had never seen his boss so angry. At least, he had never seen her so angry at someone other than him. He looked at Savage. The sergeant gazed steadfastly at the floor. 'What happened?'

'He went to the bathroom and slipped out of an open window.'

'And no one went with him?' Umar said, and grinned at the inspector.

Don't make me laugh, you bastard, Carlyle thought. Getting angrier by the second, the Commander looked like she wanted to smack someone in the mouth.

'He was having a dump,' Savage explained, his voice so low that they could hardly hear it. 'The security guards waited outside the stall.'

'It might have helped,' Simpson said grimly, 'if you hadn't been so busy trying to chat up that reporter from BBC News.'

Savage's head dropped even lower. Poor old 'Robbie'. This time Carlyle couldn't help but smile. He loved it when Simpson lost her rag. Further infuriated, the Commander jabbed an angry finger towards him.

'I'm glad you find it amusing, John. What are you going to bloody do about it?'

Pushing himself out of his chair, Carlyle allowed himself a stretch. 'Well,' he said, trying to keep the amusement from his voice, 'I suppose we'd better go and find him then.'

TWENTY-THREE

The Collingwood family home was a solid terrace house in Highbury, not far from the former Arsenal football ground. Sitting in the gloom of the living room, Carlyle sipped from a cup of green tea and eyed Alison Collingwood carefully. An attractive blonde woman in – he guessed – her late thirties. Sitting on the sofa, her hands clamped tightly together, it appeared as if she hadn't slept a wink in the last few days.

'*Mrs Collingwood!*'

'*Can you come out, love?*'

'*Where's your husband?*'

From behind the curtains, the cries of the assembled press pack – a motley bunch of middle-aged white men with a chronic vitamin D deficiency kept at bay by a harassed trio of uniforms – merged into the general background hum of the city. Inside, it was just a normal home, with a comfortable, lived-in feel. There was the usual selection of photos and mementos but nothing that spoke particularly of Simon Collingwood's sporting career.

Carlyle was embarrassed to be here, slightly ashamed to be imposing himself on this woman at the worst time of her life – but that was his job.

He let a few moments slip past.

Then a few more.

Still she did not acknowledge his presence.

'Are you sure,' he said finally, gently, 'that you don't know where your husband is? Or where he might possibly be?'

154

The shake of her head was so slight that he might have imagined it. The tears that welled in her eyes before running down her cheeks and dripping off her chin on to the carpet were real enough.

'We've told you, Inspector, Alison had no inkling of any of this,' said Celia Barclay, family friend and now de facto spokesperson for the mute Mrs Collingwood.

Carlyle finished his tea and placed the cup and saucer carefully on the floor by the foot of his chair. 'I appreciate that. And I fully accept that the escape was a spur of the moment thing. But Simon's disappearance simply prolongs this whole,' he was going to say 'mess' but stopped himself in time, 'situation. We have his passport, so he will not be able to leave the country. There is, literally, nowhere for him to go.'

'I'm sorry, Inspector.' Getting to her feet, Barclay gestured towards the door.

'Okay.' Pushing himself out of the chair, Carlyle handed her his cup and saucer. 'Thank you for the tea,' he smiled. As she took it, he slipped past her and stepped in front of Alison Collingwood. Barclay made to protest but he held up a hand and she stopped. 'Give us one minute, please.'

Clearly not happy, Barclay hesitated in the doorway before disappearing into the hall. Dropping to his knees, Carlyle took Collingwood's hands in his. She looked at him, surprised, but did not pull away.

The tears just kept coming.

'Mrs Collingwood,' he said quietly, in the hope that the eavesdropping Celia Barclay could not hear, 'I am not here to punish you or your family.' A fat, salty teardrop splashed on to the back of his right hand but he did not let go. He was surprised that he did not feel like an idiot, kneeling there in front of a crying woman, but he knew that he had to at least try to help her. 'But I cannot offer anything that can make this any easier.'

This time he got a definite nod and a sniffle.

Carlyle tilted his head towards the curtains. 'There are a lot of people out there who have a great deal of sympathy for what

Simon has done. They understand why he did it. Many of those people would like to think that if they were put in the same terrible, terrible situation, they would have the guts to do the same thing that he did.'

'Do they?' Her voice was more of a croak than a whisper.

Carlyle said urgently, 'The thing for Simon now is that he has to deal with the consequences of his actions. It is better to do this as quickly as possible so that you can try and get through this.'

Alison Collingwood's eyes filled again.

'Do you have any other children?' He knew the answer but he asked anyway.

She nodded. 'Andrew. He's ten next month.'

Carlyle squeezed her hands gently. 'When you come out of the other side of this – and you will – he will still be young, and he will still need you.'

Collingwood began rocking gently backwards and forwards on the edge of the sofa. Still he did not let go of her hands. 'I will do my best for you, but I need you to give me an idea of where Simon might be.'

'Yes.'

Carlyle waited for more but there was nothing else. After a while, he was conscious of his knees aching and he had pins and needles in his left foot. Letting go of her hands, he stood up and placed a card on the sofa beside her. 'If you can think of anything, anything at all, please let me know. I will do what I can to help.'

As if on cue, Celia Barclay reappeared in the doorway. Carlyle said nothing as he walked past her on the way out.

It should have taken no more than thirty minutes to take the number 186 from Highbury to Highgate but, thanks to roadworks on the Brecknock Road, Carlyle had been travelling for more than an hour by the time he got off the bus. In a foul mood, he made his weary way up Swains Lane, having to jump onto the pavement to avoid being run over by a group of over-excited cyclists enjoying the 15 per cent gradient on one of the steepest climbs in the city. Fretting about Alison Collingwood, he again had the sense of grasping at too many things that were outside of his control.

Running around, achieving nothing.

In the breast pocket of his jacket, his phone was going mad but Carlyle ignored it. He didn't know what he wanted but did know that he didn't want to talk to anyone right now.

Slow down.

Slow down.

Reaching the entrance to the east side of Highgate Cemetery, he glanced at his watch. There was still more than half an hour to go to closing time, so he ducked inside, flipping his ID at the attendant to avoid paying the small entrance fee.

In less than a minute, he had left the city behind.

Nodding to a couple who were heading for the exit, he began walking further down the muddy path, away from the pressures of the day. Highgate Cemetery was, to Carlyle's mind, one of the most magical places in London. If there was one place he would like to be buried, this was it. How much better to be laid to rest in the leafy gloom, worm food, rather than being incinerated, your ashes mixed with those of strangers and stuck in some over-priced copper pot? For a moment, he fantasized about burying his mother here, although he knew that would be impossible. These days, the cemetery could only accommodate seventy new arrivals a year.

Highgate's greatest celebrity, Karl Marx, was only one of a slew of famous residents, including authors George Eliot, Douglas Adams and Beryl Bainbridge, as well as Charles Cruft, founder of the eponymous dog show, the physicist Michael Faraday and the comic Max Wall. Carlyle found a bench in front of a magnificently carved memorial to Lieutenant General the Right Honourable Sir Henry Knight Storks (1811–74). His equally magnificent *CV* included High Commissioner of the Ionian Islands, Governor of Malta, Captain General of Jamaica and MP for Ripon. And those were just the highlights. Reading through the list, the inspector felt quite the underachiever.

At the bottom was the legend: *Tomorrow do thy worst for I have lived today.*

Was that a good motto for Simon Collingwood?

Perhaps.

Letting his gaze wander from Sir Henry, Carlyle tried to let his mind go free. Clear out everything from his brain and then reassemble it in order of priority. There was so much to deal with:

Collingwood

Julian Schaeffer

Ayumi Ninomiya

His mother

How had he ended up with so much on his plate? If the solitude of the cemetery was a balm on his concerns, it failed to offer any solutions. After five minutes sitting on the bench, he felt chilled. Getting to his feet, he made his way back to the exit.

Danny Hutton lived in a modernist masterpiece overlooking the cemetery. Consumed by jealousy, Carlyle walked past the Porsche parked in the driveway and gave the bell by the front door a long, hard ring.

And waited.

Tapping the toe of his shoe on the step, he began counting. Notoriously impatient, it was a way of trying to exercise some self-restraint; he would give himself to fifty before ringing the bell again.

Forty-one, forty-two . . .

The door was flung open and he was confronted by a young woman in a sheer yellow bra and a skirt that could not have been any shorter without being non-existent. Only by gritting his teeth and pressing the back of his skull down violently on the top of his spine was he able to tear his gaze away from her chest.

'Are you all right?' the girl asked.

'Ah, yes.' Carlyle tried to focus on a spot above her head. 'I am looking for Mr Hutton.'

'He's around somewhere,' she said airily. 'Hold this and I'll go and see if I can find him.'

Carlyle was still staring at the ceiling as she thrust a cardboard placard on a wooden stick into his hands and disappeared back down the hallway.

'Dad! Someone for you!'

Carlyle looked at the writing on the sign: *It's my hot body and I'll wear what I want.*

'You can say that again,' he mumbled to himself.

First Miki Kasaba and now this. It was too much for a middle-aged man to take. Maybe he should have got Umar to come up here after all.

Then again, maybe not.

When the girl returned, Carlyle was genuinely distressed to see that she had not put on any more clothes. On a second glance, she was quite tall, maybe five eight, slim, with shoulder-length auburn hair. Pretty, but not drop dead gorgeous.

'Dad's in the shower,' she smiled, apparently oblivious to his discomfort. 'Would you like a cup of tea?'

'Yes,' he said, staring at his shoes. 'Thank you. That would be great.' Closing the front door, he left the placard in the hall and followed her into a kitchen where the glass roof had been opened to create an internal courtyard.

'Wow,' said Carlyle, happy to have something else to focus on.'This place is amazing.'

'Yeah, it's not bad,' said the girl. Slipping behind the breakfast counter, she flicked a switch to start boiling a kettle standing by the sink. 'I'm Electra, by the way. Who are you?'

Carlyle gave his name and rank, which seemed to be good enough; she didn't ask for any ID.

Electra rolled her eyes. 'Dad's not in trouble again, is he?'

Again? Carlyle ignored the question. 'Do you normally let people you don't know into your house?'

She gave him a sharp look. 'Not when they spend so much time checking out my tits.'

His cheeks burning, struggling for anything remotely resembling a witty reply, Carlyle was saved by the kettle coming to the boil.

'At least you have the decency to be embarrassed,' she offered graciously. 'Boys today can't even manage that. They seem to think life is supposed to be one long porn movie.'

'Mm.' With a daughter of his own, Carlyle tried very hard not to think about what today's boys were like.

'What kind of tea would you like?'

Five minutes later they were sitting at a glass table, sipping green tea with lemon. Of Danny Hutton, there was still no sign. Looking over at the view of the cemetery, the inspector was happy to let Electra explain about SlutWalking.

'It started in Canada when a policeman told Toronto University students that women should avoid dressing like sluts in order not to be victimized. A couple of months later, a thousand people hit the streets in the first "slutwalk". Then it spread to the US, Australia, Britain and so on.'

Carlyle nodded intently. Why would anyone want to call themselves a slut? He knew, however, to keep his own counsel.

The conversation was finally ended by the arrival of a middle-aged gent in a dark green Lacoste polo shirt and a pair of crisp Hugo Boss jeans. Danny Hutton was less red in the face than the last time Carlyle had seen him but he still looked seriously overweight. He eyed the visitor suspiciously.

'Who are you?'

'This,' Electra chipped in gleefully, 'is the policeman who's come to talk to you.'

Hutton looked at his daughter. 'Isn't it time for you to make a defiant display of your inner slut?'

Electra glanced at the clock wall. 'Oh yeah. Gotta go.' Jumping up, she kissed her father on the cheek and bounced down the hallway. Hutton's expression was that of a man who'd just been crapped on by a pigeon.

The front door slammed shut.

'A strange carry-on,' Carlyle mused.

Hutton wasn't in the mood to talk about it. His pained expression showed no sign of easing. 'Have you got any ID?'

Carlyle slipped his warrant card across the table. Hutton peered at it, grunted and waddled over to the fridge to fish out a small bottle of Evian. 'So what do you want?'

Carlyle finished his tea and waited for Hutton to sit down. He didn't oblige, downing half of the water as he strolled over to the floor-to-ceiling glass doors.

'I wanted to ask you about Miki Kasaba,' Carlyle said, keeping his irritation in check.

Hutton's watery grey eyes narrowed. 'You could have given me a heads-up.' Finishing the last of the Evian, he crushed the bottle in his fist. 'My bloody wife could have been here.'

Carlyle looked around. 'Is she?'

'No,' said Hutton grumpily. 'She's gone to Westfield – for a change.' Moving back to the kitchen, he tossed the bottle into the sink. 'As if she needs another bloody designer handbag.' He shook his head at the sheer bloody futility of it all. 'But still, you didn't know that.'

'I wanted to ask you about Miki Kasaba, and the sugar daddy website,' Carlyle said flatly.

Hutton frowned. 'What about it?'

'Miki's flatmate, Ayumi Ninomiya, is missing.'

'I know, I know.' Pulling out a chair, Hutton finally sat down. 'Miki told me about it. I reckon she's probably just off partying somewhere.'

'After all this time?'

'Inspector,' Hutton smiled maliciously, 'we are not talking about ordinary chaps here.'

'Ordinary chaps?'

'You know, the average guy you see walking down the street. Or in the pub. A bloke like yourself.'

Carlyle raised an eyebrow. 'I see.'

'Alpha males is an understatement.' He puffed out his chest. 'We are *super* alpha males. You hook up with a pretty girl you like, you might spend a year taking her round the world, shagging her brains out.' He chuckled to himself. 'I think Miki was a bit

161

jealous. You see, I had met Ayumi a couple of times through the website. She was a real fox – top, top drawer. She would have been my first choice but she said no. She had already hooked up with someone else.'

'A super, *super* alpha male?' Carlyle couldn't resist.

Ignoring the jibe, Hutton began ostentatiously picking his nose. 'There's always someone higher up the pecking order than you, always.' Rolling the snot into a ball, he flicked it across the table, missing Carlyle by a couple of inches. 'And before you ask, no, I don't know who it was.'

TWENTY-FOUR

Returning home after his adventures in North London, Carlyle was relieved to find that his father had retreated back to his bedsit. It had occurred to him that his mother's death would allow Alexander to return to the family flat in Fulham. On the other hand, the old fella had got used to his new digs over the last few years so maybe he should just stay put. Either way, it wasn't going to be Carlyle's problem.

Pulling a beer from the fridge, he padded into the living room and sat down. Next to the TV remote was a newsletter from Avalon, the medical aid charity where Helen worked. Taking a long pull on the beer, Carlyle scanned the main story: *More women die in childbirth in Afghanistan than anywhere else on the planet . . . alarmingly high rate of obstructed labour . . . chronic lack of midwives . . . the miles women are forced to walk to reach qualified healthcare*

A wave of infinite weariness washed over him. Last year, his wife had organized a family trip to Liberia to coincide with her work schedule. Carlyle had been less than enthusiastic. It was the first time he had been abroad since a package trip to Lanzarote almost a decade previously.

In the event, however, he had surprised himself by conducting himself with reasonably good grace. Now, from the safety of his European home, he could claim to have found it an educational, even a humbling experience. Not that he had any intention of ever going back.

As far as this year was concerned, he was expecting to revert to their usual week in Brighton. Boring but safe. An hour on the train, it was far enough away in his opinion.

Helen wouldn't suggest going to bloody Afghanistan, surely?

As if on cue, his wife appeared in the doorway. Carlyle tossed the newsletter onto the coffee table and gestured for her to come and sit next to him. He had to admit she looked even more exhausted than he did. He knew he should get up and make her a cup of tea, but he couldn't quite manage it. Instead, he watched as she dropped onto the sofa and grabbed his beer.

'Bad day in the office?'

Helen finished the beer and handed him back the empty bottle. 'Don't ask.' Then: 'Thank you for getting your father pissed, by the way.'

Carlyle wanted to protest but thought better of it. He considered mentioning the Russian hookers but thought better of that too. 'Sorry.' He wanted to get another beer but his legs refused to stand him up.

'The poor old soul,' Helen sighed.

'I think he's bearing up quite well,' Carlyle reflected.

Stretching out, Helen let him put an arm round her shoulder. 'It's just that genetic Scottish stoicism,' she proclaimed.

'Nothing wrong with that,' said Carlyle somewhat defensively.

'And another thing,' Helen said out of the blue. 'You have to go and see the priest.'

Carlyle forced himself up. 'What?'

'Father Wotjek Mac . . . Mac something at St Wulstan's in Fulham.'

'Who? What?' On his feet now, he realized he was going to need that beer.

Pulling her mobile from the back pocket of her jeans, Helen scrolled down her text messages. 'Mac–ius–zek. Maciuszek. He's Polish.'

Carlyle felt his tiredness ratchet up a notch. 'What the hell's he got to do with anything?' he snapped.

'Alexander said your mother was Catholic.'

'News to me.' As far as he could recall, his mother had never expressed any religious beliefs of any sort. The woman had been far too . . . no-nonsense to believe in any of that kind of airy fairy, hocus pocus crap. 'She certainly wasn't a *Polish* Catholic.'

'Plumbers, priests.' Helen shrugged. 'It's what they do in Poland.'

'Stereotyping a nation.'

Helen, who prided herself on being the most politically correct member of the family, shot him a sharp look. 'There are worse things to be known for. Anyway, St Wulstan's have agreed to conduct the funeral service and I assume that *you* weren't proposing to shop around.'

'Fair enough,' Carlyle nodded. 'I suppose we should be grateful that she didn't express a desire to be buried back in Scotland.'

'So you have to go and speak to the priest about what to say.'

Realizing that it would be too churlish to protest, Carlyle accept his allotted task.

'I'll text you the number. Don't forget to give him a call.'

'Of course not. Looks like we've got a wedding *and* a funeral to go to.' He explained about Umar and Christina.

'That'll be nice,' Helen smiled, 'especially after all the other stuff.' She gestured towards the kitchen. 'Now go and get us both another beer.'

Joe Rowan leaned on the desk, playing a game called Angry Birds on his iPhone. His kids had shown him how to play it a week ago and now he was hooked.

'Sarge?'

'Huh?' Rowan launched a bird from a slingshot, groaning when it missed the egg-stealing pig and smashed into a concrete slab.

'*Sarge.*'

Reluctantly, the desk sergeant looked up to see WPC Sarah Williams standing in front of him. Williams was a good-looking girl but a bit thick. She also liked to complain. He warily looked the WPC up and down. Williams had married an accountant a year or so ago. Already, around the edges, you could see that she was beginning to go to seed. Rowan was surprised that she hadn't popped out a sprog by now. An image of Williams and her bean counter trying to make a baby popped into his head and he smirked.

The WPC gave him a funny look. 'What?' she asked, the gormless Celtic accent overriding her Estuary English.

'Er, nothing.' Rowan pushed the image of a flushed and sweating Williams from his head and shuffled some papers on the desk in front of him. 'What is it?'

Williams jerked a thumb over her shoulder. 'There's a bloke chained to the railings outside with a pair of handcuffs.'

'Jesus,' Rowan complained, 'not another stag party, is it?'

'He's an old bloke.'

'Old blokes get married too, stupid buggers.'

The landline sitting next to the computer on his desk started ringing. After some deliberation, Rowan picked it up.

'Charing Cross . . . I see . . .'

Williams watched his face grow serious. He looked her up and down without any hint of his usual lasciviousness and she wondered what she had done wrong.

'Can I have your name, please? Hello? Hello?' Biting his lower lip, Rowan returned the receiver to the cradle and began bashing at the keyboard next to the screen. A member of the public, fed up at the delay in being seen, knocked on the glass doors that separated the desk from the waiting room.

Not looking up, Rowan hit the keys harder.

The man banged on the door with his fist.

Williams gave him the hardest glare she could manage. 'We'll be with you as soon as possible, *sir*.' She turned back to the desk, leaning forward to try to see what was on the screen.

'What is it?'

Taking a half-step backwards, Rowan scratched his head for the longest time.

'Sarge?'

'The guy chained to the railings,' Rowan said finally, 'did he have any ID on him?'

'I dunno,' Williams shrugged. 'I haven't gone through his pockets. He's really pissed off. Keeps swearing at me in all kinds of different languages.'

'Okay. Call the Fire Brigade. Get them to free him and then you bring him in here. I need to talk to him.'

Refreshed by eight hours of solid kip, it was a relatively cheery Inspector Carlyle who bowled up on the third floor of Charing Cross police station well before 8 a.m. He was surprised to find his sergeant already at his desk.

'Another restless night?'

'Savage is looking for you,' Umar grunted, not looking up from his copy of the *Metro*.

'Has he found Collingwood yet?'

'Nope.'

Well he can sod off then, the inspector thought with a deliberate lack of charity. 'Simpson will be pleased.'

Umar slurped noisily from a large mug of tea. On the side was the legend: *World's Best Dad*.

You're getting a bit ahead of yourself there, sunshine, Carlyle thought. He wasn't big on superstition but he would like to see the baby out safe and sound before Umar started flaunting his parenting skills. 'She's got other things to worry about.'

'Huh?'

Umar turned the paper so that his boss could see the story he was reading. The headline read: NAMED AND SHAMED. 'Eight hundred people outed Dino Mottram online as one of the people who'd got a super-injunction,' Umar grinned.

Even squinting, Carlyle couldn't read the text of the piece, so he retreated to his chair.

'Yes, indeed,' Umar continued. 'Mr Carole Simpson has been revealed as the quote unquote "leading businessman" who entertained three ladies of the night while on a business trip to Dublin, pleasuring himself with a state-of-the-art sex toy while conducting a board meeting over the telephone.'

Carlyle thought about that for a moment. 'What's a "state-of-the-art sex toy"?'

Umar scanned the remainder of the article. 'That is not explained.'

'Probably just as well. Poor old Simpson. She really does know how to pick 'em.'

'I guess her wedding is off then,' Umar mused.

'I guess so. But you never know, stranger things have happened.'

'Simpson's never going to put up with something like that.'

'Probably not.' Not really caring one way or another, Carlyle was distracted by the sight of Angie Middleton puffing up the stairs. Middleton really was a big girl and the effort looked considerable. By the time she reached his desk, the inspector was worried that she was about to have a stroke.

'Lift not working?' he smirked.

Shaking her head, Middleton wiped a bead of sweat from her brow. 'Exercise regime,' she panted.

Carlyle glanced at Umar but his sergeant had returned to his paper.

'Don't overdo it, will you?' From the look of her, there was no danger of that. He tried – and failed – to imagine what a thin Angie Middleton might look like.

Finally she recovered her breath enough to speak. 'I was looking for you.'

Here we go, Carlyle thought. Suddenly he didn't feel so refreshed. 'Simpson?'

'No.' Unable to stand any longer, Middleton perched on the edge of his desk. His personal space wasn't so much infringed as obliterated. 'Do you remember a guy called Fassbender?'

Pushing himself back in his chair, Carlyle squinted at her the way you might squint at an eclipse of the sun. 'Paul Fassbender? Yeah, I remember him. Long time ago. Really long time ago. What about him?'

Middleton shifted her weight from one enormous buttock to another. 'He's downstairs. In one of my cells.'

TWENTY-FIVE

Carlyle did not have to repair to the Archives to dig out any decaying files or reread any yellowing notes to recall Paul Fassbender. The case had not been an **important** moment in his career, nor had it taken up a huge amount of his time. It had been neither triumph nor disaster. It was not even an experience that resonated with him at the time. But the details had stayed with him. In fact, its place in his memory had grown over time. Now, it was one of those cases that he knew that he would remember long after he had retired. More than that, it was one of those cases that had shaped both how he thought about himself and how he viewed the world around him.

Fassbender had been a German doctor working for the National Health Service at St Mary's Hospital in Paddington. During his time in London, he started a relationship with a married woman called Samantha Sands.

When Fassbender returned to Germany, Samantha went with him. After a tug of war with her husband, their thirteen-year-old daughter, Lillian, went too.

It took Carlyle a moment to recall the husband's name.

Daniel.

Daniel Sands.

For the unfortunate Daniel Sands, the nightmare was just beginning.

After a year living at Fassbender's home near Munich, Lillian died suddenly. She had spent the day horse-riding. The coroner declared that the cause of death was an overdose of sleeping

169

tablets. However, there was evidence of sexual activity. Daniel Sands, convinced that Lilian had been raped and drugged by her stepfather, began a campaign to have Fassbender charged with her murder. For her part, Samantha had stood by Fassbender, claiming that her ex-husband was delusional.

Carlyle could still recall the first time he had seen Daniel Sands, a small and crumpled figure in a creased suit, his tie at half-mast standing in Bethnal Green police station. The contrast with the man standing next to him, his lawyer, Martin Gevorkyan, couldn't have been greater. The second-generation Armenian, tall and imposing in a crisp navy suit, radiated calm and authority. Sands radiated defeat and despair.

Gevorkyan's office was next to one of the last remaining Second World War bombsites on the Mile End Road. He had made his name as a defence lawyer who was not scared of representing some of the most notorious criminal bosses in the East End. That he had taken Sands on as a client was really quite surprising. So too was his passion for the case. Gevorkyan was a man not known for taking anything too seriously, accepting victory and defeat in the courtroom with the same rueful smile. In this instance, however, he fought his way grimly through a succession of hearings for the best part of two years until he found a judge at the Royal Courts of Justice who would issue an international warrant for Fassbender's arrest.

Back then, John Carlyle had reached the rank of sergeant. He was doing a short and unhappy stint on the front desk at Bethnal Green. When Gevorkyan marched his client into the police station and demanded that the warrant be immediately executed, Carlyle had been the only officer willing to schlep over to Germany and bring Fassbender back. For his trouble, he got to spend three days wandering around Munich before being told off by a stern judge who ruled that the warrant was invalid and declared that he was wasting the court's precious time. Sergeant Carlyle never even clapped eyes on the good doctor. Indeed, it was only when he returned to England that it was properly explained to him that the Germans had refused to extradite Fassbender on the grounds that a Munich court had already dismissed the case due to lack of evidence.

Back behind the front desk at Bethnal Green, he was a sitting duck. A furious Gevorkyan berated him for not getting his man, much to the amusement of Carlyle's passing colleagues. Standing behind his lawyer, Daniel Sands had looked on, the expression on his face growing increasingly bemused.

'This is not justice!' Gevorkyan thundered, a comedy Cockney accent at odds with his swarthy features.

Not looking at either man, Carlyle could only shrug. 'It was a matter for the court. All I did was to serve the papers.'

Calming down slightly, Gevorkyan placed a meaty hand on his client's shoulder, as if to stop him floating away on a current of despair. 'I will never give up on this,' he said solemnly. 'Never.'

Gevorkyan had kept his promise. When he died – crashing a motorbike while on holiday in Greece – he was still working on the case.

And Daniel Sands? Carlyle realized that he didn't know if the man was still alive. Six months after the Munich debacle, the distraught father had been arrested trying to buttonhole the German Ambassador at a charity event being held at the Café Royale on Regent Street. Shirley Bassey had been providing the entertainment. When the Ambassador, a nasty little man with a highly dubious CV, had blanked him, Sands made a grab for the microphone halfway through 'Diamonds Are Forever'. For his trouble, he ended up with two broken fingers, a nasty cut under his right eye, a night in the cells at West End Central and a police caution. The story had merited two paragraphs in the *Evening Standard*. That was the last he had heard of the unfortunate man.

Firing up his computer, the inspector began searching one of the media databases used by the MET. A couple of minutes later he was fully up to speed with developments. Sands was still alive, still chasing Fassbender.

For his part, the German doctor was still a trouble-magnet.

Ten years after Lillian's death, Fassbender had been accused of raping a fifteen-year-old girl in his surgery. At his trial, according to the press reports, he remarked: *'I would not say that she was particularly enthusiastic but I did, however, believe that she was consenting.'*

Found guilty in that case, Fassbender had received a three-year suspended sentence and was banned from practising medicine. He unsuccessfully appealed the decision twice.

The publicity that the case generated led to three other women coming forward to claim that he had also assaulted them as teenagers. None of those cases came to trial.

When he was finally imprisoned, it was for illegally practising as a doctor. After serving nine months in a German prison he retired to Italy. According to a couple of brief newspaper reports, Samantha Sands was still with him.

And now he was downstairs.

According to Middleton, Fassbender had been found chained to the railings outside the police station at 2 a.m. He had been beaten and was rambling and incoherent. The duty desk sergeant had decided to put him in a cell for his own safety.

'What does the CCTV show?'

A pained expression crossed Middleton's face. 'It's broken.'

'Still?' Carlyle made an effort to sound outraged.

'Someone's supposed to come take a look at it next week.'

'That's handy.'

'Sorry.'

'Not your fault.' Carlyle closed his eyes and began thinking it through.

How had Fassbender arrived downstairs?

That wasn't too hard to guess.

How could an injured old man be chained to the railings of a police station without anyone noticing, never mind intervening?

Best not to dwell on that.

So what should he do next?

The original warrant had long since expired. That didn't mean a

172

new one couldn't be issued. There was no statute of limitations on murder. Technically, Fassbender was still a wanted man.

Could they hold him?

Leaning across his desk, the inspector hit a few keys on his keyboard and watched as the phone number he required popped up online. Then he picked up the receiver and carefully punched it in.

The call was answered on the second ring. 'Criminal Team.' The voice on the other end of the line was young, female and harassed.

'Nathalie Kelvin, please.'

'I'll just see if she's around. Who's calling, please?'

Carlyle identified himself and settled in for a long wait.

Nathalie Kelvin QC was the joint head of the Criminal Team at 48 Doughty Street Chambers, one of the top legal outfits in London. The Criminal Team comprised sixty-two dedicated specialist criminal practitioners, including twenty-two Queen's Counsel. For more than thirty-five years they had represented defendants in some of the most difficult and demanding cases, appearing at every level of the domestic courts and in all of the international tribunals. The team combined substantial forensic expertise with specialist knowledge of every category of national and international crime, from terrorism and homicide to money laundering and sexual offences.

Kelvin herself had represented a broad range of high-profile clients, including internet activists accused of publishing US military secrets, and environmental protestors who exposed the illegal work of undercover police officers. Carlyle had first come across her when she had been a member of Paul Fassbender's UK legal team. In the years that followed, he had watched her career take off with some interest.

After five or maybe six minutes, someone finally picked up the phone.

'This is Nathalie Kelvin.' The QC's tone was even more brusque than that of her colleague.

Carlyle, who had been busy surfing football news online, almost dropped the handset. Recovering his poise, he patiently explained who he was for a second time.

'What can I do for you?' There was nothing in the woman's voice that suggested she remembered him.

'I am ringing about a Mr Paul Fassbender.'

There was a pause.

'It was a case you were involved in a while ago,' Carlyle offered. 'He was a client.'

She recognized the crucial distinction in less than a heartbeat. 'Past tense?'

'Yes.'

'What timeframe are we talking about?'

'Something over twenty years ago.'

'Inspector,' Kelvin said crossly, 'do you realize how many cases we handle here? I deal in the law, not ancient history.'

'I know, but—'

She cut him off in mid-sentence. 'How do you spell the surname?'

'His? Or mine?'

'Both.'

Carlyle duly obliged.

'Let me check my records. What is your interest in Mr . . . Fassbender?'

'He's in one of my cells, downstairs.'

There was a pause that suggested the name was more familiar than Kelvin was letting on. 'Has he asked for me?'

Carlyle adopted a relaxed tone. 'I don't know. I haven't seen him yet.'

Kelvin's tone became even sharper. 'It's a bit premature to be ringing me then, don't you think?'

'I was—'

The line went dead and he sat there listening to the dial tone.

After a while, he returned the phone to its cradle, slowly got to his feet and allowed himself an extended stretch.

'Well,' he said aloud to himself, 'I suppose it's time to go and see the man himself.'

TWENTY-SIX

Listening to the retreating steps of the desk sergeant, Carlyle leaned against the cell wall while Fassbender eyed him warily. Sitting on his bed, with the remains of his breakfast at his feet, the old man was wearing a navy fleece and a pair of grey jogging pants. On his feet were a pair of box-fresh New Balance running shoes. His face was tired, grey and unshaven. His thin silver hair was in need of a comb. There was a cut on his left cheek and his right eye was puffed up. His dishevelled state made him hard to age but Carlyle assumed he was somewhere north of seventy.

'Paul Fassbender?'

'Who are you?' The accent was harsh but the voice hardly wavered. 'Why am I being kept here?'

'Mr Fassbender—'

'Dr Fassbender.'

Folding his arms, the inspector adopted his most official monotone: 'You are wanted for questioning in connection with several serious alleged offences.'

The old man shook his head dismissively. 'This is England. *I* am the victim here. I was abducted and violently assaulted.'

'How did you get here?'

'What does it look like? They kidnapped me. Brought me here from Italy.'

'But how did they get you into the country?'

Fassbender scowled. 'Why don't you ask the people who did it?'

Carlyle's eyes narrowed. 'Who did this to you?'

'There was a young guy. I'd never seen him before. He must have had help.'

'Can you give me any more details?'

'Pah!' Fassbender dismissed the question with an angry hand. 'They don't matter. I know who put them up to it. *You* know who put them up to it.' It was almost as if the words were choking him before he managed to spit them out. 'You should have arrested the old fool already. Or do you not enforce the law in this country any more?'

'If you want to make a complaint—'

'I do. You can be sure of that.'

Nodding, Carlyle pushed himself off the wall. 'Then it will, of course, be investigated thoroughly. However, I would also like to ask you a few questions.'

Fassbender stared at him with his good eye. 'Am I under arrest?'

Carlyle trotted out the answer that he had rehearsed upstairs. 'Not at this time, sir. But if you decline to speak to me I will have to review that situation.' It was as far as he could go without laying himself open to a raft of potential charges himself, starting with wrongful arrest and false imprisonment.

For a moment, Fassbender contemplated the floor. Finally he looked up. 'I want to speak to my wife.'

Carlyle nodded.

'And get me my lawyer.'

Angie Middleton smiled at him as he appeared at the desk. 'How did that go?'

'Fine.' Carlyle made a face. 'He wants his lawyer.'

'Fair enough.' They both knew that only a total idiot would consent to helping the police with their enquiries without having their brief present. Whatever else he was, Fassbender was not stupid. Next to Middleton's computer was a half-eaten jam doughnut sitting on a paper plate. Looking at it longingly, she dipped her right index finger into the sugar on the plate and lifted it to her mouth.

'Part of the diet?' Carlyle teased.

'I told you,' she said sharply, 'I'm not on a diet, I'm on an exercise regime.'

'Oh yes.' Carlyle smiled benevolently, knowing that – whatever she called it – it wasn't going to work.

Middleton licked the last few grains of sugar from her finger. 'Want me to sort out the lawyer for your guy downstairs?'

Carlyle glanced at his watch. He would have to be ready to start any questioning as soon as the lawyer arrived; otherwise Fassbender would be out of that cell faster than Middleton could make her doughnut disappear. Once that happened, the only thing stopping the doctor heading straight back home would be his lack of a passport. Presumably, being the efficient bastards they were, the Geman Embassy could sort that out in a matter of hours.

He looked enquiringly at Middleton. 'How long do you think we can realistically leave it?'

Now it was her turn to make a face. 'A couple of hours, max. I certainly couldn't go off shift without having sorted it.'

'Okay. Give me two hours. I need to go out but I will be back by then. Let me know *immediately* if there's a problem.'

'Will do,' Middleton said obediently. But she was looking at the doughnut, not at the inspector. Shaking his head, Carlyle headed for the door.

On his way out, the inspector popped into the gents. Standing at the urinal, he felt his phone start to vibrate in the breast pocket of his jacket. Fishing it out with his free hand, he hit the receive button.

'Carlyle.'

Down the line came the sound of muffled sobs. In one of the stalls, a toilet flushed.

'Hello?'

More sobs.

Jamming the handset between his shoulder and his ear, Carlyle gave his tool a quick shake and zipped himself back up. 'It's okay,' he said quietly, 'take your time. I said I would do what I can to help.' Not stopping to wash his hands, he stepped out into the corridor.

The sobbing stopped.

'Mrs Collingwood?' The inspector was fairly sure he knew who he was talking to.

'I have an address,' she whispered.

'Hold on.' Carlyle fumbled in his pockets for a piece of paper and something to write with. To his relief, he came up with one of his own tattered business cards and a badly-chewed school pencil belonging to Alice. 'Okay, I'm ready.'

It was a house in a place he'd never heard of. Scribbling it down, he read it back to her but the line had already gone dead. Dropping the phone back into his pocket, he rushed for the exit, all thoughts of Paul Fassbender now gone.

The address he had been given was for a cottage on the edge of a village on the South Downs, a couple of hours' drive from London. Carlyle quickly commandeered a Range Rover from the garage at Charing Cross and told the driver, a constable called Andy Grayson, where he wanted to go.

'And put your foot down,' the inspector barked.

'Yeah right,' said Grayson as he rolled out of the station and into traffic that was at a standstill. 'There are roadworks all the way round Trafalgar Square and down Whitehall. It's totally buggered.'

'Great.'

Ten seconds ticked past. twenty. The lights along the road turned green. Still nobody moved. Some genius, three cars in front, was blaring rap music out of his stereo so loudly, it felt like the road itself was vibrating.

'For God's sake.'

Grayson drummed his fingers on the steering wheel. 'Want me to roll the sirens?'

Carlyle scratched at the back of his hand. Inappropriate use of sirens was frowned upon, if only because the practice was both widespread and the source of regular public complaint. To do it only five yards from the station was not smart. On the other hand, he was in a hurry.

'Do it.'

'Cool.' Grinning, Andy cranked up the volume and wound down his window. He stuck his upper body out of the car and waved his arms around. 'Get out the way, you berks.'

'Andy,' Carlyle admonished him. 'Leave it out.'

The constable settled back into his seat. 'Do you want to get out of here or not?'

'Fair point.' Carlyle shut up and watched as the drivers in front of them tried to edge on to the pavement to get out of the way. Still waving his arms in encouragement, Grayson edged them forward. It still took them another couple of minutes to get past the National Gallery and on to Trafalgar Square. Eventually, after driving the wrong way up the Mall and past Buckingham Palace, they found clearer roads.

His temples throbbing, Carlyle knew that his headache was going to be a bastard. The noise from the siren wasn't helping. Opening his window as far as it could go, he touched Grayson on the shoulder. 'You can turn it off now.'

'Yeah?'

'Yeah.'

Somewhat reluctantly, the constable complied. But he kept driving hard, getting other drivers to pull over out of their way wherever possible.

After little more than an hour and fifteen minutes they were free of the city entirely.

'It's like a different world out here, innit?'

'Yeah,' Carlyle agreed. 'The land that time forgot.'

They were cruising down the main street of a place that looked like it had come straight out of an advert for real ale or whole-meal bread – a Soho advertising executive's idea of a 'traditional' English village.

'I come from a place like this,' Grayson said cheerily.

'I'd keep that to yourself.'

The constable brought the car to a gentle halt to allow a couple of geese to saunter across the road as they headed for the duck pond in the middle of the village green. 'I bet they don't even have a Starbucks,' Carlyle mumbled to himself. His headache had gone and the air was fresh. But he was missing Covent Garden already. He pointed to the only sign of life they'd seen so far, a small café at the far corner of the green. 'Pull up over there.'

Lucy's Diner was basically the end house on a small terrace where the ground floor had been turned into a café. Outside, two small tables sat underneath a green awning that sagged worry-ingly in the middle. The front door was open, but there were no customers and no signs of life.

'Wait here a minute.' Releasing his seatbelt, Carlyle opened the door and stepped out onto the road. Stretching, he walked ten yards up the road and then back again. After so long sitting in the car, it was good to know that his legs still worked. Then he headed towards Lucy's.

Inside the café, it was a good ten degrees warmer than it had been outside. As far as he could see, the place was empty.

'Hello?'

Rustling came from somewhere in the back. After a few moments, a woman popped her head out of the kitchen.

'Sorry, just coming.' The head disappeared again.

'No problem.' Carlyle nodded indulgently. After all, he was deep in the sticks and you had to make allowances.

Another minute or so passed before the woman reappeared, wiping her hands on a tea towel. 'Sorry.' She was blonde and pretty, with clear blue eyes and a strong jawline. He guessed early thirties. 'I was working in the back.' Her English had an accent, possibly East European. Maybe all the Poles coming over here didn't stay in London, after all.

'Are you Lucy?' Carlyle smiled.

'What?' For a moment, the woman looked confused, then she smiled back. 'No, no, that's the lady who owns it. I am Anna. I just work here.' She tossed the tea towel over her shoulder. 'What would you like?'

Carlyle ordered a green tea – happy, for once, not to be paying London prices.

'Take away?'

'Yes, please.' He let her hand him a paper cup.

Producing a selection of coins, he asked for directions to the cottage.

'Ah,' Anna said, staring him straight in the eye as she dropped the money into the till, 'you must be police.'

'What?' Carlyle tried to appear surprised.

Anna shrugged. 'You look for the rugby player, no?'

Carlyle gazed around. The place was empty. Grayson was still sitting in the car, watching him through the window. Even so, he still lowered his voice. 'Have you seen the rugby player?'

Anna took a step backwards, clearly now regretting her conversational gambit. 'Are you police?'

'Yes, yes.' Placing the cup on the counter, he pulled out his ID and let her study it. 'I'm a policeman from London. I'm looking for Simon Collingwood. Have you seen him?'

Anna shook her head. 'No. No one's seen him. But everyone knew his family used the cottage for their holidays. When he escaped, people have been saying the police would come to take a look.'

Carlyle felt his headache returning. He took the lid off his cup and sipped at his tea. 'So,' he said slowly, 'where do I find this place?'

TWENTY-SEVEN

Who would ever call their house 'Sunnyside Cottage', Carlyle wondered grumpily as he wandered up a narrow, unpaved track about five minutes' walk out of the village proper. Elegant elm trees lined both sides of the path – under different circumstances, it would have been another picture-postcard moment. The inspector seriously doubted if he could live somewhere with such a wet moniker. On the other hand, Winter Garden House was no great shakes either.

'Get a grip,' he mumbled to himself. 'You have got more important things to worry about.' For the third time in the last minute, he pulled out his mobile and studied the screen with exaggerated care as if he could will a signal.

'Of course there's no bloody coverage; you're in the middle of nowhere,' he chuntered. Maybe he should have thought this through better. 'Why would you need a mobile? All you're doing is marching off to find an axe murderer in the middle of nowhere.' And maybe he should have told Umar. 'Idiot.' Or brought Grayson along, rather than leaving him to enjoy Anna's Polish cooking.

Fed up with the complaints of Moaning Carlyle, Calm Carlyle tried to take over his thoughts. 'Don't be a drama queen. Collingwood is basically harmless.'

'Unless he comes after you with an axe.'

'But you didn't rape his daughter, did you?'

'Good point.'

'Are you talking to yourself?' asked a voice behind him.

Carlyle almost jumped out of his skin. 'Jesus. You scared me shitless.'

'Sorry.' Simon Collingwood gestured towards the trees with the small axe in his right hand. 'I was cutting some wood and I heard you coming up the road.' He looked healthy and relaxed. Middle England personified. In his white and green check shirt, faded jeans and sturdy boots he could have walked straight out of a Boden catalogue.

Carlyle eyed the axe nervously. The blade looked decidely sharp.

Collingwood looked in the direction that the inspector had come. 'Where's the cavalry?'

Carlyle considered lying but didn't see the point. 'There's no one else; it's just me.'

Collingwood smiled warmly. 'That's kind of you, Inspector. I appreciate it.'

'Er, my pleasure.' It sounded stupid, but Carlyle didn't know what to say.

'Did Alison tell you where to find me?'

Carlyle nodded.

Collingwood smiled sadly. 'I thought that she would. C'mon,' he pointed further up the path with the axe. 'The cottage is just up here. Let's go and have a cup of tea.'

In keeping with the rest of the place, Sunnyside Cottage looked like it belonged on the front of a chocolate box or a calendar extolling the joys of the English countryside. A small, two-storey whitewashed building, it even had a thatched roof. Inside, the ground floor had been opened out into one large open-plan space with a kitchen at one end and a large fireplace at the other. Sitting at a cheap pine table, Carlyle sipped reflectively on his second tea in quick succession. Outside, the silence was broken only by the sound of the wind in the trees and the occasional cry of a bird. Feeling a long way from home, he missed the background hum of the city with a grim intensity.

Finishing his own drink, Collingwood placed the empty mug in the sink and moved over to the fireplace. Since coming inside, he had left the axe on the table, as if inviting the inspector to make a grab for it. But Carlyle had given that idea barely a second thought. The rugby player was younger, bigger and fitter than he was. Suppose that the inspector managed to get his hands on the weapon? He didn't fancy his chances of being able to use it. Just as important, Carlyle had no inkling of Collingwood's intentions. He was an intelligent man operating under great stress who had shown no ill-will to anyone other than the men who had attacked his daughter. The inspector had come here in the first place because he thought there was a good chance that Collingwood would simply give himself up. Even now, he was happy to let things take their course and see how they played out. Maybe Grayson would come looking for him. Sometimes you just had to wait and see.

'We've come here every summer for, I don't know, the last six or seven years.' Collingwood gestured around the room. 'The kids really like it. It's so different from London.'

Carlyle nodded. He wondered what Alice would make of a place like this. Probably be bored after about ten minutes.

'It belongs to the guy who runs the rugby club,' Collingwood continued. 'He doesn't know I'm here at the moment, of course, so you should keep him out of this.'

'I understand,' Carlyle told him. 'I'm not looking to cause trouble for anyone else. I said to Alison that I would do what I could to make things easier, and I meant it.' He took a last mouthful of tea and put his mug down on the table. 'But we need to deal with these issues.'

Collingwood held up a hand. 'Do you think I should have killed them?'

Carlyle coughed. 'I can't answer that.'

'What would you have done?'

'I don't know.'

Collingwood gave him a disapproving look. 'That's not much of an answer, Inspector.'

'It's the only answer I can give.' Carlyle scratched his left ear. 'Please God, never let me be in a situation like that.'

'But if you were,' Collingwood pressed.

'But I'm not,' Carlyle snapped, feeling irritated for the first time. Maybe he had indulged this man too much. 'It is pointless hypothesizing. We can talk around it forever but it doesn't do either of us any good. *What ifs* are for people with too much time on their hands.'

'If I get banged up,' Collingwood laughed, 'I'll have plenty of time on my hands.'

Yes, Carlyle thought, *I suppose you will.*

Collingwood's face then hardened into a stern mask. 'Prison is just not for me. I'm not going back.'

'I can understand that,' Carlyle smiled sadly. 'But you have to. It is the only way that everyone can get through this.'

Irritated, Collingwood said, 'I thought that you understood.'

Half-expecting Bambi to appear through the trees, Carlyle gazed out of the window. He turned back to face Collingwood. 'I think I do.'

'But you came to take me back.'

'Yes. You go back to go forward. That's the way it is sometimes. Your family—' For the first time, he saw real anger in Collingwood's face.

'The family is gone.'

Shifting in his seat, Carlyle shrugged. 'You don't know that.'

'It's over.' Collingwood pawed at the carpet with the toe of his boot. 'We are getting a divorce. Alison says I'm an animal for what I did.' Tears welled in his eyes. 'What *I* did.' Sniffing, he wiped his nose on the back of his hand.

What should he say now? John bloody Carlyle, all his wisdom used up. 'They still need you,' was all he could manage.

'I won't be much use in prison,' Collingwood snorted, 'will I?'

This time, Carlyle couldn't think of anything to say at all. Scanning the room, he caught sight of a telephone, sitting on the floor by a moth-eaten sofa. Following his gaze, Collingwood said, 'I'm *not* going back.'

Carlyle took hold of the axe handle and stood up. 'I need to make a call.'

'I don't think so.' Barrelling across the room, Collingwood pulled back a fist. A row of scarred knuckles hurtling towards him was the last thing the inspector saw before the lights went out.

He was woken by a woman's screams. Distant at first, they got closer and closer until he could hear what she was saying, some strange foreign language. Carlyle opened his eyes and stared up at the ceiling. It was blurry and indistinct. After a moment, he realized that he had lost his spectacles. Rolling on to his side, he pushed himself up from the carpet and looked around until he found them under a chair. The right lens had been cracked but they were wearable.

'Another trip to the opticians beckons,' he grumbled, as he slipped the specs back onto his nose. Pulling himself up by the chair, he staggered over to the sink and took a drink from the tap. The dull pain at the base of his skull was growing steadily and he splashed some water on his forehead.

'Are you okay?'

He turned to see Grayson standing in the doorway.

'What happened?' the constable asked.

Ignoring him, Carlyle stormed out of the cottage. The sun had fallen behind the trees, leaving them in an ethereal twilight. Ten yards beyond Anna, the body of Simon Collingwood turned gently in the evening breeze, his feet almost touching the ground.

Grayson appeared at his shoulder. 'I checked for a pulse – nothing. You wouldn't have thought that branch would have been able to hold his weight. Who is he, anyway?'

Anna's cries had now reduced to steady, undulating sobs. 'Get her out of here,' Carlyle said quietly, 'and call an ambulance.' He watched a squirrel run past the sobbing Anna and climb up the tree from which Collingwood was hanging. 'I'll make a few calls from inside and we'll try and get this wrapped up as quickly as possible. Then, hopefully, we can get back home.'

* * *

Glancing at his watch, Detective Superintendent Quentin Pinkey felt like crying. The first suspicious death on his patch for well over three years – a celebrity axe murderer to boot – and it had to happen on the very day when the Police Choir were holding their annual charity concert. Proceeds from this year's event were going to the local Samaritans. Pinkey felt like giving them a call himself. There was no way on God's sweet earth that he was going to get away from the crime scene in time to take part.

Pinkey, not a bad tenor even if he did say so himself, was a leading light of the singing group and had put the best part of four months' effort into preparing for the event. With a programme that included Will Todd's 'Christ Is the Morning Star', John Ireland's 'Greater Love Hath No Man' and Walford Davies's 'God Be in My Head', it was sure to be the highlight of the singing calendar and he was galled beyond belief that it might go ahead without him.

Equally galling was the fact that a fellow officer had strayed on to his patch without extending the basic courtesy of letting him know in advance. It was easy to take an instant dislike to the monosyllabic inspector from London who stood before him, explaining how the axe murderer came to be hanging from a tree. It did cross his mind that the London cop and his sidekick might have been down here on some vigilante mission but they looked like a right pair of wimps – even two-on-one they didn't seem capable of it. Where did the Met find these people? It was no wonder that the capital was drowning in crime, vice and depravity. His wife wanted them to take the kids up there for a week in the summer to see the sights but Pinkey knew that he should put his foot down. A trip to Fuerteventura was a far better bet; easier on the wallet and safer too.

Arms folded, he began humming 'Morning Glory, Starlit Sky'. What was the guy called again? Carlisle? What kind of a name was that? Looking the inspector up and down, Pinkey tutted silently. The guy was clearly a complete berk. 'All right,' he muttered, 'tell me what happened again.'

How many times do you need it explaining? Tired and hungry,

Carlyle shot the provincial plod a sharp look. He was just about to articulate his feelings about his colleague's mental acuity when he was saved by the phone starting to ring. Pulling it out of his pocket, he stared at the screen in disbelief. The top left-hand corner showed a signal strength of two bars. Where did that come from? Rooting himself to the spot in case the coverage disappeared again, he turned away from the plod and hit the receive button. 'Carlyle.'

'Where the hell are you?' Angie Middleton hissed. 'I had to get Fassbender a lawyer. I can't keep him here any longer.'

'Okay, okay.'

In the background, someone started shouting. There were a few seconds of general hubbub before Middleton came back on the line. 'Sorry about that.'

'Tough day?'

'Total crap,' she said, with conviction. 'Not helped by your man in the cells.' She lowered her voice again. 'Anyway, Fassbender's lawyer has told him to say nothing. He is refusing to make a complaint about the people who beat him up. The bloke just wants to get back home as quickly as possible.'

'We can start our own investigation,' Carlyle countered. 'How long will it take him to get a new passport?'

'I heard his lawyer say that the Embassy will be able to sort travel papers by tomorrow.'

Damn Germans – they lived up to expectations every time. 'Fine. Tell them that we will want to speak to him tomorrow.'

'I doubt they'll go for that.'

'Just tell them,' said Carlyle, irritated. 'Say that we are treating this as an extremely serious matter and that I expect them to be at the station at eight tomorrow morning.'

'Okay.' The desk sergeant sounded dubious that such a tactic would work but Carlyle was insistent. His mind was racing. A plan was forming. For the first time in days, he felt like he knew what he wanted to do.

'And Ange . . . Ange – hello? *Hello?*' He looked at the screen.

The signal had gone again. 'Bollocks.' No matter. Now he had to find Grayson and get back to the city as quickly as possible.

Dropping the phone back in his pocket, he turned to face the local plod, saying, 'Sorry mate, got to go.'

The rural copper looked like he wanted to kill him; he was about to say something but the inspector held up a hand.

'An emergency.' Carlyle broke into a jog. 'Sorry about the mess here, but if you need anything else, give me a bell. Should be a doddle. You'll be a real hero for sorting this out.' Picking up speed, he moved away, not waiting for a reply.

TWENTY-EIGHT

Around thirty miles out of London, a coach carrying a group of Chinese tourists had gone into the back of a beer tanker. Only one of the three lanes was still open. As the traffic slowed to a crawl, Carlyle stomped on the floor in frustration.

Bobbing his head along to Snoop Dogg's 'Sweat' on the radio, Grayson gave him a *What can you do?* kind of shrug.

'Turn that racket off,' Carlyle growled. 'I need to make a call.' Rooting around in the pocket of his jacket, the inspector pulled out his 'private' mobile and switched it on. The Nokia was one of the cheapest, most ubiquitous pay-as-you-go models on the market. Carlyle had bought it with cash and he topped it up with cash at random newsagents well away from his usual haunts. He didn't flash it around and he gave the number out to very few people. Even then, he changed both the phone and the sim card every three or four months. This didn't guarantee secrecy, not by any means, but it meant that he could be reasonably sure that no one could easily check his calls. The phone gave him some measure of privacy and for that the hassle and cost was worth it. Relieved to find that he had a full signal, he waited for the contacts to load, pulled up a number and hit call.

'Sutherland.'

'Brian, it's John Carlyle from Charing Cross police station.'

'Yeah.' On deadline, *The Times*' Crime Editor was not in the mood to chat.

'I've got something for you – it would be an exclusive.'

Sutherland grunted non-committally. In the background, Carlyle could hear him still pounding away on his keyboard. Bracing himself, he explained the Fassbender story in less than thirty seconds.

'I remember,' said Sutherland, sounding vaguely interested. 'It was quite a story at the time. I was on the *Observer*; they had money back then. Hold on.' He stuck his hand over the receiver and for the next few seconds there was the sound of muffled voices. Then: 'You still there?'

'Yeah.'

'And this is all kosher?'

'Totally.' Carlyle watched as they finally slipped past the scene of the accident. There was beer everywhere but from the relaxed demeanour of the assembled ambulance crews, the inspector deduced that no one was seriously hurt. Once past the mess, they immediately picked up speed.

Grayson moved the Range Rover back up through the gears as he swung past a woman in a green Skoda. 'We should be okay now.'

Carlyle nodded and turned his attention back to the call. 'I saw Fassbender this morning,' he told Sutherland. 'He'll have to go to the German Embassy in the morning to get a new passport.'

Dangling the prospect of a day two story in front of the journalist.

'And no one else has this?'

'No one.'

'Okay,' Sutherland sighed. 'We can probably give it five hundred words with a picture. I'll call you back in a minute for some colour.'

'Call me on this phone.' Carlyle slowly dictated the number.

'Fine.' Sutherland clicked off and Carlyle looked over at Grayson. 'You didn't hear that.'

Moving smoothly into the outside lane, Grayson pushed their speed up past seventy miles an hour. 'No problem.'

'Good.' Carlyle put the Nokia away and took out his 'official' handset, a BlackBerry. Against his better judgement, he called Simpson. Normally, he could rely on getting her voicemail but, for once, the commander pounced on his call.

'Inspector,' she said icily, 'I hear that you've been enjoying a day out in the provinces.' Carlyle began to explain but she cut him off. 'I have heard what happened. Doesn't the word "protocol" mean *anything* to you, John?'

'I just—'

'Or what about the words "common" and "sense"?'

'Boss—'

'You just wanted to run around, pissing people off as usual.' Simpson certainly sounded mightily hacked off. Her mood couldn't be down to him alone, could it? Then he remembered the drama of love rat Dino Mottram playing away and smiled to himself. The Commander clearly had a lot of crap to deal with at the moment. Maybe he should cut her some slack.

'Sorry, boss,' he said gently. 'I know that you've got a lot on your mind right now.'

'What's that supposed to mean?' Simpson shrieked.

'Nothing, nothing,' Carlyle said hastily. 'At least the Collingwood case has been dealt with.'

'And what about the man who was shot in the park, Julian Schaeffer?' Simpson snapped.

Good question, Carlyle thought. 'We've got nothing much, so far. No sign of the shooter. We're still looking at the wife.'

'I hear that she's using Abigail Slater.'

'That's right.'

'More good news,' Simpson grumbled. 'Don't let her take you to the cleaners again.'

Again?

'Keep me posted.' Simpson ended the call.

Carlyle gritted his teeth. 'Bastard.'

'Who, Simpson?' They were still in the outside lane. Grayson slowed as he came up behind a black BMW.

'Eh? No, no,' Carlyle said quickly. 'Someone else.'

Eyeing him in the mirror, Grayson grinned, clearly enjoying the inspector's discomfort.

The BMW moved back into the middle lane. Carlyle gestured at the road ahead with his free hand, saying, 'Just drive.' Returning his attention to his phone, he began searching for an address. 'I need to get back asap.'

Grayson did as instructed, dropping Carlyle off on a West London street that was lined on both sides with modest terraced houses. When the inspector was a boy, this place had been a slum. Now, the only way he could afford to live on any of the surrounding streets was if he won the lottery. Stepping off the pavement, Carlyle bowed his head and approached a door with the lion's head knocker. Knocking twice, he waited.

As it opened, he lifted his head to meet the gaze of an elderly man standing in the door way.

A knowing look passed between them.

Finally, Carlyle spoke. 'Do you remember me?'

'Of course.'

'Were you waiting for me to turn up?'

'Yes. To be honest, I thought you might have been here rather sooner than this.'

Carlyle smiled. 'I was out of town. I have literally just got back now. I assume that you know why I'm here. Maybe we could talk inside?'

Nodding, Daniel Sands stepped aside and invited the inspector into his home. 'The lounge is off to the right.'

Arriving in the room, Carlyle stayed on his feet.

'Please, take a seat.'

The inspector held up a hand. 'I'm fine like this, thank you.' After all that time spent in the car, he was happy to keep his legs working. Pacing the carpet, he took in the sparse furnishings and the small, chunky TV on a dresser in a corner, possibly the last CRT set left in the whole of the capital. Sands's house might be worth a fortune, but, inside, the place looked like it hadn't been touched for the last thirty years.

Next to the dresser was a small bookcase, overflowing with histories of the Second World War and the Cold War. On the top shelf was the room's only photograph. It showed a young girl. She was looking into the camera, smiling. The inspector didn't need to ask who she was.

If Sands caught him staring at the picture he didn't mention it. He stood in the doorway, the genial host. 'Would you like a cup of tea?'

Carlyle smiled wearily. 'It's been a long day. A green tea would be great.'

Sands's brow furrowed in concern. 'I only have peppermint, I'm afraid.'

'That'll be fine.'

'Good.' Sands shuffled into the kitchen. After another quick glance round the room, the inspector followed. Watching the old man fill the kettle and take a box of tea bags from an overhead cupboard, it struck him that Sands looked basically as he remembered him. Dressed in a baggy brown shirt and green corduroy trousers, the man didn't seem to have aged much in the quarter century or so since they had last met. Maybe that was because he had seemed so haggard last time around.

The kettle came to the boil. Carlyle let Sands drop a tea bag into a mug with a picture of the House of Commons on the front and fill it almost to the brim with boiling water. 'Thanks.'

Sands nodded and filled another mug for himself.

Resting against the lip of the sink, Carlyle stirred his tea. 'So,' he said, 'how did you get Paul Fassbender back into the UK?'

Sands looked down at the blood-red slippers on his feet.

'I'm just curious,' Carlyle pressed gently. 'Kidnapping a man and smuggling him into the country takes a lot of money and planning. Not to mention the balls to chain Fassbender to the railings right outside my police station.'

A small smile played across Sands's lips.

'You didn't know?' Carlyle took a mouthful of tea. 'We found him right on our doorstep.'

'Paul Fassbender.' Sands stared into his mug. 'It was all such a long time ago.'

'Yes, it was.'

'And yet it seems so fresh.'

'The day is long,' Carlyle mused, 'but life is short.'

'Sorry?'

'It's just a saying,' the policeman said hastily. 'I think that I can understand what you are getting at.'

'What I mean is that justice must be allowed to take its course.' Sands lifted his gaze slightly, without quite making eye-contact. 'Don't you think that's right?'

'I thought that it had.' But the words felt like ashes in Carlyle's mouth. He washed them away with some more peppermint tea.

'How could anyone say that?' Sands's voice had started to tremble. 'Mr Fassbender has spent decades hiding from the truth. He has never faced the charges that were placed in front of him.'

Stepping over to the sink, Carlyle rinsed and placed his mug on the draining board, next to an expensive-looking wooden block containing six yellow-handled kitchen knives. 'After all this time, you know that he may not go to jail?'

'I am aware of that possibility.' A steely glint appeared in Sands's eye. 'I will deal with that, if it happens.'

'What does that mean?' When Sands didn't answer, Carlyle added, 'You know that you will probably end up facing charges yourself, after what has happened.'

The eyes went back to the floor. 'I am serene.'

This time tomorrow you might not be, Carlyle mused, *if you're stuck in a cell and Fassbender is sitting happily back at home*. 'Who helped you on this?' he asked. 'I want to speak to your accomplices. Apart from anything else, they need to explain how they managed to smuggle Fassbender into the country.'

Sands lifted his head to reveal a sad smile. 'I am sorry, Inspector. You will have to forgive me. I simply am not able to answer any of your questions on this occasion.'

'Fine.' The inspector pulled a scrap of paper from his pocket and handed it to Sands. 'Brian Sutherland is a journalist on *The Times*. He knows about the case and is expecting your call. Whatever happens with your legal fight, I think you'll have to argue your case in the court of public opinion.' He patted the old man on the arm. 'Thanks for the tea. I need to get going.'

Sands showed him out.

'Someone will be round to see you tomorrow,' said Carlyle, opening the door.

'Thank you.'

What could you possibly be thanking me for? Standing on the doorstep, the inspector waited for his eyes to adjust to the light.

Sands hovered on the doorstep. 'I just wondered . . .'

'Yes?'

'What would you do? In my situation, I mean.'

Carlyle turned to the old man and frowned. 'It's impossible to know that. I cannot begin to imagine—'

'Your best guess,' Sands interrupted politely, 'based on what you know. If you found yourself being tested like this, how do you think you might react?'

'My best guess,' the inspector smiled wearily, 'is that I honestly don't know.'

TWENTY-NINE

On the way home, Carlyle stopped off at Jubilee Hall for a work-out. He tried to make up for his lack of diligence in the exercise department by putting in a brutal half an hour on a cross-trainer, driven by a concentrated blast of Stiff Little Fingers' new album on his iPod.

Pleasantly surprised not to have incurred a cardiac arrest, Carlyle finished his session and took a long, hot shower. On the way out, feeling shattered but virtuous, he nodded at a famous actor who was sitting at a table in the café and tried not to gawp as he passed the studio where a belly-dancing class was in full swing. Approaching the exit, he took out his work phone and called Umar.

'Hey,' his sergeant said cheerily. 'I hear that you've been having fun in the sticks.'

Carlyle grunted. 'I've already had Simpson on.' Pushing his way through the turnstile, he nodded at the girl behind the reception desk and started down the stairs to the exit, careful not to trip over his feet as he did so. 'She was relatively sanguine by her standards.'

'I think she's got other things to worry about than you,' Umar commented. 'The word is that she's dumped Mottram. The wedding's off.'

'Makes sense,' Carlyle observed. 'A bloke like that, with all that cash, is always going to play away.' Pushing through the front door of the gym he stepped onto the Piazza. It was almost 10 p.m. but there were still plenty of tourists milling about, and a busker outside the Transport Museum who was busy murdering Lou Reed's 'Perfect Day' had attracted a half-decent crowd. The inspector immediately executed a 180-degree turn, nipping down an alley to get away from the racket. Turning east on Tavistock Street, he belatedly remembered his conversation with his wife about Umar's upcoming nuptials. 'Oh, by the way, Helen is very excited about *your* wedding. We are looking forward to it.'

'Great,' Umar replied, but there was a distinct lack of enthusiasm in his voice that made Carlyle wonder if he'd found someone else to do the honours. There was just no pleasing some people. 'Anyway, I wanted to talk to you about Julian Schaeffer.'

'Yeah?' Carlyle's stomach rumbled and he wondered what he would find in the fridge at home. Maybe he should pick up a pizza on Drury Lane. Or some filled pasta.

'We're not making much progress, I'm afraid.'

Big surprise, Carlyle thought glumly. It was a thoroughly professional hit. Professionals, as a rule, don't get caught.

'So I've decided to re-interview all of Iris Belekhsan's work colleagues tomorrow,' Umar continued, 'and I was hoping you would come along, to see what you make of them.'

A trip to the dentist's. Great. Crossing Bow Street, Carlyle decided against the pizza. 'What time?'

'Ten.'

'Okay.' He should be done with Fassbender by then – assuming the guy actually turned up. 'Where is it?' Umar gave him an address just off Wigmore Street, near Oxford Circus. 'Fine. I'll see you there.'

In the fridge at home he found enough smoked cheese to make a sandwich and enough orange juice to half-fill a tumbler. He was enjoying his feast when Helen appeared in the kitchen.

'I've booked you in to see Father Maciuszek at ten thirty tomorrow,' she said by way of introduction, 'at the church.'

'What?' Carlyle dropped the last of the sandwich into his mouth, chewing carefully before swallowing.

Leaning against the frame of the door, his wife folded her arms. 'He's the priest.'

'That doesn't work for me,' he snapped, cutting her off. 'Tomorrow is a total nightmare.'

'For Christ's sake, John.' Helen took a step forward, looking like she wanted to thump him. 'Your mother is due to be buried in three days and you haven't even phoned him.'

Three days? Urgh. He was completely losing track of time. Still hungry, he wondered what else he might find to eat.

'I explained to Father Maciuszek that you are a policeman. He understands that things are really busy but this has to come first.'

'Yes.' Carlyle wiped a crumb from the corner of his mouth. Now was clearly not the time to argue.

Helen looked at him suspiciously. 'So you'll go? It should only take a half an hour.'

Plus the best part of an hour to get there and another hour to get back, he thought sourly. *My day will be totally ruined.* Opening a cupboard, he found a packet of Jaffa Cakes. Lifting it off the shelf, he gave it a shake. Plenty inside. He smiled.

The Lord may taketh, but the Lord giveth as well.

'He just needs some background about your mum,' Helen continued, 'some bits and pieces he can use in the service.'

'Okay.' Carlyle stuffed a Jaffa Cake into his mouth, whole. Couldn't his dad do this? Maybe the old bugger was still off somewhere trying to get laid. He grinned at the thought.

'What's so funny?'

'Nothing, nothing.' A piece of Jaffa Cake flew out of his mouth and landed on the floor.

Helen gave him a disapproving look.

'Sorry.' Bending down, he picked it up and stuck it back in his mouth.

'John.'

Grinning, he stepped over and gave her a quick cuddle, promising, 'I'll see the guy tomorrow.'

'Good.' Happy again, she turned back down the hall. 'I'm going to watch the news. A cup of white tea would be nice. And don't forget to take the bag out.'

The clock by the bed said 6.19. Snoring gently, Helen pulled the duvet over her head when he kissed her on the cheek. Yawning, Carlyle slipped out of the flat and headed for the station.

It had rained heavily during the night, washing the streets. There was an invigorating chill in the air that helped further improve the inspector's mood. Walking through the Piazza, he felt that he was seeing the city at its best. Dropping on to the Strand, he managed to arrive at Eat – one of the many café chains that covered London – just as they were opening up for the day. Ten minutes later, he stepped through the front doors at Charing Cross, flat white and brioche in hand, to be confronted by a weary-looking Naohiro Ninomiya.

Pushing himself off the bench, the man extended a hand. 'Inspector Carlyle.'

Carefully grasping the brioche and the coffee in his left hand, Carlyle shook his hand. 'Mr Ninomiya.' He gestured at the clock on the wall with his chin. 'It's a bit early.'

The place was empty and silent as the grave but still Ninomiya looked around nervously. 'I wanted to apologize for the other night,' he said in a voice so low the inspector had to strain to catch it. 'I hope your father is all right.'

Now it was Carlyle's turn to look around furtively. The last thing he needed was his father's peccadillos being broadcast around his workplace. He took a sip of his coffee, enjoying the bitter taste on his tongue. 'There is nothing to apologize for,' he said, smiling kindly. 'The matter has been dealt with. I don't want you to worry about it.'

Ninomiya nodded but still seemed far from reassured. Carlyle gestured for him to sit back down and joined him on the bench. Placing the cup beside him, he opened up the brioche and offered a bite to the Japanese. Ninomiya shook his head.

'No, thank you.'

Good answer, thought Carlyle cheerily as he took a hearty bite. He let Ninomiya watch him eat for a few moments before asking, 'Have you seen Miki yet?'

'Not yet. We are having breakfast in . . .' Ninomiya glanced at his expensive watch, 'just over three hours.'

That sounded about right, Carlyle thought as he finished off the brioche. Ms Kasaba didn't strike him as an early riser. The thought of the nubile Miki happily snuggling in her double bed popped into his brain and he pushed it firmly away. Wiping his hands on a paper napkin, he balled up the rubbish and deposited it next to the cup. 'I met with a friend of Miki's,' he said, thinking carefully about his words. 'It was a useful conversation which may help me find out some more things about your daughter.'

'Do you think . . .'

Carlyle placed a hand lightly on Naohiro Ninomiya's shoulder. 'I don't think anything. One conversation leads to another and we may end up with something, we may not.'

Ninomiya stared at his shoes. 'Should the original investigating officer not have discovered this . . . person?'

Quite possibly, Carlyle thought. Inspector Watkins and Sergeant Savage were sinking in his estimation faster than the bloody *Titanic* after it hit the iceberg. Lifting his cup, he sucked every last drop of coffee from inside. 'As far as I can see, the initial investigation was done properly. In accordance with all relevant protocols. It is not uncommon for other things to come up at a later stage. Anyway, I still need to make a few more enquiries.'

'How long will that take?'

'I don't know, a couple of days, maybe a little longer.'

Ninomiya scratched his head. 'I was thinking of going home.'

Carlyle got to his feet. He had a nice caffeine buzz going. Another coffee – not to mention another brioche – was in order. 'Given that you're here, I would suggest holding on for a few more days. Talk to Miki and I will see what I can do today. We will talk again and take a view on what else can be done.'

'Thank you, Inspector.' Ninomiya stood up and once again offered his hand. 'I am very grateful for your assistance.'

'It is nothing.' Carlyle gently ushered him towards the door. 'Just do me one favour?'

'What?'

'Stay away from the hookers.'

The second coffee was good, if not quite so good as the first. There was no such problem with the brioche. Feeling happily full, if a little guilty, the inspector trotted up the stairs and headed into the station to start his day for the second time that morning.

'I am looking for an inspector called . . . Carlyle.'

Approaching the desk, he saw a tall, grey-haired man hovering over Joe Rowan at the front desk.

I'm Mr Popular this morning, the inspector observed unhappily as he took a step forward, saying, 'I'm Carlyle.'

The man turned and jabbed him in the chest with a rolled-up copy of *The Times*. 'And I suppose you had nothing to do with this?'

Resisting the temptation to arrest him on the spot, Carlyle took the man's paper. Opening it up, he had to keep a straight face. Brian Sutherland might have only managed two hundred and fifty words – rather than the five hundred promised – but he had got them on the front page. With a photo of Fassbender, the 20-point headline read: SEX CRIME FUGITIVE DUMPED OUTSIDE POLICE STATION. 'Sex crime fugitive' – Sands would doubtless like that. After scanning the story, he folded the paper up and tossed it back to his accuser. 'And who are you?'

The man seemed vaguely offended not to be recognized. He stuffed *The Times* into the side pocket of a briefcase overflowing with papers. 'Sidney Hardy. I'm Paul Fassbender's lawyer.'

Carlyle looked around. 'So where is your client?'

Hardy was clearly intent on working himself up into a state of high dudgeon. 'As you well know,' he spluttered, 'there is no requirement for Mr Fassbender to present himself to the police at

202

this time. He is not suspected of any crime. In fact, he is the victim here.'

Carlyle could have taken issue with any of the lawyer's points. Instead, he let them slide. 'Our investigations are continuing,' he said evenly. 'If your client is not here at the appointed hour I will make an application for a warrant for his arrest.'

'Which you won't get,' Hardy snorted.

'We'll see.' Carlyle shrugged.

'You'd better be careful, Carlyle.' The lawyer poked a gnarled index finger towards the inspector's face.

Rowan looked on, curious as to how his colleague would react.

'You are encouraging a sad, delusional old man to play the role of vigilante,' the lawyer continued. 'You're condoning home invasion, assault, false imprisonment, kidnapping and malicious prosecution. You might even be considered an accessory after the event.'

Looking past Hardy's left shoulder, Carlyle caught Rowan's eye. 'Looks like I'm going to need that warrant.'

Rowan picked up the phone. 'Shall I get hold of de Castella?' Judge Evan de Castella was the first port of call whenever anyone at Charing Cross needed a warrant in double-quick time. User-friendly, he was always available – the kind of guy who gave the legal profession a good name.

Unlike Mr Hardy.

'Thanks.'

'There are journalists camped outside the German Embassy,' Hardy said coldly. 'This is further harassment of my client. If you delay Mr Fassbender's return to Italy by as much as one minute, I can guarantee, at the very least, that we will launch a civil action.'

Rowan dialled a number and began speaking, sotto voce, into the receiver.

'There is no need for all this hostility.' Carlyle gestured at his watch. 'Your client still has time to make his appointment.'

'You are incredible.' Grabbing his bag, Hardy pushed away from the desk, heading for the door.

'So I'm told,' Carlyle laughed.

Hitting the lock release mechanism, Hardy turned and gave the Inspector one final glare. 'Given that you like to play games with the media, you should also know that if you drag Nathalie Kelvin's name into this, she will make it her mission to have your job.'

I've never heard that threat before. Carlyle wondered about the connection between Hardy and Kelvin. Maybe they worked together.

'Inspector,' He looked over to see Rowan offering him the handset. 'I've got the judge on the phone.'

Resisting the temptation to give Hardy a smack, Carlyle turned to take the call.

THIRTY

After finally escaping the station, the inspector headed west. Arriving early for his appointment at St Wulstan's, he took up a seat on a bench under a listing oak tree outside the church. Thinking about his mother, he considered what he might say to the priest. The sun was shining and the small courtyard provided an oasis of calm that seemed, somehow, to keep even the relentless hum of the city traffic at bay. If it hadn't been for the fact that his phone started ringing, the place would have been perfect. The caller ID told him that it was Umar. With some reluctance, he answered it just before it went to voicemail.

'Yeah?'

'Where are you?' the sergeant asked.

'Sorry, something came up.'

'But I'm here at the Wimpole Dental Surgery with a dozen people to interview,' Umar whined. 'I wanted you to check them out.'

Stop moaning. It's not like I'm trying to muck you about. Carlyle said, 'I know. Look, I should be able to make it over there in an hour or so. Get started and I'll join you as soon as I can.'

'Okay.' Umar sounded like a sulky teenager, which made the inspector smile.

'Is Belekhsan there?' he asked.

'No. Funnily enough, she isn't coming in today.'

'Big surprise,' Carlyle grunted. He wondered if he should give Abigail Slater a call, if only to yank her chain. Maybe later. 'See you later.' Ending the call, he pulled up another number. Before he could hit call, however, he was conscious of someone coming towards him. Putting the phone away, he looked up.

'Mr Carlyle?' Carlyle thought about it for a moment. Not many people called him 'mister'. Nodding, he got to his feet, extending his hand.

'I am Father Maciuszek.' The fresh-faced young man had a firm handshake and an easy smile. With curly brown hair, brown eyes and a dimple on his chin, he looked about sixteen but presumably was somewhere in his mid-twenties. In his free hand was a small spiral notebook and a red pencil. He gestured for the inspector to sit back down. 'My condolences for your loss.'

'Thank you,' Carlyle mumbled.

The priest sat down beside him. 'I have spoken to Alexander and to Helen,' he said, his voice betraying only the slightest hint of an accent. 'They tell me that . . . erm . . .'

It took Carlyle a moment to realize that the priest couldn't recall his mother's first name.

'Lorna.'

'Yes.' Father Maciuszek smiled apologetically. 'They told me that Lorna was a good woman.'

'Yes.'

'Was she a practising Catholic?'

'To be honest,' Carlyle replied, clearing his throat, 'well, obviously, I haven't lived with my parents for a long time, so . . .'

The young priest touched him gently on the arm with long, feminine fingers. 'But she was a good woman.'

Meaningless platitudes. 'Yes.'

'When I get up to speak about her . . .'

Carlyle launched into his spiel. 'I would simply say that she came from Scotland to London to work hard and try to make a better life for her family. Back in the 1950s, that was a big deal. These days, you would hardly think about it but then, there was a lot of pressure to stay put. I don't think that the rest of the family in Scotland were very happy about the move. Especially her own

mother. But that's the way she was, a woman capable of taking –
er – difficult decisions.'

'Yes, yes,' the priest nodded enthusiastically, making notes in
his notebook. 'That's good.'

'She and my father were together for a long time.' Carlyle wondered if Alexander had mentioned the divorce; probably not. He
ploughed on, listing a few randomly chosen facts – jobs, hobbies,
friends. Not much of a life really but without it, he wouldn't exist.
Running out of things to say, he came to an abrupt halt.

Father Maciuszek looked at him expectantly for a moment or
two before closing his notebook and shoving it into his pocket.
'That was very helpful. Thank you.'

'Good.' Glad it was over, Carlyle quickly got to his feet.

Smiling, the priest got up. 'I will see you before the service.'

'Yes.'

'In the meantime, I hope that your father is bearing up.'

'He is bearing up well, thank you,' Carlyle replied stiffly.

'Good. He should know that he can call on me at any time,
should he need to talk.'

'Thank you.' Carlyle began shuffling back towards the real
world. 'I will let him know.'

Heading back into Covent Garden, it would have been quicker to
take the tube. However, the inspector didn't feel like going much in
ground, happy instead to sit at the back of a number 19 bus as
it made its way through an infinite set of roadworks towards the
West End. Stuck in a traffic jam on the King's Road, he called
Brian Sutherland at *The Times*.

'I saw it made the front page,' said Carlyle after Sutherland had
picked up the phone.

The Crime Editor grunted in a manner suggesting that old news
was of no particular interest to him.

'Any developments?' Carlyle asked.

'I've spoken to Sands. Is he going to get arrested?'

'Dunno.'

'It would be helpful if you could find out.'

Carlyle sighed – once you feed the beast, it always comes back for more. He told Sutherland: 'Fassbender didn't turn up to the station this morning. He's refusing to co-operate with our investigation.'

'That's a surprise.' Sutherland laughed shortly. 'I've had his lawyer on threatening me with all sorts.'

'Sidney Hardy? He's a twat.'

'He's a lawyer. Anyway, I've got a snapper down at the German Embassy to see if Fassbender turns up. No sign of him yet.'

'He'll need to go there sooner or later to get his passport.'

'You would have thought so,' Sutherland replied. 'But he seems more scared of us than he is of you.'

'Most people are.'

There was the sound of voices in the background. 'Look, I've got to go,' the journalist said.

'Just one thing,' Carlyle added hastily. 'Ask Hardy what his connection is with Nathalie Kelvin QC.'

There was a pause while Sutherland placed the name. 'Kelvin's a heavy hitter,' he said finally. 'What's she got to do with all of this?'

'She was on Fassbender's legal team when he originally got off. She doesn't want anyone making the connection.'

'Interesting. I'll see what I can find out.' Sutherland ended the call and Carlyle looked up. The bus had moved less than ten yards during the course of his conversation. No skin off his nose. Given that he was going to the dentist, he was in no particular hurry.

The Wigmore Dental Surgery occupied the ground floor of a new glass and steel development two blocks north of the John Lewis department store on Oxford Street. It was bright, clean and friendly and stocked the biggest range of toothbrushes that Carlyle had ever seen in his life. Next to the reception desk was a waiting area for patients which was dominated by a large aquarium running the length of the back wall. Off to the left, a corridor led to a number of treatment rooms. Carlyle listened carefully for the sound of drilling but none was forthcoming. Somewhat disappointed, he gave his full attention to the fish.

'Pretty, aren't they?' The inspector turned to face a petite blonde woman with a healthy tan and sparkling blue eyes. Her hair was pulled back into a ponytail and she was wearing a crisp white smock and white trousers. A name tag attached to the smock told him that her name was Celina Morrow-Jones.

'Huh?'

'The fish.'

'Ah, yes.'

She pointed at a yellow fish with black spots. 'This one is a Dwarf Puffer.' There was a trace of a foreign accent but he couldn't place it. 'They come from Kerala in India.'

'I see.' His interest in things aquatic more than sated, the inspector moved away from the tank. 'I'm—'

'I know,' she said cheerily, pointing down the hall. 'Your colleague is in the blue room.'

'The blue room?'

'Third door on the left. Follow me.'

'Thanks.'

Stepping into the consulting room, he was surprised to see Umar sitting in the dentist's chair with a paper bib under his chin and a sheepish look on his face.

'What the hell are you doing?'

The sergeant finished gurgling with mouthwash and spat it into the bowl attached to the arm of the chair.

'Sergeant Sligo was overdue a clean,' Celina explained cheerily, 'especially as he has his wedding coming up.'

Carlyle shot Umar a disgusted look. 'Nice to see you two have been getting acquainted,' he said grumpily.

Celina stepped over to a workbench behind the chair and picked up a small dish containing a pile of what looked like orange mud. 'He just needs a polish and then he'll be done.'

Christ, thought Carlyle, *if Simpson could see us now.*

Umar pointed at a pile of papers on a chair in the corner. 'Take a look at those. I'll be out in a minute.' A terrible whirring noise filled up the room as Celina advanced on Umar's open mouth. Grabbing the papers, Carlyle beat a hasty retreat.

It took him little more than five minutes to scan through the information that Umar had gathered. It basically consisted of two lists: one was the detailed information of the people who worked at the surgery – names, contact details, work history, National Insurance numbers; the other contained simply the names of each patient, with a set of initials next to each, which presumably denoted whose patient they were. Focusing on those with 'IB' next to their name, the inspector went up and down the list a couple of times. Nothing jumped out at him, so he went back to staring at the fish. After about thirty seconds, he grew bored with that, so he started up a game of Word Mole on his BlackBerry. He had reached Level 14, with a score of 1,523 when Umar finally reappeared, flashing his new, improved smile.

'Save it for the ladies,' Carlyle growled. 'Let's go and get something to eat.'

Repairing to Bar Remo on Princes Street, Carlyle ordered Pasta Napolitana and a bottle of sparkling mineral water.

After much deliberation, Umar went for egg and chips and a cup of tea. He watched the waitress shuffle off and turned to his boss. 'Can you cover lunch? Celina wiped me out. The clean and polish cost me £115.'

'It's an expensive business.' Carlyle tried to think back to the last time he had been to visit his dentist. It had to be a couple of years, easily. The thought of having someone root about in your mouth and then paying through the nose for the privilege was just too much to bear. He tapped the pile of papers that were sitting on the table. 'How did you get this?'

Umar made a face. 'We're not supposed to have them. Patient confidentiality and all that. Celina printed them off for me as a favour.'

'Nice girl.'

Umar grinned. 'Yeah.'

'Shame you're getting married. Pretty girls will just have to pass you by from now on.'

'Hm.' The waitress arrived with their drinks. Umar sipped his tea and contemplated his fate.

Carlyle poured some water into a glass and gulped it down. 'Anyway, there doesn't seem to be much here.'

'In the end, I got to speak to eight of the staff. Three of them told me that Iris Belekhsan's new boyfriend was one of her patients.'

'I thought we knew that already.'

Umar shrugged.

Carlyle flipped back through the lists. 'Which one? There are about two hundred names here.'

'A guy called George McQuarrie.'

'M, M, M . . .' Carlyle ran his finger up and down the list until he found him. G.W.P. McQuarrie. The inspector stared at the name for several seconds.

George William Peter McQuarrie.

Well, well, well.

At last, they could be on to something. The inspector sighed happily as the waitress placed Umar's plate of food in front of him. The sergeant hesitated, waiting for his boss's food to arrive, but Carlyle signalled for him to get on with it. 'Dig in, smiler,' he grinned. 'You've got a busy afternoon ahead of you.'

THIRTY-ONE

Ivor Jenkinson bent forward and squinted at the video playing in a small window in the top right-hand corner of the screen. Shot in night vision it was green and grainy, but he could still make out what was going on. Just about. 'Is that what I think it is?'

'Yeah.' Sitting in front of his computer, Joe Donnelly let out a small, embarrassed laugh. Pushing his glasses back up his nose, Donnelly turned to face his boss. 'That guy: is he really shagging that donkey?'

Now it was Ivor's turn to laugh nervously. You saw a lot of weird stuff on the internet but there were some things that could still make you squirm, especially if you watched them with your staff. 'Is there any sound?'

'Nah.' Donnelly scratched his left nipple under the Jesus and Mary Chain T-shirt he was wearing. 'They reckon this was shot by American Special Forces on patrol in Iraq or something.'

Ivor rubbed his chin thoughtfully. 'Amazing.'

Joe pointed at the screen. 'The donkey looks a bit bored, to be honest.'

Sam Gilzean appeared at Joe's other shoulder to see what all the excitement was about. She had arrived for work an hour late this morning – looking seriously hungover to boot – but had clearly decided to brazen it out. 'What kind of donkey is it?'

'Eh?'

'Is it male or female?'

'Dunno.' Joe contemplated the question. 'Why?'

'No reason,' Gilzean replied casually. 'Just wondering if it was straight sex or gay sex we were watching today.'

Ivor felt the contents of his stomach threatening to come back up and swallowed hard. 'Do you think it's real?'

'Nah.' Sitting back in his chair, Joe stuck his hands on his head. Suddenly conscious of the nasty odour emanating from Joe's armpits, Ivor took a step backwards. 'I'm sure that the CIA or whoever faked it up. Good fun, though.'

'Okay.' The smell was getting worse. Breathing through his mouth, Ivor began beating a hasty retreat. On the screen the terrorist/freedom fighter/whatever was still giving it his best shot, so to speak.

'It looks real to me,' Gilzean mused. 'Anyway, if they were going to fake it, wouldn't they have the donkey fucking the guy, rather than the other way round?'

'Assuming it's a male donkey.'

'Of course.'

'Enough,' Ivor squawked. He was getting really worried about the burrito now. 'Just don't send it to the clients by mistake.'

Joe laughed. 'The dirty bastards would probably like it.'

'Speaking of which,' Sam pointed at the glass wall which gave them a view of the lifts and the reception area.

Ivor looked up. 'Oh, great.' A short, crumpled middle-aged bloke was standing by the unmanned reception desk. Without doubt an unhappy punter. He could spot them a mile off. The kind of loser who couldn't score in a brothel. Only the real losers turned up at the office. Most months you would get one or two. The kind of guys with the self awareness of an amoeba, who could demand a blow job from a Cheryl Cole lookalike *and* their money back with a straight face. He really should have stuck that *NO REFUNDS* sign up on the wall.

The donkey video disappeared from the screen as Joe began typing furiously.

Ivor tried to look ingratiating. 'Sam.'

'No way.' Patting Joe on the back, Gilzean beat a hasty retreat. 'I'm busy. Anyway, you're the boss. He's your problem.'

'Bollocks.' Ivor plastered something approximating to a smile on his face and put his best foot forward.

The man eyed him suspiciously. 'Mr Jenkinson?'

Ivor nodded and automatically extended a hand. 'That's right.'

The man thrust a card into Ivor's hand. 'We need to have a word . . . in private.'

Glancing at the card, Jenkinson grimaced. 'I see. Come this way.' Turning, he set off down a long corridor, leaving Carlyle to follow.

At the end of the corridor, Jenkinson opened the door to an office that had been fitted out to a much higher standard than the rest of the building. Framed posters for video games *L.A. Noire* and *Halo* hung on the wall behind a cherry veneer desk, and sliding glass doors opened out on to a small terrace. Dropping the inspector's card onto the desk, the man sank into an oversized black leather chair.

'Please.' He gestured for his visitor to take the other chair. On the desk stood what looked like a model toy soldier. Picking it up, Jenkinson weighed it in his hand.

Peering at the figure, Carlyle tried to work out what precisely it was.

'It's a 1/6th scale *Berserker Predator* collectible.' Jenkinson waved it around aimlessly. 'You know, from the movies.'

What kind of bloke collects toys? 'Very nice,' Carlyle said politely.

'It's quite rare.' Jenkinson carefully placed the Predator back on the desk. 'So, what can I do for you,' he glanced back down at the card, 'er . . .'

'Inspector,' Carlyle said patiently.

'What can I do for you, *Inspector*?'

'Well . . .'

'Are you here in a professional or a *personal* capacity?'

'Sorry?'

'Are you a Leafhopper client?' Jenkinson asked hopefully.

'Oh,' Carlyle responded, catching his drift. 'No, no.'

'Okay, so what are you after?'

'I am here about a woman called Ayumi Ninomiya.'

Jenkinson looked at the Predator for enlightenment. When none was forthcoming, he listened to the inspector explain about the missing girl.

'What I need,' Carlyle concluded, 'is a list of men that Ms Ninomiya hooked up with through the site.'

Having seen this request coming a mile off, Jenkinson plastered a contrite look on his face. 'I'm sorry, Inspector. I would like to be able to help you on this. However, all of our records are confidential.' He smiled weakly. 'Data protection and all that.'

'I can appreciate that,' Carlyle smiled back, 'but under the circumstances, I was hoping . . .'

There was a knock and a young woman stuck her head round the door. Jenkinson impatiently waved her away. He turned back to the inspector. 'It's got nothing to do with me, I'm afraid. It's in the contract.'

Wondering just how far he would be able to ram the Predator up Ivor's arse, Carlyle gritted his teeth. 'You want me to get a warrant?'

Ivor scratched his left earlobe. 'You can try.' Pushing himself up from the chair, he picked up the figure and signalled towards the door with it.

Carlyle gestured for him to sit back down. 'Alternatively, I could go and have a word with Harriet Botto.'

Ivor Jenkinson placed the Predator carefully back on the table for a second time.

'I checked her out.' Putting a nasty smile on his face, Carlyle turned the knife. 'She still lives in St John's Wood.'

Jenkinson ran the back of his hand across his forehead. 'That was a long time ago.'

'Ivor, come on. There's no statute of limitations on *rape*.' Pleased with himself, Carlyle sat back in his chair. He'd done some homework, for once, and it looked like it had paid off. Seven years ago, Ivor Jenkinson had had a fling with Botto, a married co-worker at his previous business. Botto's husband accused Jenkinson of rape.

When the police were not able to persuade arriet to give evidence, her husband divorced her. Jenkinson had then gone off and married someone else.

At the mention of the r-word, Jenkinson jumped slightly in his chair, as if he'd been given a mild electric shock. 'I didn't—'

'That would be a matter for a jury to decide,' Carlyle said solemnly. 'The Met is currently reviewing all outstanding serious sexual assault and rape cases. As far as we are concerned, so-called "guilt" or "innocence" don't come into it.' Jenkinson's bottom lip began to tremble; suddenly he looked like he was about eight years old. 'The key issue is the likelihood of a conviction. Can we get a result? And your case is in the green pile.' Carlyle paused. He was making this bollocks up as he went along and didn't want to get too carried away.

Jenkinson belatedly realized that he was supposed to ask a question. 'What's the green pile?'

'Good to go.'

A strangled groan slipped from Jenkinson's throat as his eyes lost their focus. *Stay with me*, Carlyle thought, somewhat disconcerted that his little spiel was having quite such an effect. He pulled his chair up to the desk and leaned forward. 'My colleagues in charge of the case reviews have identified Ms Botto as a priority case for interview. That means that they intend to re-interview her and ask her to finally make a formal complaint.'

Tears welled up in the other man's eyes. 'Can they do that?'

Carlyle made a face. 'I think they're looking to speak to her next week.'

'Oh God.'

'The green cases are chosen very carefully. They only go for the ones they really like the look of. There's something like a ninety-five per cent success rate in getting them to court.'

Jenkinson's head slumped on his chest. 'And then?'

'To be honest?' Carlyle tried not to grin. 'Having gone carefully through the file, I'd say there's a good chance you'd end up with four to six years.'

Another electric shock. He looked up. 'In prison?'

'I'm afraid so.' Carlyle paused again. 'It's pretty tough for rapists.'

Jenkinson started to sob. 'But I'm not . . .'

'And once you get out, you'll have to remain on the Sex Offenders Register. Or, alternatively, I can make this go away.'

Jenkinson looked at him doubtfully.

'Inspector Kelvin Smith is in charge of this case,' Carlyle burbled. 'Kelv is a good mate of mine. He owes me a few favours, too. I can easily get him to flip you into the red pile.'

Reclaiming his Predator, Jenkinson clutched it to his breast as if it would protect him from the evil forces of the state.

'So what do I have to do?'

'All I need,' said the inspector, reasonableness personified, 'are a few names and phone numbers.'

Ten minutes later, he had a sheet of A4 paper containing four names and addresses, along with emails and contact details. Ivor Jenkinson had recovered some of the colour in his cheeks. The Predator remained inscrutable. The inspector glanced down the list. 'Are these all of the people Ayumi Ninomiya met up with from the site?'

'Well,' Jenkinson began, 'we can never give a one hundred per cent guarantee, of course, but Leafhopper has this special security feature for the benefit of its female members. You can chat online with potential sugar daddies, but if you agree to meet up with anyone in person, we ask you to use our unique "hooking up" feature which allows you to log where and when the date is taking place, so that there is a record if,' realizing that he was digging himself into a hole, he coughed, 'er, something goes wrong.'

Carlyle arched an eyebrow. 'And do things go wrong?'

The worried look returned to Jenkinson's face. 'It is like anything else in life . . .'

I've yanked the guy's chain enough, Carlyle thought. 'Okay, okay.' He held up a hand. 'Are these the only guys, as far as you know, who Ayumi hooked up with through the site?'

Jenkinson nodded. 'Yes, with the caveat that she might have met others and just not recorded it.'

'I understand. At least this is a start.' Carlyle thought about it for a moment. 'How many people did she hook up with online without going on to meet them?'

'Something like a hundred and seventy, give or take.'

'Jesus. That's a lot of flirting.'

'We have almost three thousand five hundred blue chip sugar daddies signed up,' Jenkinson said proudly.

A cyber meat market. Carlyle shook his head.

'It's not just about sex,' said Jenkinson defensively. 'We've had one wedding already.'

Carlyle raised an eyebrow.

'Unfortunately, it only lasted three months. But still.'

Good God. Maybe he *should* talk to Harriett Botto; a few years in jail might do this odious little prick some good. At the very least, the inspector was tempted to grab the Predator and beat Jenkinson around the head with it. He glanced again at the sheet of paper in his hand. 'What's this at the bottom?'

'That's your login and password,' Jenkinson said slyly. 'I thought you might want to give the service a go.'

Carlyle shot him a look.

'Free, of course.'

'Hm.' If Helen somehow got to hear of this, she would have a fit. The Predator looked like he was going to kill himself laughing. The inspector got to his feet. 'Thank you for your co-operation.'

THIRTY-TWO

'Speak.'

'Gideon? It's John Carlyle. I'm looking for Dominic.'

As far as the inspector knew, he was the only person who called him Dominic. To everyone else, including his long-term sidekick and fixer, Gideon Spanner, he was just 'Dom'.

There was a grunt on the other end of the line, followed by the sound of footsteps and some voices in the background. Finally, Dominic Silver himself came on the line.

'Inspector,' he said warmly. 'Good to know you are still alive.'

'Yeah,' Carlyle said ruefully.

'How long's it been?'

'Since our little trip?' Carlyle tensed up. 'Six months, give or take?'

The 'little trip' had seen Carlyle and Silver, along with Gideon, cross the Channel to kill a French gangster called Tuco Martinez. On that journey, the inspector had crossed a very clear line, something he hoped he'd never to have to do again. Returning to his 'normal' life, he had kept his distance from Dom.

'It was six months yesterday.'

'Yeah?' Carlyle wished it was much longer. 'Look, first things first.' He recited his new pay-as-you-go number, waiting patiently while Dom scribbled it down.

'We should get together,' his old friend said.

'Good idea.' Carlyle tried to inject some enthusiasm into his voice. The business with Martinez had taken him outside of the law, much further outside of it than he had ever thought he would go. That in itself wasn't Dom's fault but it was the kind of risk that you took when you had a mate who was a drug dealer. 'But things are really busy right now.'

'I know what you mean,' Dom laughed. 'I've retired and things are still frantic.'

'You what?'

'I've retired – well, more or less.'

Better late than never, Carlyle thought to himself. 'Good.'

'You were right. I shouldn't have tried to get back into the drugs business. Trying to work with our French friend was a big mistake. So, basically, I've cut everything back now. It's just Gideon and me and we provide a very occasional *family and friends* type of service. Most of the rest of the business has been parcelled out to other operators.' He mentioned a few names that Carlyle had never heard of.

'Ah well, you know what you're doing.'

'Always, Johnny boy,' Dom chuckled. 'Always. My new side-line is art.'

Carlyle took a couple of seconds to process this piece of information. 'Art?'

'It's just another selling gig,' said Dom cheerfully. 'I've got some great up and coming artists on my books – Abbruzzi, Bezmiller, XTX, Cecil "Pop" Ivy – and a great showroom on Cork Street. You should come and have a look.'

'Okay.' Carlyle belatedly remembered the reason he had called in the first place. 'Look, I wondered if you could help me.'

'Of course.'

'I'm trying to track down George McQuarrie.'

'Bloody hell. He's a right thug. Make sure you take some back-up.'

'I have to find him first. Any idea where he knocks about these days?'

'Sure. I see him round and about quite often. He likes to go to a place called the Signal Bar on Duke Street in St James's. His dad still has some offices round the corner.'

'Thanks.'

'My pleasure. Look, we're having a reception at the gallery in a couple of weeks for a new opening.'

'Yes?' Carlyle couldn't manage to sound even remotely interested.

'Yes. It's a new Max Slater installation called *Taking on the House*. It's about how we disseminate and deconstruct pre-digital cultural paraphernalia in the post-digital age.'

Post-digital? *Where? What? When?* The inspector himself was still struggling into the digital age and wasn't too thrilled about it.

'Why don't you come along? Bring Helen and Alice. Eva and the kids will be here.'

'Sounds good. I'll definitely try.'

'Okay. I'll get Eva to give Helen a call. Just try to avoid getting beaten up by George McQuarrie in the meantime. I'll see you at the reception then.'

'Great.' Ending the call, Carlyle wondered about Dom's new career in the art world. If he was finally going legitimate, the inspector could surely put up with listening to a whole new lexicon of bullshit. Maybe their relationship – which went all the way back to the early 1980s – would survive, after all. The thought made him feel glad.

Having set Sergeant Savage the task of tracking down the guys on Ivor Jenkinson's list, Carlyle found Umar in the basement of the station, picking over a plate of lasagne in the canteen.

'How's it going?' Carlyle placed a can of Coke on the table and pulled out a chair. By way of response, Umar shovelled a massive forkful of pasta into his mouth. 'Still not getting any sleep, eh?' Chewing thoughtfully, Umar nodded. Carlyle pulled the ring on his can and waited for him to swallow.

'Not a bloody wink.' Umar stabbed his fork into the remains of the lasagne. 'Can't remember the last time I got laid either,' he said dolefully.

Welcome to the real world.

The young man shook his head sadly. 'It's got to have been a week, at least.' Another slab of lasagne disappeared into his mouth. 'I have made some progress with regard to Julian Schaeffer, though.'

'Oh?'

'Yeah.' Umar wiped a piece of tomato sauce from his mouth with a napkin. 'He wasn't exactly Parent of the Year.'

Picking up his Coke, Carlyle tilted back his head and emptied the can down his throat.

'He wasn't making child support payments, even though his wife had threatened him with the MPA.'

'Good luck with that,' Carlyle grunted. The Maintenance Protection Agency was supposed to chase absent fathers for their payments. Billions of pounds in debt, with a massive backlog of unprocessed cases, it had long since become a national joke. The money it brought in was almost matched by its insane running costs. The Government was always being urged to dissolve the MPA and transfer its responsibilities to HM Revenue and Customs. His stomach started to rumble. He realized that he really should have gone for the apple pie. Then he had an epiphany – he *would* go for the pie. Pushing back his chair, he got to his feet.

Umar waved his fork in Carlyle's direction. 'And he had been arrested.'

The inspector sat back down. 'Tell me more.'

'Well,' Umar dropped the fork back on to the plate, 'in the last year, his wife has rung the police three times to complain about his allegedly threatening behaviour.'

Carlyle nodded. They should have picked up on this earlier but he let it slide.

'The third time, he was arrested outside the family flat and taken to West End Central. In the end, no charges were made.'

'Okay,' Carlyle sighed, 'but they were still getting on well enough to share looking after the girl.'

'Only after Westminster Social Services had done an investigation,' Umar pointed out.

'Which concluded what?'

'Nothing in particular.'

'Big surprise,' Carlyle scoffed. 'It's almost always impossible to get to the bottom of what happens behind closed doors.'

'Yeah,' Umar agreed. Both men knew that trying to deal with domestic arguments was a nightmare. When trust and goodwill went out of the window any concern with truth went with it. 'But when it comes to Rebecca, I get the impression it was more a case of pass the parcel than anything else.'

'Poor kid.' Carlyle told himself he should give the girl's grand-father, or step-grandfather or whatever he was, a call. Ironically, Ronald Connolly was the only one who seemed to give a damn about the kid. He stared morosely into his cup. 'Doesn't get us much closer to why anyone would want to shoot the father, though, does it?'

'No.'

'Next steps – we need to speak to George McQuarrie.' Carlyle mentioned the name of the restaurant that Dominic Silver had given him. 'Find out about his relationship with Iris Belekhsan. Had he met Julian Schaeffer? What did he think of him?'

'Who he thinks might have offed him?'

'Exactly. Savage is upstairs checking some other stuff for me. Take him with you.'

'Surely I can manage that on my own?'

'Absolutely not.' Carlyle wagged an admonishing finger at his sergeant. 'This guy is a brute. His father – Arthur – was a well-known Soho bookie and property developer thirty odd years ago. He was famous for – allegedly – having three guys tortured and shot in a basement in Windmill Street. Never convicted, of course; apart from anything else. the bodies were never found. George had the public school education and the posh vowels, but that was never going to be enough to override his dad's DNA. Sadly for Georgie boy, though, he's not as smart as his dad. He's been sent down twice, for Assault and Actual Bodily Harm. He's a big bas-tard too, so take some support. I would come along but I need to check on the Paul Fassbender situation.'

Lifting his mug, Umar took a mouthful of tea. 'Angie was telling me about that. Sounds like a right blast from the past.'

'Yeah. It's a strange one.'

'Some vigilante pensioner.'

'Daniel Sands is just an old bloke who wants justice for his child. Any half-decent parent would feel the same.' Carlyle waved his index finger at the sergeant. 'Just you wait till Christina drops that sprog, then you'll know what I'm talking about. The minute you hold that baby, it will hit you like a bolt of fucking lightning.' He let out a long breath. 'Until then, it's impossible to understand.'

'Sounds like you support the guy.'

Carlyle got to his feet and stretched out his arms. 'And why shouldn't I?'

THIRTY-THREE

Back upstairs, Angie Middleton was perusing the latest copy of some celebrity magazine. Another minor member of the royal family was getting married and the world was supposed to stop turning so that everyone could fall to their knees and tug their forelock. Carlyle smacked the back of the mag with his hand.

'Why do you read that stuff?' he asked.

'Because I like it,' she grinned, not looking up. 'Not all of us around here are stuck-up London liberals, you know.'

The inspector laughed out loud. 'You know, that might be the nicest thing that anyone in the Met has ever said to me.'

'Get over yourself.' Middleton turned a page. 'Commander Simpson is looking for you, by the way.'

'Isn't she always?' Carlyle quipped. 'I'll give her a call later on.'

'No need.' The voice was accompanied by a gloved hand descending on his shoulder.

Middleton quickly shoved her reading material underneath the desk as the inspector wheeled round to greet his boss.

'Commander.'

The look in Carole Simpson's eyes suggested a headmaster who'd just caught the boy who was responsible for the graffiti in the school toilets. 'Come with me,' she said firmly, striding off down the corridor. Carlyle exchanged a joky *Oh shit* glance with Middleton, who shrugged apologetically before quickly returning to her reading.

Simpson had already reached the stairs. 'Hurry up.'

'Yes, boss,' said Carlyle. Giving a mock salute, he jogged after her.

Keeping up a more than brisk pace, the Commander led him to the first floor. When she stopped abruptly in a corridor lined by meeting rooms, the inspector almost ran into the back of her.

'Sorry.'

Turning, Simpson smiled.

At least she's in a good mood, Carlyle thought, grateful for small mercies.

'Now, John,' she said, standing close to him, keeping her voice low, 'I am having a good day today.'

Where the hell was she going with this, Carlyle wondered. Not happy with having his personal space invaded, he stared at his shoes. They were badly scuffed. Had he ever polished them? he asked himself. Probably not.

'People are doing what they are told.'

'Er, good.'

'For a start, I told Dino that I was leaving him,' there was more than a trace of relish in her voice, 'and that the wedding was off.'

Poor old Dino, Carlyle thought. *He's probably getting over the disappointment by banging a couple of lithe bimbos as we speak.*

'What's so funny?'

'Nothing.' Suppressing a grin, he looked up. 'I'm glad you were able to sort things out, one way or another.'

'The point is, he took it without complaint and did what he was told without protest.'

She'd lost him again. Carlyle reverted to a thoughtful nod.

Raising her index finger, Simpson pointed down the corridor, to the second door on the left. 'So when we go in there, I want you to do the same.'

Carlyle scrunched up his face in confusion. 'You're dumping me?'

'If only I could,' Simpson sighed. She pointed again at the door. 'No. We are going in there and I am going to tell you what to do and you are going to smile, say, "Yes, Commander", walk back out of the room and execute my orders with immediate effect.'

'Execute your orders?'

Simpson nodded.

'With immediate effect?'

'Yes. Do you think you can get your head round that?'

Carlyle scratched his chin. 'I suppose so,' he tutted, 'at least on a theoretical kind of basis.'

'John.' Simpson took half a step backwards as if she was getting ready to punch his lights out.

Carlyle held up a hand. 'No, no. I get it.' He set off down the corridor. 'Let's give it a go. After all, there's a first time for everything.'

Opening the door, he let Simpson enter before stepping inside behind her. The room was small, almost completely filled by the rectangular table in the middle which had three chairs along each side. The chairs on the near side were empty. The chairs on the far side were filled by Paul Fassbender, his lawyer, Sidney Hardy, and a fierce-looking woman of late middle-age in a classic Chanel suit. On the table in front of Fassbender was a crisp new German passport. Simpson stayed on her feet, so Carlyle also stood, hands behind his back, eyeing each of the trio in turn. The looks he received from them suggested that they would happily have had him disembowelled on the spot.

Just as well that life is not a popularity contest, he thought.

Simpson cleared her throat. 'I think that you gentlemen both know the inspector,' she said, her tone brisk and businesslike. Fassbender and Hardy nodded and the Commander gestured to the woman.

On reflection, he thought that she looked a bit like Coco – circa 1965 – but maybe that was just the suit.

'Inspector, this is Nathalie Kelvin QC.'

Now it was Carlyle's turn to nod brusquely. Hardy started to say something but Simpson quickly cut across him. 'I have reviewed the situation here,' she said, rushing her words in a way that told him she was nervous, 'both the original case history and the events of the last few days.' She nodded at Fassbender. 'Once again, I can only express our sympathy for your most unfortunate ordeal.'

Harrumphing, the doctor folded his arms.

'I can assure you,' Simpson continued, 'that we will make all reasonable efforts to bring those responsible to justice.'

'You know who is responsible,' Fassbender protested. 'You know where he lives. Why hasn't he been arrested yet?'

'I have applied for an arrest warrant for Mr Sands. It should be ready by the time we finish here.'

Pushing back his shoulders, Carlyle stared at a spot on the ceiling.

'The inspector will go directly from this meeting to execute that warrant and bring Mr Sands to the station for questioning.'

'I'm afraid,' Nathalie Kelvin sighed, 'we have no confidence in the inspector's ability to perform his duties in a professional and rigorous manner.'

'We?' Narrowing his eyes, Carlyle gave her a hard stare. 'In precisely what capacity are you present?'

'She is an interested observer whom we are happy to accommodate,' Simpson hissed. She looked along the faces on the other side of the table. 'And the inspector here is one of my very best men.'

Pardon? Carlyle tried not to look surprised at this rare endorsement.

'Indeed, he is one of the most successful officers in this Force.'
Steady on.

'Plus, he has extensive experience of the background to this case.' She turned to Carlyle and smiled. 'Are you ready to collect Mr Sands?'

Carlyle's heart sank. 'Yes, Commander.'

Was it his imagination or did a look of surprise ghost over Simpson's face as he delivered his lines?

She cleared her throat. 'Good. Bring him back here as quickly as possible.'

'Yes, Commander.' He had to resist the urge to salute. Simpson shot him a look that said *Don't overdo it.*

Ignoring the hostile looks coming from the other side of the table, he turned and opened the door.

'Oh, Inspector?'

'Yes?' He half turned to see a look on Nathalie Kelvin's face that would curdle milk.

'If – ever again – you try to feed my name to the newspapers, I will have your guts for garters. And the rest of you for medical research.'

Thanks a million, Brian Sutherland, the inspector thought angrily. Ignoring the grimace on Simpson's face, he ducked out of the door and fled down the corridor.

Carefully pouring the last of the wine into her glass, the large man on the opposite side of the table arched his eyebrows enquiringly. Haley Devlin blushed violently. 'For God's sake, George,' she whispered, 'I'm not giving you a hand job. No way.'

The girl's embarrassment only made George McQuarrie even more excited. He gestured around the empty booths of the dimly lit Signal Bar. 'But we're the only people here.'

'What about the waiters?'

'When was the last time you saw one? They're all in the back having something to eat. Don't worry, no one will catch us.' Not that it would bother him if they did; he'd always quite enjoyed an audience.

Still blushing, she shuffled up close on the banquette.

'George McQuarrie?'

As Umar and Savage approached the table, the man looked up, annoyed. His female companion jerked backwards, sitting up straight as she wiped her hand on a napkin. Umar stepped in front of Savage and flashed the couple his ID.

Pulling the table towards him, McQuarrie shifted in his seat. 'What do you want?' For once, Carlyle was right; he was a big bastard – easily six foot two and by the looks of things in quite good shape as well. Even with the two of them, it could be a struggle if he put up a fight. Umar glanced at Savage, wondering if his partner could take a punch. Maybe, he thought ruefully, they should have brought some uniforms along for the ride. He thought about calling the station but discarded the idea immediately. It was too late now.

Dressed immaculately in a Richard James grey pinstripe, with an off-white shirt open at the neck, McQuarrie eyed the policemen suspiciously from under a mop of curly blond hair.

Umar adopted his most formal tone. 'We need you to come with us, please, sir.'

'Oh you do, do you?' McQuarrie grabbed his wine glass and gave them a mock salute before throwing the last of the drink down his neck.

'We just have a few questions.' Savage leered at the girl.

McQuarrie placed the glass back on the table. 'But do you have a warrant?'

'We can get one,' said Umar lamely.

'Well, fuck off and get one then,' McQuarrie roared, going red in the face.

Hayley looked anxiously at the two policemen. 'George, for God's sake.'

'They can piss off,' McQuarrie harrumphed. Grabbing her hand, he pulled it onto his lap. 'Now, where were we?'

'George,' her face went crimson, 'please.' She tried to pull her hand away but he gripped it tightly. 'Ow, let me go!'

A waiter stuck his head out of the kitchen door to see what was going on then quickly disappeared again.

'Release the lady's hand, Mr McQuarrie,' Umar said firmly.

'Or what?' McQuarrie sneered, rubbing her hand against his crotch.

'Or I will arrest you for sexual assault.'

'And,' Savage grinned, 'we will let your little friend here know what we want to talk to you about.'

Umar scowled at his colleague as Hayley finally jerked her hand free.

'What *do* you want to talk to him about?' she asked.

'The murder of Julian Schaeffer.'

The girl looked at him blankly.

230

Savage jerked his thumb at McQuarrie. 'Schaeffer's the husband of one of his other girlfriends.'

Umar shook his head. 'Well done.'

'Oh, for Christ's sake.' Jumping to her feet, Hayley squirmed out of the booth and fled towards the door.

'I'll see you later on,' McQuarrie shouted after her, apparently amused by the scene.

By way of reply, Hayley waved the middle finger of her left hand in the air as she disappeared into the street.

'Thank you for that,' McQuarrie grimaced as he readjusted his trousers.

'Our apologies for interrupting your lunch,' said Savage, with a complete lack of sincerity.

'It wasn't the food I was worried about.'

'So, are you coming?'

McQuarrie thought about it for a moment.

Umar gestured at the clock on the wall behind the table. 'C'mon, let's go.'

Shaking his head disgustedly, McQuarrie got himself up from the table. 'Okay, okay.' Turning away, Umar took a step towards the door. As he did so, something seemed to trip in the big man's brain. Grabbing the empty wine bottle by the neck, he smashed it off the side of Umar's head. Umar staggered but did not fall. Rushing forward, McQuarrie punched him twice in the face, sending him flying across a nearby table. His blood up, McQuarrie pounced on the statuesque Savage, sending him straight to the floor with a vicious head-butt that pulverized his nose.

'Fuck!' Rolling on the floor, Savage held the crimson mask of his face. Trying to force himself to his feet, Umar only succeeded in vomiting all over his jeans.

Realizing that neither policeman was about to get back up, McQuarrie paused to admire his handiwork and get his breathing back under control. Tossing the wine bottle onto the banquette, he kicked Savage twice in the ribs, promoting another outbreak of screams from the hapless sergeant. Trying not to make it seem too obvious, Umar rolled behind the collapsed table in order to escape the same fate. In the distance, he could hear the sound of approaching sirens. Someone in the kitchen must have called 999. The sergeant gave silent thanks for the immediate response of his colleagues.

Looking up, he realized that he could only see out of his left eye. McQuarrie caught his gaze. 'Saved by the bell.' He wiped a bead of sweat from his brow. 'If I ever see either of you two bastards again,' he said, stepping over Savage's prostrate body as he strolled towards the door, 'rest assured, I will kill you. And that's a promise.'

'Fuck you too.' Rolling on to his back, Umar stared up at the ceiling with his one good eye, waiting for the sirens to drown out the sound of Savage's moans.

THIRTY-FOUR

As he said he would be, Daniel Sands was sitting outside the Diana Memorial Playground watching a steady stream of children enter the front gate of the Peter Pan-themed area. Ordering a double espresso from the kiosk, the inspector glanced down the list of rules, painted on a board by the entrance:

- Supervise your children at all times
- Glass bottles or jars are not allowed
- Cycling, rollerblading and ball sports are not allowed
- Smoking is not permitted in the playground
- Alcohol is not permitted in the playground
- Only registered Assistance Dogs will be permitted

That just about covers it, he thought, as a smiling member of indeterminate origin handed him his coffee. It was piping hot and he took a cautious sip. Sharp and bitter, it would do. Holding it carefully, he walked over to Sands's table, sat down and gave a nod of acknowledgement.

'Nice spot.'

'I like it.' Sands smiled sadly. 'Of course it wasn't here when . . .' His voice trailed away and the inspector gazed into his coffee.

'No.' When Carlyle looked into the man's face, he was shocked to see that Sands had aged ten years or more in the last twenty-four hours. Seemingly, he had made the transition from a lively pensioner to a frail old man waiting for his health to fail. The inspector wondered if he would be able to cope with what was to come. He had promised Simpson that he would obey her instructions to the letter, but he seriously doubted if he could be responsible for bringing Sands in. Maybe he would have to let the Commander down again.

'The problem is,' Sands said ruefully, 'if you're a man sitting here on your own, everybody wonders about you.'

'Yes.'

As if on cue, two young women walked past, each pushing an expensive stroller that looked as if it might have been designed by scientists at NASA. Without breaking their conversation, they looked the two men up and down suspiciously. While Carlyle glanced away, Sands gave them a modest wave. Blanking the greeting, the women quickened their stride as they walked away.

'See what I mean?'

Carlyle nodded.

'Everyone is in their own little bubble.' Sands gestured at the retreating women. 'They push their kids around in nine-hundred pound buggies and gabble away to each other on their mobile phones and then they look at me and think: Who is that man? Why is he hanging round a playground? Is he a pervert? Is he playing with himself under the table? Is he going to try and steal my child?'

'It's a public park,' Carlyle said. 'You have every right to be here.'

'Yes and no.' Sands sighed.

Finishing his coffee, Carlyle placed his empty cup on the table only for a gust of wind to almost blow it away. Snatching it back, he crumpled it in his fist.

'If you are a parent there is always the fear – always,' Sands said.

Carlyle knew exactly what he meant. 'Yes.'

'The great terror – for all of them – is that something could happen to their child, just as something happened to mine.' Sticking his hands into his pockets, Sands leaned back on the bench. 'Of course, I only ever had the one. I often wonder if having more makes you worry less about each one individually.'

It was something that Carlyle often thought about too. So much of his life, his hopes and fears were tied up in Alice that it scared him. It scared him because he knew that he could only protect her so far, for so long. It also scared him because he wondered if, ultimately, not being able to suppress his fears made him a bad father. Gazing skyward, he watched a lone cloud scudding across the sky, heading east. Lost in thoughts about his own family, he felt sick to his stomach that he could do nothing to help this man.

For a while they sat in silence, listening to the happy screams of the children playing on the pirate ship and the climbing frames.

'Mr Sands,' Carlyle said finally, 'I am very sorry about this.'

Daniel Sands reached over and gave him a comforting pat on the arm. 'Don't worry about it, Inspector. None of this is your fault. I don't really know how we quite ended up here.'

Carlyle smiled sadly. 'Me neither.' He felt the caffeine buzzing in his system and wondered how this thing would play out. Nothing came to mind.

'It should never have come to this.'

'No.'

They watched a couple of laughing girls, maybe eight or nine, running towards the playground gate.

'In just over three weeks' time, it will be Lillian's birthday. She would have been thirty-seven.' Sands's eyes filled with tears as he gazed into the middle distance, focusing on something that Carlyle could not see. 'It's funny,' he sniffled. 'On the one hand, she will always be the child you remember her as.'

Carlyle stared at the pigeons.

'On the other, you can't help but wonder, if she was sitting here now – what kind of woman would she be? Would she have been a lawyer? That's what she talked about. Would she be married? Would she have children of her own?' A fat tear ran down his cheek. 'Would I have been a granddad?'

A plane floated across the sky, heading for Heathrow, low

enough for Carlyle to be able to make out its Qantas logo. Trying to banish thoughts of his own hopes and fears, he pondered what Daniel Sands had said. Maybe, after what had happened with Lillian, Sands should have had another kid or two; found a new girlfriend and got her knocked up as quickly as possible; found something else to occupy his time – use up his energy, burn up his fears.

He let the jet glide beyond his line of vision. 'We have to get going.' Standing up, he dropped his crushed coffee cup in a nearby bin.

'Yes.' Sands got to his feet.

'Do you have an Oyster card?'

Sands looked at him quizzically. 'Yes.'

'Good. We'll take the tube. No cars, no flashing lights. We'll go in the back way, in case there are any press.' He glanced at his watch. 'The station should have called your lawyer by now – they'll get him to meet you there.'

Sands nodded. 'Thank you. But a lawyer is optional. I will be pleading guilty to the charges. The authorities may not bring Fassbender to justice, but at least I can name and shame him in open court.'

Carlyle put a hand on the old man's shoulder. 'I am telling you, you have to think about this very carefully. You must speak to your lawyer before doing anything rash.' He realized that he had no idea who Sands's lawyer was; he sincerely hoped that it was someone decent.

Sands shook his head. 'You don't understand.'

'I never said that I did,' said Carlyle, a bit too sharply. 'Look,' he sighed, moderating his tone, 'you can tell your story on the steps of the police station just as easily as you can from the witness box.'

'I want people to know what I did,' Sands said doggedly. 'I won't tell you who helped me, of course, but I want everyone to know that it was me behind it. I want them to know that I didn't give up. And I want people to ask why, even when that monster was handed to the police on a plate, he was still able to walk free once again.' He looked enquiringly at the inspector. 'And maybe you can tell them.'

'That,' Carlyle said quietly, 'is a question way above my pay grade.' Despite his pig-headedness, he still admired the old man's boundless determination. Maybe he had got it the wrong way round; maybe that was the very thing keeping him alive.

So many *maybes*.

They resumed their walk, leaving the calm of the park behind for the grubby urban chaos of Bayswater. The lights were against them as they reached the road. Sands nudged Carlyle as they waited at the crossing.

'You know he did it, don't you?'

Carlyle shrugged as a taxi barrelled by, inches from his face. 'None of us *know* anything.'

'But there's the evidence.'

'You can interpret the evidence almost any way you like – that's what lawyers do. They construct a story and try to sell it – sell it to the police, to the judge, the jury, to the press, to their client.' The lights changed and he took Sands gently by the arm, leading the old man across the road, towards Queensway tube station, and back to Charing Cross police station, to face the music.

THIRTY-FIVE

'Are you sure that you want to sign this?'

'Yes.' Sands gestured for the inspector to hand him the biro. Carlyle glanced at Sands's lawyer, a fresh-faced chap called Gavin Potts. Frankly, he would have preferred to see a lot more grey hairs. There was very little doubt that, if it came to it, Nathalie Kelvin QC and her flunkies would make mincemeat of the young fellow.

Avoiding eye-contact, Potts showed no emotion either way. 'I have explained to my client the implications of his statement,' he said mechanically, the nervousness discernible in his voice. 'He has made it clear that this is how he wishes to proceed.'

Nothing like having your brief on your side, Carlyle thought unhappily as he handed Sands the pen. 'Sign at the bottom and initial each page please, sir.'

'Yes.' Sands took the pen and scanned the typed-up statement. Carlyle watched as he applied his spidery scribble at the bottom.

'There, done.' Replacing the cap, Sands laid the pen on top of the statement and sat back in his chair. After a moment's reflection, he looked at the inspector. 'I have always taken full responsibility for my actions,' he said quietly.

Carlyle nodded, wondering if that made the old man a mug – or a hero.

'It's just a shame that other people don't do the same.'

Yes, thought Carlyle. *Yes, it is*. Getting to his feet, he reached over the desk and picked up the pen and the statement. 'Okay,' he sighed. 'I just need to go upstairs and get this processed. Please wait here.'

Potts nodded. 'We will, of course, be making an application for bail before sentencing. Mr Sands is not a flight risk. Nor does he pose a threat to anyone – in the wider sense.'

Carlyle raised an eyebrow. 'And in the narrower sense?'

'The court should take into account that my client's only objective was to bring Mr Fassbender into the hands of the UK authorities, which he has done. Any disappointment that Mr Sands may feel as to the way in which the authorities have dealt with the matter thereafter should not obscure the fact that he has never sought to take the law into his own hands.'

'I am not sure that Fassbender and his legal team would see it like that,' Carlyle replied. Sands was staring into space, as if this conversation had nothing to do with him.

Potts batted away the comment with a wave of his hand. 'However they respond, I hope that you will be able to support our request to the court.'

Carlyle turned and headed for the door. 'I'll see what I can do.'

Less than five minutes later, Carlyle stood in front of Paul Fassbender and his lawyer, Sidney Hardy. He was beginning to feel like a character in a Brian Rix farce, running frantically from room to room trying – and failing – to keep everybody sweet. At least he hadn't lost his trousers – so far, at any rate.

No longer present was the Coco Chanel lookalike, Nathalie Kelvin QC. Having made her point, she presumably had more important matters to attend to.

'This is simply not good enough.' Fassbender looked angrily from Carlyle to Simpson and back again.

'Sir,' said Simpson through clenched teeth, 'Mr Sands has signed a full confession.'

'Hardly a *full* confession,' suggested Hardy.

Fassbender smacked a fist on the table. 'You also have to arrest the man who kidnapped me on the orders of that demented madman.'

Simpson shot a glance at Carlyle but the inspector was determined to keep his mouth firmly shut. Arms folded, he stared out of the grime-streaked window, trying to look inscrutable.

'I want justice.' Fassbender was working himself up into a fury.

With a bit of luck, the old bastard will have a stroke. Carlyle still couldn't resign himself to the fact that Fassbender would walk.

Again.

Hardy placed a calming hand on his client's forearm but Fassbender shrugged it off angrily. 'You people are just not trying.'

'Mr Sands has made his statement,' Simpson repeated. 'He will appear in court later today or tomorrow. Our investigations regarding the other person or persons involved in this matter are continuing. In the meantime, sir, you are free to return home.'

Fassbender muttered something to his lawyer, who made a face.

'So what precisely can you tell us about the investigation that will give my client and myself comfort that the man who assaulted Mr Fassbender and drove him across Europe in the boot of a car will be caught and punished?'

The room was hot and stuffy and the Commander was beginning to go red in the face. She looked like she wanted to smack both of them. Carlyle tried not to smirk. 'Our enquiries are continuing,' she said, reverting to her best bureaucratic monotone. 'That is all that I want to say at this stage.'

A pained expression crossed Hardy's face, as if he had just had a spike shoved up his backside. 'I think—'

'And *I* think,' Simpson countered, coming closer to losing her cool, 'that the Metropolitan Police Force has extended every courtesy to you and your client.' Hardy tried again to speak, but she continued talking over him. 'This is a police matter and you have to leave it to us.'

'If I leave it to you,' Fassbender sneered, 'nothing will happen. Even the old fool himself will probably manage to escape jail.'

Then he won't be the only one, Carlyle reflected.

'My apologies, sir,' Simpson replied, 'but I don't see that you have any alternative other than to accept my assurances that we are acting professionally and in good faith, with your rights and interests very much in mind.'

'Good faith?' Fassbender mocked. 'I very much doubt that. I will go to the court. I will speak to the judge. I will *demand* justice.' He made it sound as if it was something completely within his power and control. Raising his eyes to the heavens, Hardy tried to control the grin that was creeping around the edges of his mouth.

Simpson bowed her head. A bead of sweat trickled down her temple. 'Very well.'

'And I will make sure you do your job,' Fassbender continued, waving an admonishing finger at both the inspector and his boss. He was on a roll now and he wasn't going to let the minions off the hook. 'I will come here every day until you find this wretched vigilante and his associates.'

You do that, Carlyle thought. *You bloody do that.*

'Very well,' Simpson grimaced. 'We will let you know when the time of the court hearing is confirmed.' Without waiting for a reply, she turned to the inspector and pushed him towards the door.

In the corridor, Carlyle held his tongue until they were out of earshot.

'That went well,' he said, letting out a long breath.

'Yes,' Simpson said snarkily. 'Thank you, John.'

He looked at her askance. 'How was that my fault?'

'Don't start.' Simpson rubbed her temples in a futile attempt to massage away a brutal headache.

Not for the first time, they were bickering like an old married couple.

Carlyle smiled at the thought.

Simpson rubbed harder. 'What's so bloody funny?'

'Nothing.' Carlyle gestured back in the direction of the interview room. 'At least I kept my mouth shut.'

'I suppose I should be grateful for small mercies.' Giving up on the temples, Simpson rolled her shoulders, letting out a small sigh in the process.

As he watched her, the inspector went through his mental To Do list.

'*What*?' Simpson glared at him angrily.

Looking away, Carlyle caught sight of a pretty WPC walking down the corridor towards them carrying a couple of outsized box-files in front of her. Another new arrival, from Balham apparently. Reynolds was her name, something like that. As she approached, he gave her the 100-watt Inspector Carlyle smile. Eyes focused on the middle distance, she blanked him as she walked past.

'Ah,' Simpson grinned, 'the mysterious Carlyle charm. Bestowed only on the chosen few.'

Lengthening his stride, Carlyle pushed his way through a set of double doors. 'I'll see you in court for the Sands hearing,' he said gruffly. 'First I need to go up to UCH.' She shot him a quizzical look and he quickly filled her in on Savage and Umar's run in with George McQuarrie.

When he'd finished, Simpson looked more irritated than concerned. 'Are they okay?' she asked, her tone suggesting no more than a bureaucratic level of interest.

'Yeah,' Carlyle replied.

'You could sound happier about it.'

'It's nothing serious. Umar's got a black eye and a couple of cuts. Savage has got a couple of cracked ribs.' He paused, for effect. 'The main reason for going up there is to stop them hitting on the poor nurses.'

Simpson looked distinctly unamused.

'Joke,' he said lamely.

'What about McQuarrie?'

'We're tracking him down.'

'Make it quick,' Simpson snapped. 'And go easy on the over-time. As always, there are issues with costs.'

'Of course,' Carlyle nodded. 'The girl George was with when we tried to pick him up has given us a couple of addresses and I'll

242

have another chat to Iris Belekhsan. She might be a bit more talkative when she finds out that she was only one of Mr McQuarrie's various consorts.'

'Good.' Simpson seemed satisfied with that.

'It may be,' said Carlyle, trying to balance sucking up to the boss without actually promising anything, 'that this is the important breakthrough on the Schaeffer shooting.' Pushing their way through another set of double doors, they reached the front desk, which appeared deserted.

'We'll see,' said Simpson, stopping at the desk. 'McQuarrie didn't pull the trigger, though, did he?'

'No.' Carlyle took another couple of steps before stopping, indicating his desire to be on his way. 'He was on holiday with Belekhsan at the time.' He hopped from foot to foot, as if he needed to pee. 'But he would know how to make it happen.'

Just then, Angie Middleton appeared from a door behind the desk. Simpson glared at her but said nothing. She turned back to the inspector instead and said, lowering her voice, 'What about motive?'

Carlyle shrugged. 'What, you mean other than the fact that they were going through a bitter, protracted divorce and they hated each other more than anything else on earth?' He didn't want to admit that his team had been too distracted by other matters to spend time going through the boring stuff, like checking for life insurance policies.

The Commander looked at him enquiringly.

'It'll be the usual,' Carlyle burbled on. 'Sex or money. Or sex *and* money. We just need to fill in the blanks.' He cast a quick glance at Middleton. Eyes glued on her computer screen, the desk sergeant bashed a couple of keys on her keyboard, trying – and failing – to make her eavesdropping less obvious.

'Well,' said Simpson firmly, 'I suggest that you get on with it.'

'Yes.'

'And what about the child?'

'For the moment, Rebecca remains in the care of her mother. I want to speak to both Social Services and the grandparents about what we should do if—'

'It's going to be a hell of a mess,' the Commander interrupted, cutting him off, 'if the mother gets arrested for killing the father.'

'I know. You couldn't make it up.'

'I suppose we'll just have to cross that bridge when we get to it.'

Carlyle caught Middleton's eye and grinned. 'Yes, I dare say we probably will.'

THIRTY-SIX

Sergeant Savage had been kept in for observation. Instead of being sent home with some top-drawer painkillers and a login for NHS Direct, he was tying up a bed in University College Hospital, at a cost of several thousand pounds a day.

No wonder the National Health Service was doomed.

Dutifully following the signs to the Stanley Bowles Ward, the inspector found himself in a room full of zombified geriatrics. The guy in the nearest bed to the door, headphones clamped to his skull, was watching TV, singing along to an advert. The other patients were prone in their beds, staring into space.

Looks like the drugs trolley has just been round, Carlyle observed.

'Excuse me, sir?'

The inspector turned to see a male nurse, a thirty-something white skinhead, eyeing him suspiciously. When Carlyle explained what he was looking for, the skinhead told him, 'This is the Armfield Ward.'

'Okay,' said Carlyle through gritted teeth. 'How do I find Stanley Bowles?'

'It's at the other end of the Osgood Wing,' the nurse said unhelpfully, gesturing back the way that Carlyle had come. 'Follow the signs.'

Trying to ignore the smell of disinfectant, the inspector reversed down the corridor. After several minutes of hopeful wandering, he turned a corner to find Umar playing on his BlackBerry.

'Where have you been?' The sergeant finished sending an email and gestured at the line of beds on the other side of the doors. 'Robbie's in there. We've been waiting for you for ages.'

'It would have helped if I hadn't spent the last hour,' Carlyle moaned, shamelessly exaggerating, 'traipsing round this bloody hospital trying to find you.' Looking through the window, he could see Savage sitting in the third bed from the door. He was wearing one of those green paper gowns that they give to patients without any pyjamas. Reading a copy of the *Standard*, he looked perfectly content. 'How is he?'

'He'll live,' said Umar, still fiddling with his BlackBerry. 'Sorry we made such a hash of things.'

The apology surprised the inspector. He had assumed that he was going to get blamed for sending the two of them up against McQuarrie without more back-up. He quickly regained his composure before his sergeant could look up. 'These things happen,' he said graciously. 'Don't worry about it.' He looked Umar up and down. The guy looked like he'd been in a fight – which he had – but the damage to his pretty-boy good looks was strictly short-term. In a week or two, there should be nothing to see; he might have to postpone the wedding photographs though, Carlyle thought with a smirk, saying aloud, 'How about you?'

'I'm fine,' Umar said, putting the BlackBerry away. 'Savage got the worst of it.' On cue, Savage looked up to see the inspector standing by the door. Pushing his way into the ward, Carlyle stepped over to the bed with Umar in tow.

'Good to see you survived then,' he said, by way of greeting.

Folding the *Standard* in two, Savage winced at the memory. 'He was a big bloke.'

All thoughts of his own culpability completely forgotten, Carlyle shot Umar a sharp look. 'I told you that before you went out.'

'Yes,' Umar protested, 'but—'

'Do you know how much it's going to cost, to track the bastard down?' Carlyle whined.

Savage tossed the paper on the bed. 'At least we know who did it now.'

'Maybe,' Carlyle shrugged.

'He must be in on it,' Umar said. 'Why else would he have run?'

'Because,' Carlyle laughed, 'he's a dickhead.'

A middle-aged female nurse appeared by the bed and handed Savage a jumbo box of painkillers. 'Take a couple of these when the pain gets too much,' she told him. 'No more than eight in one twenty-four hour period, though.'

'Okay. Thanks.' Waiting until the nurse had turned and walked away, Savage ripped open the box, popped a couple of the tablets from their silver foil, threw them down his throat and swallowed.

Glancing up, Carlyle saw the clock above the door. There were too many things to do and he had to get going. 'How did you get on with the sugar daddies?' He tried not to look too impatient while Savage washed the tablets down with a swig of water from the plastic bottle on the table by the bed.

'Spoke to one,' the sergeant said finally, taking another drink from the bottle. 'Left messages for two. Not got to the fourth one yet.' He ran Carlyle through the list. 'I've updated my notes at the station.'

'Okay.' Carlyle realized that it would have been too much to hope for, that they might have sorted out the Ayumi Ninomiya case as well. 'Well,' he gave Savage an understanding smile, 'I suppose it's some time off for you.' As in: *Get your arse out of that bed and get back to work.*

Not obviously picking up on the inspector's coded message, Savage nodded and beamed.

Carlyle tried another smile. It didn't come naturally and he could feel his cheeks starting to ache. 'I'll chase the rest of these guys down.' *On my own.*

'Thanks,' Savage replied cheerily. 'I should be fine in a couple of weeks.'

'Take all the time you need,' Carlyle managed before his smile became too obviously a grimace. 'See you later.' Patting Savage gently on the arm, he nodded at Umar. 'C'mon, pretty boy, let's get going.'

247

* * *

Dismayed, WPC Alison Titchfield listened to the sound of her colleagues – PCs Smith, James and Henderson – romping up the stairs like a mini-herd of baby rhino. The suspect, if he was in the building, would have heard them coming a mile off and doubtless bunked out of a window. Titchfield wondered if she should step back out on to the street to try to intercept anyone trying to flee but no, she had been told to stand at the bottom of the stairs, so stand at the bottom of the stairs was what she would do. Scarcely three months into her first posting and the young WPC had already learned lesson No. 1 in the Metropolitan Police rulebook. *Do not, under any circumstances, act under your own initiative.*

Especially if you are a woman.

It was something that was drilled into you day after day after bloody day. And when you weren't being reminded of it by your male colleagues, you had plenty of opportunities, standing around in hallways, on doorsteps and on street corners, to reflect on it on your own. Titchfield watched a mouse appear from a gap in the skirting board and run away from her down the hall. From upstairs came the sound of more banging and shouting as the boys tried to find the right flat. *You should have let me go up there*, Litchfield thought sourly. Apparently the bloke they were looking for had put two sergeants in hospital. Smith, James and Henderson could easily go the same way. They were big but they were stupid. They should have left the job of tracking down Mr George McQuarrie – whoever he was – to her.

More shouting was followed by the sound of a door being smashed.

Bloody hell, Titchfield thought, *what a total racket.*

The neighbours were probably already dialling 999 and asking for a SWAT team to be sent over immediately.

Better get their retaliation in first. Titchfield lifted the radio clipped to her body armour and hit the call key.

'Sounds like we've found the target. All under control, over.'

'*Roger. We've just had a call this second from a neighbouring property. Reports of a disturbance, over.*'

'It's just us,' Titchfield snapped, angry at being right. 'Nothing to worry about, over.'

'*Understood, over.*'

Shaking her head, Titchfield let go of the radio just as an almighty scream came hurtling down the stairs, followed almost immediately by another.

It looked like they'd found their man.

For a moment, the young WPC was caught in two minds. Stay put – or go to the aid of her colleagues? A third blood-curdling scream made up her mind for her and she ran up the stairs, taking them two at a time.

Less than five seconds later, she was on the first-floor landing looking at a short hallway containing three doors. Two of the three were firmly shut but the middle door – Flat 5 – was hanging on its hinges. As Titchfield stepped towards it, a massive figure bounded out, heading for the stairs. Without thinking, the WPC took a step sideways to get out of the man's way. As she did so, however, she left her right foot sticking out, catching his trailing leg as he flew past.

'Shiiittt.'

Suddenly conscious of her elevated pulse, Alison Titchfield watched as George McQuarrie disappeared over the edge of the stairs. There was a satisfying series of bumps and screams and then silence.

Taking a moment to compose herself, the WPC calmly made her way back down to the ground floor. By the time she reached McQuarrie, he was moaning, in a heap in the hall. The mouse reappeared from its bolthole, took a look at what was going on and then made itself scarce. A bruise was already coming up on McQuarrie's forehead and he was holding his knee.

'My leg.' He tried to force himself up but when Titchfield put her boot in the small of his back he went down again without much in the way of protest. Pulling a set of handcuffs from her belt, she dropped on one knee and secured his left wrist to the pipe of the hallway radiator. Job done, she got to her feet and brought the radio back to her lips.

'Suspect apprehended, over.'

'*Good work, over.*'

'Thanks,' Titchfield grinned. Then, glancing back up the stairs, she realized that it was ominously silent on the first floor. 'Looks like we've got some injuries, though,' she continued. 'You'd better send an ambulance, maybe two, over.'

'*On the way, over.*'

Flipping himself onto his back, McQuarrie tried to yank his hand free.

Titchfield shook her head. 'Behave.'

He looked up at her through two slits for eyes. 'You bitch!' he hissed. 'My kneecap is broken or something.'

'Just be grateful I don't break your other leg,' Titchfield said sweetly. Turning away from the captured suspect, she headed back up the stairs. The ambulances would be a while yet; she'd better see how the boys were getting on.

THIRTY-SEVEN

Wishing she could have a cigarette, Hilary Green finished her latte and tossed the empty paper cup into a nearby bin. Annoyed that she didn't miss, Carlyle eyed her suspiciously. He had known the Westminster Social Services Case Officer for four or five years now but their working relationship remained perfunctory, with neither side having much time for the other, nor for the institutions that they represented. As far as the inspector was concerned, the council's social workers were just a bunch of lame civil servants whose only thought, if and when they clocked on in the morning, was how quickly they could clock off. For her part, Ms Green – a fifteen-year veteran of cleaning up other people's mess – saw the police as all too ready to pass the buck, running away from difficult cases and leaving the dirty work to Social Services.

Collecting up her papers, Green swept them into an oversized red handbag. Glancing at her watch, she cursed under her breath. Carlyle, standing at the window with his arms folded, pretended not to hear. He didn't have to pretend not to care.

'I don't have time for this.' Zipping up her bag, Green stood up straight and placed her hands on her hips.

'Sorry,' Carlyle said, clearly not giving a toss. Out of the window, he watched a couple of detainees being placed in the back of a security company van. 'Maybe you can dump it on Camden.'

'I tried that already,' the social worker sighed, 'but the girl's given home address was in Westminster, so it looks like I'm stuck with it.'

'Unlucky. So what are you going to do?'

'We'll just have to see what happens.'

'Huh?' Carlyle looked back at Green, trying to give her his full attention. He had asked for this meeting, after all; insisting that she come to Charing Cross police station to discuss Rebecca Schaeffer in the only slot he had free in his day. Not for the first time, it struck him that Green was an incredibly unattractive woman. She must be in her early forties now, he thought, and looking every year of it. At least she'd given up on the bottle-blonde look that she'd had when they'd first met. If anything, that had made her look even older. Now her natural brown was streaked with grey, which went some way to softening the permanently sour expression on her face.

Perfect for a social worker, really.

Green shot him a look full of weariness and suspicion. 'Until the mother is charged – as you know – we will not do anything.'

Now it was the inspector's turn to sigh. 'I'm just trying to plan ahead.' Now that George McQuarrie was back in custody, he wanted to move in on Iris Belekhsan as well. There was a flight risk to consider, however. He didn't want her to up sticks and head off to the arse end of nowhere – particularly with the kid in tow. If that happened, it could take years to get her back. Worse, if she chose her destination wisely, she might never be sent back.

He glanced at his watch. Daniel Sands was due in front of the beak in just over twenty-five minutes. The hearing would doubtless start late but he didn't want to risk missing it. It was a brisk fifteen-minute walk to Horseferry Road Magistrates' Court but it could easily take another ten minutes to get in. He cursed the closure of the courts at Bow Street, just a couple of minutes away. The site had lain empty for years now, with the plans to turn it into another luxury hotel stymied by the financial crash.

Looking disgruntled, Green pulled a phone from her pocket and began typing a text message. 'You're wasting your time. We'll just have to see what happens.'

Carlyle grunted. Why did he bother with these people? Gritting his teeth, he gave it one last go. 'If the mother was responsible, she will face some serious jail time. That is only right and proper. But the child is the person who is suffering most from all of this. I do not want her interests to get lost in the legal process. She should not go into care if there is an alternative.'

Green sent her message and looked up at him as if he was an idiot, which he probably was. 'I'm surprised you dragged me over here for this,' she said coolly. 'There's really nothing I can do.' Resisting the urge to wrap his hands around her neck, Carlyle glared at the woman. But for Hilary Green, it was water off a duck's back. Hauling her bag over her shoulder, she headed for the door. 'If you take the mother into custody,' she repeated, grabbing the handle, 'Social Services will have to be fully involved . . . even before the matter goes to court.' She shot him a superior look. 'To be honest, I'm not sure we should have given the police the leeway that you've had to date in this case.'

Sod you, too, thought Carlyle.

'The bottom line,' she said as she pulled the door open, 'is that it is by no means certain that the Local Authority will let the daughter stay with the grandparents.'

'But—'

Stepping out of the door, Green held up a hand to cut him off. 'Indeed, given the circumstances . . .'

Carlyle felt the anger rising in his throat. 'So she can stay with her mother, who may well have organized the murder of her father, but not with her grandparents? Iris is using Rebecca as a kind of human shield. She is banking on the fact that I won't chase her and risk the kid going into care. Anna and Ronald Connolly are my way around that.'

Green looked at him with a mixture of sadness and loathing. She held up the thumb and forefinger on her right hand, like a teacher addressing a terminally dull pupil. 'A, you don't know whether Ms Belekhsan was in any way involved in the murder of Mr Schaeffer. B, Mrs Connolly is still so heavily sedated she can't look after anyone.'

Carlyle scrunched up his face in anguished protest. 'Oh, come on.'

'And, C, the "grandfather" Ronald Connolly is not a blood relative. He has no rights and no one has even assessed his ability to look after the child.'

Carlyle made to protest further, but she ploughed on.

'Do you even know how old he is? What kind of health he is in? Have you checked him against any of the databases? Is he safe? Is he capable?'

Rather him than Social bloody Services, the inspector thought dourly, letting his gaze fall to the floor.

'You're listening to your gut instinct. Well, good for you. You've met with the guy for what? Twenty minutes at the most? An hour? Is that really enough on which to base such an important decision?' Suddenly, she was on a roll, enjoying the conversation. 'Anyway, who are *you* to judge?'

Embarrassed at being taken to the cleaners by a social worker, Carlyle protested, 'I don't want to be the bloody judge!'

'Sounds like it to me.'

'It's just that no one seems to be looking out for the kid in all of this.'

'This is not your problem, Inspector. It goes without saying that everything will be done according to the regulations.' Readjusting the shoulder strap of her bag, Hilary Green gave him the kind of patronizing look he'd had to endure for the whole of his working life. 'It's not our job to take sides.' With a final smirk, she slid into the corridor, letting the door close slowly behind her.

The City of Westminster court, to give it its proper name, was a seventies monstrosity; a soul-destroying box of a building with all the charisma of George Orwell's Ministry of Truth. Situated a few minutes from the House of Commons – and close to New Scotland Yard – it doubtless gave the politicians and Met top brass some sense of satisfaction that justice was being meted out on their doorstep. Not for much longer, though. As he skipped through the front entrance, Carlyle wondered if this would be his last ever visit. Like Bow Street, Horseferry Road had been sold to developers. In future, the inspector would have to spend more of his valuable time schlepping up to the newly refurbished magistrates' court on the Marylebone Road to have his days in court.

Parking any thoughts about the vagaries of property development, the inspector slipped as quietly as he could into the back of Court No. 6. The Daniel Sands hearing had already started and the public benches were surprisingly full, swelled both by members of Her Majesty's Fourth Estate as well as random onlookers, curious to see what a geriatric vigilante looked like. Catching sight of Simpson sitting inconspicuously at the far end of the back row, he made his way slowly along the line of observers, finally forcing a big man in a rather tatty-looking pinstripe suit to shuffle along the bench so that he could squeeze in next to the Commander.

'Sorry I'm late,' he mumbled as he forced Fatso to cede another inch.

'You haven't missed much,' said Simpson, nodding in the direction of Paul Fassbender who was sitting half a dozen rows in front, next to his lawyer, Sidney Hardy. Nathalie Kelvin QC was strikingly absent, no doubt a reflection of both her camera shyness and pressing business elsewhere.

'No sign of Coco then?

Simpson kept her eyes front. 'Sorry?'

'Nothing.' He followed Simpson's gaze. There was a pause while the judge, a woman, scrutinized some papers. 'Who's that?'

'Julie-Anne Castor.' And when Carlyle looked blank, Simpson hissed, 'Just another middle-class, middle-brow know-nothing.'

The inspector had to stifle a laugh. 'You're getting very cynical in your old age, Commander.'

'I suppose,' Simpson huffed, 'that's your idea of a compliment.' She gestured back towards the bench. 'She's a staunch supporter of Edgar Carlton.'

'Aha.'

Edgar Carlton was a politician – the Prime Minister, no less; now well ensconced in his second term. He had survived remarkably well for a man who brought together nothing more than a watery blend of traditional upper-class incompetence and twenty-first century digital 'activism'. Carlyle's job had brought him into contact with the great man on one memorable occasion, on the eve of Carlton's first election as PM. The experience had left him bruised, unhappy and extremely lucky to still have a job.

'Not exactly a character reference, is it?' he whispered.

'No.'

The irony of it was that Simpson had been something of a fellow traveller at the time. Back then, her husband had been a major donor to Carlton's election campaign. That was before the fraud convictions, jail and terminal cancer. Somewhere along the line, the Commander seemed to have lost her enthusiasm for the great Carlton Project. Some people just didn't have any staying power.

Grinning to himself, Carlyle watched the judge scrunch up her face as she went down the page, line by line. Not a very fast reader either, by the look of things. While the delay continued, his gaze returned to Paul Fassbender. He estimated that the doctor was only fifteen feet from Sands. The inspector could almost feel the waves of hostility radiating from the elderly German as he looked ready to pounce on his nemesis.

'If he causes a disruption,' Carlyle mumbled, 'or tries to attack Sands, I'll have him straight back to the cells at Charing Cross.'

'Don't push your luck, Inspector,' Simpson admonished him. 'We've wasted enough time on this already.'

There's nothing like a bit of support from higher up the food chain, thought Carlyle glumly. Finally, Judge Castor put down her reading and signalled to the defence that they should make themselves heard. The inspector looked on, distinctly unimpressed, as Sands's lawyer got somewhat unsteadily to his feet and began reciting a list of reasons why his client should be allowed bail. The gist of the argument was that Sands had done his worst and posed no further threat to anyone. Under normal circumstances, the inspector would have scoffed at the lot of them; but these were not normal circumstances. Carlyle watched intently as the judge, head bowed, made copious notes. To her left, Fassbender squirmed on his seat, the expression on his face like that of a man being repeatedly pricked by a needle.

He's going to do something stupid, thought Carlyle, more in hope than expectation.

Leaning towards him, Simpson whispered: 'How's the Schaeffer case going?' The inspector began filling her in, only to get an elbow in the ribs for his trouble.

'Ssssh!' the fat man implored. 'I'm trying to listen.'

Carlyle glared angrily at the cheeky sod before bringing his boss up to speed.

'So how are you going to play it?' Simpson whispered after he had finished.

'I think I'll have another talk to the wife first. McQuarrie can stew for a while. If nothing else, we have him for Actual Bodily Harm against five police officers.'

Simpson shook her head. 'That man is a prize idiot.'

'We should always be grateful for prize idiots,' Carlyle replied. 'Think of what our clean-up rates would look like without them.'

'I remember his father.' Simpson removed a piece of lint from the sleeve of her jacket 'Arthur McQuarrie was a complete bastard but at least he had a decent amount of common sense.'

'Yeah.' Carlyle glanced up at the judge. The prosecution now took to the stand and began painting a picture of Daniel Sands as a cross between Jack the Ripper and Carlos the Jackal. Unmoved, Sands himself sat staring into space. 'Kids today, eh?'

'Yes, indeed. All the time, effort and money spent on young George's education and he still turns out to be a useless little git.'

Carlyle adopted the pained visage of the worried parent. 'What can you do?'

'Makes me glad that I never had kids.' Simpson turned to look at the inspector. 'What about you?'

Eh? Where had that come from? 'No regrets at all,' Carlyle said quickly. 'Having Alice was the best thing we ever did, by a million miles.'

'Then you're very lucky, John.'

'I know,' Carlyle smiled, genuinely happy at the thought. 'Alice is doing well. She'll be fine.'

'Good.' Simpson looked as if she wanted to say something else but hesitated. 'By the way,' she said finally, 'I was sorry to hear about your mother. My condolences.'

'Thank you.' Carlyle bit his lip, shocked to realize that he had essentially forgotten about his 'loss'.

Simpson put a gloved hand on his forearm. 'I will come to the funeral, of course.'

'Thank you,' he mumbled. 'I appreciate it.'

Thankfully, their conversation was interrupted by the sharp bang of the judge's gavel.

'Goodness me,' said the fat man, to no one in particular, 'that's a turn-up for the books.'

Carlyle looked up to see Paul Fassbender remonstrating angrily with Sidney Hardy. The lawyer was trying, with no great success, to usher his client towards the exit.

'By the look of it,' the inspector grinned, 'Mr Sands made bail.'

As he approached the door, Fassbender caught sight of the police officers and started cursing in German.

'Paul,' his lawyer remonstrated, 'calm down.'

'Don't push me.' Fassbender waved his index finger angrily past Hardy's right cheek. 'These people,' he shouted, his voice trembling, 'they are the ones to blame.' A couple of journalists pushed past Carlyle, tape recorders aloft, trying to record the show. The inspector resisted the temptation to give one of them a sly kick as they edged by. 'They flout the law. It is shameful. Truly shameful.'

'Go on,' Carlyle murmured to Simpson, keeping his eyes on the furious Fassbender, 'let me nick him.' A restraining hand was clamped on his shoulder.

'Just leave it,' Simpson said firmly as Fassbender was finally hustled out of the door with the hacks in tow. 'Let's not make a difficult situation any worse.'

'All right,' Carlyle conceded, knowing that he'd had his fun. Turning round, he looked back towards the benches at the front – but Daniel Sands had already left.

THIRTY-EIGHT

Walking back through the front doors of the police station, the vague sense of satisfaction that he'd felt at Sands's small victory in front of Judge Castor had evaporated as Carlyle caught sight of his other lost cause – Ronald Connolly. In an instant, the inspector was struck by a mental image of the person he himself might become in twenty years' time – small, unobtrusive, slowly disengaging from the world around him. Pushing the image from his brain, he stopped to let a woman with a buggy go past him on her way out. Connolly, with his back to the door, had not noticed the inspector's arrival. More than a little overdressed for his surroundings in a grey suit, he was sitting, legs crossed, reading a copy of the *Daily Telegraph*, politely ignoring the dosser eyeing him from the bench opposite. It would be easy enough to slip back out without Connolly noticing; go round the side and in the back entrance.

For a moment, he hesitated. Then the drunk stood up, started yammering something incomprehensible and began slapping at the *Telegraph*, trying to get Connolly's attention. The wino's probably a *Guardian* reader, the inspector decided. Recovering the power in his legs, he stepped forward to rescue the old man.

Taking Connolly down to the canteen, Carlyle bought some teas and installed him at a quiet table before running through the latest developments. 'So that's basically where we are,' he concluded, sipping at his green tea. 'You and your wife have to start sucking up to Hilary Green and Westminster Social Services, big time, if you are to avoid the risk of Rebecca perhaps going into care.'

Sipping his English Breakfast blend, Ronald Connolly nodded thoughtfully. Placing his cup back on its saucer, he looked up and asked the question that had brought him down here. 'So you think Iris was behind Julian's death?'

Carlyle shook his head, saying, 'Sorry, but I cannot go into any of the details of the investigation, sir,' replaying the kind of bland stock phrase he'd used a million times in his career.

Connolly stared into his tea, waiting for the 'but'.

'But,' Carlyle said carefully, happy to oblige, 'it would be wrong of me to tell you that anything has been ruled out at this stage. We are still pursuing all possible avenues of enquiry.'

'I understand.' A thin smile crept around the edges of Connolly's mouth. He lifted the cup halfway to his mouth and then put it down again. 'Anna's taken it very badly.'

Carlyle nodded.

'You can imagine – Julian was her son.'

'Yes.'

'She is on quite strong medication. Even so, the things she says about Iris; they never really got on. I don't suppose that is much of a surprise. You know what they say – no mother ever thinks that her daughter-in-law is going to be good enough for her boy.'

'No,' Carlyle agreed, 'I suppose not.'

This time when Connolly lifted his cup he did take another mouthful of tea. 'She is absolutely convinced that Iris is to blame for all this.'

The inspector gave a helpless shrug.

'Which is why,' reaching into the inside pocket of his jacket, Connolly pulled out an envelope stuffed with papers, 'she asked me to bring you this.' He placed the envelope on the table in front of Carlyle.

'What is it?'

'A will. And some insurance policies.'

Carlyle stared at the envelope. *Bloody hell, Umar*, he thought, *you should have picked these up days ago.*

'I haven't looked at them in any detail,' Connolly continued, 'but as far as I can see, everything goes into a trust for Rebecca. Anna is beside herself at the thought that Iris will end up controlling the trust.'

It all comes down to money in the end. 'How much?'

'On the policies?' Connolly let out a long breath. 'Maybe half a million or so.'

Carlyle wondered what the small print said about getting gunned down in a playground. Knowing insurance companies, there would be something.

'Anna thinks Julian's total estate will be worth more than five million, once you sort out the property and the business.'

Five million? That was more than enough of a motive for murder. Carlyle allowed himself a low whistle.

'Death duties will take a chunk, though,' Connolly pointed out.

That still leaves quite enough to lead someone to kill, the inspector reflected. He idly wondered how much he himself was worth dead – a lot less than that.

'How did Mrs Connolly come to have these documents?'

'I'm not sure.' Connolly lowered his gaze. 'I think she had them for safekeeping.'

Mm. Iris Belekhsan would be looking for these. Or maybe she had her own copies. Either way, it was something they would have to quiz her on.

'Anyway,' Connolly went on, as if the idea had just floated into his head that second, 'it's a motive, isn't it?'

Carlyle scooped up the envelope and pushed back his chair. 'Thank you for this. We will take a look.' He got to his feet and waited for Connolly to do the same. 'Now, what I need you to do is liaise with Social Services.' Rummaging around in the pocket of his jeans, he fished out a card belonging to Hilary Green and handed it over. 'Whatever happens with this investigation, the one thing I want to ensure is that Rebecca is not left high and dry.'

Connolly looked like he was going to say something then

thought better of it. Navigating his way between a couple of chairs, he let the inspector shepherd him out.

When Carlyle got home, Helen was sitting on the sofa, reading the evening paper. On the TV, as was her wont, she had the BBC's rolling news channel with the sound muted. Planting himself next to her, Carlyle glanced at the screen. A pretty blonde reporter was standing on the steps of a New York courtroom. She was explaining the latest twist in the case of a French politician who had been arrested for the alleged rape of a hotel chambermaid. The story had been running for weeks; it was like something out of a Tom Wolfe novel.

'God bless the French,' Carlyle chuckled, snuggling up to his wife. 'They can never keep it in their trousers.'

Helen grunted in a manner that suggested the peccadillos of some randy foreigner were not worthy of her attention, at least not when she was busy reading an analysis of the latest humanitarian crisis taking place in the Gaza Strip. Avalon, the medical aid charity for which Helen worked, operated in Gaza – when it was deemed safe enough to do so. Of course, 'safe' was a relative term. Avalon currently had a group of twenty volunteers working in the territory. In the last year, one had been killed and three badly injured. Inevitably it was a serious business that took a considerable physical and emotional toll on all of the staff involved. He let her read on in peace. A couple of minutes later, a huge sigh signalled that she was finished. Helen folded the paper in half and tossed it onto the coffee table. 'So, how was your day?' she asked.

'The usual.'

The news moved on to a report about a games console launch. Helen shot him a look that said, *Is that it?* Normally, Carlyle was quite keen to discuss his cases with his wife – she was insightful and he valued her advice. But occasionally, when things got too much, he tended to clam up. Not good. He knew he should force himself to outline at least one of the problem cases he was currently facing. But which one?

'The thing with the kid isn't getting any better.' Draping his feet over the end of the sofa, Carlyle dropped his head into her lap. Pulling off his glasses, he glanced at the blur of the TV screen. It was impossible to make out what was going on. He liked it better that way. 'It's a total mess.' Helen listened intently, gently stroking his hair, while he explained his unsuccessful attempts to insulate Rebecca Schaeffer from the mess that her parents had created. 'The frustrating thing is that I can see exactly how it's going to play out but there's nothing I can do about it.'

'You just don't have any leverage.'

'I know, but—'

'So you'll just have to wait and see what happens.' Helen leaned over and tenderly kissed him on the crown of his head. 'Maybe the mother had nothing to do with it.'

'Right.' Carlyle snorted.

'If she's a successful dentist,' Helen went on, 'it doesn't sound as if she needs the money.'

Better double-check that, Carlyle thought. He'd never heard of a dentist who wasn't rolling in cash – why else would you spend your whole life looking in other people's mouths? But you never knew. 'Maybe. Whatever. She and the boyfriend are the only suspects we've got.'

Helen resumed stroking his hair. 'And what's the boyfriend like?'

'He's a right thug.' He explained about George McQuarrie resisting arrest and his ruck with the two sergeants.

'Poor Umar. Will he be okay for the wedding?'

Carlyle let his eyelids droop. 'He'll be fine.'

'What should we get them for a present?'

'God. I've no idea. What do you think?'

'Why don't you speak to him about it? There are always things you need when you're first starting out.'

'I suppose,' Carlyle conceded. 'They've been living together for a while, though.'

'Even so.'

'I'll ask him. You know, I had a funny thought today.'

Helen stopped stroking his hair. 'Oh yes?'

Hearing the wariness in her tone, Carlyle hesitated. But it was too late to go back now. 'I wondered if we should think about leaving London.'

She pushed him up. 'You've got to be kidding!'

'It was just a thought; I wasn't—'

Helen jumped to her feet, an annoyed look on her face. 'What the hell would we do out,' she waved her arm in the direction of the window, 'out *there*?'

'It was just a—'

'Don't mention this to Alice, she'd have a fit.'

'I wasn't—'

'For God's sake, John,' she huffed, heading for the door, 'you really do come out with some really stupid stuff sometimes.'

As she disappeared into the kitchen, Carlyle lay back on the sofa, wondering if he should put his glasses back on. After a while, he decided against it.

THIRTY-NINE

'Helen was wondering – what should we get you for a wedding present?'

Stuffing the remains of a croissant into his mouth, Umar chewed for a regulation six, seven, eight seconds before swallowing. Washing it down with a mouthful of coffee, he let out a satisfied sigh.

'Any thoughts?' Carlyle persisted.

'I dunno, really. Maybe I should talk to Christina.'

Christ, how complicated could it be? 'Why don't you email me her mobile number and I'll get Helen to speak to her direct?'

'Good idea.'

'Is everything sorted?'

'Yeah, yeah.' Umar recited the time and the place. 'All you guys have to do is turn up. We'll do the ceremony and then grab some lunch.'

'Sounds good.' Taking a sip of his espresso, Carlyle gave his sergeant the once-over. In the gloom, he looked fine. The bruising had already gone down quite a bit. There shouldn't be a problem on the big day. Even if there was, presumably he could be Photoshopped back into shape.

They were sitting in a cramped booth at the back of the Monmouth Coffee House, just off Seven Dials in the north-west corner of Covent Garden. Carlyle scanned the room, watching a single barista expertly work the trio of red Gaggia Deco machines lined up against the back wall. Feeling the caffeine begin to kick in, he tried to summon up his usual enthusiasm for London life. He feared he would fail – and then he caught the eye of a devastatingly pretty Asian girl, tall and dark, with her shoulder-length black hair swept back into a ponytail. Under a cream mac, with a large black patent-leather handbag slung over the left shoulder, she wore a charcoal-grey business suit and cream blouse, buttoned at the neck. Her heels clacked loudly on the wooden floor, demanding attention. The inspector was not the only man in the place who had clocked her, but he alone had her eye as she made her way towards them.

Maybe London wasn't so bad, after all.

The look on the woman's face hardened as she approached their table. Before he could turn to see what the boss was gawping at, Sergeant Umar Sligo felt a hand on his shoulder.

'Umar?'

Looking up, he jerked away from the woman, spilling coffee all over the table. Carlyle began taking remedial action with a stack of napkins.

'They told me I might find you here,' the woman continued, pulling up a stool and plonking herself down on it. She had a clear Manchester accent. 'I've been looking for you all over the place.' Carlyle tried not to appear too interested as he finished mopping up the coffee.

'Niamh,' Umar stumbled.

'Niamh?'

'This is my boss, Inspector John Carlyle.'

Niamh looked Carlyle up and down. She couldn't have looked any less impressed if he'd just dropped his trousers. 'Whatever.'

Trying not to look too apologetic for his existence, Carlyle dumped some sodden napkins on the table and offered a hand. He held it in mid-air for a few seconds until it was clear that she was not going to shake it.

'This,' Umar gestured, somewhat embarrassed, 'is Niamh, my sister.'

A sister, eh? Carlyle edged forward on his seat, wondering

if some of his sergeant's mysterious backstory was about to be revealed. He looked at the woman. 'Niamh Sligo?'

'Niamh Grieg, actually.' She waved a finger at the inspector to show her wedding band. 'I got married, unlike some people.'

Carlyle turned to Umar, who looked about as comfortable as an endoscopy patient, mid-procedure. The inspector was torn between politeness and curiosity.

As if reading his mind, Niamh Grieg, née Sligo, glared at him. 'I need to talk to my brother.' It struck Carlyle that she was not one of those women who looked good angry. Indeed, his perception of her attractiveness had plummeted from the moment she had opened her mouth. Despite all his better judgement, he actually found himself feeling sorry for Umar. Sucking the last dregs from his espresso, he returned the demitasse to its saucer. 'We're actually on duty at the moment,' he said smugly.

'What?' Niamh glanced around. 'In here? You're just having a coffee.'

Umar stared at the floor, in traditional *I wish the ground would swallow me up* pose. Leaning across the table, Carlyle tried not to grin as he said quietly, 'We're undercover.' Still looking down, Umar half-stifled a laugh.

Screwing up her face, Niamh managed to make herself look even less attractive. It was one of the most remarkable transformations Carlyle had ever seen. 'Bollocks!' she snapped. 'You're just bunking off.'

Carlyle quickly scanned the room. At the table by the door, less than twenty feet away, a pair of white-haired grannies were sitting nattering away in a foreign language over their guidebooks.

'See those two by the door?' he whispered.

Niamh followed his gaze. 'Yeah.'

'Suspected people traffickers.'

Umar coughed.

'No way.' Niamh looked more than doubtful. 'They're just two old ladies.'

Carlyle scoffed. 'It's a great disguise, don't you think? They bring in young girls from . . . er . . . Romania, promise them visas, jobs, working in places like this and then make them turn tricks.' *Turn tricks* – a crass Americanism. He stole a glance at Umar who was now gripping the table tightly, looking like he was about to piss himself. *Breathe, boy, breathe.* 'We've been trailing them for over a year now. So far, this is as close as we've ever got.'

Umar composed himself enough to chime in, 'It's true.'

'If we lose them,' Carlyle continued, unable to resist gilding the lily, 'we'll be in deep trouble. Thousands of man hours have gone into this investigation.'

Clearly unconvinced, Niamh looked from sergeant to inspector and back again. 'So,' she said finally, 'should I go?'

A wave of relief passed over Umar's face. 'Yes.'

But Carlyle hissed to the girl before she could get up: 'No, *no*. Stay put, for God's sake. Don't draw attention to us.' Umar shot him a dirty look but he ignored it. 'Keep talking to your brother. What did you want to ask him about?'

Niamh returned her gaze to her brother and the matter in hand. 'Sandra wants to know what's going on.'

She's not the only one, Carlyle thought. He made a show of staring at the grannies, who were now consulting a copy of *Time Out*.

'How many times?' Umar complained. 'I've told her what's going on.'

'Well,' Niamh replied, 'she doesn't think that you've told her anything.'

'And you came all the way down here to tell me that?'

'Tony is down here for a conference. I tagged along.'

Umar looked at the inspector, who kept his own counsel. By the door, the grannies were packing up their books and getting ready to leave.

Niamh followed Carlyle's gaze. 'Don't you have to follow them?'

'Nah.' Carlyle watched one of the old ladies wave to the barista as they walked out. 'The team outside will do that.'

'Anyway,' Niamh continued, 'Sandra still thinks that you and she are getting married.'

'You what?'

'So do Mum and Dad.' Eyes blazing, the bearer of bad news seemed to be rather enjoying her brother's discomfort.

'But I've told her a million times . . .'

'Well, Umar,' she patted his hand patronizingly, 'she obviously hasn't got the message. She's coming round for dinner with Mum and Dad and Tony and me on Saturday night – maybe you should come up and sort it out.' Getting to her feet, she swung her bag over her shoulder, nearly knocking the head off the guy sitting at the next table. 'Anyway, I've done my bit. Now I can get on with my shopping.' She shot Carlyle a withering look. 'And *you* can get back to your white slavery ring or whatever it is.'

Niamh Sligo walked out of the door of the Coffee House, hesitated and then turned left, no doubt heading for the consumerist delights of the West End. Letting out a long breath, Carlyle counted to ten before turning to his sergeant.

'So that was your sister?'

Umar had to think about it for a moment before nodding. 'Yeah.'

'And who's Sandra?'

'An old girlfriend, up north.' Umar stared unhappily into his empty cup. 'I finished with her ages ago.'

Carlyle stared at him intently.

'Well, a while ago.'

'What about Christina?'

'What about her?'

'Does she know about all this?'

Umar shook his head.

'Well,' said Carlyle, happy to adopt the elder statesman role now that the opportunity had presented itself, 'I suppose there's no need to trouble her with that, what with everything else that's going on.' He tried not to grin, failing miserably. 'Even so, it looks like you've got a few loose ends to tie up before your wedding.'

* * *

Abigail Slater gave Carlyle her standard 'look' – a noxious mixture of disgust and amusement that made her nostrils quiver. The inspector thought back to the untimely demise of her erstwhile boyfriend Christian Holyrod and his lips twitched.

'Is something amusing you?' Slater demanded.

Carlyle's grin grew wider. 'Not really.'

'Good.' Slater straightened the papers on the desk in front of her. 'Then maybe we can begin.' They were sitting in the offices of Stiff, Smithers & Mongolsson, in a room identical to the one he'd been in before, maybe even the same one. Slater was flanked by Iris Belekhsan and Kieron Sterling. Today, the young assistant, resplendent in an Ozwald Boateng two-button mauve suit, had passed on the earring.

Out of the window, Carlyle watched a trio of red cranes hauling some iron girders into position at a building site in the City. Despite the travel eating up more of his day, he had been happy to schlep back to SS&M. This was a conversation best not had at the station. He rolled his pre-printed ID badge into a tube and tapped it on the table. 'First things first,' he said, not looking up. 'Your client has to surrender her passport or she will be deemed a flight risk.'

'That is completely unnecessary,' Slater scoffed, 'as you well know.'

The inspector focused on Belekhsan. She held his gaze with a cool look that gave little away. Two, three seconds passed before she reached over and opened the zip of her handbag on the floor.

'Iris.' Slater put a hand on her arm. 'That will not be necessary.' Belekhsan shrugged it off with more than a hint of irritation.

'It is nothing.' After several seconds of rummaging, she pulled out one of the new-style British passports and tossed it across the table. 'Here.'

Carlyle stuck out his left hand to stop it skidding off the table and onto the floor. 'Thank you.' Opening it up, he checked the details.

Iris Ada Morin Belekhsan.

Thirty-four years old.

The passport had only been renewed six months earlier.

He looked at it carefully. It told him nothing. 'Did you get this for your holiday?'

A brusque nod was all he got in reply.

'Okay.' Carlyle shoved the passport into his jacket pocket. 'Let's get down to it.' He knew that he couldn't trust Slater one inch. But he could appeal to her self-interest and that of her client. 'We will need to have a formal conversation at the police station very soon.' Carlyle paused as Sterling began scribbling on a yellow A4 pad. 'First, however, I wanted to discuss some things off the record.'

Slater looked at him slyly. 'And what might these "things" be?'

'It has to be *completely* off the record.' Carlyle nodded at the pad. 'With just you and your client.'

'Very well. Kieron, if you wouldn't mind . . .' The associate was already out of his seat and halfway to the door. Clearly, the youngster was used to getting kicked out of meetings when they started becoming interesting.

Looking around the room, Carlyle waited for the aide to leave and the door to close behind him. 'And you are not making any recording of this conversation?'

'My, my, we are paranoid today, aren't we?' Slater licked her lips. 'This had better be good, Inspector. But, no, for the non-existent record, there are no recordings of this conversation being made.'

'Okay.' He would just have to take her word for it, however uncomfortable that made him feel. He looked at each woman in turn, trying to at least give off a vague vibe that he knew what he was doing. 'As you may know, George McQuarrie was taken into custody last night.'

'Yes, of course we knew that,' Slater said impatiently.

From Belekhsan, however, he began to detect the first signs of unease.

'I expect that he will be charged in the morning.'

'With what?' Slater demanded.

'With a range of things,' Carlyle said blandly. He focused his gaze exclusively on Belekhsan who, this time, would not meet his eye. 'I believe we have enough to link him to the shooting of Julian Schaeffer.' It was an outright lie but he hoped that he could get them to a position where they believed it too.

Slater stroked her chin thoughtfully. 'I will be interested in seeing the evidence.'

Ignoring her, Carlyle moved on to his pitch. 'On that basis,' he said, 'I can do one of two things.' Finally, Belekhsan looked at him. 'Either I can arrest you as well, for conspiracy to murder, in anticipation of Mr McQuarrie implicating you, which I am sure that he will do.' There were definite signs of concern in those dark eyes now. 'Or you can get your retaliation in first, as it were, and lay it out for me, explaining how the whole thing happened and how Mr McQuarrie was the driving force behind the shooting of your husband.'

Sitting back in his chair, he folded his arms and waited for their response.

FORTY

A cold wind gusted off the Thames, causing Umar to shiver. Standing amidst a group of maybe twenty yachts in the marina at St Katherine's Docks, he looked up at Tower Bridge which had been opened to let some naval ship head further upriver. Even at this distance, he could make out the lines of traffic queuing on the south side of the bridge, and the odd, futile blast of horn made its way towards him on the wind.

The sergeant was feeling sorry for himself. Not only did he have his family problems to deal with, but the inspector had dumped the Ayumi Ninomiya case on his desk as well. With Savage still enjoying the hospitality of the Stanley Bowles Ward at UCH, Umar was left to track down the remaining sugar daddies that the girl had met through the Leafhopper website. After four hours chasing his tail, he had managed to rule out one of the three outstanding men – a banker who admitted meeting Ayumi once but then ditched her because, quote unquote, 'her tits weren't big enough'. Of the two that were left, one was a film financier who was apparently in Los Angeles on business. That left Ivan Borloo, a 'green entrepreneur', whatever that was, who ran a consultancy called NoN (Now or Never).

Umar had presented himself at NoN's suitably fashionable Spitalfields offices to be told that Mr Borloo was rarely present. Indeed, looking across the large open-plan space that NoN rented, the sergeant counted twenty desks, all of which were empty. The only member of staff on duty – a pretty red-haired receptionist called Valerie – was more than happy to chat.

'So where is everyone?' Umar asked.

'Oh,' said Valerie, 'the consultants aren't tied to their desks. They spend most of their time on the road.'

'What do they do, exactly?'

'Not sure,' Valerie said merrily, as if it were a feather in her cap to be oblivious to whatever it was her employer was actually selling. In her early twenties, she sounded like she was from South Africa. Under her Chipmunk T-shirt, she looked very pert indeed.

Umar found himself smiling brightly, until he remembered that he was in enough trouble already. 'Is the business doing well?' he asked, taking a precautionary step away from the reception desk.

Valerie looked at him blankly. 'I've no idea.'

'But Mr Dorloo's loaded, isn't he?'

'Oh yeah. But that's the family money. His family made a killing in uranium mining.'

'Nice.'

'And now he's trying to give something back.'

'Uh-huh?'

'That's why he lives on his boat.'

Obviously.

Shivering, Umar cursed the fact that he didn't have an overcoat. To his left, an almost empty tourist boat made sluggish progress as it headed towards Docklands and the Thames Barrier. As he walked along the jetty, reading off the names of the various boats – *Milky J, Bertie's Delight, Lunar Lady*, a series of 30-, 40- and 60-foot single-mast yachts – he thought about Niamh's unscheduled appearance in Seven Dials. If it wasn't for the fact that Inspector Carlyle took such obvious delight in his discomfort – he was a bit of a bastard like that – Umar would have been worried about his charmless sister mouthing off in front of his boss. The question was, should he take her advice and go up to Manchester at the weekend? Try to sort out the situation once and for all?

When confronted with a seemingly intractable problem, Umar liked to try and break it down into manageable parts. In this case, he placed the ex-girlfriend on one side of the ledger and his parents on the other. He felt annoyed about Sandra. They had gone out together for the best part of three years. To be frank, that had been about the best part of three years longer than he had originally envisaged dating her. With the benefit of hindsight, he could see that he had left it too long to pull the plug. However, he hadn't counted on Sandra Norris's tenacity. He must have sat her down and told her what was happening at least four times. On each occasion, however, she would simply reappear a week later as if nothing had changed.

In the end, he had opted for a drastic course of action. One of the reasons he had come to London was to make it clear that they were over. After more than a year, Sandra continued to peddle the myth that somehow they were couple. Of course, she had a willing audience in his parents, who both thought he should have been married long ago, living in Prestbury or some other Cheshire bolthole, with a rapidly expanding brood.

Umar was a little embarrassed that he hadn't mentioned the London wedding to his folks – hadn't even mentioned Christina – but he knew that if he did, they would just give him endless grief. Better to present them with a fait accompli once it was all done and dusted.

He shook his head angrily. Umar liked to think that he was a fairly laid-back kind of a guy, but it irritated him beyond belief that he was unable to escape the dead hand of other people's expectations. *Why can't they just live their own lives*, he wondered. For a moment, he considered the scene around the dinner table if he broke the news – 'I'm marrying my American girlfriend' . . . no, 'I'm marrying my *pole dancer* American girlfriend in London, who just happens to be *eight and a half months' pregnant*.'

The thought of tossing that little hand grenade into a pot of his mother's stew made him grin guiltily, leavening his dark mood, at least for a couple of seconds.

Maybe he could even take Christina with him.

No, no, no, don't get too carried away. That could cause a riot.

He was suddenly conscious of music coming from one of the boats, some kind of Techno that he didn't recognize. Easing out of his own problems he turned his attention back to the boats – *Lucky Dollar*, *Crazy Dog*, *Anne Sinclair* . . .

Anne Sinclair.

The music was coming from the cabin of Ivan Borloo's boat, which was just a short distance from where he was standing. Umar tried to peer inside but it was small and dark and impossible to see who was there.

'Hello?' His words were carried away on the wind.

'*Hello?*'

Still no response.

He looked down at the small platform on the back of the boat, maybe three feet from the jetty. Should he jump on? He wasn't sure he wanted to risk it. Up above, to some appreciative honks from the traffic, Tower Bridge began lowering. He was still girding his loins for the leap onto the boat when a small figure appeared from the cabin. Despite the chill, she was wearing only a pair of Guess jeans and a white cotton vest with a massive Armani Jeans logo emblazoned on the front. Standing upright, she took an extended toke on a massive joint and smiled at the sergeant.

'Hi,' she giggled, offering him the joint.

Umar shook his head. He had never been much of a smoker.

Suddenly feeling the cold, she shivered.

Umar gestured towards the cabin. 'It's freezing out here, Ayumi. Let's go inside.'

Carlyle looked at the number on the screen of his phone – Umar. Ignoring the call, he dropped the handset back in the breast pocket of his jacket.

Abigail Slater decided that they had all sat in silence long enough. She had not even made the pretence of needing to discuss his offer with her client. 'I think,' she said, 'that we will need some time to consider this.'

Keeping his gaze on Iris Belekhsan, Carlyle said, 'I'm sorry. The investigation is moving along at its own pace now. The evidence will be presented to the DPP and then the matter is completely out of my hands.' Turning back to Slater, he made a hopeless gesture with his hands. 'And I know,' he added, almost as if it were an afterthought, 'that Social Services are ready to take Rebecca into care this evening if your client is arrested.'

Slater's eyes narrowed. 'Is that a threat, Inspector?'

'Of course not.' Carlyle tried to look offended. 'It is just another factor that has to be taken into consideration . . .'

'That's enough.' As if waking from her stupor, Iris Belekhsan slapped a palm on the table.

'Iris,' Slater protested.

'Shut up, Abigail!' Belekhsan reared up. Carlyle smiled; he was beginning to like Iris just fine. Slater glowered at Carlyle but said nothing. 'George will try and pin it all on me, for sure. As the inspector says, I might as well get my retaliation in first.'

The sun was shining and it was a very pleasant twenty-one degrees. The inspector had clear ideas about the optimum temperature for London living: anything below fifteen degrees was too cold; above twenty-five was too hot. This was a city built for around twenty, which it got, God knows, all too rarely. When the weather was right, however, everything else seemed to follow; tourists were less of a nuisance, waiters were friendlier, the traffic moved relatively freely – even his caseload seemed to lighten.

Today, however, there was no 'seemed to' about it. Sitting outside the Café Lido on Charing Cross Road only a few hours after Iris Belekhsan had comprehensively grassed up her boyfriend, Carlyle was feeling pretty pleased with himself. His main outstanding cases seemed to have sorted themselves out, which was a major result. The dramas of the last few days were drawing to a close and for once, his desk was relatively clear.

He looked over at Alice, greedily sucking on a can of Diet Coke, and said, 'Don't tell your mother.' He sometimes thought that Helen was more worried about their daughter having fizzy drinks than she ever had been about her doing drugs. It was an exaggeration, but not really that much of one.

Alice nodded and continued slurping away. Half-term beckoned. The inspector wondered whether they should try to get away to Brighton for a few days. They could stay with Helen's mother. It was a bit of a squeeze, but doable; he would have to be on his best behaviour but he was sure he could manage it for forty-eight hours or so – thirty-six at least.

Finishing his double espresso, he contemplated ordering another. But there was no point in being too wired. Maybe he should have a green tea instead. Still in two minds, he placed his demitasse on the saucer, sat back and closed his eyes, listening to the comforting hum of the city.

'*Real men take NO for an answer.*'

'*My dress can't say yes.*'

The inspector opened his eyes as a group of maybe a hundred scantily clad women of various ages turned the corner of Shaftesbury Avenue and began marching down the middle of the road, in the direction of Trafalgar Square. Traffic quickly began backing up in each direction. The inevitable cacophony of horns started up and there were a number of distinctly un-PC comments directed at the protestors from a group of teenage boys leering on the pavement.

'*Jesus loves sluts.*'

Carlyle scanned the crowd for Electra Hutton-Sunningdale. If she was there, however, he couldn't make her out. Scattered among the protestors were a few men, looking suitably sheepish. He caught sight of a banner that said *Sluts Pay Taxes* and laughed out loud. Alice shot him a look.

'Shouldn't you do something?' She seemed embarrassed by the whole thing.

'Me?'

'Aren't they breaking the law, marching down the street like that?'

Carlyle shrugged. He couldn't give a monkey's. Personally

speaking, he was quite happy for women to parade in the middle of the street in their smalls as often as they liked.

'It's, like, the second one they've done this week.'

'I'm not a traffic cop,' said Carlyle grumpily, signalling to the waiter for another espresso. The crowd was now passing the café. A large blonde woman in a pink bra and lime-green lycra cycling shorts stepped over to their table and handed Alice a leaflet.

'Thank you,' said Alice, suddenly English politeness personified.

'Why don't you come and join us?' The woman glared at Carlyle as she made the invitation.

'*Leave her alone,*' he wanted to say. '*I'm her father.*' But he kept his mouth shut.

Blushing, Alice shook her head and took another mouthful of Coke. To Carlyle's relief, the woman moved on. Alice scanned the leaflet, reading aloud: '*We are protesting against a culture that is too lenient when it comes to rape and sexual assault . . . that shames women for behaving in a healthy and sexual way.*' She looked enquiringly at her father.

'Wear what you like,' Carlyle told her. 'But keep up with the karate lessons.'

Alice nodded and went back to reading the leaflet.

The demonstration moved on. Already he had to struggle to make out the protestors as the rest of the city closed in around them.

'What do *you* think?' he asked his daughter.

Scrunching up the leaflet, Alice dropped it into the empty ashtray. 'I think,' she declared, 'that I don't want to walk down the street in my underwear.'

While his daughter went off to Charing Cross Road library, Carlyle walked over to the station. As he jogged up the front steps, he was nearly knocked over by Umar coming the other way.

'Sorry,' Umar shouted, not slowing his pace, 'gotta go. Christina's waters have broken.'

'But—'

'I know, I know.' There was a look of genuine fear on the sergeant's face. Stopping at the foot of the steps, he hopped from foot to foot. 'She's more than two weeks early. I thought that your first kid was always supposed to be late?'

'You never know.'

'Anyway, I'll give you a call.'

'Okay.'

'Oh, and the Ninomiyas are on the second floor.'

'Which room?'

'Don't worry.' Umar waited for a taxi to pass and skipped across the road. 'You'll hear 'em.'

'Let me know if we can help with anything,' Carlyle shouted after him, but he was gone.

Carlyle was surprised to see Simpson standing outside Meeting Room 6, arms folded, listening to the angry voices inside, yammering away in Japanese.

'Did you see Sergeant Sligo?' she asked, by way of greeting.

Carlyle nodded. He gestured at the door. 'How long has this been going on?'

'About twenty minutes.' Simpson raised her eyes to the heavens. 'His relief at finding his daughter was quickly superseded by anger at the way she has behaved.'

'To be honest,' Carlyle said, 'I can understand where he's coming from.'

The shouting went up another couple of decibels. By the sound of things, Ayumi was giving as good as she got.

'How could she disappear for so long without anyone having a clue where she was?'

'According to the statement she gave Umar, she and her boyfriend went sailing round the Med and only got back the day before yesterday.'

Carlyle tutted. 'What about her bloody mobile phone?'

'Dropped it over the side, apparently. She didn't know anyone was looking for her, so didn't bother to call her flatmate or her dad.'

'Great.'

'I know.' The look of abject frustration on Simpson's face told him that she was working out how much police time and money had been wasted on this particular wild-goose chase.

'Ah well. At least it's a happy ending. Imagine if we'd found her dead in a gutter somewhere.' As if on cue, the shouting from the meeting room subsided.

'Now that they've finished playing Happy Families,' said Simpson, already walking away, 'get the loose ends tied up and get them out of here. I don't need to see the final report.'

As the Commander disappeared through the set of double doors at the end of the corridor, the shouting started up again. *Bloody Umar*, thought Carlyle grumpily, *leaving me holding the baby*. Bracing himself, he reached for the door handle.

FORTY-ONE

'What's this?' Helen held up a scrap of paper with a user-name and a login ID scribbled on it. He had dropped it onto the kitchen counter, along with the rest of the contents of his pockets. Knowing exactly what it was, Carlyle tried not to blush.

'It's a login for a website called Leafhopper.' Cursing himself for not shredding it earlier, he quickly explained the backstory of Ayumi Ninomiya, Ivor Jenkinson, the owner of site, and Ivan Borloo, Ayumi's sugar daddy.

'Hmm.' Helen stared at the bit of paper.

Adjusting his tie, Carlyle tried to remind himself that he'd done nothing wrong. He tried not to feel guilty or look shifty.

Helen let him stew in his own juices for several seconds. Not for the first time, he thought that she would have made the better cop of the two of them. 'And . . .' she said finally, 'have you given it a go?'

'Huh?' Staring at his shoes, he could no longer prevent the blush. 'No, no.' He forced his head up, conscious of the nervous smile playing across his lips. 'We found the girl. It wasn't necessary.'

'No?' She gave him a superior look.

'No,' he said firmly.

'I suppose,' she said, trying not to grin herself, 'that you don't really have the *sugar* to be a sugar daddy, do you?' She slipped the piece of paper into her jacket and stepped over to straighten his tie. 'Anyway, c'mon. We have to get going.'

Father Maciuszek doubtless did his best, but the funeral service for Lorna Gordon was feeble at best. A twenty-something Polish virgin talking solemnly about people he knew not and things he could not possibly comprehend. Aside from family, there were only two other mourners in the gloom of St Wulstan's – an ancient-looking woman who Carlyle suspected was a full-time funeral attendee, and Ken Walton. Walton was an avuncular man in his seventies who had been his mother's boyfriend for a while when she split from his dad. Despite her promise, Commander Simpson hadn't made it.

The whole thing took a total of thirty-five minutes.

It seemed like an eternity.

The mood was grim, rather than sad. If his mother had been watching, she would probably have lapped it up. As the curtains closed, and the coffin lurched off towards the gas fires, Carlyle went to loosen his tie, only to be stopped by a harsh look from Helen to his left. On his right, Alice looked down blankly at the words of Psalm 94. The whole thing seemed utterly pointless. It struck him that he'd never been to a funeral that hadn't been profoundly depressing. Maybe, when his time came, if he wasn't allowed into Highgate Cemetery, he should get Helen to have him cremated immediately. No mess, no fuss and everyone just goes on with their lives.

Getting to his feet, he took his wife by the arm and they began walking out at a suitably funereal pace. Behind them, he was surprised to see his father fall in with Ken Walton and begin chatting in what seemed like a friendly manner. 'I hope he's not inviting him to the wake,' he whispered to Helen.

'Why not?' She squeezed his arm in gentle reproach. 'It's good that they can talk – very mature.'

'A bit late for that,' Carlyle grumbled as he stepped towards the light.

The wake was held in an upstairs room of a nearby pub called the Sinking Ship. It had been chosen by his father. Carlyle had no doubt that the Palm Court of the Ritz Hotel would have been more to Lorna's taste but, hey, she wasn't here. As he suspected would happen, Ken Walton tagged along, so the five of them – Carlyle, Helen, Alice, his father and Walton – sat down to the worst of 'traditional' English pub fare of tinned tomato soup followed by roast beef and boiled potatoes.

Ignoring the hostile glances of his wife, Carlyle took refuge at the end of the table with a pint of Stella Artois. He was contemplating a second pint when he remembered that he hadn't switched his phone back on after the service. Christina must have been in labour for about twenty hours by now, and he wondered how Umar was getting on. He grinned to himself as he keyed in the security code. Immediately the phone started buzzing in his hand. The screen informed him that he had four missed calls.

'John,' Helen complained, picking at a boiled carrot. Alice had her head in a book about vampires. The old men ate slowly, methodically, in complete silence.

Dialling his voicemail, Carlyle held up a hand. 'Sorry. I think it might be Umar, about the baby.' There was only one new message.

'Inspector, I thought we had an agreement. What the hell is going on? Call me immediately.'

Deleting the angry voice of Abigail Slater, Carlyle put his phone away. A spasm of pain went through his abdomen as the Stella mixed with the beef. It sounded like his deal with Iris Belekhsan was coming apart at the seams. That might explain why Simpson wasn't at the funeral. He needed to get back to the station to see what was going on and whether there was anything he could do about it.

Jumping to his feet, he jogged round the table and told his wife: 'Sorry, work crisis.'

Helen's face darkened.

His father placed his knife and fork carefully on to the plate. 'Is it something serious?'

''Fraid so, Dad,' Carlyle nodded, grateful to the old fella for helping him out.

Alexander smiled. 'You'd better get going then. I'll settle up for this lot.'

'Thanks.' Carlyle quickly shook Walton by the hand and gave Alice a peck on the forehead. Then he placed a hand on his father's shoulder and gave it a squeeze. 'And thanks for sorting all this. I think it went well.'

Looking down at his plate, his father's face was blank. 'Yes. I think we gave her a good send-off.'

Carlyle glanced at Helen but she was still glowering at him so he quickly looked away. 'You're right, Dad,' he lied, squeezing Alexander's shoulder again. 'I think we did.'

Carlyle headed back to the station at a steady clip. Not wanting to be buttonholed again by Abigail Slater, he nipped in through a side entrance. Approaching the front desk from the rear, he sidled up to Angie Middleton who, as usual, had her head stuck in some celebrity magazine.

'Ange,' he hissed. Flipping the page, the desk sergeant didn't look up. He crept closer to the desk. 'ANGE.'

'Eek!' Middleton jumped an inch into the air. 'What are you doing?' she squealed. 'Creeping up on me like that; you'll give me a heart attack.'

'Sorry,' Carlyle said meekly. 'Where's Simpson?'

She looked at him suspiciously. It was not a question that you often heard from the inspector. 'Upstairs. On the third floor, I think.'

'Ta.' Carlyle wheeled around and walked right into Abigail Slater.

She pushed him away angrily. 'Where the hell have you been?'

He thought about mentioning his mother's funeral but decided against it. You didn't play for sympathy with someone like Slater. 'Where's Iris?'

'Downstairs,' Middleton interjected. 'She's scheduled to be taken to Holloway later this afternoon.'

Damn. Things really were slipping away from him. Slater

started to say something but he held up a hand. 'Stay here,' he said, trying to inject some authority into his voice. 'Let me see what I can find out. I will be back in five minutes.' He turned back to Middleton. 'Ange, can you arrange some tea for Ms Slater?' The desk sergeant gave him a *get it yourself* look but he faced her down. 'I'll be right back.'

The inspector found Simpson in a meeting room overlooking the courtyard. She was on her mobile when he burst in. He hesitated in the doorway but she signalled for him to come in and sit down, while she finished her call.

'He's just arrived now.' She looked at Carlyle while talking into the handset. There was an excited burst of chatter from the other end of the line.

'Well, he *was* burying his mother.' She rolled her eyes to the ceiling.

Cremating her actually, Carlyle thought.

'So you should try and cut him some slack. Whatever's happened, the DPP have made their decision; it's a matter for them now.'

Carlyle's heart sank. If the Director of Public Prosecutions had decided to go ahead and charge Iris Belekhsan, it was game over for his attempts to save Rebecca from the clutches of Westminster Social Services.

More indistinct chatter emerged from the handset.

Simpson began to look really annoyed. 'You know about Slater as well as I do, sir. Whatever claims are being made, the fact is that the inspector has run this case professionally and expeditiously. He has done a great job.'

Carlyle tried to look modest. But it was true, wasn't it? He was the one who had made the connection between Belekhsan and McQuarrie. After that, it all came together quite nicely, whatever the collateral damage.

After patting himself on the back, he tuned back into the conversation.

'*I* will deal with Ms Slater,' Simpson was saying with what seemed like genuine relish. 'Yes, of course I will keep you fully informed. No, there will be no fallout, I can guarantee it. Okay. Good. Thank you.'

Finally, she ended the call and dropped the handset on the table. 'Who was that?'

'The Deputy Commissioner.' Simpson didn't say which one. 'He's been getting earache from Abigail Slater about your "deal" with Iris Belekhsan.' She frowned. 'What the hell were you doing?'

Carlyle tried to look nonplussed. Hadn't she just said he'd done a great job? 'I just wanted to try and make sure the daughter was looked after in all of this.'

'For Christ's sake, John.' She picked the handset off the table and for a moment he thought she was going to chuck it at his head. 'You can't try to do a deal with someone suspected of employing a bloody hit man to kill her husband.'

'That's one way of looking at it.'

'It's the only way of looking at it,' Simpson thundered.

Digging in, Carlyle folded his arms. 'Look . . .'

Simpson cut him off with a wave of her hand. 'And with Abigail Slater, of all people. I know you think that she's some kind of joke after what happened with the mayor . . .'

Despite everything, Carlyle grinned. Happy memories.

'But she still has access to a lot of people. She can cause plenty of trouble.'

'It was a perfectly reasonable approach.'

'Not the way she tells it.'

Well aware that Slater might try to drop him in it, he had his story ready. 'You and I both know that George McQuarrie was probably the instigator of the Julian Schaeffer killing, thinking that he could make some serious money out of it. The kid has already lost one parent. Social Services won't let her stay with her grandparents. Should I really just toss her into Care, saying "tough luck"?'

Simpson said crossly, 'You really do take your damned pragmatism too far sometimes, don't you?'

Carlyle waved a hand in the air. 'Why does no one care about what happens to Rebecca?'

'That is just not your problem,' Simpson insisted. 'McQuarrie's statement clearly implicates Belekhsan.'

McQuarrie's statement? *You should have left that to me.* Carlyle groaned. 'Who did the interview?'

'Thomas.' Chief Inspector Lesley Thomas was a twenty-year veteran who had worked out of Charing Cross for the last three years. Carlyle didn't know her that well but he knew she had a good rep as a solid cop. 'I've watched the video. It was always going to be enough for the DPP.'

'But still, that's not the matter in hand.'

'It is, as far as they're concerned,' said Simpson patiently. 'Think of it from their point of view: if they tried to let Belekhsan skate, they'd get chopped up into little pieces in court, never mind the newspapers.'

'So what about the Connollys?' Carlyle knew that he sounded like a pig-headed fifteen year old, but he kept going.

'You know the various different issues that Westminster Social Services have with Mr and Mrs Connolly.'

The inspector gave a reluctant nod.

'She is not currently deemed fit and his age and medical history are also issues.'

'Medical history?'

'He had a minor stroke a couple of years ago.'

'He looked fit enough to me,' was all Carlyle could think of to say.

Simpson got to her feet, signalling that her patience was not infinite. 'Well, I suppose we should all be grateful that you're not a doctor then, shouldn't we?'

Unable to manage a smile, Carlyle stood up, too. 'So that's it?'

'Chief Inspector Thomas will oversee the final report for the DPP,' was Simpson's final word on the matter.

The inspector nodded.

'And, as I told the Deputy Commissioner, I will look after Abigail Slater.'

'Thanks.' Genuinely grateful, he didn't feel the need to ask the Commander what she had in mind.

Simpson gestured towards the door. 'You've had a hell of a lot on your plate recently, John. Maybe you should take a few days off.'

'Good idea.' This time Carlyle did manage a smile. 'Maybe I will.' He thought about Inspector Sophie Watkins and Savage and Umar, all of them off for one reason or another. Bloody hell, at this rate the station wouldn't have anyone left. But they would cope; they always did.

FORTY-TWO

Standing in the Tesco on Garrick Street, Carlyle thoughtfully eyed the bottles of spirits lined up on the shelf just above his head. Not a great drinker, he hadn't kept a bottle of Jameson's at home for at least a couple of months. Still, needing to unwind, he had an inkling that a little drink might go down nicely this evening.

To aid his decision-making process, the supermarket was offering a fiver off a bottle. 'What's not to like?' he mumbled to himself as he placed one in his basket, alongside a bunch of bananas and a jumbo pack of Jaffa Cakes. Joining the self-service queue, he looked up at the rolling news playing on the TV hanging from the ceiling. A ticker along the bottom of the screen informed him that French police had arrested a dozen fishermen accused of smuggling illegal immigrants into the UK. Maybe that was how they got Fassbender in, Carlyle mused. In truth, he didn't care much one way or the other. Border security was not one of his great passions.

Returning his attention to the basket, the inspector was belatedly struck by the random and, frankly, rather dissolute nature of its contents. Not wanting to be subjected to an inquest into his eccentric choice of purchases when he got home, he decided to ring Helen and see if there was anything else they needed at home. Putting the basket on the floor, he fumbled for his phone. Pulling up his wife's number, he hit call just as the handset started vibrating in his hand.

'Helen?'

'Hello?'

Bollocks. Carlyle realized that he had mistakenly taken the incoming call. 'What is it, Ange?'

For once the desk sergeant was all business. 'You need to get over to Belgrave Square – quick.'

The inspector arrived to a cacophony of horns. A corner of the square had been taped off and traffic was backed up in all directions. The rush-hour was in full swing and the mood was turning ugly as drivers began to comprehend the severity of the delay.

Inside the police cordon, he counted more than a dozen emergency vehicles. A uniform intercepted him as he ducked under the tape but Carlyle quickly flashed his ID and was allowed to proceed.

'Inspector!'

It took him a moment to recognize one of the uniforms who had been on duty on Rosebery Avenue when Pippa Collingwood had been run down by a mail van.

'What happened?'

'Two old guys started going at it in the middle of the road.' The PC gestured towards the white screens that had already been set up on a section of pavement. 'One of them had a knife.'

Carlyle's gaze followed a trail of blood snaking across the paving stones, trickling into the gutter. Nearby, a pair of paramedics were in deep discussion by the side of an ambulance. Their lack of urgency told its own story. Leaving the constable to try and keep the gawkers at bay, he walked over to the screens and peered inside.

The body lay in the recovery position, although all attempts at resuscitation had clearly failed. Squatting down, the inspector looked directly into the dead man's face. Was there a wry smile on his lips – or was he just imagining it?

A female forensics technician appeared at the gap in the screens. 'Sir,' she said politely, 'I need you to step outside.'

'Of course.' Carlyle slowly stood up.

'We haven't made an ID yet.' The woman pointed at the body with a latex-sheathed finger. 'Do you know him?'

'Yeah.' Carlyle did not go into any further detail.

'Nasty business,' the woman observed. 'The knife was still in his chest when we got here – it was driven almost all the way through his body.'

'Crime of passion,' Carlyle mumbled.

The tech looked at him blankly.

'What kind of knife was it?'

'Small kitchen knife. Looked expensive. The kind you get from Heal's or John Lewis. Serrated blade. Yellow handle.'

Carlyle thought back to the collection of knives in Daniel Sands's flat. 'Where is the other guy?'

'They're treating him in one of the ambulances. He's only got minor injuries, as far as I know.'

Carlyle nodded. 'Has he been arrested yet?'

'No idea.'

'Okay, thanks.' Taking one last look at the corpse sprawled on the pavement, he turned and walked away.

In charge of the scene was a detective inspector from Victoria called Paula Willmer. Carlyle knew her in passing, although, as far as he could recall, they had never actually worked together. Standing next to a police Range Rover, talking on her mobile, Willmer caught sight of him as he approached, signalling that she was just wrapping up her conversation.

Carlyle hovered at a respectful distance, staring at the tarmac in an attempt to keep all of the surrounding chaos at bay.

Finishing the call, Willmer stuffed the phone back into the breast pocket of her jacket. 'What are you doing here?' she asked.

'It's my case,' said Carlyle, 'kind of.'

'Really?' Willmer's face brightened. 'You mean you're going to take it off my hands?'

'If you don't mind.'

'Mind? Are you kidding? I'd be delighted.' She looked as if

she might spring forward and give him a kiss. Carlyle took a step backwards, just in case. 'I've got more than enough on my plate as it is without having to deal with a murder investigation. Apart from anything else, my husband's supposed to be taking me to dinner tonight. It's the first time in more than six months we've had a "date". If I cancel, he's going to go spare.'

'I can understand.' Carlyle tried to recall the last time he'd taken Helen out. It certainly wasn't in the last six months. On the spot, he made a vow that he would take his wife to dinner at the next possible opportunity. Not tonight, though.

'I owe you a big favour for doing this,' Willmer smiled.

'Not really.' Carlyle gave her a ninety-second version of the Lillian Sands story. 'It should be fairly straightforward to deal with.'

'Bloody hell. That sounds complicated enough to me. Anyway, it's all yours.'

'Thanks.' Carlyle's phone started vibrating. He checked the incoming number.

Umar.

He hit receive and stepped away from Willmer. 'What news?'

'A baby girl. Six pounds, seven ounces.'

'Congratulations.'

'She's perfect,' Umar gushed. 'Born just over an hour ago. I think we're going to call her Ella Jane.'

'That's great.' Carlyle watched another couple of techies in their white boilersuits head towards the screens. 'How's Christina?'

'Doing well. Everybody's fine. Tired, but okay.'

'Good, good.'

'I think we're gonna have to postpone the wedding, though.'

'Don't worry about that,' Carlyle laughed. 'You can do it whenever.'

'Yeah. In the meantime, there's just one thing I wanted to ask you about.'

Carlyle lifted his gaze to the heavens. 'Yes?'

'About my paternity leave . . .'

294

'We will take care of all that. You look after mum and baby and we can sort out the details later.'

After offering further congratulations, Carlyle finished the call and made his way over to the nearest of the ambulances. The back doors were open, allowing him to look inside at the old man sitting on the gurney. The front of the man's shirt was stained almost black. His hands were covered in blood that was not his own and a bloody palm print had been smeared across his forehead. The expression on his face was a mixture of anger, confusion and exhaustion.

Blood, the inspector thought, *will have blood*.

It took several moments for the man to realize that he was not alone.

'This is your fault,' he growled.

Carlyle said nothing.

'You should have stopped this from happening. You knew that idiot was stalking me.'

'You killed him,' Carlyle pointed out.

'He came out of nowhere with the knife in his hand. I had to defend myself. What else could I have possibly done?'

'Save it for the judge.' Carlyle began fumbling for the handcuffs in his back pocket.

Struggling to his feet, the man lashed out, aiming a dirty shoe at Carlyle's head. But his target was too far away and he only succeeded in kicking over a small tv monitor before slumping back on to the gurney. 'There was no alternative,' he wailed. 'He would have killed me; pre-meditated murder was what it would have been.'

Pulling out the cuffs, the inspector cleared his throat. 'Paul Fassbender, you are under arrest for the manslaughter of Daniel Sands.'

Fassbender looked on in silent fury while Carlyle read the caution.

'You do not have to say anything, but it may harm your defence if you do not mention, when questioned, something you later rely on in court. Anything you do say may be given in evidence.' The inspector paused. 'Do you understand?'

Fassbender's eyes narrowed. 'I understand perfectly.'

'In that case, sir, please step out of the ambulance.'

As Carlyle waited for Fassbender to comply with his request, he felt a fat raindrop explode against his skull, followed by another. Looking up at the darkening sky, he uttered a selection of curses. He was always getting the weather wrong. 'Why,' he muttered to himself, 'didn't you wear your bloody raincoat?'